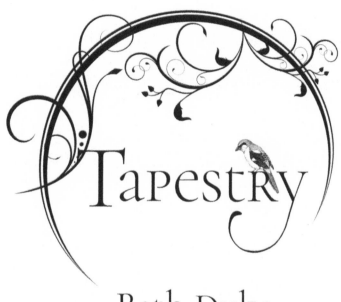

Beth Duke

TAPESTRY
Copyright © 2020 by Beth Dial Duke

ISBN 13: 978-0-578-64448-6 (paperback)

www.bethduke.com

A feather's not a bird

the rain is not the sea

a stone is not a mountain

but a river runs through me

"A FEATHER'S NOT A BIRD"
BY ROSANNE CASH

For Jason and Savannah,
my finest gifts to the future

One

SUNNYVALE, TEXAS

Gossip is the most valuable currency in a small town. It's the reason the elderly widow waits in her front yard for the mail carrier. It's why the hardware store clerk quits stocking a shelf and rushes to see his neighbor near the nuts and bolts bin. It causes three women to maneuver themselves around a shampoo bowl and listen while they await their turns at the hair salon.

They're about to get paid.

On this particular morning, Celia Harris was walking to her own mailbox when she received an early Christmas present: the glamorous Kara Lee Darling from the mansion located two miles, one massive antique black and gold European wrought-iron gate, and half a universe away. Mrs. Darling was walking arm in arm with her bodyguard, smiling up at him and gesturing to a stand of oak trees. Celia noted her tight chestnut-brown leather pants and mink-trimmed cream sweater, then glanced down at her own floral housedress thrown over a pilled wool turtleneck. She jumped into a pile of leaves behind the sycamore in the front yard, praying no snake was hiding there. Celia had been terrified of lurking serpents her entire sixty-three years on this earth.

Mrs. Darling was as stunning as everybody said. She really *did* look like a movie star; tall, dark-haired and flashing a brilliant smile with teeth like perfectly matched pearls. She had a figure any eighteen-year-old would be praying to develop, though she had to be in her thirties. And those eyes. The sparkle in them was visible from here.

Celia's jaw dropped when the two reached the trees and Mrs. Darling leaned her head back to kiss the burly bodyguard, a local boy named Deacon Jones. Deke had been in Celia's Sunday School Class when he was just a moon-eyed boy. She inhaled deeply, smelling the waxy crayons she'd loved those children with, right out of her own pocket.

Now he was all moon-eyed at Mrs. Darling and cradling the back of her fancy Dallas hairdo with his hand all dug into it. Darling, my foot, Celia thought. *That woman is a Jezebel, all pushed up against a tree making out like a teenaged hormone bomb.*

Celia shook her head, peeking around to see how long they'd have the audacity to carry on. Those leather pants wouldn't fare too well rubbing against hundred-year-old oak bark. She hoped they'd catch on fire right there.

Mr. Pete Darling was a transplant from some other state but Southern and generally embraced by most of the county. He owned a pipeline company and employed Celia's husband as well as a cousin or two. At least a thousand people in Texas alone worked for him, no telling where all else.

So Celia knew he was in the hospital, fighting for his very life, this Tuesday morning.

Nobody at the beauty shop was going to believe this. She wished she had her iPhone to try and get a picture.

Mrs. Darling and Deke didn't kiss long enough to suit Celia. They must have been in a hurry, and worried someone might see them, even way out in the country.

Well, she sure had.

When Celia peeked around again, Mrs. Darling was grinning straight at Celia and blowing an exaggerated kiss from Christian Dior-ed lips to her outstretched palm, lowering her fingers like a laser to point precisely at Celia's pounding heart.

Two

EUFAULA, ALABAMA

I peered over my grandmother's narrow shoulders at her computer screen. She was scrolling through ancient Native American recipes that featured corn hand-ground with a mortar and pestle. Some future meal was probably going to be excessively crunchy, and I made a mental note to bring home emergency backup food. I kissed the top of her head and said, "I love you, Grammy," then hurried to pick up my keys and get out the door to work.

"Have a good time, Little One. I love you, too." My grandmother never called me anything but "Little One", though I'm a twenty-one-year-old woman named Skye who towers over her. It didn't matter that I was off to work a restaurant shift, either, she was always going to wish me a "good time."

I paused on the way out to look at the kitchen countertop photo of my dad, Larry Smith. He had a beautiful grin and looked so handsome in his uniform, surrounded by small Afghani children.

One of them got him killed a few weeks after smiling innocently for the camera, blown to pieces by a six-year-old boy who led him to an IED by begging my father for help with some emergency. Of course he obliged the kid he'd handed a chocolate bar the week before.

I was a tiny girl when that happened, a world away.

I touched the photo's brass frame for luck, the same as every time I left the house, silently promising him I would find his relatives. I knew they'd want to meet the daughter he left behind.

I replayed last night's discussion in my head as I drove the leafy boulevard of historic Queen Anne Victorians and Greek Revival mansions that stood between our modest neighborhood and Eufaula's downtown.

After years of avoiding the subject, I'd dared to ask about my father's family again.

"Skye," Mama had said, "I don't know how to find them, honey. We've been over this a thousand times." She'd run her hands through her hair the way she did when she was on the verge of tears.

Grammy had chimed in, "Your father and mother were very much in love, and spent every minute they could together when he was stationed at Fort Benning. He asked her to marry him just a few months after they met. They would have been married when he came home from his tour, you know that." She paused to look at my dad's photo, which loomed much larger in that kitchen than seemed possible for any 8"x10" picture. "But we never met his family. We don't even know their names." She looked at my mother, clearly worried about the pain the subject caused her. "And Larry made it clear they wouldn't approve of him just showing up with a wife and child. He was planning to tell them eventually, but never got the chance."

I'd leaned toward Grammy with my palms up, exasperated. "But surely he had friends who could've told Mama who they were—"

"No," my mother said, a little too loudly. "No one was ever able to tell me anything beyond the fact they lived up north. Larry wasn't close to his family, and he barely talked about them to anyone. And since we weren't married, the Army wouldn't release any information to me. I'm sorry, Skye." She shrugged. "All I know is what I've told you: there were a lot of military men in his background. Like, his great-great-grandfather was killed in World War I. He was a British soldier. Larry's great-great-grandmother and his great-great-grandparents on the other side all came to New England to join relatives sometime after that. I only remember it because he joked that his ancestors fought against the colonists in the American Revolution, and they were so bitter it took them a long time to let go and immigrate."

"British, Mama? If you ever told me that, I must've been too young to remember. No wonder I love *Wuthering Heights* and *The Pillars of the Earth* so much. You don't know where in Britain they came from, do you?" I cocked my head to one side, hoping she'd keep going. This was the most she'd ever said about my father and his family.

"I have no idea, Skye." Mama bit her lower lip.

"Then please, Mama, just tell me about him, his favorite color, what he liked to eat, a movie he loved…"

My mother rubbed her eyes with her fingertips, then let her face fall into her palms for several seconds. She glanced up at me and stood to leave. "I'm sorry, Skye, I can't."

Grammy watched her walk away from us, her worried eyes telling me to leave Mama in peace. "Little One," she whispered, "Maybe someday. Even thinking about those memories is too hard, and she knows she'll go to pieces if she talks about them."

I nodded. "But Grammy, you knew him."

"Not much, though, honey. Your mom knows all the things you asked. Maybe if you give her time, she'll open up." She patted my arm and moved to the couch, where we spent the rest of the evening in mutual silence, pretending to watch something on TV.

My own high cheekbones and honey-colored skin were reflected in my grandmother's and mother's faces, but not my dark gray eyes. I needed to know where they came from, what my dad's people were like. I loved my grandmother and mother with all my heart. We had a wonderful home together, the three of us, but ours was so different from my friends' lives. There may have been divorces or separations, but at least they knew all about their dads and families, and theirs were far closer to normal than what I knew.

My grandmother was convinced she was descended from the Alabama Muscogee Creek based on her often-admired cheekbones and the geography of her hometown. She knew Eufaula had once been Creek land. She'd heard some vague references to Indian ancestry when she was a child. She added all that up and reached the conclusion she was an authentic Native American. Her real name was Verna Willis, but she insisted on being called Sparrow. According to my mom, my long-deceased grandfather steadfastly refused to indulge her

"Indian nonsense" and probably died from a curse rather than a heart attack.

Sometimes Mama and I simply referred to her as "The Sparrow." The Sparrow knew and loved the casinos owned and operated by the Poarch Band of Creek Indians nearby, and it didn't hurt her feelings one bit to think she might partake of their profits someday if she could qualify as a member of their tribe.

I was pondering all this as I parked my car and walked into the restaurant where I waited tables most evenings. An idea began to take hold, sidetracking my thoughts as I moved between dining room and kitchen all night: I could talk Grammy into ordering DNA test kits for the two of us, thereby clearly delineating what I inherited from my father's side and giving her an opportunity to prove her Native American background.

It had been discussed, but my grandmother always put it off. Mama and I believed The Sparrow was afraid her chromosomes would let her down. She'd be devastated if she could never dance around the living room to her beloved "Indian Outlaw" with the same frenetic joy again. Grammy felt a strong connection to that song and harbored an entirely inappropriate crush on Tim McGraw, too.

I would convince her we could do it together, and it would be fun. I began mentally preparing my sales pitch for Grammy as I grabbed an order from the kitchen.

"Get back in here!" Manny screamed. "You forgot the queso dip for seven. What the hell, Skye?!"

Manny was a Mexican tyrant-chef who made a great many U.S. dollars per year yelling a heavily accented "Skye!" at me while I pushed half-price margaritas on tourists and prayed tequila touched their tipping hearts. Table seven was an older couple, probably passing through town to admire the tourist row of stately homes. The wife was on her second margarita and I could tell by her smile she was a twenty-percenter, at least.

"Is this restaurant a former bank?" the lady asked. "It looks like it." Her eyes tracked the fancy crown molding that edged the high ceiling.

"No, ma'am, it was a jewelry store. You're sitting next to a display case." I waved at the glass door and shelf, once used for diamond necklaces and now holding a cheap Mexican pottery vase Manny hoped people would believe pre-Columbian.

"Would you like another margarita? I know I'd love one." I chuckled conspiratorially, sure she'd say yes, though my babyface was inviting a lecture on underage drinking. Her husband offered me the empty chip basket, smiling at me and then his slightly buzzy wife. "Bring her another margarita, and I'd love some more chips and salsa to go with the queso dip, please."

"Yessir." I nodded and winked at Josefina Cuervo, who actually looked great for an ancient. My guess was fifty, older than my mom, at least. She probably had a talented plastic surgeon. These two had a Jaguar parked out front.

Manny stood at the kitchen entrance, arms crossed, surveying his kingdom. Most of the bright red vinyl booths were empty, but it was only 5:30. "Cheer up," I told him. "You know this town loves your cooking, and your cheap margaritas more. Wait until dinnertime before you get all depressed. Besides," I added, "Mama will be here at six." My mother paid no attention whatsoever to Manny or any other men. No one could compete with the memory of my dad.

Manny allowed himself a small grin at the thought of my mother, the woman he'd worshipped from afar for the eight months she'd waitressed part-time with me. Most of the time he wore a look so devoid of expression that people assumed he was angry by default, a classic case of resting bitch face. Mama thought he looked like a younger George Lopez, who was on some sitcom she used to watch.

He nodded at my pitiful cluster of customers. "This week has been bad, though. Maybe we have to close."

Manny said this once a week. He never meant it. I rolled my eyes and headed to pick up the *muy importante* magic margarita tip potion, which eventually led the kind gentleman at table seven to leave thirty dollars cash for me.

Happy wife, happy life.

I took my cigarette break after Mama showed up, sitting on a chair behind the restaurant with our neighborhood beggar dog, "Rusty" according to his tag. There was nothing rusty about him; he was some kind of Australian Shepherd mix with a scruffy black and white coat. He made the appetizer rounds every evening. I'm betting old Rusty went home looking starved but stuffed with everything from stale bread to zucchini from the vegetarian place down the road. I slipped him a little steak I'd picked up on the way out. He licked my hand and trotted off toward Burger King.

One more satisfied customer.

I answered a text from Jeff, my on-off high school boyfriend who'd gone to Auburn to study accounting. He was going to try to get home this weekend. How hard could it be to drive an hour? *There is no try* I shot back, softening it with a heart emoji.

U should b here with me, Skye

Not this, again. Jeff knew I had no desire to go to college. I hated the classroom in high school and the entire semester I'd spent at community college. I was much happier with my nose in a book, learning on my own. I didn't need or want a degree, and definitely not the debt I'd rack up getting one.

I was preparing a brief "texture" in response (Jeff's term for my periodic text lectures) when Manny screamed. "Skye!" (it sounds like "es-cah-YEE"). I crunched out my Marlboro and went to see how busy Mama was. I'd take over tables as needed.

"What's up, Manny?" I washed my hands clean of Rusty drool and cigarette smell (bad for tips), then took a look at the dining room. Mama was juggling several booths, and Manny was trying to cook and watch Mama at the same time. Poor man was going to slice his finger off someday if Lisa Willis didn't pay him some attention.

THRee

DALLAS, TEXAS

Kara sat at her husband's side, clasping his hand and willing him to wake up. The stroke's full effects were unknown, and Pete's doctors had kept him in a medically induced coma for days to prevent further damage from brain swelling. Today was the day he was to come back to consciousness.

On the other side of the room sat Gerald Davidson, acting CEO and a major shareholder of PFD Pipelines, Incorporated, Pete's company. Gerald was a solid-looking man of forty, graying slightly at his temples. His dark blue eyes were lined by years of warm smiles. He was the consummate charming businessman, Pete's trusted friend and confidante.

Gerald was, by his own admission, the "best damn lawyer in the State of Texas." He handled Pete's legal matters, and that was all the best-damning he needed to do.

Kara knew he could strike like a viper when it suited him. She was never sure where she stood with Gerald, since it was he who helped Pete construct the ironclad prenup that insisted their marriage had to last ten years for her to be entitled to "marital assets" in a divorce, or in the event of his death. Gerald had argued for *twenty* years and lost to Kara's hands on Pete's shoulders, massaging them gently in the conference room.

Pete's company was premarital property, and Kara wouldn't see her chunk of the pipeline empire without that ten years. She'd earned every penny already as far as she was concerned, standing at Pete's side during press conferences after one of his pipelines blew up in New Mexico and the whole damn world watched it on an endless CNN loop. She'd endured the protesters waving signs about PFD killing children. She'd sat through three years of court proceedings that somehow, miraculously, left most of the company intact.

Her husband was a large, balding, introverted, boring, business-obsessed man, but he was all hers. Kara had managed to change Pete's mind about a lot of things, like the ridiculous female bodyguards he'd originally hired to protect her. She'd also talked him into leaving the tornado-target ranch he adored in Oklahoma, furnished in Early Antler, and building a home more suited to her taste near Dallas.

They'd celebrated their sixth anniversary in Italy in July. Kara wished she'd kept Pete from eating his way through Tuscany to Sicily like a rampaging Hun.

She had at least four hundred million reasons to love and support her husband. Kara lifted his hand to her lips and whispered, "Pete, please wake up. It's me, baby, it's your Kara." Pete didn't blink or raise a finger. Kara wiped a tear from her cheek and glanced at Gerald, who was watching her like he always did; with a healthy mix of lust and distrust.

She knew how to address that, at least. She stood and tugged her black knit dress into place, making sure the tiny gold chain belt was hanging across her flat lower belly and above her hard-earned round butt cheeks. Kara walked to Gerald like he was the only man in the world, her deep brown eyes sparkling and locked on his, her hips moving like precision weapons. She took his hand in hers and said, "I know you must be tired. I'm getting you a coffee and something sweet. Call me if he moves a muscle, Gerald, okay?" He nodded mutely. She turned to be sure he'd have the maximum time to watch her walk away, and as always, she did it like she'd just thrown a match over her shoulder onto a pile of gasoline-soaked trash.

"She's gone, Pete," Gerald said as the door closed. Pete Darling opened his weary eyes and blinked. "And I can't keep the nurses quiet much longer. You're going to have to let Kara know you're awake."

Pete whispered, "I want to hear what she asks you, Gerry, thinking I'm off in La-La Land." He closed his eyes and exhaled. "She's the most beautiful woman in the world. Most of the time I'm—"

"Most of the time you're scared to death of her, Pete." Gerald finished.

"I love her, Gerry. We both know she can be a little flirtatious, but that's because men stare everywhere she goes. Kara can't help the effect her beauty has. I guess I'm still insecure, worrying over nothing."

"Well, you're going to have to let her see you're okay, Pete. You can't wallow in this bed pretending to sleep, spying like the Law & Order: Special Betrayal Unit. They brought you around six hours ago, and it shows, buddy. Plus they're going to haul you off to physical therapy tomorrow and get that left side working."

Pete grimaced. "I don't know what's worse, worrying about my wife wanting to bust our prenup or Brunhilde coming to kidnap me at seven tomorrow morning."

Gerald laughed. "Her name is Denise, and she's a pretty young thing. Just kind of... muscular, that's all."

Kara Lee Evans Darling moved through hallways and sidewalks with crowds parting like a Ferrari was driving through. Men gaped and women did, too, until they turned to smack their husband's arms. She sailed past a nurse's station and smiled at a young intern into bumping the desk's counter and fumbling his iPad.

Deke was waiting where she'd stationed him, on a couch in the main lobby. He threw down a dated copy of *Guns & Ammo*, following her into the stairwell.

"How is he?" He cocked his head like a confused puppy, unsure whether to display loyalty to his master or his mistress. *Poor Deke*, she thought. *I may have broken him.* Kara dragged a long red fingernail down his chest, stopping just above his belt. Then she stepped back and said, "Mr. Darling will wake up any time now, and I'll be by his side. You go to the office and wait to see if he needs anything there. Understand?"

Mr. Darling. Deke swallowed the urge to say anything more, along with his pride. "Yes, ma'am." He opened the door for Kara and watched her saunter off to the cafeteria.

FOUR

EUFAULA, ALABAMA

Mama and I found my grandmother wearing a fringed fake-suede shirt and matching ankle-length skirt, stirring something suspicious on the stove. It was nine-thirty p.m., and at least eighty degrees outside.

"Mom, really?" Mama turned her face to the ceiling. Maybe she was begging the ancestors for patience.

"I got it from the eBay, Talisa." Grammy whirled a few times to show off the skirt's flare, waving her wooden spoon. She blew me a kiss and said, "*Hesci*, Little One." It sounded like hiss-jay, and I knew it meant hello because I'd helped her find the Creek Language and Traditions website.

"It looks like a Halloween costume." Mama was shuffling through the day's mail. She threw it all into the garbage can under the sink. "I'm afraid to ask what you're cooking."

"I am cooking a cornmeal soup, and it's going to taste great," Grammy replied. "It has to sit for a few days to sour, and it's called *sofkey*."

"Uh huh," Mama said. "And are we supposed to eat this for supper in a few days?" She was leaning on the back of a kitchen chair, tired but pretty. Her hair was long like Grammy's, but brown instead of snow white. I thought Grammy Sparrow's hair was amazing. She wore it in a braid that met her waist, and when she brushed it at night, it was soft as kittens.

"Can if you want to. It's mostly to put in a bowl by the front door to welcome visitors." Grammy had gone back to furious stirring.

Mama shot me a look. "Mom, you're going to have to stay off that website. This is getting crazy. Even the purest Creek Indian doesn't make some weird sour glue soup for visitors in 2018. Besides, what visitors?"

"Maybe that Mexican lowww-tharrio of yours, Talisa," Grammy chuckled. "You should invite him over."

"He is not interested in me, and your soup would scare him back to Juarez. It's less frightening than fermented cornmeal slush." My mother glared at me, since I'd obviously told Grammy too much about Manny's crush on her.

"What's so scary about Juarez?" I asked.

"Nothing now, I guess, but it was the murder capital of the world ten years ago. Manny said he has nightmares about the drug cartels."

"You sure have learned a lot about Manny," I told her, and immediately regretted it. Mama announced she was going to bed, tired of the two of us "ganging up on" her. She took her purse and phone, heading off to her room at the end of the hall.

Grammy muttered, "That one is stubborn. Won't even use the name I gave her."

"I think Talisa is a pretty name, too, but if Mama wants to call herself Lisa, you should understand that, Grammy. Especially since you only added the 'Ta' when you read it in a book after she'd been Lisa until third grade."

"It means 'beautiful waters' in Muscogee Creek, and she's an Aquarius—"

I laughed at her and she laughed back. "Let's stick to one realm at a time, okay?" I said.

"Deal." Grammy turned the stove off. I could smell corn and something vaguely like dill pickles.

"Why can't you cook more Alabamian food, like chicken and dressing or potato salad?" I asked her, but made sure she saw I was smiling when I said it.

"Little One, this soup was Alabamian before the chicken and dressing people came. Our people *were* Alabama. We *are* Alabama."

"Chicken and dressing people, huh? Grammy, you used to work full time at Walmart and ride a Harley. Do you remember that?"

She nodded. "I remember that and all the generations that came before me. I remember my great-great-great-great-grandfather, who was a chief and his daughter was a princess."

"All this started two years ago, when you went to that casino." I raised my eyebrows as high as they'd go. "Now you *remember* these ancestors?"

"It is a gift," she answered, pouring the glop into some ceramic pot she'd painted with bright yellow stalks of corn. She placed the pot on an old bedside table she'd dragged out of the garage and put by the door. "Someday you will understand we are not whole until we know the ones who walked before us.

They beat in our hearts and feel with our fingertips. We are the result of all who loved us into being, Little One."

"Do any of my ancestors know how to make decent mac and cheese through your fingertips?"

Grammy laughed. "Tomorrow is Saturday. I'll bake some chicken and dressing, too."

"*Mvto!*" I hugged her tightly as the smile dawned on her face. "That's right, mutt-OH, Grammy. I can visit a website, too."

"Only I don't know how to say 'you're welcome'," she fretted.

"We'll find out," I said. I looked down the hallway to make sure Mama was still in her room. "Grammy, I know how important your Creek ancestry is to you. And you know how important it is to me to find out more about who I am. Let's finally do something about it and order the DNA kits we've talked about. You're going to have to be brave to do it, but you can confirm your Native American heritage once and for all. It's simple these days." I paused to look for any sign of agreement and didn't see it. "And mine can be my birthday present from you. I know it's expensive, but it's what I want more than anything in the world. You're the one who's taught me I need to know the ones who came before me."

She nodded. "That's true. I've been too afraid of disappointment, Little One. But if we do this together... well, let me think about it, honey. I'll get on my computer tomorrow and find out more." She shook her head. "But what if I find out I've been wrong?"

I held her face between my hands. "Grammy, this test is a secret between you and me. No matter what your results say, they'll stay between you and me if you want. You'll always be the most precious grandmother in the world, Creek or not. And you can keep studying the culture and wearing the clothes and cooking the crazy recipes. I would never tell a soul, okay?" I kissed her forehead. "I'm going to take a shower and try to call Jeff before bed. I'll see you in the morning."

"Good night, Little One."

I left my grandmother at the living room window, staring at the stars of her Alabama.

Five

SUNNYVALE, TEXAS

Deke and Joseph, Pete's bodyguard, jumped from the car to help Mr. Darling out. Pete slapped away their outstretched hands, sliding his right leg onto the driveway and picking up his left with his massive hands. The hospital had informed him he must adhere to a low-fat, low-sugar, low-salt, low-taste diet. His six feet and five inches of height didn't excuse his three-hundred-ten-pound weight.

Bourbon was off the list. No sex for at least eight weeks. Five new prescriptions, and none of them were for fun. Worst of all, Kara had heard every discharge instruction and possessed a small book of papers detailing the doom.

He considered asking his bodyguards to shoot him, maybe somewhere on the grass for easy cleanup. Instead, he shuffled along as well as possible with one arm around each man's

torous left leg dragging slightly and moving
nquilized snail.

ver that snail to Denise four times a week
ecution, the price of being allowed to run
___ from home. Gerry was doing an adequate
job, but things were heating up in Oklahoma. No way Pete was
delegating a seventy-million-dollar project to anyone, not even
Gerry, who was first and foremost a lawyer.

Deke helped deposit him into a newly-delivered clunky,
multi-motorized leather recliner—a salute to infirmity disguised
as a La-Z-Boy football watching venue—and it wasn't even
near his desk. Kara perched opposite him in a deep blue velvet
and mahogany Chippendale corner chair he'd shelled out
several thousand for. *Well, here we are, these two chairs representing
us perfectly,* he thought. His stomach rolled.

Kara got up to swing the conveniently attached invalid
table around for him, placing his laptop and cell phone on it
and kissing the top of his head. "I know you want to get to
work, baby. I'll leave you for an hour and check back. Is there
anything I can get you in the meantime?"

Pete was torn between a cyanide capsule and a pizza.
"Maybe later. I'm anxious to get back to this Oklahoma thing."
He watched Kara sweep out of the room, long, wispy sleeves
on her blouse sailing beside her like ladies-in-waiting.

Pete opened the laptop and began reading updates from
his men in Okmulgee. None of it was good. Cassie Deer and
Franklin Weatherford had their lawyers throwing up every
possible stumbling block, including five new ground
penetrating radar demands near the proposed pipeline route.
If they found one bone, one scrap of human remains, one
freaking pottery shard, his project would be held up for
months, possibly years. The casino people were already
demonstrating against the pipeline, dredging up the explosion

in New Mexico. Damn it all, they were building a route for crude oil. Nobody was going to see an explosion from it, ever.

The most galling part was that this contract was mostly for repair to existing lines, composite wrapping to ensure leaks *didn't* happen. The rest was diverting to new routes when repair wasn't possible. The environmental nuts should be thanking him. Instead, they would be harassing his crews.

If they ever actually got to dig.

Pete loved Oklahoma, but it was looking like his worst enemy right now. He dialed the first of several contacts in his phone, a senator who lived in a fine Tulsa house Pete considered at least ten percent his own.

Kara was making a call from her private gym room on the third floor. She leaned on the treadmill and waited for Gerald Davidson's young legal associate, Stephen, to pick up.

"Yes, Mrs. Darling?" He sounded like he'd run to the phone. Good.

"You can call me Kara, Stephen. I'm wondering if we could meet at O'Malley's about five this afternoon. There's something I'd like to discuss with you in absolute confidence. I presume attorney-client privilege would extend to such a meeting?"

"Are we discussing legal matters?" Stephen recalled the last time he'd seen Kara Darling, when he delivered some papers to her husband's hospital room. She'd seemed to be appreciating more than his law degree.

"You might say that," Kara said. "Dress casually. We'll go for a ride."

Something told Stephen he should infer more than one meaning from that statement. "I'll be there," he told her, his hand shaking slightly.

At precisely five o'clock, Kara drove her black Porsche 911 Carrera into the O'Malley's parking lot. Stephen was leaning against his standard-issue Texas Ford F150. He wore tight jeans and a black cowboy hat with new Lucchese boots.

Good, he understood casual. He looked even better than she'd hoped.

She glided the car up and lowered the passenger window. "Come on, we don't have much time."

Stephen settled in, trying not to appear impressed with the car or Kara's low-cut shirt. "Where are we going?" he asked.

"Little place I have near Mesquite. No one knows about it. I bought a house and a few acres with my money after Pete and I married." Kara's eyes were locked on the road, trying to maneuver through traffic. "I told Pete I had to go get a broken acrylic nail fixed. I can get away without an escort because the goons hate the salon and the snickers in Vietnamese." She downshifted and sped around a cement truck. Stephen felt the G-force rearrange his internal organs.

Kara glanced at him. "What's the matter, Stephen, don't you like to go fast?"

Stephen summoned all thirty years of his worldly experience with women and tried to sound sexy. "In a car, yes." He let his gaze follow the mostly open neckline of her silk shirt, wondering what one more button would unleash.

Kara just raised her eyebrows and nodded. She said nothing until they pulled into the garage of a modest old home surrounded by towering oaks and not much else. Stephen figured the nearest neighbors must be at least half a mile away.

She'd read his mind. "It's very private. I come out here to think in peace." She lowered the garage door and Stephen followed her into the kitchen. He was disappointed when she headed straight for a living room chair, indicating he should sit on the couch. This was starting to feel less like a seduction and more like a job interview.

"Stephen," she began, "I know you've only been working at Gerald's firm for a year. You're taking home about eighty thousand, not bad, but you still owe Baylor more than twice that." Kara leaned toward him and the blouse fell just the tiniest bit more open. Stephen allowed himself a view of black lace and creamy skin.

"So, Mrs., umm, Kara, you want to hire me away from Davidson and Associates?"

Kara let her smile unfold gradually, holding his eyes to hers. "Not at all, Stephen. I want you to have a bright future with Gerald. All I need is a little help. I can make it very much worthwhile for you, both in billable hours and some cash on the side."

"And what help do you need, Kara?"

"I need you to provide me access to Gerald's schedule. I want to be updated with any information you can get me on his personal life, particularly whom he's sleeping with since the divorce. I want to know his travel plans. I want to know his strengths and his weaknesses."

"Why wouldn't you just hire a private detective?"

"Because a private detective isn't going to help me get Gerald off PDF Pipelines' Board of Directors. You are, when he begins misplacing important documents and screwing up everything Pete tells him to do."

"You want me to deliberately destroy the man who gave me my first job." Stephen stood and shook his head. "That isn't going to happen, Mrs. Darling. I'm not your guy."

"Gerald will be just fine, Stephen. He's made millions from my husband's company over the past few years alone. Wouldn't you like to be earning that kind of money?" Kara rose from the chair and stepped right in front of him, staring into his eyes. "Do you know where the word 'sabotage' comes from, Stephen? During the Industrial Revolution, French peasants would throw their *sabot*—wooden shoes—into machinery to grind it to a halt. They knew their jobs were being taken by machines. It was a survival tactic."

"That's a myth," Stephen muttered. Kara was slowly scraping her long red fingernails from between his legs up the front of his jeans. He cursed himself for his little gasp and the way his body reacted. For several long seconds, he was aware of nothing in the world but those fingernails.

"Then it's a hit and a myth, Stephen," she whispered. "Because I'm pretty sure that sensation was a hit for you."

SIX

EUFAULA, ALABAMA

G rammy and I had a system in the Piggly Wiggly: I gathered the items she specified all over the store while she pushed her buggy from neighbor to neighbor to talk for an eternity. I wasn't allowed to approach frozen foods until she was sure there was no one else she wanted to catch up with.

She was still wearing the fake-deerskin outfit from the previous night, refusing to acknowledge both the Alabama heat and the dropped jaws from strangers. Her friends knew to expect rampant Indianism. Everyone else, not so much.

I made a mental note to buy her moccasins for Christmas. Her old ones from a Cherokee, North Carolina souvenir shop had holes in them, so she had on some very clash-y white Crocs. I was betting she planned to glue beads on them.

When at long last she issued Frozen Food Approval, I joined her at Willie Sue's checkout line with two armfuls of

Birds Eye vegetables, a carton of ice cream and a touch of my own freezer burn. Willie Sue was a talker unless the manager was watching. I looked around, desperately hoping he'd show up. Nope. My grandmother and the cashier were fully engaged in a detailed discussion about an old classmate with arthritis who was moving to Florida.

Time of My Death from Boredom: 2:12 p.m. Central Daylight Time. I could only hope the chicken and dressing would revive me.

I started the car while Grammy educated our bag boy about Alabama Muscogee Creek history, finally handing him her usual fifty-cent tip. I assume he went back inside and quit.

"That was fun, Little One," she said, buckling her seat belt. "Thank you for driving."

"You know, I grew up thinking all grandmothers called their granddaughters 'Little One'," I told her with a laugh. "Is it short for something, like 'Little One Who Stinks like Diaper' or 'Little One Who Runs like Armadillo'? 'Little One—'" I slowed the car for some tourists crossing the street to the Shorter Mansion.

"I have called you that from the moment I first saw you in the hospital," she said quietly. "It *is* short for something. It's short for 'Little One Who Brings Pure Joy'." She was dabbing her eyes a little.

I am such a jerk. "I'm sorry, Grammy. That is beautiful and I love you so much." I reached over and held her tiny bird-bone hand in mine. "You are the best grandmother in the world. I'm just being stupid because Jeff keeps ghosting me. He's too busy to talk, doesn't text back, it's too loud in the Student Center—"

"Maybe you should surprise him in Auburn," she answered.

"I'm too scared of finding him wrapped around some skanky sorority girl. A Lilly Pulitzer hoe. Vera Bradley tats on an engineering major."

"You have a vivid imagination, Little One." She chuckled. "But if you're right, aren't you better off? Wouldn't you like to know the truth?"

"Actually, no, I wouldn't. Not right now. And please don't tell Mama. She's never been a Jeff fan in the first place."

"No, she hasn't," Grammy said. "Your mother is very suspicious of any male and their motives. I reckon she's been through too much."

Well, *that* was intriguing. "She won't talk to me about her experiences with boyfriends or dating or anything like that. Mama acts like there was never anyone in her life but my dad, and she won't say more than a few words about him. What happened to her, Grammy? Why can't she open up about him? Is it just too painful a subject because he died?"

"It hurts her to think about your father, Little One, because of the horrible way she lost him. Someday I'm sure she'll tell you all about it."

We were turning into the driveway. "You go on in," I told her. "I'll get the groceries." I watched her wipe some sweat from her forehead. "And maybe you should change into some shorts or something."

"The ancestors must have had skimpier versions of this," she agreed. "I'm 'bout to burn up."

"The eBay version is probably less breathable than deerskin," I offered.

Her eyes lit up. "Maybe I can—"

"No, Grammy. No one is going to skin deer for you to make an outfit. And who's going to tan it? And sew it?"

"Well, I'm going to look on the computer." She sprinted to the house, the idea burning a hole in her faux-suede pocket. My mother passed her on the way in and grabbed a bag of frozen stuff. "What's up with her?" she nodded at the door closing behind Grammy.

"It's too hot in the Creek today." I laughed and Mama sniggered with me.

"Thank God. She needs to take that mess off. And how is she gonna wash it?" Mama wondered.

"Presumably on a rock by the river." I slammed my ancient Toyota's trunk closed. "Never a dull moment here in our teepee."

"Jeff is home, Skye. He came by the house. I told him to text you, but he said he's going to be busy all afternoon. He'll get in touch tonight."

I tried to act like I knew all about Jeff and his presence in Eufaula and my stomach wasn't flopping like a landed bass. "Oh, okay. Was he alone? Was Eddie with him?"

"He was alone. Said he's going back tonight and if he doesn't get to come by, he'll text you when he gets to Auburn," Mama said.

Well, there was my answer. If he'd come all the way home and didn't plan to stay with me tonight, our on/off relationship was definitely way, way off. I blinked a few times and told myself he wasn't worth crying over. I felt tears running down my face anyway.

Mama set her Piggly Wiggly bag on the trunk and hugged me. "You deserve so much better than Jeff Turley, Skye." She pulled the Bluebell Peaches & Homemade Vanilla ice cream out of the bag. "Come on. We'll get two spoons."

I trudged behind her. I'd known Jeff would find someone at school who would be too much of his world there; someone who'd speak Auburn like a private language they shared. She'd throw toilet paper rolls at trees with him after football games and dance with him at Skybar. That's probably where he met her. *Cruel irony.* She'd have money for tuition and probably never waitressed in her life. Two perfect parents and a grandmother who didn't dress like Pocahontas for trips to the Piggly Wiggly.

Mama called back over her shoulder, "Manny asked me to fill in for Debra tonight. She's sick with something. I'm going in about five."

I bet Manny paid Debra to be sick. "Okay, but you're going to miss chicken and dressing. I think Grammy's cooking macaroni and cheese, too."

"Well, I didn't feel I could say no. Manny tries to give me hours whenever he can, because he knows I don't make enough at the Huddle House."

"Mama, you really are oblivious." I set the groceries on the counter and took the spoon she offered me, digging into the ice cream.

"Do you really think Manny likes me like that?" Mama said it without a trace of humor.

I shook my head. "How did you ever manage to reproduce?" I let her get one more spoonful of ice cream and then placed it in the freezer. "Of *course* he likes you, and you terrify him every time you act the slightest bit interested in anything he has to say. The only reason I get away with talking to Manny like I do is because I got you to work with me three nights a week. He's been fixated on you since the first time you walked through the door."

Mama shook her head as she closed the cabinets. "I just don't see it. He and I are too different."

"How do you even know that? All you do is pick up serving plates and smile at him occasionally. Did you know he plays soccer on Sunday afternoons at the park? And his mother lives with him. She's like, ninety, and doesn't speak a word of English. Manny takes good care of her, too. He has two nieces in town, and one celebrated her *quinceañera* Friday night. Manny went after we closed up. He's a nice guy, Mama, and he thinks you're perfect."

"He said that?" Mama's eyebrows rose to the ceiling.

"No. But I know he thinks it. You should try to get to know him a little."

She appeared to be considering it. "I just don't think he's my type, Skye."

"What *is* your type? Do you have a type? Is any man good enough for you, or was it only my father?" I tried desperately to take the words back as soon as they left my mouth.

Mama stared a hot, furious hole into me. She turned to grab her purse, phone and keys and slammed the kitchen door after her. Now I had two reasons to be miserable.

Seven

SUNNYVALE, TEXAS
Two months later

"**D**amn him to hell. You tell him we will not change one thing. Henry Littlefeather or Littlefreaky or whatever his got-damn name is. They can line I-40 sitting on their spotted ponies and throw flaming spears at my trucks. The pipeline is going through. I will not be threatened by these people *anymore!*" Pete stopped for a sip of water, the nastiest substitute for Coca-Cola on earth. "And keep the media away from them, Cory. Do your got-damn job." Pete threw his cell phone across the room as Kara opened the door of his study.

She bent to pick up the phone and handed it back to him. "You do realize you're begging for another stroke, right? You're like a man in a lightning storm waving a golf club at the sky, Pete, screaming at the heavens to be fried extra-crispy."

"I can't get anything done in Oklahoma, Kara. I need to be on the ground there, not directing a bunch of high-priced pussy millennials from this chair. Nobody in that tribe is going to listen to Cory, the Pipeline Data Analyst Who Knows Jackshit about Handling Things in the Real World—"

"Language, Pete, please," Kara said. She settled into her chair and continued, "Why don't you send Gerald to Okmulgee? He's a veteran at dealing with this stuff."

"He doesn't wanna go, Kara, and I don't blame him. It's a whole other thing with the Muscogee Nation involved. I need a good PR man like Johnny Bible, who quit, by the way, as soon as he saw where this shi—this stuff—was headed. Nobody wants to take on the environmental nuts *and* Indians, whoops, *Native Americans.* That's considered insanity these days."

"Did they find artifacts?" Kara leaned forward, chin on her fist.

"No, that's the hell of it. We're clear on bone fragments and beads and feathers and wigwam pieces—"

"You know, you could try to sound a teensy bit less sarcastic, Pete. The Muscogee are right to protect their ancestral land."

"Thanks for your support." He rolled his eyes. "Look, Kara, we aren't trying to disturb any sacred sites or artifacts. We aren't anywhere near them. I'd understand better if we were. The tribe is fighting because they think we'll be disruptive near a couple of their casinos, and a lot of them seem to believe the pipeline is dangerous. It's not gonna explode, Kara, and it's sure as hell not going to leak crude. Not with my crews doing the work."

"It's been three months, Pete. You could go. Your physical therapy is down to once a week, and you're barely limping, baby. There's no reason you can't be in Oklahoma. I'll go with you."

Pete shook his head slowly. "I have been warned to stay as far out of the spotlight on this as possible, Kara, after New Mexico. My name and face are giant red flags to anyone who knows about the explosion and the children who died. And that's pretty much everyone with a TV or computer. Otherwise I'd have been there weeks ago. Johnny's final advice to me was to stay as low-profile as I can and not go anywhere near the Muscogee Creeks. They'll publicly eviscerate me as a forked-tongued lying white man. Doesn't matter what I say, I can't say it directly to them. That's exactly what they want: a horrible face to put on the pipeline project, a poster child for greed and ineptitude."

"You weren't responsible for that explosion, Pete; the court decided that. You aren't greedy or inept."

"Didn't stop me from having to pay millions, though, Kara, or from the company's reputation and value crashing," he answered. Pete ran his hand through what remained of his hair. It surprised the hell out of him how much worse the scalp-to-hair ratio had grown over the past decade, even though he saw it each day in the mirror.

"And look how well you've fought back, baby. I am really proud of you and all you've accomplished." Kara walked over and knelt by Pete's recliner, smiling the way she smiled at him when something very, very good was about to happen. "So," she said, pushing a button, "how far back does this thing go, exactly?"

Pete was snoring softly in bed beside her hours later. Kara threw a big t-shirt on and padded out of their room, closing the door as gently as possible. She called a number only she knew, one that rang a burner phone carried by Stephen Dykstra.

"Yeah, hello?" he sounded cobwebby, so she gave him a moment. "It's, umm, really late."

"Are you alone?"

"No," Stephen answered. "I'm not."

Kara tapped her nails on the kitchen counter. "Then *get* alone, Stephen. I'll wait." She heard him mumble something and a grunted female response in the background.

"What do you have to tell me?" Kara demanded.

"And I miss you, too, Kara," Stephen snapped. It had been two weeks since she'd finally, *finally* let him get beyond high-school level make-out sessions. Kara had disappeared after that, leaving Stephen obsessed and hating himself for it, waiting for the next time he might get to see her. But she only called, and at the most ridiculous moments, like this one. He glanced toward his room, where the sleeping girl he'd brought home from the bar tonight had a delicate hand with long red fingernails hanging off the side of his bed.

"Not much," Stephen admitted. "He's still with a nice divorcee from his country club. Her name is Sheila, and he talks about her a lot. She has two kids—"

"You are boring me to tears, Stephen." Kara yawned loudly into the phone.

"I told you, I can't get anywhere near the files you want me to. There's no way. Nothing is going on at the office. His secretary is pregnant, but it's not Gerald's, if that's what you—"

"Pregnant?" Kara interrupted.

"Yeah," Stephen said. "I only know because she's been sick a lot—like, super-throwing-up-constantly sick—and he's been using some lady from a temp agency in Ft. Worth while she's taking several months' leave. She's nice. I think her name is Esther or Edith or something. She reminds me of my grandma."

"That's great, Stephen, thank you." Kara glanced up, sure she'd heard Pete moving around. "Good night," she whispered. "Maybe I'll see you in a dream. I hope so."

Stephen snapped the cheap phone shut and headed back to wake Cassidy or Chrissie or whatever the hell her name was. He was more than ready for her again.

"Hello, I'm Jenny Tyson," Kara extended her hand to Mr. Edwards of Brownhill Staffing Group. "I appreciate your meeting me on such short notice." Kara shook his hand firmly and settled into the chair across from him, adjusting her navy blue suit skirt and crossing her ankles in a dainty, ladylike gesture.

"How can I help, Miss Tyson?" Darrell Edwards took in the Louis Vuitton briefcase, the shiny short French manicure, the supermodel face. He leaned forward and shifted a few items on his desk.

"Well, as I mentioned, our firm will be working closely with Davidson and Associates for the next few months in Dallas. I'm not at liberty to discuss the case, of course, but it's one that is going to require utmost discretion. We represent a really high-profile client in Los Angeles."

"I understand." Darrell nodded. Kara noticed he was staring at her light pink lip gloss. She was giving Mr. Edwards several seconds to appreciate her lips and also consider what movie star client she might represent.

"We want to hire your best legal secretary, someone with at least ten years' experience, for several months while we're working with Gerald Davidson. I'm supposed to interview candidates personally, with some questions of a confidential nature. I hope you understand."

"Well, Miss, we already have a temp placed with Mr. Davidson, a…" he glanced at his computer screen, "a Mrs. Esther Reynolds."

"Oh, I know, Mr. Edwards! She is lovely and doing a fine job. I'm afraid she doesn't fit our needs on this case, though. We're prepared to pay her for every week she's been contracted in advance, and a generous bonus, too." Kara extended a check for a whopping sum and allowed Darrell to look at the figure and calculate his cut.

"So… you're firing Esther?" He looked stunned.

"Not at all. We're just looking for a temp who's better suited to this case. I'm sure you understand. Our circumstances are extraordinary, and we have to be very discreet. In fact," she leaned forward and spoke in a low voice, "my boss wants you to tell Mr. Davidson that Mrs. Reynolds is no longer available, and you're sending someone to take her place. We also need you to explain to her, as well, if you wouldn't mind."

"Why wouldn't your firm simply tell Mr. Davidson?"

"We don't want to come rolling in from California and start dictating things. That would be a bad start, and our client would be unhappy. It's enough that he or she's going to be required to travel back and forth to Dallas several times."

Darrell considered this, and then the beautiful lady who sat in his office, beaming at him like his wife hadn't in thirty years. Esther Reynolds would get plenty of money, he'd get a cut of both placements, and he might even get some movie star gossip, eventually. He told Kara, "It'll take me a few days to round them up for interviews. Is there anything you'd like to specify?"

"Just the legal experience, a clean background, and highly trustworthy, Mr. Edwards. I'll take it from there. Oh, and don't mention this to Mrs. Reynolds or Mr. Davidson yet. We should have someone in place before you tell either of them."

Darrell Edwards rose to shake her lovely, soft hand one more time. "I'll call you at the number you gave me, Miss Tyson. Should be Thursday or Friday, and I'll set up our conference room for your interviews."

"Thank you, Mr. Edwards." Kara winked at him. "I knew you'd help us out. I hope to see you soon."

Eight

It was a good time in The House of the Sparrow. Mama still insisted Manny wasn't her 'type,' but she came along with Grammy and me to watch Sunday soccer matches. She was reading the latest *People* magazine, though, while Grammy and I cheered for goals and sweaty bare chests.

Grammy liked watching all those young bodies running past, and I liked watching Whitman Appleby. He'd been a minor football star in high school, one year ahead of me and oblivious to my existence, even though I'd bumped into him once and dropped a milk carton on his foot at lunch. I knew how to charm the men.

Whitman had planned on an athletic scholarship to Auburn or even Alabama. His dream had crashed into two semesters of community college and a full-time job at Home

Depot. His girlfriend, seated about ten feet away, seemed to think he was David Beckham with darker hair and an Alabama accent. Occasionally she would squeal loudly at some play he made. He'd turn his head toward her and grin, and I'd catch a little solar flare from it.

Manny managed to play the first half before coming out of the game. "I'm too old for this," he said, mopping his face with a paper towel from the snack table. Mama smiled up from the latest Kardashian lip enhancement news and Manny plopped onto the grass near her chair at a respectful distance. Mama immediately buried her head in the magazine again.

Those two were never going to get anywhere, I decided. About as much chance as Whit and Skye announcing their wedding in Paris, closest friends only, event hashtag WhitAndSkyeLiveAppleyEverAfter...

"Aren't you going back in?" Grammy asked Manny. She'd come to sort of like him after three Sunday afternoons and even ventured into *Oro y Cena* for a vegetarian plate last week. I helped her look up the Spanish on her beloved computer: Gold and Dinner, a nod to the former jewelry store.

"No, I've had enough and need to get home," Manny replied. "I'll see you *mañana*, Lisa and Skye. And *Mamacita* Sparrow, you should come too," he added with a wink. "Extra caramel on the flan for you." He walked off to his truck, a little cocky at her beaming response.

Why could the man flirt with my tiny old grandmother but not Mama?

Whit trotted over during the halftime break and kissed Squealy Girl. I nodded at Grammy and she elbowed Mama it was time to leave.

The next morning's mail brought the most exciting thing we'd seen in weeks: DNA testing kits for Grammy and me. Mama was off at Huddle House already, so we sat and drooled into our test tubes together, giggling like we were on a top-secret mission.

Well, we kinda were. Mama would probably find something to disapprove of, whether it was Grammy's quest for Creek Nation membership or my own curiosity about my father's family. Yeah, it would definitely be that. I was still supposed to act like my gray eyes and five feet nine-inch height were somehow conjured by petite, brown-eyed Lisa Willis via magical chromosomal incantation.

We finished and sealed the little cardboard cartons for mailing. I'd drive up to the box outside our post office on the way to work and deposit them like the little time bombs they were. Those samples would tick for at least four weeks and then change our world, I was sure of it.

"Well, that's that," Grammy said. "What if I'm no more Creek than the Queen of England?"

"It will be our secret, like we said. Or, you won't have to eat *sofkey* ever again, Grammy," I laughed. "And it will be much easier to find clothes." Her ensemble today featured the fake deerskirt and a Navajo-looking orange and brown blouse from Walmart. She'd added lucky silver bear earrings just before we did the test.

I loved her with a fierceness I couldn't describe and wanted her DNA to show exactly what she believed. Anything less would break her heart. I blinked hard to keep tears away.

"What ever happened to that bowl of *sofkey*, anyway?" I asked her. One night we'd come home and it had simply disappeared.

"I gave it to the road crew on 431 to fix potholes," Grammy said. "I tasted it and decided the ancestors must've hated their visitors."

The restaurant was slow, even for a Monday night. We were closing in twenty minutes and Mama had the only table left, a man and woman who'd been eating and drinking for at least an hour and a half, taking full advantage of Manny's cheap margaritas by the pitcher. I was waiting to help Mama clean up, standing out back with one of my occasional Marlboros and gazing at the night sky.

"Skye!" What could Manny possibly want from me? I'd already done more than my share of cleaning and setting up for tomorrow, damnit. By the time I got into the kitchen, the dishwasher, Joe, had already gone home and Manny was nowhere in sight.

I entered the dining room and tried to puzzle out the scene in front of me. Mama was sitting with the man at her booth, his hand clenched around her wrist. Manny was holding his hands up, as if surrendering. I heard him say, "Let the lady go. Let her go right now. I am warning you."

Mama looked terrified. The man's wife or girlfriend was staring down at the table like she'd witnessed this sort of thing before. "Dan, please," she mumbled.

"I ain't going anywhere until she brings me the right change, hombre. I gave her a hundred-dollar bill, and she only brought back fifty-eight dollars. That's bullshit." Dan glared at Manny. He looked about forty, a beefy, florid guy in the kind of shirt tourists wore for local bass fishing.

"I told you to let her go." Manny's hands were lowered now, and I could see him clenching and unclenching a fist. I started to walk closer, but he shot me a look that commanded me to stop. Should I call the police? I couldn't decide.

"I'll let her go when you bring me the rest of my change. Shoulda known better than come to an illegal alien restaurant. Get back to Mex—"

"Who wrote the Federalist Papers?" Manny yelled. His accent was getting stronger by the minute. I fully expected curses in Spanish to start rapid-firing.

"What the hell are you talking about, man? Just give me my money. I don't know nothing about—"

"Madison, Hamilton, Jay, and Publius," Manny said, counting them on his fingers, triumphant. "You know how I know that? It was on the citizenship test I passed six years ago." He paused and watched the man's puzzled face revert to anger. "Now, you drunken asshole, are you gonna take your hand off her, or am I going to make you?"

"I want my money and I'll leave, Pedro." He sneered and gripped Mama's arm harder. I could see the whiteness of his knuckles.

Manny's hand shot past Mama like lightning, grabbing the man's hair and slamming his head to the table. Mama jumped up and ran to my side, crying.

Manny squatted next to the booth, never releasing his hold on the man's head. "Now here is what you are going to do, eh? You are going to leave this restaurant with fifty dollars, because you are gonna tip the lady eight of them. You are never going to come here again, or I will call the police and tell them you attacked my employee, a woman half your size. And if you are ever seen near her again, anywhere, anytime, I will gut you like a fish."

The man was still motionless on the table, but his wife was halfway to the door. "Do you hear me?" Manny growled.

The man nodded as well as he could and Manny released him. He threw the tip on the table and spat at Manny's feet. Manny stood impassively, offering nothing in return. He followed the man to the door and locked it behind him, turning to face us.

My mother squeezed my hand to let me know she was okay, though I could feel her shaking and she was openly sobbing now. I realized I'd been holding my breath. I exhaled slowly, my eyes fixed on the door, terrified the man would come back.

Mama walked to Manny and threw her arms around him in a tight hug, her forehead pressed to his shoulder. I watched until it felt too personal, when she leaned back and kissed him, long and hard and unmistakably like he was very much her type.

Nine

SUNNYVALE, TEXAS
Two months later

Two hundred and eighty characters: the exact number required for complete character *assassination*, Pete thought. Specifically, a tweet reading "My former boss Gerald Davidson, @gdavidsonlawfirmdallas exposed himself to me and tried to get me to have sex with him in his office. Do not let him or anyone else get away with this. Please understand how helpless we feel. Believe women! #MeToo #assault #believewomen #sexualharrassment #MeTooInDallasTexas #justiceforvictims"

It wasn't just there, glaring from his laptop; it was in the *Dallas News*. Gerry's picture would likely be slathered all over TV tonight, too, along with the words of his anonymous accuser "JDoe02051982", who had filed a police report already.

"What does Gerald say?" Kara asked, shaking her head.

"He's blindsided. This woman is a temp who's only been working in his office for six weeks. She never let on she was unhappy in any way, and Gerry is positive she can't have a personal ax to grind with him. She isn't looking for money." Pete paused and stared at the screen. "He didn't do this, Kara. I know Gerry, and this isn't him."

"Men do things other men would never suspect, Pete." She caught his sharp look and backpedaled. "I mean, I don't think Gerald is capable of this either. He's a very... umm... *tactile* man, but I don't believe he'd actually expose himself—"

"What do you mean, 'tactile man', Kara?" Pete stared at her.

"Just that he, you know, sometimes hugs a little too long or maybe hangs onto my hand an extra beat. It's nothing. He's just... friendly." Kara shrugged and sat down.

Pete turned back to Twitter, where the likes, retweets, and sympathetic comments were piling up way too fast. "This whole MeToo thing has gotten way out of hand," Pete said. "Anyone can ruin another person without any evidence at all."

"If she went to the police, surely they'll determine nothing happened?" Kara tilted the end of her sentence up into a question.

"I guess. The thing is, the damage is done. Gerry won't be able to walk away from her accusation. He's being interviewed by the cops this afternoon, and all he can hope for is damage control after he clears his name."

"He can straighten this out, and it'll be quickly forgotten. I'm sure everything will be fine." Kara seemed confident, so Pete held some hope for his friend, attorney and board member.

"I'm going to fix lunch, Baby. Would you like a Perrier with lime to go with your salad?" Kara had her hand on the doorknob.

No, I want a triple scotch. "Yeah, that would be great, thanks." Kara knew something Pete and Gerry didn't, and she smiled a little on the way to the kitchen. LeeAnne Byrd had described a medium-sized mole to the police, something she couldn't un-see in the whole horrible picture she related in her report. The mole was located about three inches east of Gerald Davidson's penis. It was oval, about as big as a Tic-Tac.

His ex-wife Kristin was a bit angry over her divorce settlement. She wasn't thrilled about Gerald's new Mercedes or his trip to New Zealand last fall, either, the trip she'd looked forward to making with him since helping put him through law school in the previous century.

Kristin had been delighted to describe that ugly mole to Kara, and would have furnished a photo if she'd had one, Kara suspected. Hell hath no fury like a woman scorned by crappy alimony and a five-year-old Lexus in need of new tires. She'd discarded the throwaway phone used to get the details from Kristin, destroying any possible connection between them. LeeAnne was all set, too, because she was only halfway to the twenty thousand dollars she was promised. Kara had the added insurance of LeeAnne's filing a false police report, the gravity of which a legal secretary should certainly appreciate.

It had all unfolded with exquisite timing, as Gerald's pregnant secretary had stopped throwing up and was due back on the job tomorrow.

"Are you *insane?*" Stephen had shrieked into her ear. "You're destroying Gerald's reputation with some ridiculous story concocted by a temp you placed in his office? You don't know this will backfire *all over you? Jesus,* Kara, Mr. Davidson will know LeeAnne was a plant, he'll know he was set up—"

"I have no idea what you're talking about, Stephen," she'd replied. "I'm as surprised by Gerald's behavior as anyone." Kara had hung up the phone with an eye roll at his dramatics.

Now she considered her worst-case scenario: Gerald Davidson somehow forcing the truth about LeeAnne's hiring from Darrell Edwards. Kara sincerely doubted Darrell would get her in trouble. She'd been very careful to explain the delicate nature of her intervention at Brownhill Staffing, and how her firm couldn't alienate Davidson and Associates. They were going to be working side by side, and it was extremely important he never tell about their asking for a better-suited legal secretary. He couldn't even reveal he'd been approached; their involvement with Gerald's case was completely confidential. If Kara wasn't mistaken, Mr. Edwards would do just about anything for the woman he knew as Jenny Tyson from Los Angeles. Plus, he'd probably want Brownhill Staffing's good name as far from Gerald's scandal as possible.

Besides, she mused, even if Gerald found out the truth, it would be far too late for him. Kara could manage any fallout with Pete. Kara could manage *anything* with Pete. She smiled and placed a couple of extra egg slices on today's Cobb salad. Her husband deserved them.

Gerald Davidson issued an official statement strongly denying the accusations against him, depicting them as a crude attempt to defame an innocent man. He allowed the press to speculate on whether he'd been under a demand for money in exchange for his unnamed employee's silence. He'd retained an attorney in case criminal charges were brought by LeeAnne Byrd, whose identity remained unknown to the world. Gerald was going into the office as usual, where most of his firm's long-time clients, good old Texas boys to the end, stood by his side. He was still best-damn-lawyering for Pete. He was golfing on Wednesday mornings and Friday afternoons. Sometimes he'd catch someone looking at him strangely at the club and tell himself the gossip would slither forward to the next victim soon.

His girlfriend, Sheila, refused to believe the slander against him, though she'd yet to hear of the police report's Mole of Damnation. For one brief moment, he'd been sickened to think she could have given that detail to LeeAnne.

He knew better. It could have been any of a few women he'd been with since the divorce. There were likely vengeful vipers in the group. He'd been pretty remote with most of them after getting them into bed.

The only thing that had significantly changed in Gerald Davidson's life was his regretful resignation from the PFD Pipelines Board of Directors, which was unavoidable under the volatile circumstances. He'd told Pete and a tearful Kara he completely understood the need to step down. He truly wished them the best with their continuing public relations battle in Oklahoma, and privately felt some measure of relief he wouldn't be involved.

Kara lay with her head on Pete's chest, idly stroking the few wiry hairs there. She was trying to think of the best way to introduce her latest idea. All she'd decided was that their bed was a good place to begin the discussion.

"Baby," she said, "what are you going to do about the board vacancy?"

Pete yawned and threw an arm over his eyes. "I have a couple of candidates in mind."

"Is one of them a woman?" Kara asked.

"No. No, one of them is not a woman, Kara. It's a construction business. It's populated almost exclusively by men. My board's mostly made up of guys I trust from years of association, with ties to the oil and gas pipeline industry."

"And that's how it should be, Pete. It's just," she rolled onto her stomach and faced him, "this is the right time for PFD to show some diversity. Your public face is a bunch of older white guys—"

"We have a black man on our board, Kara. Lewis Hill from Montana. He's been with us since 2011."

"Yes, I know, Baby. But it's time you put a more progressive image forth for the company. You should consider a woman. Women are leading businesses all over the world. Governments, too. Look at Hillary Clinton. She was almost our President—"

Pete groaned. "Not the way to win me over, Kara."

"Pete. Not just any woman. A woman who wants nothing but success for your company. A woman with a master's degree in engineering who had a brilliant career before she met you. I was Summa Cum Laude at *Vanderbilt*, Pete. I have dark hair, dark eyes, high cheekbones, and likely a little Native American blood. Don't you see? I can help you in Oklahoma. Let me work for PFD, if not on the board then as an executive officer—"

"It'd just look like I'm throwing my wife onto the board in a token gesture, Kara. They wouldn't respect that or welcome it, either. And there's no way I'm giving you a company job. We agreed when we married that you would stop working."

"I know, and I'm fine with that. But you should either put me on the board or a woman who's almost as wonderful as I am." Kara smiled and touched her finger to Pete's lips, silencing him. She trailed the fingernails of her other hand down the front of his body, making sure she had the last word.

Pete responded as quickly and reliably as any dog Pavlov ever met.

Ten

EUFAULA, ALABAMA
Six weeks later

"*El amarillo es bonito*," Manny sang in a terrible approximation of *Twinkle Twinkle Little Star's* melody.

I sat back and crossed my arms. "You *do* realize at least seventy-five percent of us at this table know you're hinting at yellow, right? Including your partner, Mama?"

"Oh, I know Spanish, Little One," Grammy nodded at me. "I also know cheating. Manny, table talk is against the rules, but if you're that desperate, know that we'll still beat you." She winked at me and tossed a piece of popcorn into her mouth. "We do every time, whether you tell your partner what's in your hand or not."

It was the fourth possibly rainy Sunday afternoon in the past six weeks, and Manny had fallen into the habit of playing Rook with us instead of soccer, using the threat of rain as an

53

excuse. No one objected to this, as he invariably showed up with tamales or burritos for supper. We'd taught him the game, and he'd quickly latched onto the macho-swagger aspect of winning a hand.

Except he rarely won.

It gave him a great way to spend time with Mama, though. The demands of running the restaurant made that difficult, and their courtship excruciatingly slow. It was also awkward and featured too many meaningful glances for my taste.

At least Mama had a boyfriend which was more than Grammy or I could say.

Also included in Sunday afternoons and evenings: Manny's mother, Luz, who sat in a corner staring at us when she wasn't watching an Español news channel in the next room. She rarely smiled and never spoke a word to anyone but Manny, and that was in such accelerated Spanish we didn't stand a chance of deciphering it. If he was trying to force her to warm to us by dragging her along to the house, she seemed to be thawing at a glacial pace.

Manny's yellow "hint" to Mama accomplished nothing. Grammy and I beat them for the third time that day. Grammy rose and triumphantly waved the score sheet at Manny's face, then took the popcorn bowl to join Luz on the couch and stare at the TV. I smiled at the two old ladies crunching *maize* kernels, one of them utterly clueless what the TV was saying but too polite to ask about changing to an English channel. Sparrow was due to decide she had some Aztec in her any minute now.

Mama sat gazing at Manny like he'd just presented her a ginormous diamond instead of a card game loss.

I went off to my room to await dinner in an hour or so. If necessary, I'd walk back out playing a kazoo to keep from stumbling upon those two making out by the kitchen sink.

Hours later, Luz and Grammy were snoring softly on the couch in front of Tom Selleck's moustache emoting on the television. Mama and Manny were in the backyard doing God knows what. I was trying to decide how to salvage my Sunday night when my friend Angie texted me to come join a bunch of people having a bonfire at the lake. I tiptoed to the kitchen table and wrote a quick note telling Mama where I'd gone, because I had no desire to behold the horror behind the house.

As I turned the door handle, Manny's mom whispered in perfectly understandable English, "Be careful, Es-cah-yee." She smiled at me and I nodded, trying not to look bewildered. "I will, Miss Luz," I whispered back. I closed the door and laughed. Wait until Sparrow found out she could talk Luz's ear off and be understood.

Angie and about eight other people waved when I drove up. They were sitting around the fire sharing beer and lies. Somebody's phone was playing Luke Bryan or Florida-Georgia Line or some generic country-poppy crap through a Bluetooth speaker. I spotted Greg Varnadoe sitting slightly apart from the rest.

Greg was one of the kids who'd been nice to me when we were tiny, vulnerable minnows in first grade. I was different. My dad was dead. I lived with my mom and grandmother. Danita Dawson, forever dressed in some expensive and adorable outfit, was worshipped by all the boys and girls. Her smooth, shoulder-length blonde hair swung like a satin curtain when she turned her head. Her father owned some lumber company, and she lived in a fancy two-story house that sparkled at night, all lit up for everyone to see when they drove through town. She was the undisputed queen of our school universe.

And she hated me. I was never sure why, but she'd whisper behind her hand when I walked by and laugh with her friends. I had no idea what it was about me that offended Danita, but it was constant. I came home in tears more than once. Mama told me not to pay Danita any attention. Grammy wiped my tears away and explained that Danita was in need of an exorcism, and her mother was, too, until Mama interrupted her and she walked away with her hands in the air.

Greg, whose family had moved to town from Huntsville just before school started, was similarly outcast and wandered the lunchroom looking for a friendly place to sit every day. Usually, he ate alone. One day, in the bright glare of Danita's spotlight, he was brave enough to sit with me and Angie, who was almost as unpopular as I was and my only friend. He plopped down and pushed his black-framed glasses up his pudgy nose, trying not to look fearful as he braved our territory. "I saw Danita Dawson eat a booger one day when was walkin' to the girls' room," he announced under his breath. "No one believes me, but it's true."

Of course it wasn't true. Danita Dawson didn't even have boogers. But Greg was our friend and ally from that day forward. He had a pretty nice social life going by middle school, playing football and soccer and forever ceasing to be pudgy. He started "going out" with Caroline. That made him a safe friend, always off-limits, middle-school-married and risk-free for Angie and me to hang around. We did until Caroline took over his life. She directed where and when Greg did everything, but Angie and I had something passing for boyfriends of our own by that time.

Greg spotted me, then patted his lap and invited me to occupy it. He was cute but an inch or two short of my minimum height requirement, plus he'd been with Caroline since time began. I chose a hay bale a couple of feet away.

"What's up, Skye?" Greg asked, slurring a tiny bit. "You look good. You and Jeff still together?"

He knew damn well we weren't. "No, we split up a couple of months ago." I accepted the Bud Light he extended toward me. "And I presume you and Caroline are still engaged?"

He laughed. "I guess, maybe. Don't see her much since she joined the Guard."

"The Guard. The *National* Guard?" Caroline had been almost invisible when she turned sideways in high school and completely incapable of one burpee or chin-up when we graduated.

"Yeah. She's gettin' a signing bonus of twenty thousand if she sticks with it. She's off at basic training for three more weeks in Anniston." He chugged the rest of his beer.

That explained his willingness to host me on his lap. "Good for her," I said. I wondered if the Guard would want me. I was in pretty decent shape for someone living on tortillas and refried beans.

"Yeah, Caroline's gonna get training to be a pharmacy tech. She'll have a little break after Basic, then she'll be gone to Texas for months."

"That's great, Greg," I said, and I meant it. Maybe I should quit margarita-ing tourists and talk to a recruiter about actually doing something with my life.

His eyes were beer-tear shiny in the pale moonlight. "No, it's not. I mean, it is for *her*, and I'm glad for Caroline. I don't think we'll end up married or even together after all this, though. She's leavin' me behind, stuck in my daddy's cow pasture. I freakin' *hate* cows, Skye. I hate the farm and every cowshit-covered thing on it."

I had no idea how to handle drunk-Greg, so I just sat there.

Now he was tossing whatever was at hand into the fire: his cigarette butt, a small rock, wads of hay. I'm sure he would have been grateful for a firecracker. I watched him slide off a braided leather bracelet, no doubt a gift from Caroline, and hurl it into the flames. Greg half-smiled at me and said, "You know, I had a crush on you senior year."

I laughed up a magic force field against the direction this was taking. "No, I did not know that. Besides, you were with Caroline."

"We've been together since sixth grade." He shook his head. *"Sixth grade.* That is ridiculous."

"I don't think it's ridiculous, Greg. I think it's really sweet. There aren't many couples who can say they've been—"

I stopped suddenly because he'd leaned in to kiss me. I jumped up and nearly fell backward over my hay bale trying to dodge him. "Hey, Greg, don't... you don't want to do that. You have a fiancée—"

"I'm sorry, Skye, I really am. It's been a bad day. Bad month or two. Bad *life.* Just forget it." He stood with his hands in the air and turned to walk away toward the lake.

Damn it. I glanced over at Angie, who was now oblivious to everyone but the guy she was kissing. Everyone else had parted off into couples or was working hard at it, and I might as well have been miles away. I was going to kill her for failing to mention she'd invited me out here for Greg Varnadoe.

I watched him, profiled against the lake and city lights, swaying a little, hands in his pockets. I did the only thing I could do with a clear conscience; I followed him to make sure he was okay.

"Greg, how long have you been drinking today?" I asked, hand on his arm.

"I dunno. Maybe two or three o'clock." He shrugged and pulled my hand away, dropping it into the air. "We were fishing. Kenny brought me out here and then Angie showed up and they were all over each other." He swiped at his face.

"I miss Caroline, ya know? I miss her and she's gone and I feel so stupid. I'm twenty-one and all I am is tired and sad and Caroline doesn't care. She keeps talking about all these *people* she's met, only I know most of them are guys—"

"Greg," I interrupted. "Let me take you home."

"Nah," he said, "I'm okay. I don't wanna be by myself at the apartment tonight, so I'll chill here. You're a nice girl, Skye. You're better off without that dumbass Jeff Turley, too. You're too good for him."

"So I've heard," I mumbled. "Here's the thing, Greg: I won't leave here without you tonight. You can come home with me. I'll make up the couch for you." Surely the old ladies had vacated the couch by now. Manny would have taken his mom home.

He stared. "Really? You'd do that for me?"

"Yeah. Now let's go."

"Okay, just let me grab a couple of Bud Lights." I let him stop by the cooler, then led him to my car and closed him in. No one even noticed we were leaving, or didn't care. "Don't open those until we get out of the car, Greg," I said, fastening my seat belt. I smacked his hand as he was fumbling with the beer. Greg leaned his head against the passenger window and was asleep before we arrived at the House of the Sparrow.

I woke to Grammy banging pots and pans as loudly as possible around eight the next morning. Mama would be gone to work, and Greg would be holding his head and begging for death about now.

By the time I threw on some clothes and walked out, she was sitting next to him on the couch. Greg held a small plate of freshly baked biscuits. He was a faint shade of green, but Grammy ignored that and prattled on. "So you see, there are two wolves inside you, and they fight constantly. The light and the dark, the good and the bad." She nodded at Greg to be sure he understood.

"Yes, ma'am." Greg was looking back and forth from the biscuits to me. I had no intention of rescuing him. I walked into the kitchen and poured a cup of coffee, listening as I stirred it.

"And the young man asks the chief which wolf will win the struggle," Grammy continued, "the dark or the light?" She paused for effect. "And the chief says, 'the wolf you *feed*.'" Grammy waited for her message to penetrate and then glanced over at me. "Morning, Little One. I was telling your friend about the two wolves."

"Yes, I heard that. Greg, isn't that a great story?"

"Sure is, Skye. I'm going to remember that." Greg looked at the biscuits like they were fresh cow pies. "Skye, I really need to get going to help Dad today. Could you give me a ride to the farm?"

"Sure thing." I grabbed my keys as Greg thanked Grammy for her hospitality and the nice breakfast. She hugged him and whispered something I couldn't hear.

"You eat any of those biscuits?" I asked as he collapsed into the passenger seat.

"No. I'm never eating again. Never drinking, either."

"Well, I hope you take that story of the two wolves to heart, Greg. Those are Grammy's greatest words of encouragement from the ancestors, and she only pulls them out for serious cases like you."

"I'm taking them to heart, Skye, I promise." He waited a beat or two, rubbing his temples. "But anyone who's ever had a Facebook account has read that story a few hundred times."

We both dissolved into laughter. I decided Greg was going to be okay once he plowed through this hangover. It was likely his father would notice and *literally* make him plow through it.

I delivered Greg to the end of the driveway and got out to tell him goodbye. "You scared me last night, Greg. If you ever even think of hurting yourself, you have to promise you'll call me, or call someone for help. You promise or I'll blow this car horn for three solid minutes."

"I promise," he said, and I believed him. "That was a lot of beer and a little heartache you heard talking. I'm going to talk to Caroline, and no matter what happens, I'll be okay." He hugged me. "And Skye? Thank you. Thank you for being the right person in my life at the right time. I mean it, you know?"

"I know." I pecked his cheek and drove away feeling like I'd fed the right wolf in *me*, at least.

Grammy was staring at her computer when I walked in. "Come look! The results are in the email!" She was about two inches from the monitor, squinting to read. I enlarged the screen for her.

Ethnicity Estimate

England, Wales and Northwestern Europe	55%
Ireland and Scotland	27%
Native American Muscogee Creek	14%
Spain	4%

Wow! Congratulations, Grammy, you were right all along. This is wonderful news!" I'd believed along with her, but it was great to see the results.

"I still can't join the Poarch Creek Nation, though, Little One, can I?" Her eyes were filled with tears, both happy and disappointed.

"No, Grammy, they require you to be at least one-quarter Creek. Plus, they said they wouldn't even accept DNA testing on its own. We'd have to produce all sorts of other stuff. It doesn't matter. You're as Creek as you always knew, that's what's important." I stroked her beautiful white braid.

"No. Tim McGraw. I'd really hoped to meet him backstage at a casino concert."

"That was an extremely long shot, Grammy, but he'd love you if he met you. No casino money, either. But you still have me and Mama."

"Yes, Little One, and you are the most precious things in this world to me. Is your friend Greg all right? He was pretty surprised when I started banging the baking pans, but he was nice about it and very polite. Thanks for slipping the note under my door. If you hadn't, I might have shot him."

I may or may not have rolled my eyes at the notion of Grammy taking her shotgun to an innocent, hungover boy on her couch. "I think he is. I'll check on him in a couple of days, but he's in a much better place than he was last night. Thank you for cooking him breakfast." I was pulling up email on my phone to see if my DNA results were in. I clicked on the link and had a hard time hearing what Grammy was saying as I tried to figure out what I was seeing.

Ethnicity Estimate

England, Wales and Northwestern Europe	57%
Ireland and Scotland	27%
Native American Muscogee Creek	10%
Spain	4%
Benin-Togo Sub-Saharan Africa	2%

Additional Communities

Greater Mobile, Alabama, African Settlers

"Little One? What's wrong? What is it, honey?" I heard her from the bottom of a deep pool. I was drowning. I couldn't breathe.

My mother had lied to me. She'd been lying to me my whole life, and I held the proof in my shaking hand.

Part Two

A River Runs Through Me

Eleven

EUFAULA, ALABAMA
August 1996

P ete felt at home gazing across Lake Eufaula. He'd spent much of his youth on Lake Eufaula in Oklahoma, and while the surrounding terrain was vastly different, the lakes echoed each other. His mother had told him there were Alabama family connections, too; a great-great-great-grandmother or someone had lived in the state. Her name was lost to time, but Pete liked to think his genes held a memory of this place. Maybe his ancestors were Native Americans, forcibly marched to Oklahoma in the last century. It made sense.

The contract PFD held here was the most important of his career: almost one hundred miles of natural gas line repair and replacement from Eufaula north up 431. So far it was going better than he'd hoped, and they were ahead of schedule.

Pete popped open a beer and waited for the sunset, when they'd start grilling burgers. He'd brought his crew out here for a well-deserved Saturday afternoon break. Most of them were fishing, but that didn't interest him. He'd been watching two women sunbathing on beach towels. One of them looked several years younger than he was, but perfectly legal. He'd caught her glancing his way more than once. She had dark hair, a curvy body, a criminally tiny pink bikini, and a sweet smile she revealed every time her friend said something funny. *Her friend is either a professional comedian, or this girl is trying to get my attention.*

Nothing was going to happen, because Pete Darling was terrified of talking to females. The girl was probably looking his way because he was six feet five inches tall—had been since high school— a feature that, along with his wide forehead, had earned him the nickname "Lurch". Pete shifted uncomfortably in his plastic lawn chair. He hadn't had a real relationship since college, and that was fifteen years ago. Every ounce of time and attention had gone into PFD Pipelines. It was finally, gloriously paying off here in Alabama.

The occasional women in his life were scattered along the path of construction projects all over the country. Invariably, they'd approached him, usually in a bar. Pete couldn't start a conversation with a woman any more than he could summon the Loch Ness Monster from Lake Eufaula.

For years he'd been registering in motels as "Otis Garfield" after discovering the success he'd enjoyed made people treat him differently. He didn't trust anyone, especially not a woman who might discover he owned a company worth millions of dollars.

In public he was just Pete, one of the crew, another construction worker humping it to a weekly paycheck. It fit his personality better than designer clothes or a flashy car. His crew appreciated it, too. He was watching seven of his guys enjoy the finest bass and beer Eufaula had to offer. Two others, Tim and Randy, sat near him and enjoyed the sun. Pete noticed Randy occasionally stealing a look at Pink Bikini and her friend. Like most of his workers, Randy was married. It made for an easier time on the road than guys constantly on the prowl.

Pete took a satisfied gulp of beer and closed his eyes, inhaling fresh pine. One of the guys yelled about bait, a bird screeched from a nearby tree, a cloud covered the scorching sun, and for a few blissful moments Pete drifted off to sleep.

He woke at the sound of his name. "Pete? Pete! Can you give us a hand?"

Pink Bikini and Female Comedian, a wisp of a girl, were standing next to an old blue-and-mostly-rust Datsun 280Z twenty yards away. Several of his crew had crowded around, looking under the hood and making manly noises about the engine. Pete walked over, wondering what he could possibly contribute to the conversation. He doubted the Datsun had a broken gas line.

"Hi," Female Comedian said, "I'm Lisa. This is my friend Emmy." Pink Bikini with Newly Added Bathing Suit Cover waved at him. "They said you might know what's keeping my car from starting."

Pete glared at the guys, who knew full well his knowledge of internal combustion engines ranked slightly below his knowledge of crochet patterns. He could see a couple of them stifling laughter.

"Any of you check out the battery?" He directed his question at Randy, who generally had some sense about him when it came to cars.

"Yeah," Randy replied, "Battery's fine, alternator's fine. It's not electrical."

Pete turned to Keith, who was small enough to sandwich behind the steering wheel. "Go see if it's flooded."

Randy bit his lip. "It's fuel-injected, Pete. Don't think that's the problem. Maybe an injector is clogged."

Pete chose to nod at him rather than bellow, *Why the hell did you call me over here, asshole?*

"Okay, well, if it won't start we'll call you ladies a tow truck," Pete said. He produced his tiny new flip phone from a pocket. The thing looked like it was meant for a Barbie doll.

"It won't work out here," Lisa said. "Besides, the only tow truck in town on Saturday is Lee Reese's, and he's gone to visit his sister in Phenix City."

Pete marveled at the efficacy of small-town Alabama grapevines for a minute. He threw his keys at Randy. "Well, we can give you a ride if you'd like. Randy, take my truck and give these ladies a lift into town."

Randy tossed the keys back. "Pete, we've all had too much beer and bourbon to drive anywhere right now. You haven't."

Damn him. So *that's* why they'd called Pete over.

Emmy piped up, "We don't really have to be back for a few hours—" She was looking at Pete all gooey-eyed, obviously looking for an invitation.

He surmised he was supposed to notice it was almost seven o'clock, and the ladies might be hungry. He stifled a groan and muttered, "Well, I was going to grill some burgers. Why don't you two stay with us for supper?"

Emmy answered him in a voice dripping Alabama sorghum syrup. "Oh, that's so sweet of you!" She glanced at Lisa. "We'd love to join y'all if you don't mind."

Emmy installed herself in his former chair next to Randy, enthralling him with every word. Lisa chose to help Pete at the

grill which was the biggest curse of his day. He tried desperately to think of a polite way to suggest he could manage
fine by himself. The little woman stood between the cooler on
the picnic table and him—barely the height of his lower
biceps—forming hamburger patties and chattering nonstop
about her job, her ex-boyfriend, her favorite TV shows, her
late father, her mother's motorcycle, her own useless car, her
longing to travel the world, her preference for hamburgers and
hatred of hot dogs…

Pete found it worked out just fine if he nodded along,
murmured an occasional "yeah", and concentrated on the grill.
By the time darkness fell and the soft lights near the lake
clicked on, they had served a fine meal of cheeseburgers,
potato chips and Doritos to everyone but themselves. Pete
grabbed a beer for courage and sat with Lisa at a picnic table
under the stars of Alabama. He was thrilled to find she could
eat without talking, so he could sit quietly and enjoy the soft
lapping of the lake and Lisa's smile between bites.

When they finished eating, Lisa drank two beers and grew
even less chatty. She didn't look at Pete, her eyes fixed on
Emmy and the others down by the water. Pete was horrified
to see she was crying.

"Umm, hey, are you all right, Lisa?" She didn't answer. This
was much, much worse than endless talking. Pete reached a
long arm across the table and tentatively touched her shoulder,
trying to break her out of whatever female hysteria she was in.

"Yeah, I'm sorry. My dad died a few months ago from a
heart attack. I mean, it's not like we were even close. He was
quiet and reserved, not a hugger, you know? It kind of came
back to the surface tonight, that's all. We used to come out to
this lake every once in a while." She palmed tears up from her
eyes. "I'm sorry. I didn't mean to spoil the mood."

"There's a *mood?*" Pete laughed softly, and Lisa rewarded him with a smile.

"You seem really nice," Lisa said. "I've mostly only known boys I grew up around. You're the first grownup with a y chromosome I've talked with in a long time."

"I am flattered." Pete looked at Lisa and saw a lively intelligence in her eyes, which were a beautiful dark brown. There was a kindness to her that relaxed him a little. He hadn't felt comfortable around a woman since he could remember.

"I'm not sure what part of the state, but I have ancestors who lived in Alabama," Pete was surprised to hear himself revealing anything personal.

"Oh, yeah? We're probably related. No, wait, please don't start the cousin jokes. That will definitely spoil the mood." Lisa rolled her eyes and giggled. "Look, it's Saturday night. I'm alone, you're alone, we should do something fun. Have you ever been to the Grand Canyon?"

"I really don't know you that well, Lisa—"

"No, wait, I'm serious. There's a canyon about twenty miles from here, out in the sticks, and it's beautiful. It's like a little Grand Canyon."

"Lisa, I hate to disappoint you, but it's dark." Pete swept his hand around him, eyebrows raised. "It's dark and they'll be closed."

"Of course they'll be closed. That's half the fun." Lisa jumped up. "Do you have a flashlight?"

"Of course I have a flashlight. I work construction, and I have that y chromosome, remember? But we won't be able to see anything—"

"Trust me. We used to sneak in there at night when I was in high school. It's so pretty, and I promise you'll see the canyon, or a piece of it. Come on. Tomorrow is Sunday. You don't work on Sunday, do you?"

Pete shook his head. "No, I don't work on Sunday." He glanced at his crew, all gathered around Emmy, who seemed perfectly happy to be surrounded by men. "I guess I could get the guys to make sure Emmy gets home safe."

"I'm absolutely sure you could." Lisa nodded at the group by the lake. "Why don't we just tell them you're going to drive me? I bet they can take a hint."

Pete regarded her for a minute. "You don't even know me, Lisa. Are you sure you want to ride off into the sticks with a stranger?"

"You know what? You're right. Let's start with ice cream from the Burger Barn and take it from there. Canyon cancelled. The police are probably patrolling over there tonight, anyway."

"You might have mentioned that."

Three trucks left the lake that night. One was a crew truck driven by Randy that took Emmy home; another delivered the rest of the crew to their motel. The third held Pete Darling, Lisa Willis, and the first glimmer of Skye.

Lisa didn't have even a vague idea she might be pregnant until Pete and his crew were at least fifty miles away, staying in a rented house near somewhere in rural Alabama.

They'd only seen each other four times, the second on a weekend when Pete took her to see *Sling Blade* at the theater. She despised the movie; he liked it, and as usual he'd been mostly silent the entire evening.

On their third Saturday night, they went to Providence Canyon. Pete guessed it held a passing resemblance to the Grand Canyon, but he really didn't care. They found some soft grass and laid a blanket under the black sky, which revealed the Milky Way and a billion stars when their eyes adjusted. They were hungry for each other by then, though Pete knew he'd be leaving town in a matter of days.

He didn't tell Lisa. He held her like she was precious to him. He cradled her face in his hands and lied in complete silence, without ever saying a word.

The next Saturday he was distant at the restaurant she'd chosen. Lisa talked for both of them, from appetizers through dessert.

He'd kissed her goodnight and told her he'd enjoyed their time together, but he had to leave. Pete lived on the road, going from project to project. Construction was the only thing he knew, et cetera. It was a hundred more words than he'd said all through dinner, and all it did was sting. It was clear he didn't mean for them to stay in touch. If Pete had been the tiniest bit more open and articulate, he would've explained to her that he was completely devoted to building his business. That meant constant travel, and *that* meant relationships were impractical if not impossible.

Lisa took it as the cold dismissal it was.

The motel where Pete and his fellow construction workers had stayed in Eufaula had no record of anyone named Pete Darling or Peter Darling or anything close. Obviously, he'd lied about the few things he'd told her.

Lisa rubbed the small bump of her belly as she walked to her mother's front door. She was only a few months along but baggy clothes weren't going to disguise a pregnancy on her tiny frame much longer. She had to tell Verna, who was barely past crying regularly after losing Lisa's dad. They both were.

Now she was going to hurt and upset her mother all over again, inflict a fresh wound where she had barely healed.

She found Verna sitting in front of the television, which she kept on in the background every waking moment. Lisa figured her mother could stop watching *The Price Is Right* long enough to be informed she was going to be a grandmother, so she grabbed the remote and turned it off. She plopped onto the couch.

"Mom—" she began.

"How far along are you?" Verna asked quietly.

"You *know*? How could you know? I've barely started believing it myself." Lisa searched her mother's face in wonder.

"I just *know*, Talisa. You are carrying light and love in you. My mothers and grandmothers whisper—"

"Mom, please. No magical Muscogee matriarchy right now."

"Okay, I heard you throwing up when you stopped by one morning and you haven't asked me to pick up tampons for months." Verna crossed her arms and leaned back into the couch cushions, eyes on the ceiling.

"You're not mad?"

"How can I be mad? Every day I work, cry, talk to these walls, and try to figure out what I'm going to do with my life." Verna patted her daughter's hand. "Now I know."

"I haven't told anyone. And Mom, the father is someone I slept with once, and he dumped me and left town. I have no idea where he is or if I even know his real name."

"His real name," Verna answered, "is Walking Anal Cavity. We can call him Wally for short."

By the time Skye was born, Lisa had moved back into her mother's house and settled into a routine: Verna, who now insisted her name was Sparrow, kept the baby while Lisa worked as a waitress during the day. Most nights Sparrow worked a cashier shift at Walmart and she took in the occasional sewing project. Between the two of them, with a house paid off by Nate Willis's insurance money, they made ends meet.

The routine worked beautifully until one day at work when Lisa met a gorgeous soldier on leave from Fort Benning. From that moment on, all she wanted was time. Time with Larry to discover everything about him, time to watch Larry play with Skye until she thought her heart would burst with happiness, time to make love with this man who made her feel what she'd never dreamed possible. Larry was guns and muscles and flowers and laughter and kindness and beauty—the man left people smiling wherever he went.

She had never felt as safe as she did within his arms.

The day he shipped out to Afghanistan she cried and clutched her daughter. Skye patted her face with little starfish hands, smearing her mother's tears and smiling. Larry promised he'd be home in a year and they'd be married. Skye would have a little brother and a Golden Retriever puppy. Lisa and their family would travel with him to live on bases around the world, maybe Japan, maybe Germany. She would explore Neuschwanstein Castle with Larry. They'd take Skye to Disneyland, to Kyoto, to London.

When the uniformed men came to the door, Lisa thanked them. They didn't have to do that; she wasn't family. Larry must have put her name on a form somewhere.

She walked back to her room and stayed there for three months, where the woman who'd met and loved Larry Smith died with him.

Sparrow forced her to eat, forced her to see Skye every day, forced her to go to a therapist, eventually forced her to get a new job and move forward.

She could never force Lisa to look at her daughter without remembering what she'd lost, though. Every year, every milestone, everything beautiful thing Skye did or said: those were all numbered as things Larry would never be there to love with her.

Twelve

Mama sat at the table with her hands over her ears, silently enduring every word I hurled at her. I hadn't stopped yelling since she walked in the door.

"How could you do this to me? How could you lie about the most important thing in my life? My father didn't even *look* like the man in this picture frame, did he? Mama? Was he white? Was he black?" I brandished Larry's photo like a weapon.

"What?" Mama looked up, puzzled. "Of course he was white. I don't know what you're talking about."

I replaced the photo on the kitchen countertop and slammed my phone down in front of her face. "Look. See that? Benin-Togo. Sub-Saharan. African settlers in the Mobile, *Alabama* area. That's not Larry Smith's British, New England, '*up north*' somewhere, is it, Mama? You told me my father had never been south of the Mason-Dixon Line before you met him."

"That was true. Fort Benning was the first…" She saw my eyes and shifted her gaze down to the table. "Skye, I admit it, I lied. I did it to protect you. Larry loved you like you were his own. He adored you—"

"Who is he?" I interrupted. "Who is my father? Is he dead, too, like Soldier Boy there?"

I stopped talking as a throw pillow hit the side of my head. Grammy had come in from the living room. "SKYE!" Grammy screamed. "Sit *down* and show respect for your mother. You have no idea what she's been through."

The pillow was surprising, but Grammy had never, *ever* called me by my name. I had been Little One, even when I was in trouble.

I glanced at Grammy and slumped into a chair opposite Mama, arms crossed. I was shaking all over.

"Your *biological* father," Mama began, "is a man I met the year before you were born. He was a construction worker in town for a month or two. I didn't know that when I—"

"Oh, God. You screwed some stranger and I'm the result. It's so much worse than I thought," I spat the words at her. "What is his name? Does he know about me? *Does he even know about me?*"

"No," Mama said quietly. "I never got to tell him. The name he'd given me turned out to be fake. The motel staff where he'd been staying had never heard of Pete Darling. By the time I knew I was carrying you, he'd left town, and I had no idea how to locate him." She was crying, but I didn't feel the least bit of sympathy.

"Pete. Pete *Darling*. That's what he said his name was?" I rolled my eyes. "And the motel didn't recognize the name. So you just, what, decided he was CIA and never tried to track him down?"

"Skye." Mama shook her head. "It was obvious he didn't want to be with me under *any* circumstances. He dumped me and left town with no way for me to find him."

"And you thought I'd be better off believing some guy you met later was my father. You had to know I'd find out." I shook my head and stood to leave.

"No, Skye, I had no way of knowing DNA testing would come along and blow up people's lives. I never dreamed you'd have reason to suspect Larry wasn't your biological father. He was *such* a good man, Skye—"

"Don't. Not another word about Saint Larry."

Grammy had had enough. She sat at the table and pulled me back down next to her. "Little One, you are a smart girl, not an idiot. Two percent DNA doesn't necessarily mean someone would look like a distant ancestor. I know you know that."

"Yes," I allowed, "I *do* know that. But Mama has been so weird about my father, about Larry, so unwilling to talk about him… I always suspected she'd been lying to me. All the test did was make me absolutely certain."

"Are you as angry with me as you are your mother? Because I've been lying to you, too," Grammy turned and placed her hands on the sides of my face. "We tried to do what was best for you, your entire life. Your mother and I have never wanted anything but your happiness. That is a truth you feel all the way to your bones, Little One."

"I don't know what I believe anymore." At that point the dam broke and I started crying. All my anger dissolved into sadness, the last thing I wanted. It was so much easier to hold on to white-hot resentment than share my hurt with either of them.

Mama reached across the table. "I'm so sorry, Skye. Every year it got harder to tell you, and by the time you were grown I started to worry you'd never forgive me. I didn't know what difference an absentee father would make after you turned eighteen. It made more sense to me to keep it all a secret." She came around the table and hugged me, with Grammy's arms encircling us the best she could from my side.

After my heart rate slowed a bit, I took a ragged breath and asked Grammy, "Why did you encourage me to do the DNA test, knowing it might show something that pointed to my real father?"

"Because I never dreamed it would, Little One. I thought you'd see the same thing I'd see, with some minor European variation."

"I made my results public online, Grammy. The DNA ethnicity thing is just one part of this. I'll find blood relatives eventually, and they'll help me track my father down. It's only a matter of time."

Grammy and Mama exchanged a look. I could practically see twenty-one years of worry morphing into a terrible new concern: loss. Would I want to leave them and be with my father? Would I move to Wisconsin or California or New York? Did I have brothers and sisters? Another grandmother or two?

"I love you both very much," I said. "I'm sorry I yelled at you, Mama, and I understand you did what you thought was right. I get that." Both of them were sniffling. "But you know me well enough to know I won't be happy until I figure this out and get answers. I'm going to start looking now." I reached for my phone and walked off to my room. Neither of them said a word down the hall after me.

Google showed me two hours' worth of Pete Darlings all over the country, from an FBI analyst to a bakery owner. Obviously, the name wasn't going to help much, even if it was authentic.

The answers lay with the genealogy website, which revealed nothing at all.

Yet.

I decided to concentrate on my African history, browsing websites about Benin-Togo. It was immediately apparent what that area's main export was in the 19th century: people. Human beings captured by the Kingdom of Dahomey and forced into slavery in many parts of the world, some I'd heard of and some I hadn't.

Including Mobile, Alabama. Around two a.m., long after Grammy and Mama were asleep, I found contact information for a noted scholar and researcher of African-American genealogy named Frazine Taylor.

I could never have imagined the truth bomb she would drop on me just three weeks later in her Montgomery office.

"So," Ms. Taylor began, "you have a fascinating ancestry to trace, particularly because many records are extant, which is unusual for families like yours in Alabama." She pushed a sheet of paper across the desk to me. "You're descended from an original settler of Africatown, now known as Plateau, near Mobile. Her name was Dolly in Alabama, but in her native Africa she was called *Bamijoko,* which is a Yoruba name meaning 'stay with me'. It's usually given to newborn girls in families who have lost daughters." She tilted her elegant head to one side, clearly echoing my puzzled look. "I'm guessing you don't know anything about Africatown, or African Town, as it was once known. So let's start at the beginning."

"Yes, please." I sat back in my chair and listened carefully.

"In 1860, the international slave trade had long been illegal. There was a man who came to Alabama from Maine to make his fortune; his name was Timothy Meaher. It's said he made a wager with fellow businessmen he could bring a shipload of Africans into Mobile and sell them, right under the noses of customs authorities. Meaher spent a great deal of money disguising his schooner ship, the *Clotilde*. Underneath, she was outfitted for human cargo and to store the food and water necessary for an additional hundred passengers. The *Clotilde* also carried a bag of gold to bribe officials if intercepted."

"Would the law have been well enforced at that time?" I asked.

"Yes, in terms of international slave transport. There were ships patrolling from several countries, including the U.S., to intercept slavers. If they recovered people, they were mostly repatriated to Sierra Leone and had to find their way home. Many came from the Benin region you've seen referenced. But once the captives were landed in this country, they could be sold discreetly. Meaher stood to make a very great deal of money with this voyage. He hired a Canadian captain named Foster to sail to Africa. Foster bargained for and purchased approximately one hundred and twenty-five prisoners held by the King of Dahomey."

"And my ancestor was one of them?"

Ms. Taylor nodded. "She endured a horrific voyage across the Atlantic, hidden in a compartment below decks that was crammed with people. Each held a tiny space in the darkness. They were given only enough nourishment and water to stay alive. Many were seasick and temperatures could reach one hundred and twenty degrees at the height of the day. The stench was nearly unendurable, as you can imagine. No thought or allowance was made for waste removal or any sort of cleanliness. The men were cruelly shackled, but Bamijoko was a young woman, so she was spared that. Overwhelming the Africans' horror at their conditions was the despair they felt at being separated from their loved ones and knowing they'd likely never see their homes again. It's what each of them stressed over and over, for all the years that followed: they longed for the land they'd been forced to leave."

My stomach knotted at the thought of what they'd endured, a heartbreaking homesickness that had to be a constant, physical ache. And they'd suffered it along with countless other cruelties. My hands were clenched into fists in my lap.

"How did they come to be captured in the first place?" I asked.

"The King of Dahomey made raids on villages for the express purpose of capturing people for sale. Even after the slave trade was banned, he still ran a very profitable illegal business, exporting mostly to Cuba and some Caribbean islands in the second half of the century. His soldiers would seize men and women and march them to be held in *barracoons*, like crude holding cells, until they were sold or traded. The ones who resisted were decapitated, and the soldiers displayed their heads to the people they'd captured as they walked to their destination. It was a gruesome and grueling journey to Dahomey." She paused to examine my face. "Are you okay?"

"Yes, I'm just trying to take this all in." I blinked away tears and attempted to smile at Ms. Taylor politely.

"So, Meaher," she continued, "he brought these captives into Alabama around 1860. They were the last known shipment of slaves to arrive in the United States. Your ancestor, Bamijoko, was renamed Dolly and worked primarily in Meaher's own household. It appears she was responsible for sewing and cleaning. Incidentally, in her culture, sewing would have been a skill the men practiced, not the women. Dolly learned sewing and how to clean a large house that must have overwhelmed her. She lived in quarters underneath the Meahers' porch."

She slid another piece of paper toward me, documenting the census of African Town in 1866. "Dolly was emancipated by the government in 1865, and she and her fellow shipmates immediately began trying to find a way to return to Africa. When it became clear that was impossible, the Africans decided to form a town of their own, preserving their native Yoruba language and customs. They largely kept to themselves, venturing out only when necessary for trade. Dolly took back her Yoruba name, shortening it to Joko." She pointed it out on the census form. "She married a fellow former slave named Charles Broadhurst, who appears to have been born in Alabama. The town thrived for many years, but eventually its descendants moved on, many of them to new parts of the country. It was remarkable in every way, though, and utterly unique. The courage and wisdom of the people who founded Africatown can't be overstated, nor their sacrifice to earn the money necessary. The best known of them was Cudjo Lewis, interviewed by Zora Neale Hurston. There are a number of books on the subject—I'll give you the titles—and I'm sure you'll find more about Joko in them." She smiled at me. "I know it's a lot to process. What questions do you have?"

"Well," I began, "Since I had absolutely no idea of my African heritage, I have to wonder if Joko's children or grandchildren left Africatown, and when they married white people. I mean, it seems unlikely after what you told me about how the African community was determined to keep to itself."

"You're right," Ms. Taylor answered. "Joko remained in Africatown until her death in 1908. Her children continued to live there, but her grandson Garrett fell in love with a woman named Bettie Guffey who grew up nearby; Bettie was both white and Creek Indian. Anti-miscegenation laws would have prevented them from marrying in Alabama, but they were legally wed in Kansas in 1922 on their way to join relatives in Oklahoma. Census records indicate most of Garrett and Bettie Broadhurst's descendants were still in Oklahoma, at least until 1950. I don't have information on all of them."

"Do you have anything on a descendant named Darling?" I asked.

"No," Ms. Taylor replied, "I don't. Is that name of interest to you?"

"I honestly don't know," I said. "It's beginning to look like it's not." I thanked Ms. Taylor and walked out in a daze, determined to read everything I could about Africatown, and visit what remained of it, too.

Thirteen

EUFAULA, ALABAMA

I watched Grammy add a fourth sandwich to a large cooler she'd packed for our day trip. It was against Verna Willis's constitution to buy food when traveling by car, so we always ended up with a cooler that weighed more than she did full of bottled water, meals and snacks. If you dared to walk out of a gas station with a pecan log, she'd glare at you until you finished it.

I hoisted the thing off the kitchen table and toted it out into the pale darkness, shoving it onto the back seat with a grunt. It was almost six in the morning, a time when Mama was used to experiencing sunrises and Grammy and I were used to deep sleep. We were not morning people. Grammy sighed and deposited herself in the passenger seat of my car like it was an electric chair. "How long did you say it takes?" She glanced at me as I buckled my seat belt. "Five whole hours?"

"It's a little less than five hours, especially if we don't stop for food. We can live off that backseat buffet for a few days." I jerked my thumb at the cooler and she raised her eyebrows and gave me her signature "you're welcome" nod.

My grandmother wore a sleeveless yellow floral blouse and white Capri pants. I raised my eyes to the heavens, grateful she hadn't had time to outfit herself in head-to-toe Kente cloth. If I hadn't invited her at the last minute she would have been wearing at least an early Queen Latifah hat.

Grammy stared out the window at the brilliant pink sky in the east and bit into a vanilla Moon Pie. I steered the car west toward Africatown.

I nudged her awake as we reached the huge bridge across the Mobile River, just in time to see the "Cochrane-Africatown Bridge" sign.

"Are you ready for this, Little One?" she said. "Look at you, you have glory bumps." Grammy ran her tiny hand along my goose-pimpled arm. The bridge went on forever, and then we saw a giant mural painted in vivid blues on our right: the *Clotilde* on the sea. Just after it was a "Welcome to Africa-town" sign. My stomach flopped a rapid beat along with my heart. I spotted the old cemetery and parked the car just inside the gate, opening the door into blast-furnace July heat. Grammy followed as I began walking up the center path, deserted and silent except for the highway traffic noise and what sounded like a hundred wildly barking dogs nearby. I widened my eyes at my grandmother and she shrugged. "Maybe they're trying to duplicate wild barking dogs in Africa. I wish we had a gazelle to throw at them."

That was such a Sparrow thing to say.

I stopped to take it all in: the cemetery wasn't all that big, and chock-full of headstones old and new. Very few flowers adorned these graves, not like our frantically decorated cemeteries in Eufaula, which were covered in an ever-changing array of Hobby Lobby arrangements. Across the street was the Union Missionary Baptist Church, its red brick soaring into a tower that was overshadowed by a massive oak. An oak that had doubtless been there when the settlers of Africatown founded the church in 1872.

Despite the screaming dogs and scorching day and the cars and trucks roaring past at sixty miles an hour, I could close my eyes and imagine my distant ancestor here at a time when this was their world. This was the Africa they created, their own village where Yoruba was spoken and the people celebrated their newfound freedom with food, memories and customs from their home eight thousand miles away.

It might as well have been the moon. Ms. Taylor had told me the "shipmates" likely never heard of the funding some received to help them back to Africa, raised by various groups trying to assist with repatriation. Though about forty people did make the return voyage from Alabama, the *Clotilde* survivors never pursued anything but a trip back that would carry them all, not as individuals, but as a family. That was impossibly expensive and the passage would probably have been too hard for the older members of the community to endure.

And this, where I stood, was where my distant Yoruban grandmother probably walked. The church across the street might be where she married Charles Broadhurst, where she worshipped in her strange, newfound Christian faith.

When I looked back from the brick church, I saw Grammy moving quickly toward a man I hadn't noticed at the back of the cemetery. He was bent over, pulling weeds from a grave. I ran to catch up before she announced her granddaughter was here to learn African dance or whatever Sparrowism she might spout at him.

He looked up and dusted his hands on his cargo shorts as we got closer. I guessed he was in his late twenties. His hair was in dreads, the ends of which were bleached blond and he'd gathered them into a sort of big topknot. His skin was a light brown and his eyes lit up as he smiled at us. I noticed he was wearing a white Auburn t-shirt and wondered if he was visiting here, too.

Leave it to Grammy to find out: "Do you live in Africatown?"

"No, ma'am," he answered in a voice so soft it startled me, "most people call it Plateau these days, but I live in Mobile. This is my great-grandfather's grave", he waved at the mass of weeds, "and I try to come over here and clean it up when I can. Are you two exploring Plateau for any special reason?" He glanced over to the fence bordering the cemetery, covered in vegetation that hid the hysterical dogs. Beyond it you could see a row of shotgun houses that had fallen into ruin years ago. I looked down a neighboring street and saw much the same; buildings that had been reclaimed by nature sitting beside somewhat newer houses that were each surrounded by chain-link fence and had seen much better days.

"Do you know anyone who lives here now?" I asked.

"No," he shook his head, "my relatives moved away a long time ago. Most folks did after the paper mills closed and they lost their jobs. There aren't many people left. Sad, isn't it? When you think how this town started out?"

"Are you descended from one of the original settlers?" I asked him. "My name is Skye, by the way, and this is my grandmother, Verna." I held out my hand to shake.

"Sparrow" my grandmother muttered under her breath.

"My name's Jimmy," he answered, "and no, not that I can prove, anyway. I think my great-great-grandparents moved to Africatown years after it was founded. I know the history, though. My granddaddy grew up in Mobile, but he said his grandfather was a former slave who moved to this town after it had been established for years. He wanted to be buried here because of that." Jimmy nodded at the church across the street. "I've been researching the history of this place for a long time. Granddaddy was convinced he was descended from the Yoruba tribe in Nigeria, which is how I got my name."

"Jimmy?" Grammy offered him her skeptical look.

"Jimi, J-I-M-I, actually, short for *Olujimi*, which means 'gift from God'."

"Oh, wow, that is so cool, *Olujimi*. What a great name. I'm here looking for the graves of my great-great-great-great-grandmother and her son. She was one of the Clotilde survivors. Joko Broadhurst."

He regarded me with an eons-long look. "Is that so?"

"Well, yeah, believe it or not, it is. I found out through DNA testing and then I was lucky enough to trace my line all the way back here. I just don't know what part of the cemetery to search."

"Well, I do. Follow me."

Grammy and I trudged through weeds and little dips in the ground, trying to avoid stepping on graves or snakes or fire ant mounds. I kept my head down and concentrated on Grammy's feet leading me for what felt like ten minutes. When I looked up, we were standing under the canopy of a big tree on a hill, surrounded by stone and concrete slabs in all directions.

"This is where the earliest graves are," Jimi explained. "As you can see, there's nothing left you can read. Your grandmother may very well be here."

"I know she is." I could feel it in my heart. I searched for any trace, any marking. It had all been weathered away long ago. I bent down and traced one of the slabs with my finger. An acorn had fallen there, and I pocketed it.

"I have to get back to work," Jimi nodded at the distant grave, "but there's one more thing I wanna show you." He walked out into the bright sunlight and we followed. He stopped in front of a flat, narrow marble monument at least seven feet tall, dedicated to Cudjo "Kazoola" Lewis, born circa 1847, Dahomey, Africa, died 1935, Plateau, Alabama. Last Survivor Slave Ship *Clotilde*, 1860. At the base of the monument were four fresh-looking jar candles, a testament to the affection people still had for the best-known of the "shipmates" who settled Africatown.

"Do people actually come here and light these candles often?" I asked him.

"Not sure, but I wouldn't be surprised. He's a legend and a local hero." Jimi crossed his arms and stared at the monument. "My grandfather never wanted him forgotten. Talked about Cudjo a lot, though he never met him. Anyway, I gotta get to work." He jumped down into the deep grass and turned around to wave as he walked off.

"Bye, Jimi, and thank you!" I called after him. I offered Grammy a hand, and we climbed down and crossed the busy highway to the church. In front there was a bronze bust of Cudjo, shaded by the nearby tree. I ran my fingers over his face, the face my ancestor had surely known. Grammy and I went and stood under the old oak for several minutes, gazing at the church. I picked up a leaf to preserve and took one last look at the cemetery where someone's dogs still shrieked a warning at visitors. Maybe they never stopped.

We drove around the neighborhood, sad to see nothing to show this was ever a thriving community. Even though some houses were definitely occupied, we didn't see a single person. The porches sat empty, no children played in the yards, the streets and sidewalks were abandoned. Even the dogs of a thousand voices couldn't be seen.

There was a sign directing us to a non-existent Information Center. Nearby we found a heavily vandalized memorial to two figures from Benin-Togo, government officials who'd visited years before. Their busts were completely destroyed and the monument's legend had been scribbled over. "Who could blame anyone for their anger at that?" Grammy noted.

I slowed down as we passed the mural of the *Clotilde* on the way out, its sunny, vibrant colors lying to the world.

"You're going the wrong way, Little One," Grammy said. "Eufaula isn't in this direction."

"That's because I have a surprise for you. We're stopping at a hotel in Birmingham tonight on the way to see something special tomorrow. And we're not eating cooler food for supper, Grammy. We'll find a nice restaurant."

"Those are perfectly good pimiento cheese sandwiches—" she began.

"Tonight and tomorrow are sponsored in part by Mama and Manny, Grammy. They wanted us to get to make this trip together."

"They wanted the house to themselves."

I laughed. "Probably that, too. Eww. Anyway, it will take a few hours to get to Birmingham, and"—I produced a pillow and blanket from the back seat—"you can nap all the way if you like."

"I want to know where we're going, at least," Grammy said, her head tilted. "Oh, no, I didn't pack clothes! I don't have anything to sleep in."

"Mama and I took care of all that. And where we're going is a secret. All I can promise is that you'll love it, Grammy, and I brought you something appropriate to wear."

"Is it another African thing?" She rested her head on the pillow and grinned at me. "Because I have Kente cloth in my suitcase, I just didn't have time to sew anything. I wanted to do a dashiki."

"You really are crazy." I giggled at her. "No, it's not African. That's all I'm telling you."

Grammy closed her eyes and at least pretended to sleep as I navigated the endless monotony of I-65. She woke to snack occasionally and handed me M&Ms and Doritos like I was five. My earbuds played all the music that normally would have had her jumping out of the car.

Best road trip ever.

By the time I brought all our stuff into the hotel room, we were exhausted and ready for real food. We walked over to a steakhouse and ordered some wine to start.

Grammy clinked her glass to mine. "To Talisa and Manny. What a precious thing, this trip with you, Little One."

"I love having you along, Grammy. This was a good day."

She sipped her wine and put her glass down. "Was it really, all of it? I worried you might be sad after what we saw in Africatown. That had to be emotional for you."

"Not really," I answered. "I mean, I pretty much knew the whole story before we went. I knew what we would find, for the most part."

Grammy looked at me expectantly.

"What? It's depressing to see the town in such bad shape. When I think of all the sacrifice my ancestor and Cudjo and the others made to create their town—years and years of it, and they started with nothing, absolutely nothing—and all the hardship they endured, yeah, that's rough. Their hopes and dreams; how they must have dreamed of a bright future for their descendants and for their town. That's definitely sad… and then when we were standing under that tree and all those graves are just blank and everything's washed away and…" Grammy reached for my hand, because I was suddenly full-blown crying in the middle of a restaurant.

"I'm okay." I wiped my face with my napkin and looked to see if anyone had been watching. "You're right, it took a while to hit me, I guess."

Grammy took a bite of buttered yeast roll and washed it down with cabernet. "Of course I'm right, Little One. I've known the tenderness of your heart since you were born. And baby, the best way you can honor Joko and all the others is to live your life as fully and joyfully as possible. She's watching you, and I think she's happy you finally found her."

"Do you really believe all that stuff, Grammy?"

"I most certainly do, Little One. The ones who came before watch over us. They delight in our happiness. No matter how many generations back. You carry the tiniest bit of Joko with you everywhere."

"That's a lovely thought." I took a long swig of wine.

"*You* are a lovely thought, Little One. A lovely thought and a lovely dream, first dreamt long, long ago."

"How did I get lucky enough to have you as my grandmother, Sparrow?"

"Probably a virgin sacrificed into a volcano way, way back. I'm well worth it."

The bottle of wine lasted all the way through chocolate bread pudding. Grammy and I slept like we'd summited Mount Everest.

We were up at the crack of nine, and after a hefty dose of coffee, ready to tackle the road. I had to make Grammy leave the pimiento cheese sandwiches in our motel room's refrigerator rather than put them back into the cooler. I convinced her we could risk food poisoning.

Also, I hate pimiento cheese.

As soon as her seat belt clicked, she demanded to know our destination.

"We're going to Florence, Alabama."

"What in the world is in Florence, Alabama?" Grammy replied.

"That's the surprise part. Do you like your Rolling Stones t-shirt?"

Grammy looked down at her chest. "Well, I've always liked the band. I fail to see how it can relate to anything in Florence, though."

"Ah. Well, Florence is near Muscle Shoals, where the Stones recorded some of their best music."

"So we're going to tour a music studio?"

"No, Grammy. And Mick Jagger isn't coming to Florence to sing for us, either. But stones are involved. That's all I can tell you."

Grammy ripped open a pack of Twizzlers and I wondered for the millionth time how she could possibly be a tiny, thin, teensy birdwoman. She smacked me on the arm with a Twizzler. "Take one. Best car food there is. No mess, not too sweet, won't make you thirsty, breaks into individual pieces for easy consumption…"

I nodded and put my earbuds in after that. It was a blissfully short drive, and we pulled up next to an abandoned cornfield to park in less than two hours.

"We came to see a dead cornfield?" Grammy asked.

"No," I spun her around, "we came to see that." We faced a small section of the Wichahpi Commemorative Stone Wall. It's over a mile long, twisting and turning its way all over the property of Tom Hendrix. The locals call it Tom's Wall. And Tom was sitting in a lawn chair in his driveway, waving at us. I'd called a few days before to tell him I was bringing my Creek grandmother.

Tom was a handsome man with high cheekbones and thick white hair. He stood about six feet tall, and his deep brown eyes sparkled as he smiled and rose to greet us. He was eighty-two-years-old and the most charming Yuchi Indian man on earth. That, in itself, would have been a wonderful treat for Sparrow, but I knew this visit would mean far more to her than getting to exercise her old-lady flirting skills.

Which she'd already commenced. When he went to shake her hand, she clasped his between her two and gazed at him like he was Tim McGraw.

"You must be Sparrow," Tom said.

My grandmother's hand flew to her chest. "You know my name? How could you possibly—"

"Rolling Stones t-shirt." Tom nodded and Grammy shot me a look. "Do you have some time to sit with me, Sparrow, before you walk the wall's path?"

Grammy perched on a chair next to him as I stood nearby, watching and listening. Tom's property was heavily shaded and cool, even in July.

"To tell you the story of the wall, I must first tell you of Te-lah-nay, my great-great-grandmother. She was a Yuchi Indian who grew up here, close to the Tennessee River. Her people believed there was a woman in the river who sang to them. They called it The Singing River."

My grandmother nodded sagely in understanding.

Tom continued, "When she was eighteen, she was forced to walk the Trail of Tears to the Indian Territory in what's now Oklahoma. It was a horrible journey many didn't survive. Te-lah-nay hated it there. She was miserable and missed her home. She said she couldn't hear singing from the river where they settled her." He paused to look at a portion of the stone wall we sat beside. "So, she walked home. It took her five years, and no one knows exactly how she found her way back. She was the only one of the many thousands 'relocated' to return."

"That is amazing," I muttered.

"Yes, it is," Tom clasped his hands together and continued. "Years ago, I decided I wanted to honor my great-great-grandmother and her journey. I couldn't think how best to do it until I met with a tribal elder who gave me the perfect answer: 'We shall all pass this Earth, only the stones will remain. We honor our ancestors with stones. That's what you should do.' And I knew it was perfect. I've spent the last thirty-three years building this wall of stone, and much of it is rocks from the Tennessee River itself. The wall is over a mile long and it contains a stone for each step my great-great-grandmother took to reach her home in Alabama. There are millions of pounds of rock surrounding you here." He waved his hand toward the wall. From where I stood, I could see it winding off down an endless path under a canopy of trees, with built-in places to sit and contemplate it all. "It's the largest unmortared wall in the United States, and the largest memorial to a woman. And," Tom nodded at my grandmother, "this is very much a woman's spiritual place. People from all over the world come to experience the wall. Actually, where you're sitting now, a famous woman wrote much of a song called *A Feather's Not A Bird* about the 'magic wall'. It's Johnny Cash's daughter, Rosanne Cash."

"I know that song! I remember hearing it years ago. You'll love it, Grammy," I said. She nodded and turned her rapt attention back to Tom, who was clearly the most charming man she'd ever met.

"So, Sparrow, will you walk with me to a special part of Te-lah-nay's wall?"

My grandmother jumped up, and we followed Tom a short distance to a section made of rocks that sort of resembled skulls.

"This is the grandmothers' wall," Tom said. "Here, Sparrow, place your hand on it."

I watched her close her eyes and then allow tears to run down her face. I put my arm around Grammy and hugged her.

"Little One, you have to do this. Touch these stones, and memories of the grandmothers who have meant so much to us come flooding back." She palmed the tears from her face.

"I have my grandmother who means so much right here," I smiled at her.

"That's not what I mean. It's like a connection with all who have come before. Like we were talking about last night." She took my hand before I could protest this hoodoo and placed its palm on the smooth stones. I closed my eyes to humor her. That's when it hit me, and I can't even explain what *it* was… I wasn't consciously thinking, just feeling the energy that flowed into me. And I was crying before I knew it, not as much as Grammy, but definitely in tears.

I opened my eyes to see Tom watching us, gently nodding and smiling. "It affects nearly everyone that way. Folks come from all over the world, and they all say they feel a connection to their ancestors here like nowhere else. Now, I'm going to let you ladies explore the rest of this side, and then I'll meet you when you come back." Tom turned and went back to his driveway station to meet some new arrivals.

"Wow," I turned to Grammy, "that was really something, I have to admit. I'd read about this place, but I thought I was bringing you here to explore the Indian heritage part, not have a second meltdown of my own." I wiped my wet cheek with the back of my hand and smiled at her.

"When will you learn, honey, that we are all woven into the past as much as the present? We're a tiny part of a tapestry so immense and beautiful, we can't imagine it." Grammy took my arm and led me forward. We trailed our fingers along the wall, pausing in the cool shade now and then to sit in the little places Tom had built in, some like small amphitheaters, every bit of it crafted of local stones. We were quiet all the way, because the place demanded reverence. On and on we walked, and I kept thinking how one man had built all of this by himself for well over thirty years of his life—heavy, hard work—because he wanted to honor his grandmother.

I didn't want to reach the end. We turned around and walked back, thinking we'd seen it all.

Tom was finishing up the story of Te-lah-nay for a German couple, the father carrying a small boy in a fancy European backpack thing. Their accent was easy to identify as they thanked Tom and set out on the path we'd just taken, nodding as they passed.

"So, did you enjoy it?" Tom asked.

"Very much," my grandmother answered. "It's astounding, what you've done here. I am so moved by it."

"Sometimes I can't believe it's been over thirty years," Tom answered. "I'm grateful I could do this for my great-great-grandmother. My wife thought I was crazy when I started it, and she's been a wonderful support all this time."

Only I could see the tiny cloud that passed Grammy's face.

"Let me show you the rest," Tom continued. "This," he pointed at a narrow rock at the bottom edge near the driveway, "was the first stone I laid here. And all around it is the top section of the wall where I've placed rocks people have brought from everywhere." He held up a glittery-looking rock shaped like a whale, a gift from a little girl that he obviously prized. There were fossils and a meteorite and a "fertility rock" Tom swore had helped a woman who touched it and then became pregnant soon after. He joked that Grammy shouldn't touch it, but I think the humor was lost on her. We walked on a bit and reached another, larger stone amphitheater, the last structure. "This is the prayer circle," Tom said. "There are a few ministers from local churches who come here to compose sermons."

Grammy immediately seated herself and told him, "We're going to stay right here a little while if that's okay."

"Of course, of course," Tom replied. "I'll be waiting if y'all have any questions on your way out."

I sat beside Grammy, who leaned her head back and looked into the oak limbs above us. "This place is truly holy, Little One. I've never experienced anything like it. Thank you for bringing me here." She patted my knee. "If you don't mind, I'm going to say a prayer before we go."

I nodded at her. It was pretty unusual for Sparrow to mention prayer, which she regarded as an extremely private thing. I held her hand as we sat quietly for a good five minutes. My mind wandered off to Africatown, to Eufaula, to Oklahoma.

I had no idea how soon I would follow it there.

Fourteen

CATOOSA, OKLAHOMA

D eke stretched his legs down the length of the oversized maroon leather couch by the oversized fireplace in the oversized living room of the oversized VIP Chief Suite Kara was occupying at the Hard Rock Hotel and Casino. He could hear her on the phone in the bedroom with Mr. Darling, painting a vivid, glowing impressionist artwork of the situation in Oklahoma that bore no semblance to reality.

He looked around, trying to decide if the suite was larger than his apartment in Dallas. Of course it was. It was designed to sleep six, and slept exactly one unless you counted the occasional guest Kara quietly ushered out into the hall at two in the morning.

These private powwows were hard to miss from his own insomnia-plagued room on the other side of a wafer-thin wall. She was a bit of a moaner, Kara. Also, she left the adjoining door unlocked, ostensibly for security. Deke figured it had more to do with her exhibitionist side. Kara Darling loved the thrill of knowing Deke could walk in on her and whoever she'd dragged from the local Creek. He wished he could warn them she was the human equivalent of smallpox-infested blankets.

He rolled his eyes at the third "my love" she worked into the conversation. Pete Darling was either the stupidest man on the planet or he wore mega-blinders in order to stay married to her. Was she hot? Like Georgia asphalt in July. He could even forgive his body for still panting after her. But damn, she could be a self-centered bitch.

So pretty, though. Pretty like angel trumpets and pink oleander, which his mother had hysterically warned him against his entire childhood.

He heard her say goodbye and sat up just before Kara floated into the room and took a split of champagne from the minibar. She was wearing head-to-toe ivory, including her beloved Christian Louboutin stilettos. Deke took a moment to mourn his masculinity, long sacrificed to the fashion education she insisted he absorb. He tried to stuff it down to wherever his pride was these days, but he helplessly recognized Prada purses and Gucci scarves against his will.

Kara poured herself a small tumbler of Moet and took a sip, setting the glass on a polished wood table to leave a ring. The maids must adore her, Deke thought.

She leaned forward, hands clasped. "I have to be in Okmulgee by two this afternoon. Have the car ready and we'll leave at one, okay?"

Deke had no idea what contribution Kara was making to the pipeline construction site, now in the process of ground preparation. Her presence as a member of the PFD Board of Directors had curbed the protests a little, though, he had to give her that. He had a suspicion what body parts she might have employed to get tribal leaders on her side. And her back. And her front. And her knees...

"Deke? Are you listening? You looked like you zoned out for a minute there." Kara smiled, a kindergarten teacher addressing her student on the first day of school.

Had she really forgotten that months ago they'd made out like post-prom teenagers? That he'd actually gotten his hand inside her blouse before Kara made him stop, insisting she couldn't betray her husband? What a laugh. Kara betrayed her husband every ten minutes. Deke had realized long ago she used sex to control whatever situation she chose. It worked spectacularly for a woman who looked like she did, spoke like she did, stared into the eyes and straight into the pants of every man she targeted. She'd left him with the slightest promise, the vaguest hint, that someday things could go further.

And Deke Jones wanted that more than anything in the world. He found himself staring at those long red fingernails as they tapped the table.

"Mr. Darling and Joseph will get here tomorrow. They'll pick up a car at the airport because Pete wants to be incognito. Probably a minivan or crossover thing, whatever moms drive." She waved her hand in front of Deke's face. "I could swear you haven't heard a word I've said."

"Mr. Darling and Joseph tomorrow," Deke replied. "What time?"

"They'll get here about three, because Mr. Darling wants to go by the site and the place they're setting up for the lay-down yard."

"Laydown yard?" Deke cocked his head to one side.

"It's the site where they'll store the pipe when it arrives and all the equipment to install it."

"They gonna have good security? These people are still mad, you know. And the national media is just waiting for something to video. Did I tell you a cameraman asked me my name?" Deke sat back and waited for Kara to explode.

Kara arched an eyebrow. "And you replied?"

"No comment. That's what I say to anything they ask. It's only a matter of time before they show up here at the hotel, though, especially if the protests crank up again. Right now they don't have anything more interesting than some people waving signs out by the site."

"I chose this hotel," Kara emptied her glass in a gulp, "because it's an hour away from the site. More than that, though, because they've assured me we'll be protected. No reporter is going to get near me here. Have you ever considered what kind of security casinos have, Deke? This place is a fortress with a zillion cameras and guards everywhere."

Cameras that capture Langdon Tiger as you kiss him goodbye wearing a fluffy Hard Rock robe, Deke thought. "Yeah, that's for real. I feel like someone's watching me all the time."

"Well, then, they're getting some sweet eye candy," Kara said, her hand on his arm. "I'm going to spend some time catching up on emails. Will you let me know when it's almost one?"

Sure, because your phone, laptop, tablet, and bedside clock won't give that info up, Kara. "Yes, I'll knock on your door," Deke answered, staring at Kara's backside as she walked away, forcing ivory silk into a rhythmic dance. That's something for the cameras, he thought, reaching for the rest of the Moet split. He guzzled it and took the empty bottle and glass to the kitchen.

Kara kicked her shoes off and collapsed onto the bed, scrolling through a secret email account she'd set up for Langdon. "Lang", he'd told her to call him. There were no messages.

She pulled a pillow to her and inhaled deeply, trying to conjure his mysterious cologne, somewhere between sandalwood and cinnamon. Kara closed her eyes and remembered how, ten nights ago, Lang had knocked on her suite's door an hour after a political dinner at a nearby restaurant. Kara had come back to her room and showered, exhausted after smiling all evening and smalltalking her way into the hearts and minds of the people. She knew she should summon Deke to answer the door, but she quietly swung it open after seeing who stood on its other side.

Because Langdon Tiger was unlike any man she'd ever met. They hadn't said one word about getting together after dinner, but the pull between them was so strong Kara didn't even pretend to be surprised when he materialized at her door. Lang was well over six feet tall with smooth, straight, pure-white hair that almost reached his shoulders. He was lean—skinny, almost—and his skin was a dark honey. Cheekbones that could cut diamonds, and eyes that reminded Kara of polished mahogany. He was wearing, she remembered, an exquisitely tailored Italian suit of navy wool and a green silk tie that looked vaguely iridescent. He smiled at her but made no move forward, just stood perfectly still, stopping the rotation of the earth for a minute.

Kara didn't speak, didn't smile, didn't welcome him, didn't bother to feign any discomfort at his dropping by out of the blue. She put her hands on his shoulders and kissed him, so tentatively it was almost just a breath on Langdon's lips. Still, he didn't move. He gazed down at her and waited until she placed her arms around his neck and opened her mouth to his. Lang didn't respond, and Kara began to wonder if she'd mistaken the reason for his visit and she'd have to scramble for her dignity. Then he closed his eyes and began kissing her, softly at first and then in a way that made Kara lose track of anything but him. He lifted Kara effortlessly and wrapped her legs around his waist, then carried her to the bed without a word. For another twenty minutes Langdon Tiger teased Kara, his lips and hands exploring her entire body. He paused and looked down at her for a few long seconds, sweeping her hair away from her face.

"I have to leave now," he whispered with a smile. Kara realized he hadn't even taken off his tie.

"Leave and I will find you and I will kill you," Kara said, fumbling with the tie and removing it. She wound it behind his neck and used it to pull Langdon down to her.

Later, she'd asked him how he'd known she wouldn't simply ignore his knock or slam the door in his face.

He'd stretched an arm above his head on the pillow and looked into her eyes. "Can you honestly tell me you didn't feel the chemistry between us the minute I touched your hand when we met days ago? That you haven't noticed me watching you, and more importantly, seen you watching me back? Tonight's dinner was three hours of visual foreplay, Kara, from the length of a table seating twenty. I felt you reaching out to me, all night long."

"Still, Lang, we don't really know each other—"

"I'm willing to bet that hasn't stopped you before." He closed his eyes.

Kara was briefly at a loss for words. "You have no right to say that to me—"

"I'm not insulting you, Kara," he interrupted. "Merely pointing out you're a sexual being, not saddled with guilt the way most of your people are. My ancestors didn't associate sex with guilt and angst like yours. You can learn a thing or two while you're here." He rolled over and stood to dress. "I hope I'll see you again," he said, tugging his suit pants up. He finished putting his clothes on, tied his tie, and strolled out of the room without another word.

Kara spent the hours until dawn contemplating what had just happened to her, pretty sure she'd met the male version of herself.

Langdon was a cabinet member of the Muscogee Creek Nation, so he and Kara saw each other in meetings designed to ease tensions over the pipeline project. Kara dutifully reported her company's progress and plans, while Lang and the others discussed their tribe's concerns in response. They consulted on local events and adjusted calendars to prevent disruptions. They identified lots of ways PFD could reach out to the community. Kara felt like a skilled diplomat navigating the line between the two. Lang was largely responsible for curbing the number of protesters PFD encountered; his word was respected and went a long way toward smoothing things for the project.

There was never the most remote indication to anyone of what happened secretly between Kara and Lang in Catoosa, Oklahoma. They were professional and regarded each other almost icily in public.

He'd been back to her room two times since that first night, both without any notice. Kara never knew when he'd show up.

All she could be sure of was that she wanted more. Always more.

Kara was startled by Deke's knock on her bedroom door. "Ten minutes till one!" he yelled. She slipped her shoes back on and pulled her hair into a messy bun, adding some Gucci aviators and coral lipstick to her ensemble. At the last minute, she threw on a gold choker with a pearl pendant—perfect with ivory. Kara smiled at her reflection and hoped Lang would show up to appreciate the way she looked today at the local community center, where she'd be presenting a generous PFD donation for an after-school program.

Deke settled her into the nondescript Chevy sedan, watching all around for any sign of reporters or protesters. They'd started using the hotel's back entrance to be extra safe. Kara thought it was a silly precaution, but Deke took his job seriously. "You look nice," he told her. Deke plugged the address into the car's navigation system and drove off as Kara looked up from her phone and nodded in response. She'd finally gotten an email from Lang: "See u soon".

Kara was surprised when they pulled up to the pale green concrete-block community center. There was a much larger crowd here for the presentation than expected. She noted the cameras of two local TV stations trained on their arrival, and, off in the distance, Lang was standing by the door. It was the first time she'd ever seen him in jeans, and he wore a black cowboy hat that made her glance linger too many beats.

Kara offered her most brilliant smile as Deke helped her from the car. She glided forth like she was emerging from a limo to step onto the Oscars' red carpet and wave at her adoring fans. And the Academy Award for Best Actress on a Reservation goes to...

She stopped to shake the hand of the community center's director and managed to sneak a smile at Lang. Kara was walking with Deke in front of her when something hit her stomach. She looked to her right instinctively, watching in slow motion as a young man threw a plastic squirt bottle to the ground and ran. Deke held her shoulders. "Are you all right? Are you hurt?" Kara looked down. Her ivory silk sweater and palazzo pants were striped with black motor oil. Deke threw his arm around her and hustled her back to the car.

Kara was crying, more from anger than anything else. Deke sped away without a look back.

"Are you sure I shouldn't have stayed at least long enough to say goodbye?" she asked Deke, who was fishing a roll of paper towels from the back seat and handing them to her, like they would make a difference.

"No. Absolutely not. It might have just been motor oil, but that was assault, and it's my responsibility to get you out of there. If the authorities want to talk to us about it, they can find us. Mr. Darling wouldn't want you to stick around after that, no matter what."

Kara nodded. "I guess you're right." She was swiping at the oil and only succeeding in grinding it into the fabric. "Oh, God, this will be all over the local six o'clock news." She threw her head back against the car seat.

"Or maybe national," Deke answered.

Kara winced at that. She pulled her phone out and checked it over and over, willing Lang to text her, to express some concern.

When the phone rang, it was Pete. Kara began to cry harder as she recounted what had just happened. Deke could hear Mr. Darling's voice, clearly outraged, and was glad he'd followed his gut and gotten her out of there.

Kara hung up and sighed. She was angrier with herself than anyone because she'd just been doused with stinking motor oil, and all she could think about was how she could convince Pete to let her stay here after this. Here, with Langdon Tiger and his magic.

Pete Darling crammed his frame into the private jet and tried to quiet his stomach. He hated flying, never got used to the brief terror of uplift and the adrenaline jolt of the plane thumping down upon landing. If that were punctuated by turbulence in between, well, much scotch would need to be poured. It was a mercifully short flight to Okmulgee Regional Airport, where a driver would pick him and Joseph up and take them to the car rental place.

He looked around at the redecoration Kara had ordered for his Cessna Citation, all-new sable brown leather he was pretty convinced she'd chosen to match her hair. It was worth it, he figured, to keep her happy. Anything to keep Kara happy. Thank God she hadn't been hurt yesterday. Pete would never have forgiven himself. At least, the oil attack had given him a solid argument on the need for his wife to come home and let someone else take her place in Okmulgee. She'd obviously generated all the goodwill she could.

The fifteen-year-old who'd thrown old, dirty 10-W30 on his wife would be in juvie long enough to think about his transgressions, and Pete's attorney told him the kid's parents were shipping him off to a military school when he got out. Turns out he was a regular at the very community center Pete was generously funding, and the center's management was anxious to condemn the little shit's actions and distance themselves. Pete was being magnanimous and not asking for anyone to reimburse them for Kara's outfit, which likely cost approximately one year of military school.

Kara hadn't left the hotel since the incident. He'd been very clear she should stay put. Deke was under orders to make sure she didn't venture out at all. Nobody was allowed anywhere near Kara's suite, either. Meals could be delivered to Deke, and they'd skip maid service for a day or two.

Pete stared out at Oklahoma's brown Arbuckle Mountains in the distance. On this trip he'd get the final details worked out so they could get started with this pipeline. A year of constant wrangling, wheedling, redesigning, donating, back-patting, faltering, regrouping effort was about to pay off, and pay off big.

And, while Pete didn't consider himself a sentimental man, he was happy to be back in his home state. He'd missed Oklahoma, and Oklahomans in particular, good old boys he could relate to. Pete white-knuckled the landing and saw a tall man standing next to a Tahoe in the distance. Since he was the only human anywhere near the tiny excuse for an airport, Pete assumed this was his and Joseph's ride.

They blinked their way into the sunshine and down the steps to the tarmac, where a forty-ish man with long white hair extended his hand for what Pete considered a ladylike shake.

"Welcome, Mr. Darling. I wanted to greet you in person. I'm Langdon Tiger, Tribal Administrator of the Muscogee Creek Nation."

Fifteen

Eufaula, Alabama

Mama walked in, threw her keys on the table, and stood behind Grammy at the stove. "Is that venison stew?" She wrinkled her nose at me and I shrugged from the couch, where I'd been watching the constant parade of daytime television in our house.

"It's not good for you to eat nothing but burritos and chimichangas, Talisa," Grammy informed her. "There are a lot of good vegetables in this stew. Remember vegetables? You ate them before you met Manny."

"Where did you get the venison?" Mama asked, peering into the pot Grammy stirred.

"Wilma's husband got an eight-point buck last December. She's emptying her freezer." Wilma was Grammy's oldest friend and sometime casino companion. They'd go off to Wetumpka every once in a while, Grammy to play slots and

Wilma to escape Joe Bill, who'd been retired from his hardware store and underfoot too many years.

Mama came into the living room and threw herself onto the couch beside me. "I'm exhausted," she sighed, gathering her hair into a ponytail, "and this heat is killing me. Half the people in the Huddle House were there just for the A/C today. Crappy tippers. What are you watching?"

"Dr. Phil is helping a five-hundred-pound woman to realize she eats because she's anxious, not hungry."

"He is not a doctor," Grammy yelled from the kitchen. "He just plays one on TV. The man drives me crazy with his platitudes. I don't know how he's still on the air. Oh, yeah, because Oprah made him one of The Chosen People—"

"You're making me anxious, Mom. Keep it up for a while so I'll actually want to eat venison stew." Mama elbowed my side. She took a carefully swaddled sugar cookie from her purse and broke it in half, glancing back to be sure Grammy didn't see her hand it to me. We got through the rest of Dr. Phil sneaking bites and chewing discreetly. About the time Grammy set the stew on the table, the news came on.

"Mute that!" my grandmother hollered. "We don't need the noise during supper."

I wondered why we needed the noise the rest of every waking hour, but wasn't about to mention it. I glanced at the screen one last time before going to the table. "Look, y'all, they're showing Oil Lady again." We stared at the TV as someone in Oklahoma got black oil thrown all over her off-white outfit. The poor woman looked terrified for a few seconds and then a burly man grabbed her and rushed her away to safety.

"They ought to arrest the guy who did that," I said.

"I'm sure they did. I think it's a great way to get the country's attention, though. That woman is probably one of the oil company's executives," Grammy said. "I mean, I'm sorry her clothes are ruined, but the Creek in Oklahoma are within their rights to protest, Little One. That pipeline is going to pass very close to their land. There could be all kinds of problems."

"Since when are you all up on Oklahoma oil pipeline protests?" Mama asked.

"I get a Creek Nation newsletter in my email," Grammy replied. "I know what's going on with my people everywhere."

"I thought you just felt it in your collective consciousness, Mom," Mama said, waving her hands in the air. "Why do you need a newsletter?"

"Do you know the Creek word for smartass, honey?" Grammy asked her.

"No, Mom."

"It's Talisa."

"Grammy, you told us Talisa means 'beautiful waters'," I said. We had variations on this conversation about Mama's name fairly often.

"Yeah, I was wrong. I got a vocabulary update in the newsletter." Grammy handed me a piece of cornbread. "And after what you saw and heard in Florence from Mr. Hendrix, I'd think you'd have more respect for the Creek in Oklahoma, Little One."

"You're right, Grammy, I do." I set my spoon down and placed my palms on the table. "I've been waiting to tell y'all," I said, "I have a possible DNA match, a first or second cousin, and I sent her a message. I don't know where she is or even her name. She could be Cousin Terry in Dothan, I guess." Cousin Terry was Grammy's deceased brother's child. She lived alone in the musty house Uncle Bert and Aunt Theresa had left her, surrounded by cats and romance novels.

"Naw, I doubt it," Grammy said. "That girl's denser than the hair on a Kardashian." She shook her head. "If Terry were any slower we'd have to go down there and water her every week. No way she figured out how to do all this DNA stuff on the computer." She shot Mama a meaningful glance. "I'm guessing this is someone from your father's side."

"I hope so, honey," Mama said, as if she actually meant it.

"Okay, everybody eat your stew," Grammy said. I dug into mine, but when it was my night to cook, we were having some kind of salad. It was way too hot for soup, free ingredients or not.

"Do we need to take a moment to contemplate and thank the spirit of the deer we're eating?" Mama was walking close to the edge with The Sparrow tonight.

"Joe Bill said he was noble and pure and kind to his mother," Grammy answered, her voice dripping honey. "Obviously, Talisa, you need extra." She ladled a bit more stew into Mama's bowl. "Are you going to Manny's tonight?"

Mama shook her head. "No, he has family in town."

Well, that was interesting. "Are they from Mexico?" I asked.

"Yeah. It's actually just one guy, his ex-brother-in-law, Marco."

"Ex-brother-in-law?!" Grammy dabbed at her mouth with a napkin. "Does that mean there's an ex-wife?"

"Yes," Mama sighed, "there's an ex-wife he married when he was just a kid. They divorced at twenty-two, no children, everything is simpatico. It's all lovely except Luz apparently worships Santa Yolanda, the beauty who stole her heart along with Manny's and never gave Luz hers back. She even has a framed picture of Yolanda on her bedroom dresser."

"Wow. So, you think Luz will try to Parent Trap them back together, only, err... mother trap them?" I said.

"Not likely. Yolanda is married to a resort owner in Cozumel and has four children. I think I'm safe."

"Maybe if Luz thinks Yolanda has a lot of money—"

We stared at Grammy and she shrugged.

"That's the other thing I found out," Mama said. "Luz is loaded. Turns out her second husband, the one who died right before they moved here, had the first McDonald's franchise in Juarez. She sold it for a ton of money, and even after splitting that up with his sons, she's pretty much set. Luz actually loaned Manny the down payment for his restaurant. He worked nonstop and barely took any money home until she was paid back because Luz was constantly stationed in a booth, hissing instructions in Spanish. Most of Manny's recipes came from her, though. She's a great cook."

"How did they end up in Eufaula, anyway?" Grammy asked.

"Manny was looking for a restaurant, any restaurant, for sale. Someone had remodeled that old jewelry store, put in a kitchen and everything, and then had to give up on it before they ever opened. Manny bought it at a bankruptcy auction."

"I remember that," Grammy said. "It was going to be The Walking Catfish. Lenny Griggs had a logo designed with a walking catfish in a top hat carrying a cane."

Mama and I laughed as we gathered the dishes to wash. "I'm kinda sorry I missed seeing that," I said.

"The logo, maybe, but nobody would have eaten a single hush puppy served by Lenny or his wife. They used to buy their herpes meds at the Walmart pharmacy." Grammy pushed her chair in and headed to the living room, walking away from her Sparrowbomb of the evening without a backward glance.

The next morning I had an Ancestry.com message waiting:

"Hi the only person I can think of is my
dad's uncle, but my mom says he never
had kids and she thinks he couldn't for
some reason.
sry lmk if I can help with anything else."

Useless. Until I saw 'Ancestry04782552' had included at
the bottom: Chloe Darling.

So, the name he'd given Mama had been real, after all.

It didn't take long to locate Chloe and her father, John,
then a nanosecond to Google my way to the exact Peter F.
Darling I'd been searching for. I found a few photos of him.
My gray eyes stared back at me from each one.

Oh, he could have kids, all right.

My father was obviously a very successful man. It looked
like he owned most or all of a pipeline company called PFD;
two of the photos showed him wearing a tuxedo at fancy
parties, an old bald guy standing next to some gorgeous actress
who seemed familiar. There was no caption on either, though.
In another he was slightly younger, dressed in full camo, and
the story identified the man with him as a senator from
Oklahoma at his private "hunting ranch" in Caddo County.

What had happened over the last twenty-two years to take
him from the construction worker Mama had known to
important gazillionaire?

None of it made sense. Or had Mama lied about this, too,
because he didn't want anything to do with me? No, I had
clearly seen she was telling the truth about not being able to
contact him after finding out she was pregnant. Her memories
of that had been written all over her face.

It was easy to find contact info for his company. I didn't
think corporate Twitter would respond to me waving a Maury

Povich paternity sign at them, though. I found an email on their website, a Facebook page, the address of their office in Dallas... but nothing on Peter F. Darling's residence. Predictable. He probably lived in a fortress, protected from realities like me.

It occurred to me I had absolutely no idea what I'd say, even if I had a way to say it. I looked up articles on contacting biological parents.

Don't act in haste. Consider the reaction you may receive. What are you hoping your father will be like? Does he have other children? Is he married? How will your new relationship affect his marriage? What do you hope to gain through this contact? Do you have health concerns to discuss? What will you do if your father wants nothing to do with you, or claims you aren't his child? Are you emotionally prepared for the consequences of contact?

That last one was easy. I was not emotionally prepared, not at all. In fact, I wished I still thought the handsome, smiling soldier in the kitchen photo was my dad.

I had a little while to consider this as I dressed to head to the restaurant to set up and work my lunch shift. I had no intention whatsoever of mentioning it to Grammy, because I knew she'd want to discuss it to death. There were eighteen minutes until Manny would declare me late and fume about it all afternoon.

"Good morning," she muttered, turning the pages of a magazine at the kitchen table. "Did you sleep... oh, lord, you found him, didn't you?" Grammy jumped up and hugged me, then held my shoulders at arms' length.

All I could do was pick up my jaw and stare. The Sparrow occasionally had flashes of insight, but this was her most impressive ever. "How did you know?"

"Just felt it," she shrugged. "I wish I could feel some lottery numbers and go to Columbus for tickets. And honey, you said you were waiting to hear from a relative on your Ancestry DNA thing last night. Your eyes are a little brighter than usual this morning. That's a tell."

"I'm going to have to work on my transparency." I kissed her cheek. "I have to get to the restaurant or Manny will yell at me."

Grammy jumped up and scooted her chair in. "Okay if I ride with you? I'm meeting Luz there. She wants me to make a dress for her, so we're going to discuss colors and fabrics and eat lunch, too. Manny is going to translate for us."

I suppressed a grin at the knowledge Sparrow still didn't know Luz could not only understand, but speak, English.

"How will you get home?" I asked as she scooted out the door towards my car.

"Youber."

"Grammy, this is Eufaula. We don't have Uber."

She closed her car door and buckled up. "Betty Wilson is bored, and she told all of us if we need a ride home from town we can just call and she'll do it for ten bucks. She was calling it Youber but I told her she should spell it E-u-b-e-r. Get it?"

"Unfortunately, I do." I patted her arm and gave her the laugh I knew she was waiting for.

"So, tell me about this man," Grammy began. "What is his name? What does he look like? Is he still working construction?" She cocked her head to one side, eyebrows raised like Spanish Inquisition flags.

So, this was why she'd jumped in my car instead of driving herself. "His name really is Pete Darling, and he looks like a tall, tubby, bald, old guy. He wasn't lying. Maybe the motel messed up or something when Mama asked about him."

"Maybe." Grammy looked thoughtful. "But I doubt it. I guess he could have been checked in under the company he worked for, and they never heard the last name 'Darling'."

"Yeah, well, that's the other thing. He owns his own company now in Texas, and it's big. They have something to do with pipelines, but I'm not sure what kind because the website isn't very specific. Maybe gas, maybe oil, maybe sewer pipes for all I know. I don't know if they manufacture pipelines or install them or what. Is that the word, install?" I shrugged as I backed the car into the street.

"He could be part of the oil thing near the Creek in Oklahoma… " Grammy closed her eyes, deep in thought or Creek telecommunication.

That's when it clicked. The beautiful actress in the photos wasn't an actress. She was Oil Lady, from the news. "Oh, wow," I said, "I think he is. I'm not sure what their relationship is, but the woman we saw getting oil splashed on her must work for his company. I saw two pictures of them together."

"Oh, honey," Grammy said. "A man that rich and he ain't good-lookin'? That's his wife, or she's trying to be."

My stomach was squirming at the thought of barging into Pete Darling's life with his perfect wife after all these years. *Hi, umm, congratulations, it's a girl. A full-grown woman, actually. Care for a cigar, or perhaps to slam the door in my face?*

I gave up trying to picture myself standing on the doorstep of his mansion, Bastardess Skye from The Heart of Dixie, battered Walmart suitcase in hand. *Oh hello, is that Megan Fox holding the martini glass behind you? My, she looks stunned.* "I'm not going to contact him. Knowing who he is is enough. My life is here with you and Mama, and his is obviously rich and full without a surprise daughter. I can't stand the thought of what might happen if he knew about me. I am not *emotionally prepared*, as Google suggests." I parked the car with four minutes to spare and started to get out.

Grammy grabbed my arm. "Little One, if you don't contact him, if you don't at least let him know he has a daughter, that's not fair to either of you."

"I'm just the accidental result of a couple of lonely nights in Eufaula, Grammy. That doesn't really constitute a daughter."

My grandmother pressed her lips together, the way she did when she was furious and trying not to cuss. "You are not an *accident*," she said, clutching my wrist tighter. "You're going to stop saying or even thinking that right now. Have you ever considered what my life would be without you? You think you're not here for a reason? You brought your mother back to life after Larry, and damn near the same for me after your grandfather had died. My world had been nothing but shades of gray, and you came with color and sound and more joy than I could ever have imagined. You gave us meaning and love and laughter. You may be many things, Hannah Skye Willis, but you are *not* an accident."

Great. Now I was crying, and I had two minutes to get inside the restaurant. Grammy swiped at my tears and continued, "And you are going to tell Pete Darling he has a daughter, because it doesn't matter what he says or does, really. You're surrounded by love, and if he doesn't add to it, that's his loss. But honey, you'll never forgive yourself if you don't contact him. You will always wonder, and wondering is hard on a heart."

Luz was waiting in a booth near the back, wearing a bright red floor-length dress embroidered with white flowers at the top. Her gray hair was in a neat bun at the base of her neck. She nodded as I walked past, a little mischief in her dark eyes.

Grammy slid in opposite her. She leaned over and said, loudly and William-Shatner style, "Are. you. going. to. get. Manny. to. translate. for. us? She waved her hands to indicate Manny's height and then toward the kitchen where I was hiding and watching.

Luz paused for a beat and responded in rapid Spanish. Grammy waved Mannyward again with a hint of impatience. Luz reached for Grammy's hands and held them, then announced, "That won't be necessary. I learned English last night."

It was fun watching my grandmother mentally review all the things she may or may not have said in front of Manny's mom over the past few weeks. When she'd rearranged her face from awestruck to normal, she announced, "Well, you're doing all right for a beginner, I guess."

"Can you duplicate this dress in white and embroider it with multicolored flowers?" Luz asked.

Grammy shook her menu open. "In my sleep with one arm tied behind my back," she replied. "And why didn't you ever tell me?"

Luz shrugged. "You never asked."

Sixteen

OKMULGEE, OKLAHOMA

Pete glanced back at Joseph after shaking Langdon Tiger's hand, the question in his eyes answered by a slight nod from his bodyguard. They climbed into the SUV, Pete riding shotgun and Joseph peering at Langdon from the back.

"Glad to have you here, Mr. Darling," Langdon said, steering towards the highway. "Your wife's made a wonderful impression on all of us and done very well establishing trust and goodwill with the tribe. You should be proud of Mrs. Darling."

"I am proud of her, Tiger. After what happened to her at the community center, I don't want her in Oklahoma, though."

"Call me Lang, please," Langdon smiled at Pete, revealing perfect white teeth. "And you must understand one troubled youth doesn't represent the rest of us. He'll be punished harshly for attacking Mrs. Darling. That was a horrible thing to do. None of us are complicit in it, Mr. Darling. The after-school program is important to so many families. They appreciate your generosity."

"Call me Pete."

"Okay, Pete. The protesters you have here now are environmentalists from outside, with only a few Creek. Your wife has done a lot in Okmulgee to calm tensions. She's taken the time to talk to people, to reassure them."

Pete found himself looking at Joseph in the rearview mirror. He was regarding the passing scenery, but his eyebrows were raised.

"You're taking us to the car rental place, right?" Pete suddenly remembered he'd just assumed so.

"Yes, but if you want, I can take you to the site for your laydown yard first. We'll be going by there in about five minutes. Good space, isolated and secure."

"Yeah," Pete answered. "That will work well." He glanced at Joseph, who didn't seem to have a problem with it.

"I was wondering if you might consider adding a couple of young Creek men to your staff there. They have experience with heavy equipment and pipe storage."

"You want me to hire people who've held this project up for months to guard my storage site?" Pete shook his head and stared out at a lake in the distance, framed by blue mountains. He missed mountains.

"Exactly why you should hire them. It'll look good for PFD, and you have my word they're well-qualified and trustworthy. Neither of them have been involved in the protests, Pete. Don't paint all of us with that brush."

"You can give their resumes to the guy in charge, Drew Tyler. Tell him to talk to me. No promises." Pete took a look at this long-haired, impeccably dressed man and wondered if either of the two prospective hires were his boyfriend.

Lang parked the Tahoe and told Pete he had to attend to a phone call, but he'd join him and Joseph in a minute. The yard was satisfactory, surrounded by new chain link fencing and well-lighted. Pete couldn't see anything to object to, especially with the initial pipeline site less than fifteen minutes away. By the time they returned Lang was just finishing his call. He smiled broadly at Joseph and Pete. "Sorry about that. My girlfriend. You know how women can be."

So he likes girls, Pete thought. Imagine that.

"Does everything look good to you?" Lang asked.

"Looks great," Pete said. He was feeling better about Okmulgee by the minute. "I'm originally from Oklahoma, you know, western part of the state. I miss it. My wife talked me into moving to Dallas right after we married. Used to have a ranch here. Did a lot of hunting. You hunt, Lang?"

"No, I'm surprisingly inept at it. Embarrassment to my ancestors."

Pete just laughed. He figured Lang's ancestors would be more embarrassed about his perfectly manicured fingernails. Lang drove them up to the car rental lot and wished them a good stay in Oklahoma. "Call me if you need anything while you're here." Pete was relieved he didn't offer to shake hands again.

"Thanks for the ride," Pete said, tapping the roof of the Tahoe. "Appreciate all you've done for us." Joseph hoisted their suitcases and Pete didn't offer to help. He wasn't about to let anyone in Oklahoma catch his slight limp, and carrying heavy objects would betray him in a second.

Kara was waiting for him in her room, as ordered. She threw her arms around Pete and kissed him.

"Are you wearing a new cologne?" he sniffed. "You smell like cinnamon."

"No. I'm wearing nothing at all, actually." Kara opened her silk robe to welcome her husband while a weary Joseph settled into the adjacent junior suite with Deke, who had lots of interesting things to tell him about Langdon Tiger.

A couple of hours later, Kara brought her laptop over and placed it on the bed next to her husband. "I have a surprise for you," she said. "I've used my time in lockup here to do some research." She turned the screen to Pete. "It was built by a Silicon Valley hotshot who discovered he really prefers shooting things in video games. Put it on the market three weeks ago. It's available immediately." The screen showed a majestic hunting lodge with mountains in the background, surrounded by acres of cleared land.

"Where is that?" Pete asked.

"That's the best part. It's exactly thirty-eight minutes from Okmulgee, thirty if you drive like I do. And it's the perfect way to celebrate this pipeline project, my darling."

She only called him "my darling" when she really, really wanted something.

"Why the sudden interest in Oklahoma, Kara? You hated it here when we married."

"I hated that *house,* Pete. This is different. It's partially furnished already. We could just move in. And I want to do this for *you.* We don't have to leave Dallas, baby. This can be our getaway. A place that's just ours, far from the office."

"And the price?"

"It's all there. Look through all the photos, Pete. I kind of have my heart set on it." She kissed him lightly on the lips. "I'm going to shower and dress for dinner. It will be heavenly to go out tonight. We'll get a great big steak."

Pete nodded and returned his attention to the laptop. The place was beautiful, he had to admit it. And he really missed his life in Oklahoma. He could easily commute to Dallas when necessary. These days, especially after the stroke, he worked from home, anyway.

He scrolled through the pictures and was already imagining adding an elk or two to the walls of the great room when Kara emerged. She wore his favorite dress, emerald green with a deep v-neck that kept him staring. A night with Kara in that dress, permission to dig into a giant slab of beef, the project going forward, and a return to living in his home state to ponder. Pete's life had never been better.

Seventeen

EUFAULA, ALABAMA

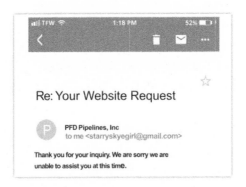

"Two weeks," I said. "It took two weeks to get a non-reply from his company." I handed my phone to Grammy, who was passing by the living room on the way back to her bedroom sewing sanctuary. She was spending almost all her time there lately.

"Well, honey," she sat across from me, "did you really think they'd put you in touch with him? What did you say?"

"It was a form I had to fill out. I just put that I needed to speak with Mr. Darling about an important personal matter."

"Like a large deposit for his bank account from a recently deceased Nigerian prince?" Grammy handed my phone back. "Surely there's another way to contact him."

"There's a voicemail maze I can't get through at his office. The one time I got an actual person to speak to me, she said he wasn't in and she couldn't take a personal message for him or connect me to his voicemail. I mailed a written letter the same day I tried the website thing. And there's no way in the world to find personal contact information. His private life doesn't exist online, or his property is registered in different names."

"Well, I guess you can't blame him," Grammy said. "I'd want privacy if I carried the burden of all that money, too. Imagine the stress."

I rolled my eyes and immediately regretted it, knowing I'd triggered my grandmother's *Wealth Is Not Money* TED Talk. She knew I'd heard it all my life. That didn't matter. The Sparrow was going to deliver, though it might be an abbreviated version if I got lucky.

"Wealth is in your heart and mind, Little One. It's the way you look at the world." She paused to wave her hand at the view of our tall sweetgum tree in the front yard which was currently deciding between bright green, yellow, or orange as its signature color for fall. "It's your thoughts, the way you experience all that surrounds you. Wealth has nothing to do with money. It's your family, your friends, the love directed toward you. No one can own the things that hold true meaning." She took her Diet Coke and started to head to her room. "And you, your mother and I are the—"

"Yeah, the wealthiest people you know. I get it, Grammy. I don't think money is quite the burden you do, though."

"It's keeping a man in Texas from knowing he has a beautiful daughter, isn't it?" She punctuated that with a final, triumphant eyebrow raise and left the room.

She had a point. All I could do was hope somehow Peter F. Darling got a look at the letter I'd mailed him, in which I'd mentioned he knew my mother, Lisa Willis, in Eufaula, Alabama in the late 1990s. I didn't introduce the topic of parenthood, leaving the reason I needed to speak with him vague. Grammy was probably right. Anything I sent him without directly mentioning my purpose was going to sound scammy. But my alternative was to tell him he had a daughter and live with the fact he never wanted to see my face.

If he ever saw what I'd written at all. I figured there were eight layers of screening between me and my biological father in his plush leather office chair, where I imagined him surveying the skyline of Dallas and hurling thunderbolts at the mortals who displeased him below.

Three more weeks passed before Mama handed me an envelope with a PFD Pipelines logo embossed in silver as its return address. I unfolded it as she and Grammy studied my face like a topographical map, searching it for peaks of joy or valleys of disappointment.

I kept myself expressionless as I read, "Thank you for your inquiry. We regret we cannot forward personal correspond-dence from this office. Best wishes, Wanda L. Miner, Corporate Relations"

I tossed the letter onto the kitchen table for them to read. Mama was the first to speak. "Skye, baby, I know you're disappointed…"

My grandmother was looking at the floor, as though some fresh answers might be located in the worn beige linoleum.

"No, Mama. I'm disappointed when Auburn loses. I'm disappointed when my car's air conditioning stops working. When my scratch-off ticket isn't a winner. When I get a stain on a new shirt. This…" I picked the letter up and wadded it into a ball, tossing it into the wastebasket under the sink. "…is not disappointment. I'm just mad at myself for listening to Grammy's brilliant advice about writing to my father. *But honey, you'll never forgive yourself if you don't contact him.*" I said it in a mocking, screechy old-lady voice and stared hard at Grammy, who was still searching the floor. She had her long white braid over one shoulder, stroking it absently. "I'm mad at myself for being over twenty years old and living in this house like it's some special lady commune. I should have been out of here a long time ago. I'll be moving as soon as I find a place." I held up both palms at them and started to back away.

"Skye, please, you're upset, you can't make decisions like that when all you're feeling is anger and hurt—" Mama reached for my arm and I shrugged her off.

"Let her go," Grammy said quietly. "Let her go, Talisa." Grammy didn't even look at me.

I went to my room and lay on my green and blue paisley bedspread trying to figure out who might need a roommate. Angie texted me back about a friend whose lease was almost up and might be looking to share a new apartment. She'd get me a number.

That was the one and only possibility I turned up after texting six people.

I studied the room I'd been living in since I was born. Everywhere I looked was a memory, shelved or stuck on the walls. My tiny speck of a life surrounded me, from volleyball trophies *"Most Improved Player"* to a photo of Jeff and me at prom, which I'd somehow left tucked into my dresser mirror after our breakup. My high school diploma Mama had framed. My tiny pink ballet shoes from exactly one year of classes at the age of six. It was all completely depressing. I gave up on sleep and re-read my library copy of *A Prayer for Owen Meany* until my eyes wouldn't stay open. Then I fell into a series of dreams in which I was late: late for class, late for work, late for an interview, late for everything and panic-stricken.

Grammy was still in her room when I got up. Mama was waiting for me in the kitchen, sipping coffee as she leaned against the counter. "It's been the three of us for so many years, baby. I can't imagine living here without you." She brushed a tear away. "But I always knew you'd leave, whether for college or a boy you fell in love with. I just hoped it would be for a happy reason, Skye, not this."

"So did I, Mama. Honestly, I wish I'd never found out about Pete Darling. I wish I still believed everything I used to, including Grammy's stuff about us women living together being some modern version of Creek matriarchy. I wish I could go back to how I felt before the stupid DNA test." I gave her an awkward hug. "But Mama, I can't go back and neither can you. I have no idea where forward is, but I don't think it's here."

"Don't decide anything too quickly, Skye," she sniffed. "Give yourself a few days and you may change your mind." Mama shook her head. "At least I'd still see you at the restaurant."

"Mama," I said, "working at Manny's has been fine with all of us living here and sharing expenses, but it won't be enough for paying rent somewhere. You know that."

"So," she rinsed her mug and put it on the draining rack, "what will you do?"

"I'll keep my job at the restaurant for now, but I'm going to look into other things, maybe the National Guard, I don't know. I'm still trying to figure out how to do life. I feel like I'm way behind."

Mama grabbed her purse and keys. "I'll tell you a secret, Skye: we all are. It never stops." She kissed my cheek and held the side of my face. "Not even your grandmother has all the answers, though you can't tell her I said that. But be gentle with her, baby. She's as torn up as you are, and making her feel like this is her fault... well, that's wrong. You know better." Mama walked out of the house and left me wearing a new, suffocating layer of guilt on top of my anger and hurt.

I knocked on Grammy's door. "Yes?" she answered.

"I just wanted to make sure you're okay in there." I leaned against the wall, listening. She was clearly shuffling stuff around her room before opening the door.

She stood gazing up at me with all the tenderness God ever gave a grandmother for her wayward offspring. I wrapped my arms around the tiny woman whose heart had nurtured me through all the ups and downs of my life, crying into the shoulder of her fleece robe. "I'm so sorry, Grammy. Please forgive me. I'm so very sorry." I was full-blown sobbing now, thinking how I'd mocked her.

"Little One, all you did was tell the truth. You don't have to apologize to me." She hugged me, then patted and rubbed my back like I was a swaddled baby. "I didn't even consider that you wouldn't hear back from him," she whispered, her voice breaking. "I do feel like it's my fault."

"No. It is not your fault." I swiped at my tears and shook my head. "I needed to try, and I did. It's over now and I can move on." I paused and bit my lower lip. "And Grammy, I think that means leaving here and living on my own. Well, with a roommate so I can afford it. Or maybe joining the military…"

I stopped as I watched her face fall, then rise back up into the most insincere smile I'd ever seen. "You *should* be out discovering the world. We've had you to ourselves longer than we deserve, your mom and I. This is your time, and if you change your mind about college, I have a little money put away. I can help."

"I'm not going to college, Grammy. I tried that, and all I learned was that I'm sick of sitting in classrooms. Aren't you the person who's always told me some of the best-educated people in the world don't have degrees?"

"That's true, Little One, but you have to consider what work you want to do. Are you planning to wait tables like your mother? To run a cash register like me? You don't need money for much, honey, but you'll have to pay the bills."

"Some of the brokest people I know have four-year degrees, Grammy. And none of them can quote Whitman or Dorothy Parker or know Sequoyah's syllabary like you and I do."

"The cure for boredom is curiosity. There is no cure for curiosity," she answered. "Fortunately, you've always been as curious as I am, with both our noses buried in books. Well, my nose is mostly in the computer for the last year or so. I never dreamed of that much information at my fingertips. It's like magic."

"You're like magic." I kissed her cheek and she waved at her sewing machine.

"I need to get back to what I was doing. I love you, baby."

"I love you too, Grammy. I'll see you after work."

I closed her bedroom door and wondered if I was making a big mistake. My life with Mama and Grammy was wonderful in a lot of ways. Maybe I belonged in this house for a few more years. It took one minute in my own room, surveying all the mementos I'd looked at last night, my museum of minutiae, to remember why I needed to grow up and move on.

I was in the National Guard recruiter's office in Dothan three days later.

Eighteen

OKMULGEE, OKLAHOMA

K ara followed the highlighted route on the GPS as carefully as possible. The navigation system didn't recognize the road she was on and it was easy to see why. The last mile had been more like a cattle path. She was staring at the red dot in the distance on the map and the dotted line pointing toward it. "Turn right," the Tahoe announced. There was no place to turn. She cursed and threw the SUV into reverse, launching a dirt cloud at the canopy of trees overhead. Kara spotted an even worse excuse for a road on her right about twenty yards back. Surely she would remember having to go through a glorified weed patch the one time she'd been driven out here.

It was taking entirely too long; she'd only bought herself an hour and a half by saying she had to go for a bikini waxing and had no intention of dragging Deke along. Pete had been distracted by a teleconference and waved her out of the room. She was blissfully free.

The house came into view about a minute later; it was situated atop a small hill, all wood and glass and not a window covering in sight. She hadn't noticed that before, but it was typical of Lang. So was the fact the entire second floor was a bedroom suite with a glass wall facing out the other side, toward every Oklahoma mountain sunset.

His pickup truck sat in the driveway.

Kara was about to burst with excitement at the news she'd come to deliver: they were closing on the hunting lodge next month. Pete was practically giddy at the idea of spending time in his home state, and Kara had already imagined a hundred ways to meet up with Lang. Her husband was on the road a lot of the time. It wasn't impossible to imagine smuggling Langdon Tiger into the lodge for a few nights.

Kara smiled to herself and reached for the present she'd brought him: a framed 8x10 of her sprawled on the bed in the hotel suite, wearing nothing but one of Pete's Oklahoma-print neckties. Kara had discreetly ordered the photo online and had it delivered to a pack & ship post office box she'd registered for such purchases. There was also a very expensive sex toy she planned to introduce Lang to in the glossy black gift bag. She was pretty sure he'd love it almost as much as the photo after today's demonstration.

She knocked on the polished oak door, its edges beautifully carved with deer and other animals. Kara had missed that detail, too, but it had been dark when Lang brought her here and she was mighty distracted. He didn't answer, so she tried the doorbell. When that didn't work, she knew he must be out back in the hot tub. She walked around the side of the house and opened a gate onto a well-landscaped path. She remembered this part; the path led to another gate in the high wooden fence surrounding the hot tub. It was sunk into a patio with rockwork that featured a waterfall at one end. There were plants all around the inside edges of the enclosure; a series of clematis vines snaked down inside the fence, trailing bright pink and purple flowers. Kara referred to it as his miniature grotto.

He was sitting in the water, just as she'd known he'd be, his tall back to Kara and his long white hair falling behind his head. She was sure his eyes were closed, the way his face was tilted toward the sun. She hoped she could sneak into his line of vision before he opened them.

Kara walked to the side of the patio, contemplating where to set the gift bag and how quickly she could get her clothes off. She began unbuttoning her blouse with her back to Lang. She turned around slowly, wearing her sexiest smile.

Kara would replay the scene that greeted her a thousand times in her mind. First she saw the girl who had the flawless golden skin of a twenty-year-old. Her hair was black, at least waist-length, flowing out and dancing atop the water. Kara hadn't seen her when she walked in because she was tiny, hidden by Langdon. He was quite naked and so was the girl. She was straddling Langdon and moving her hips very slowly, barely noticeably in the churning bubbles of the hot tub. The girl turned her face to Kara and smiled, like she was regularly interrupted having sex with Langdon Tiger and didn't mind.

Lang seemed to return to reality very suddenly, but he didn't attempt to move. "Hi, Kara," he said. "This is Nila." Nila was still smiling and apparently permanently affixed to Lang. "I wasn't expecting you," he continued. "Why don't you join us?" He grinned at Kara and then leaned his head back again; eyes closed and mouth hanging open.

What kind of drugs was the man on? Kara stared in disbelief for a few seconds. She took the five-hundred-dollar, gold-plated Eroscillator 2 from the gift bag, switched it to the "on" position, and threw it into the hot tub like she was trying to win a prize at the county fair.

Where was a thirty-dollar toaster, she thought, when one needed it?

The splash was enough to startle them both. Nila moved away from Lang and he jumped up and out of the tub. The man literally moved like a tiger, sleek and magnificent and beautiful. Kara hated him for that.

"Kara, wait!" he yelled at her. He followed her to the gate, no towel, no shame, no hesitation. "You can't be mad at me." Lang held his open palms out wide and shrugged. "Surely you didn't think—"

"No," she said evenly, "Of course I didn't. Don't let me keep you. You seem to be losing your… enthusiasm." She glanced pointedly below his waist, though he wasn't nearly as shriveled as she'd like.

"I'll see you— " Lang began.

"You won't," she said. "I was wrong to come here. Just stay away from me, Lang. I'm already tired of this game and the stakes are too high, anyway."

Lang shrugged. "You didn't tell me to expect you today, Kara. What's that you're holding?" he asked.

"A present for Pete," Kara improvised. Perfect. She'd explain she'd gone to pick it up, and the waxing was a ruse to surprise her husband with the photo. She could skip the strips she'd brought along in the SUV and the parking lot agony they'd have put her through.

This was worse.

The dull ache in her chest was something new to her, and Kara was afraid he might actually see her cry. Lang looked pretty ridiculous standing there dripping, though. She focused on that and conjured a laugh. "Bye, Lang." She turned and sashayed away with her practiced walk until she heard him slam the gate closed. Then she plodded to the Tahoe.

How stupid she'd been, thinking they had some sort of relationship. Karma, big fat karma, for all the men she'd manipulated with sex and then ignored. She'd allow herself a few more minutes of pain, but she was sure as hell going to move on to anger soon. Anger was much more comfortable to wear.

Kara never suspected she'd see Langdon Tiger a few days later under very different circumstances. Or that her anger would make everything in the world fall apart.

Nineteen

EUFAULA, ALABAMA

My grandmother was only pretending to fluff pillows on the living room couch. I saw her glance at Mama and me over and over as I recounted what Sergeant Whitaker had told me: I had one of the highest ASVAB test results they'd seen in the Dothan office. Most of my line scores were in the ninetieth percentile or higher, and I could practically choose any military career I wanted; not limited to the National Guard, either. I could enlist in the Navy and eventually become a cryptologic technician, deciphering enemy communications. I'd earn great money, and the benefits were better than I could hope for anywhere else. Best of all, I'd receive a twenty thousand dollar signing bonus when I completed training.

All I had to do was commit to a six-year contract. I could see the world. I could serve my country and find meaning and purpose in my life, which I knew was a recruitment spiel, but it sounded great.

Sergeant Whitaker told me I could go to the MEPS in Montgomery as early as next week for my enlistment—he would make all the arrangements. After he saw my test results, he'd said everything to me with the zeal of a Baptist preacher addressing a particularly sinful-looking flock on a Sunday morning.

I'd walked out of there feeling like the gold the Dothan recruiters had been panning for since they opened the office. I could see myself in a dress uniform. I could also see myself preventing a terrorist attack by decoding an intercepted message no one else could crack. I really was good at puzzles and word games. All of this led to daydreaming about working in the Pentagon.

So, naturally, The Sparrow had to perch on a chair and sing me a song of her people.

"Little One, let me tell you a story from long, long ago. Most people don't know it, but at that time the bear had a long, fluffy tail, nothing like we see on bears today. He was very proud of his beautiful tail."

I nodded and did my best to look attentive. Mama got up to get a cup of coffee, as it was clear this parable was intended for me.

"So, one day Bear is very hungry—starving, in fact—and he is walking along the lakeshore. It's very cold and almost time for Bear to begin his long sleep. He must find food. The lake is frozen already. Bear comes upon Otter, who is sitting near a small hole in the lake's ice. Otter has a large pile of fish next to him. Bear can practically taste them.

"'How did you get all those fish?' Bear asks Otter. He is eyeing Otter's dinner and wondering whether to steal it.

"'Oh, it's easy,' Otter replies. Instead of telling Bear how he dove into the hole and swam to catch them, he says, 'I just hang my tail into the hole I made in the ice. Every once in a while, I wiggle my tail around. When a fish bites it, I quickly pull him up. It's the easiest way to catch all the fish you can eat.'" Grammy dangled and swished her hand loosely in front of my face, to illustrate the fishing method and make sure I was listening, too.

"Bear peers over at the hole. 'That sure sounds easy. Do you mind if I use your fishing hole?' he asks Otter.

"Otter says, 'I have enough fish. Use my fishing hole as long as you like, friend.' Then Otter picks up his fish and walks away.

"Bear pokes his tail into the ice hole and waits. He waits and waits. Once in a while he wiggles his tail so the fish can see it. Bear waits until the sun begins to set, but not one fish even nibbles at his tail. At last, he decides to go home. He'll have to search for food tomorrow. But when he tries to stand up, his tail has frozen into the ice. He can't move. He pulls and pulls at his tail, but it's stuck tight. Finally, he pulls with all of his strength and rips off almost all of his beautiful, fluffy tail. It was gone forever. And that is why bears today have only a stub of a tail."

"Grammy," I began, "I don't see—"

"Yes, you do." She nodded at me, eyes wide. "Don't always believe what people tell you, Little One."

"That's a pretty long path to telling me you don't trust the recruiter," I shook my head at her. "You could have just said so. And I'm really proud of the test scores, Grammy."

"Of course you are, and so am I. But they tell me nothing I didn't know. You've always been brilliant, Little One. You've mostly been bored in school, and your mother and I have understood you hate sitting in classrooms." Mama nodded in agreement. Grammy continued, "There's never been any doubt of your intelligence or ability. We've just been waiting for you to figure out how you want to use them. It's a big decision."

"I know that, Grammy. And I think this is my big opportunity."

"Maybe," Mama and Grammy said in unison.

"But you both think I shouldn't rush into it."

"Actually, we think you should take your time and research more about what a military career will demand of you," Grammy said. "It's not as rosy as that recruiter is making it sound, Little One, and you know that in your heart. And there are," she glanced at Mama, "risks. You have all the time in the world. The United States Military isn't closing anytime soon. They will wait for you."

"Sergeant Whitaker says—"

"I don't care what Sergeant Whitaker says," Grammy cut me off. "What I do care about is the hopes and dreams all your grandmothers held for you, and the sacrifices they made. And you've seen that firsthand lately, so honor it by choosing something worthy."

I threw my head back. "Y'all don't understand. I feel like my world has been turned upside down. This whole thing with Larry not being my dad, and my father refusing to even speak to me... sometimes I don't even know who I am. I just want to feel like I'm moving forward."

Mama finally decided to speak up. "You're being a little dramatic, Skye. You're the person you've always been, every bit as loved and cherished as ever."

I met her eyes. "I know that, Mama, and I didn't mean to hurt your feelings. When I say I don't know who I am, it's more about where I fit into the world. I can't stay here the rest of my life. I have friends who are making good money already, and some of them have gone into the military. It's not a bad career path."

Grammy looked exhausted, and a little teary. She stood and leaned over to hug me. "It's not about money, Little One. It's about waking up in the morning feeling happy about the day ahead. It's about using your gifts wisely. I need you to promise me you'll wait one week before committing to anything. Will you do that?"

"I guess," I mumbled.

"No guessing. Promise me."

She wasn't going to go off to bed until I did, and I knew it. "I promise, Grammy. One week. And I'll do some research, too."

"Then I'll say good night." She kissed the top of Mama's head and mine. "See you two in the morning."

We watched her walk down the hall. "Is she okay?" I asked Mama. "She sure is spending a lot of time in her room."

Mama smiled. "She's fine. You know how your grand-mother is when she has a sewing project." She waited until she heard Grammy's door close. "And honestly, Skye, she's worried about you and this military thing. I'm glad you promised to slow down some. You may not want to hear this on top of that bear and otter saga, but recruiters *will* paint a glorious picture for someone like you and leave out the darker scenes." She glanced at Larry's photo, forever smiling from the corner of the kitchen counter. Mama slapped her palms on the table. "Anyway, Manny and I are going to a movie. Wanna come?"

It was the most halfhearted invitation I'd ever heard, not that I would have allowed myself to be dragged along. "No, I'm going to do what I promised and Google military life on my phone until my thumbs start marching in unison." I wiggled them at her. "Have fun." I kissed her cheek and thought how unfair it was that I kept sending my mother off on dates and no guy had looked at me in approximately forever. Maybe I'd Google nunneries for the religiously confused Baptist Great Spirit worshipper.

Manny greeted me for my shift the next night with his recently fashioned fatherly face, which was grave and serious and entirely unearned. "Your mother is worried about you," he confided as he gazed into the empty dining room, arms crossed. We had about ten minutes until opening.

"I know that, thank you so much, Manny. She talks to me, too. I'm her *daughter*." I could see I'd hurt his feelings in the way he dropped his arms and walked off to the kitchen, shaking his head.

I was a human wrecking ball lately and didn't know how to stop. If I needed confirmation, it was time for me to get out of town; I saw it in the faces of everyone I snapped at.

The first customers to step through the door were Greg Varnadoe and his friend Jackson Latimer. Jackson was great-looking; he had a beautiful smile and dark hair he kept longish. He wore a tight white t-shirt and jeans on his tall, muscular body. I caught him looking at his reflection in the mirror Luz had installed by the cash register. Unfortunately, Jackson's intellect could be herded onto the top of a straight pin. No one had been amazed when he dropped out senior year and started working at the local gym. I'd heard he was doing well there as a personal trainer.

Greg looked like he'd bulked up a lot, no doubt with Jackson's assistance. He even seemed an inch or two taller. I glanced down and realized he'd paired extra-high-heeled cowboy boots with his shirt, tie, and khakis. Why was he wearing a shirt and tie? Why did anyone in his twenties own khakis?

Greg waved as he and Jackson settled themselves into a booth, since we wouldn't have a hostess for another hour.

"Congratulate me," he said, grinning. "Remember I told you I was thinking of applying to the Eufaula Police Department?"

"You actually did it?" I wasn't aware he'd followed through, even though we texted pretty often and I saw his Snapchat stories, usually with one of the cattle on his family's farm or riding a four-wheeler through a slog of mud.

"My interview was today," he glanced down at his outfit. "I passed the physical last week, thanks to my buddy Jackson here. The runnin', the pushups, the sit-ups, the six-foot fence climb, the wrigglin' through a window… hell, they even made me push a Volkswagen for fifteen yards, Skye. I'm buyin' Jackson drinks and dinner to say thanks. You're lookin' at the newest addition to local law enforcement."

Jackson nodded and said, "Yeah" with a big smile.

"Wow, congratulations, Greg," I said, happy for him. "Y'all want to start with a beer?" I glanced back toward the kitchen.

"Pitcher of margaritas and some chips and queso would be great," he answered. "I haven't had any real food in two weeks."

"Yeah," Jackson grinned. "I'll be livin' on protein bars for a few days, but it's worth it."

"I'll be right back," I tapped my pen on their table and walked away. Greg, a police officer? Who would have believed that?

They were flicking a makeshift paper football back and forth when I returned. I demanded ID, knowing they'd laugh, but I'd sworn not to serve my friends without it. They dug in their pockets and handed them over. I was suddenly struck by how young we all still were, and it choked me up a little.

Greg poured himself a margarita and lifted his glass to me before gulping half of it down. "I start the academy next week. Already told my dad. He is not thrilled, but he's never thrilled by anything I do. My mom is convinced I'm goin' to get shot and cries every time she looks at me. It's not a great time at the Varnadoe house." He added a halfhearted laugh. "But there's no future on that effin' farm, Skye, and my dad refuses to see it. So I'm movin' on and doin' somethin' with my life." He twisted his margarita glass around in his hands. "Truth is, I always kinda thought I'd make a good cop."

I smiled at him, still the sweet boy I'd known when we were little. I wanted to cry, too. "I know you will, Greg. You'll be the best they have. What's Caroline think about it?"

"Aww, she and her soon-to-be-husband think it's great." He took another swig of his drink and glanced at Jackson, waiting for me to register his words. "I told you Caroline was gonna meet someone in the *National Guard,*" he said it in a mocking singsong, "and she did. Name's Bert. Caroline and Bert live in Texas. What the hell kinda name is Bert? Sounds like he's in his forties or somethin'."

I wasn't sure how to respond. I went with, "Well, I'm happy for her, I guess. Are you?" I looked to see if Manny had stepped out of the kitchen to glower because I was taking too long chatting. They were the only customers in the place, but it depended on Manny's mood. Sure enough, he poked his head out and nodded at me. Permission to talk to my friends, granted.

"Honestly, Skye, I haven't cared what Caroline does for months. That's the truth. It took a while, but I realized what I was really hurtin' over was losin' the future she and I were supposed to have together, ya know?" Greg paused for a minute and looked down at the table before lifting his eyes to mine. "I'm over Caroline, though, and it's mostly because of you. I think of you way more often than her."

He must have seen my mouth hanging open. "But hey, don't worry, it's all good." Greg held up his hand to direct my mind-traffic. "I just wanted you to know. I think you're pretty, Skye, and sweet and funny. And no one tells you because you're too scary. You're always spoutin' some words nobody knows or talkin' about shit we never heard of."

"Yeah," Jackson contributed, nodding.

"Who is we?" I said, too stunned to say more.

"I dunno. A few of us guys who know you, that's all. You're special, and I thought you should know that." He handed me his menu like he hadn't just thrown labels like "pretty" and "scary" at me or seemingly confessed he was in like with me. "And I want the number five combo plate," he added.

Jackson put his menu on the table for me to grab, because his brain didn't quite make it to handing it to me. "Yeah, that sounds good to me, too."

"Okay, I'll get that out to you in a few minutes." I took their empty chip basket. "And I'll bring you more chips. Is there anything else y'all need?" This was my most awkward table ever. I wanted to get to the kitchen and press some reset button to make things normal again.

"Hey, Skye, calm down. I'm telling everyone what I think of 'em before I leave for training." Greg clinked his glass to Jackson's and laughed. "But you really are somethin' special, Skye Willis. Just bring yourself back to this table over and over, and we'll be fine." Then he swept his eyes up and down my body, leering at me. Greg, my sweet Greg, had learned leering from Jackson. God, he was probably taking steroids.

I waited with Manny until their platters were ready. "Your friends out there. You tell them you are thinking about this Navy thing?"

I looked at the ceiling. "No, I didn't."

"Tell them, Es-cah-yee. See if they think it is a good thing for you to do, eh?"

"All right, I will. I'm sure they'll be happy I have the chance to do something besides wait tables. No offense, Manny."

"Oh, no, I'm not offended. But while you wait tables for me, you do the best for everybody. Go on, their food is getting cold."

I slid the hot plates in front of them, reminding Jackson twice to be careful not to touch his and burn himself. "You know, Greg," I said, looking at Manny trying to eavesdrop, "I went to the recruiting station in Dothan last week. I didn't take the ASVAB in school, so they gave it to me there. My score is high enough they're offering me a big signing bonus and a chance to do something important in the Navy."

Greg looked up from his forkful of enchilada. "That's great, Skye. You're not gonna do it, are you?"

"Why? Why is it okay for you to put yourself out there and risk your life as a law enforcement officer, but it's not okay for me to join the Navy?" I crossed my arms and glared at the fourth person to ruin my exciting news.

"I mean," Greg said, "It's fantastic you got great scores, Skye, but that just means you can do anything you want to, doesn't it? They want you to sign up for six years, right?"

"Yes, and I'll still be in my twenties when I get out, Greg." I watched Jackson do the mental math sans finger assistance.

"You're missing the point, Skye. If I hate being a policeman, I can quit or transfer somewhere. If you hate this hitch in the Navy... well, it's called a contract for a reason."

"But it all sounds so exciting," I whined.

"And maybe it would be. But you better think about sellin' that much of your life for twenty thousand bucks. I mean, I know you get trainin' and benefits, too, but I think six years of Skye Willis's life should be worth a lot more than that. It is twenty thousand, right? Same as they promised Caroline?"

"Yes," I answered. I was saved from having to talk about it more by two couples who came in. I waved goodbye to Greg and Jackson, giving them a few minutes before I knew they'd ask for another pitcher, which Greg would drink while Jackson switched to water to preserve his chiseled abs. And his driver's license.

An hour and a half later, a very sober Jackson hugged me and said, "You really are a sweetheart", which made me feel uber-guilty about regarding him as a fancy houseplant. "Think hard about your choice, Skye. I love doin' what I do, and I make a good livin' at it. I have clients in Phenix City and Dothan, too. But if I didn't have fun doin' it, no amount of money would make it worth the grind."

"And you could get hurt, Skye," Greg slurred. "I don't want you getting' hurt." He stood to hug me goodbye, too.

"Worry about yourself, Officer Varnadoe," I told him. "I don't want you hurt, either." I gave him a chaste, sisterly kiss on the cheek and watched them step out into the streetlights. They'd left me a thirty dollar tip on a forty-five dollar tab.

On Day Four of my Week of Deep Thinking, I woke to find a note from Grammy saying she'd gone to the casino with Wilma and would be back in a couple of days. We shouldn't worry about her and someone should finish the chicken casserole before it went bad. Also, the Eastons' cat was missing and we needed to look out for him. Also, we should stay out of her room because she'd left it in a mess and didn't want us to move anything. Finally, she loved Mama and me more than anything.

She'd probably had enough of the Skye-high drama in the house lately. Even I had. Mama and I spent that night *not* talking about the Navy or my generation's struggle to establish themselves or The Future. We binge-watched half a season of *The Great British Baking Show,* which forced us to drive to a convenience store for Ding Dongs and Snowballs a little after midnight. It was the most fun we'd had in a very long time.

Mama was off from the Huddle House for a couple of days. We worked together at *Oro y Cena* that night, handling a bigger-than-usual crowd. Mama said she was too tired to go to Manny's for the night, but I think she wanted some time alone with me before Grammy got back. We brought home flan for a bedtime snack.

"This has been so much fun, Skye, having you all to myself," Mama said, hugging me goodnight.

"But you miss her, too, don't you?"

"Yeah," Mama chuckled. "Everything is different without The Sparrow here. When I was very young, I thought everyone's mother read Tolstoy and made dreamcatchers to hang all over their kid's bedroom. There's just no one like her."

I smiled and turned to go to my room. "I think we're both more like her than we know. I hope so."

The next morning, Wilma called while Mama and I sipped coffee in blessed silence.

"Hey," I answered, "Are y'all having a good time? Aren't you coming back today?"

"Skye," Wilma sounded a little breathless, "I know your grandmother told you she's with me. She's not, though. Y'all need to turn on the morning news on channel six, honey. Right now, hurry. I didn't think she'd really go through with it. Verna has gone and done somethin' for you and now the whole country is watchin'."

Twenty

CATOOSA, OKLAHOMA

K ara opened Pete's suitcase and carefully placed her nude photo between his shirts and plaid boxer shorts. He'd have a happy surprise in Harrisburg, Pennsylvania, which would otherwise be a series of dull meetings Pete would complain about when he called each night. He'd be back in less than a week.

A few days had passed since discovering Nila in Lang's hot tub, a time for Kara to reflect and deeply regret she'd thrown a perfectly good gold-plated Eroscillator 2 into the water.

It pained her, this revelation that she could share any lover's attention with someone else. Kara Darling played second fiddle to no one. She would have told you it wasn't jealousy or insecurity that made her want to set that fiddle afire and throw it at Nila. It was sheer stunned outrage that Lang desired another woman while he'd been with her.

That did not happen. Not to Kara.

She would shed the memory of Langdon Tiger's body. She would rededicate herself to Pete. She would stop looking for her next conquest.

She would order another gold-plated Eroscillator 2.

And she would get her revenge.

Joseph drove Pete to the airport in the early hours of a fine September day. Pete watched the sun rise and paint an Oklahoma lake the deepest rose pink, smiling to himself at the thought he would finally leave Texas and live where he belonged. The limp from his stroke was all but indiscernible now, and Pete knew he was a lucky man to get this new beginning.

Kara had been especially sweet lately, fussing over him and acting like the tigress he'd known in bed years ago. Maybe she'd grown to love his home state and was excited about their new life there. Maybe she'd been reading sexy books. He didn't care as long as it didn't stop.

Joseph waved his hand in the rearview mirror as Pete pretended to read something on his laptop. "Yeah, what is it?" he asked.

Joseph said, "We're going by the laydown yard in a minute. Do you still want to stop there?"

Pete didn't want to stop, but he knew it would be good to put in an appearance with Drew Tyler, his man in charge. Early morning surprises had always been part of his management style. "Sure, we'll stop for a few." He closed his laptop and resumed sipping the coffee Kara had handed him as she kissed him goodbye, wearing nothing but a Sooners t-shirt and a sleepy smile.

God, he loved that woman.

They were met at the gate by a Creek kid Drew had hired, recommended by that weird Langdon Tiger. Pete still didn't know what to make of Tiger, with his elegantly manicured nails and brown eyes that seemed to laugh when Pete spoke, no matter how seriously. Langdon made him distinctly uncomfortable and Pete sensed he enjoyed doing it.

Joseph talked to the guard, who was apparently bored and disinterested until he realized who sat in the back seat. He waved them through and Pete made a mental note to ask Drew about him.

They walked into the office at precisely 6:48. Drew was nowhere to be seen. Pete and Joseph wasted five minutes searching for him before the kid abandoned his post at the gate, wandering over to ask, "Oh, are you looking for Mr. Tyler? He's coming in late today on account of his wife is feeling sick. He said he might have to take her to the doctor."

Pete swept his eyes up and down the young man. He was the prototypical American twenty-something, bored and probably dying to stare at his phone when they drove away. He was tall and fit-looking, though Joseph could break him in half with his bare hands. He wore a World of Warcraft t-shirt and jeans with holes at the knees. "What's your name, son?"

"I'm Dakota," the kid answered, extending his hand.

Of course you are, thought Pete. He shook hands with him as the kid continued, "It's great to meet you, Mr. Darling. Thanks for the job here."

"You're welcome, Dakota. You have security experience?"

"I do," he answered, "I used to work security at an apartment complex and at a warehouse in Tulsa. I have an advanced certification with this, too." He patted the holstered Glock pistol at his side.

"I see," Pete said. "Well, Dakota, tomorrow when you come to work for my company, you'll do it in jeans that have no holes and a clean shirt with no shit printed on it, okay? Mr. Tyler should have explained we have a dress code, and you can't look like a damn homeless person when you're on the clock. Do you own a polo shirt, with a collar?"

"Yes, I do." Dakota had lost his smile.

"Okay, well, that's what I want you to wear if you're working my yard, all right? We understand each other, Dakota? And tell Mr. Tyler to call me the second he drives up. If I'm unavailable, he's to keep calling until I am. Got that?"

"Yes sir," Dakota answered. "I'll tell him what you said."

Pete turned and climbed back into the Tahoe, his morning curdled like old milk.

Joseph had been working for Mr. Darling long enough to know when it was best to remain silent. He didn't even dare to turn on the radio. When they boarded the plane, he settled himself as far from his boss as possible and wished, not for the first time, he was assigned to Kara instead of her husband. He should have pretended to be gay like Deke had, the sly bastard.

Mr. Darling shook Joseph's shoulder and woke him as they prepared to land in Harrisburg, staring at him like he'd been sleeping while responsible for his safety at thirty thousand feet. He was not a damn flight attendant, he was former LSU right tackle who could back sane people off with a stern look. Pointing to exits and handing out pretzels weren't in the job description. Joseph tried to act like he wasn't annoyed, and nodded at Mr. Darling.

"We'll go straight to the state offices when we get the car," Pete said. He handed Joseph a slip of paper. "That's the address. I've spent the flight studying this Mariner thing, and I think I have a good solution for them."

Joseph recalled some reference to the Mariner Pipeline and possible environmental contamination, but he didn't know much and would rather debate Protestantism with the Pope than try to discuss pipelines with Pete Darling. The man lived and breathed his business. He read about it constantly, researched trends in fabrication, examined terrain maps, and was basically like a teen playing Fortnite when it came to pipeline stuff. It bored Joseph to tears. "That's great," Joseph said, wondering how soon he could get to his own, blessed, private hotel room. He was in for a good five hours of standing in a corner followed by dinner at whatever steak restaurant was recommended to Mr. Darling by a helpful Pennsylvanian. Thank God he didn't have to suffer the variety of kale and carrot crap Deke did most of the time.

His girlfriend, Lalique, couldn't understand why he didn't leave bodyguarding Mr. Darling and get a decent job elsewhere, so he'd have more time for her. But Joseph was making twice what he could at any job he qualified for, which was pretty much confined to being a bouncer or personal trainer. And Leeka liked the jewelry and other surprises he bought her *way* too much to push the issue.

Joseph reminded himself of all this as he hoisted their luggage and walked behind Mr. Darling to the car rental place.

Kara spent a wonderful morning shopping online and eating a scrumptious room service breakfast of eggs Benedict and a large mimosa. Later, when Pete called to say they'd landed, she told him to be sure to unpack carefully. She'd sent a little present for him.

That afternoon she dragged Deke to a Tulsa art gallery to consider furnishings to personalize the lodge. Kara selected a massive abstract oil painting of a stand of trees. It featured splashes of what Kara called Louboutin Red among the duller greens and beiges, and she thought it would be perfect over the stone fireplace. It was worth every penny to prevent a disembodied elk head from appearing there. She arranged to have it delivered and hung when they moved in next week.

They followed that with a trip to a furniture store, where Kara sat with the manager for two hours discussing accent pieces. She was building the great room around the painting, with a bold red lacquered coffee table to accompany the existing beige leather sofas. She found mahogany lamps with tasteful deer carved into their bases and ordered two to appease Pete.

The empty dining room was Kara's most exciting project. It would feature a modern, sixty-inch-long rectangular chandelier flush-mounted to the ceiling with hundreds of LED lights, Swarovski crystals, and tiny white metal butterflies suspended from it. It was the crowning touch for the white Italian marble dining room table and white velvet chairs she'd imported. Practicality be damned; they'd eat most of their meals in the more manly casual dining room left behind by the Silicon Valley guy, anyway.

Pete had told Kara he trusted her to select what was needed to make it *their* home, because, "You have better taste than any interior decorator. And you never let me forget it." It was implicit: she should customize this house so she couldn't complain constantly like she had in Pete's original beige-on-beige Oklahoma antler museum.

Back at the Hard Rock after a long day of spending money, Kara ordered a Cobb salad to eat in bed. She mixed herself a martini and told Deke to get whatever he wanted from room service and not to bother her unless the building was on fire. She'd see him around eleven the next day. She playfully informed him she planned to go back to Tulsa for an afternoon yoga class, where he could watch her from behind.

Might as well keep the help happy.

Deke banged on Kara's door at 9:15 the following morning. No answer. He continued to call her name and pound his fist, attracting the attention of a group of housekeeping staff gathered around a big pushcart down the hall. He was about to give up when she swung the door open, glaring at him. She wore no makeup and a fluffy white hotel robe.

"What?! What could possibly be so important you're doing this, Deke?" Kara spat the words at him and clenched her teeth when she finished speaking. Deke took an involuntary step back.

"Your cell's off and the desk says they can't get you on the room's phone because you ordered them not to put any calls through and something is happening that no one will tell me but it's—"

Kara grabbed his sleeve and pulled him into the room, slamming the door behind him. "For Chrissakes, Deke, stop babbling." She picked up her phone to find three missed calls from a number she didn't recognize. As soon as she pressed the green button, a man picked up.

"Hello, Mrs. Darling, I'm sorry to disturb you, but Mr. Darling is in a meeting in Pennsylvania and I didn't know what else to do—"

Kara threw her head back in frustration. "Who is this?"

"My name is Drew Tyler, ma'am, and we haven't met but I run the laydown yard outside of Okmulgee and we have a problem here."

"I'm sure you can contact Herb Larson or Dennis Wheaton, Mr. Tyler," Kara said, reeling off the names of project managers she could recall. "Why are you bothering me with this?" She plopped down on her bed and waved Deke to a chair in the corner.

"Well, ma'am, there are news crews here and I—"

"News crews? Why? What exactly is going on in twenty-five words or less, please?" Kara was drumming her red fingernails on the bedside table and staring at Deke. "Turn on the TV" she mouthed and pointed.

"There's a protester, and she says she will only get down if Mr. Darling personally comes to talk to her."

"Get down? Get down from where?" Kara rolled her eyes and yelled into the phone. "She's inside the yard? What the hell is going on, Drew? Tell me right now!"

"I don't know how she got in, ma'am, or who called the news people. I'm sorry Mrs. Darling, of course I take full responsibility, I tried to tell her Mr. Darling isn't even in town…" she didn't hear the rest of his reply, because Kara hung up as she saw the television screen. A reporter was standing at the base of a massive pyramid of stacked steel pipe. She didn't catch his words as the camera panned slowly upward to zoom in on a tiny old lady perched at the top, dressed in a fringed deerskin shirt and jeans. Great, she thought, another local Creek nutcase. Kara managed to unmute the TV, but the reporter had stopped talking and no one could hear the old lady, because a guy who must be Drew Tyler stepped into the frame and told the cameraman he needed to move back immediately. If he had to warn him again, he'd call the police. The station cut to a commercial.

He hadn't *already* called the police? This woman was a trespasser. Maybe that was better, though, she'd defuse the situation herself. Kara threw her hands into the air and told Deke, "Bring the car out back. Do you know how to find the laydown yard?"

"I think so," Deke shrugged, uncertain.

"Then look it up. Call that idiot Tyler if you need to. I'll be down in five minutes." Kara rushed to throw some clothes on and grab her makeup case and hair supplies. The reporters would probably see there was no story and move on before she got there, anyway, but she wanted to look her best.

"Wow," Deke said, rounding a bend in the road, "I was not expecting *this.*"

Kara looked up from her phone, checking for the tenth time for a return text from Pete. Her mouth formed a neat "o" at the crowd that had already gathered outside the laydown yard, lining the entrance with signs reading "STOP THE UNSAFE PIPELINE" and "NO PIPELINES ON STOLEN NATIVE LAND." Most were held aloft by local Creek, she saw, not the environmentalist crowd. She held her head down as Deke inched the Tahoe to the gate where they were waved in after he identified himself and his passenger. Several people smacked the SUV with their palms as it passed. Kara glanced back to make sure the gate was securely closed behind them.

Deke parked next to two local news vans outside a temporary office building and came around to extract Kara.

A short, middle-aged man with graying temples approached her and extended his hand after hastily wiping it on his jeans. Kara pretended she didn't see a handshake offered, nodding instead as he introduced himself as Drew Tyler. "I'm sorry about all this, Mrs. Darling. From what I can tell, a guard let this lady in last night and then admitted the camera crews early this morning after someone called to tell them she was here sittin' way up on top of that pyramid stack. She's telling everyone who will listen that she's not climbing down until Mr. Darling comes to speak to her."

She looked him up and down, clearly disgusted. "And you've not only allowed her access, you've allowed a media circus to be built around a protester."

"Mrs. Darling, I..."

Kara stalked off around the office toward the storage area without letting him finish. The first person she spotted was Langdon Tiger. He stood apart from the others, saying something into a phone he hastily shoved into his pocket when she walked up. "What the hell are you doing in here, Lang? Do you know this woman?" She squinted at the tiny person in the distance, sitting on God only knew how many thousands of dollars' worth of steel.

"The station alerted me, because she's telling everyone she's Creek. They thought I could help. She's not from around here, though." Langdon shrugged and looked at the pyramid of pipe about fifty feet away and the woman atop it.

"I don't understand why 'the stations' were allowed in the gate in the first place. Or why they aren't long gone," Kara said.

"Because someone working for PFD, in charge of the gate, invited them here. He told them there was a renewed pipeline protest being led by a Creek woman who had 'undisclosed' information. You know they're not going to pass that up. And they're within their rights to stay and cover the story."

"And do we know who the someone responsible for this damn mess is?" Kara asked.

"Unfortunately, I do. He's a local guy named Dakota Weller I recommended. And he's already been fired by Mr. Tyler there." Lang nodded at Tyler, who'd decided to keep a safe distance.

"Great. One of the guys you talked Pete into hiring, Lang. One of your local, *helpful* young men who can be trusted. Just *great.*" Kara held her palms up at him and made a shoving motion. "None of you are worth a damn, or another minute of my time. Go burn in hell, Lang, and take your *tribe* with you."

Lang stood expressionless, but reached for his phone as Kara turned and stomped over to Deke, who was watching from several feet away. "I've had it," she told him. "I don't care if the little old lady falls on her little old Creek head. I am so sick of these fucking people. You give and you give and this is the thanks you get. Motor oil thrown on you. New demands every day. None of them cares about the environment, they only care about their goddam casino money and whatever else they can squeeze out of the rest of us, and they've squeezed more than they deserve already. I've had it with every single one of them." Kara paused and looked at the woman waiting atop the pyramid. She closed her eyes and visibly calmed herself with a deep breath. "I'm going to talk her into coming down. Keep the reporters back as far as you can. I'll tell them my conversation with the woman is off the record, but I don't trust them to keep it that way." The cameramen were just standing around at the moment; Kara figured they were about to give up on the non-story unfolding in front of them.

She approached the news guys with her brightest smile, telling them she apologized for the misunderstanding that brought them there. If she could speak with the protester for a moment, there'd be nothing more for them to film. The two reporters responded the way straight men always responded to Kara and stepped back obediently to admire her in action.

The little Creek woman watched Kara come closer. "You're Mrs. Darling, aren't you?" she called. Kara detected a strong Southern accent.

"Yes, I am. And you are?"

"My name is Verna Willis, but my friends and family call me Sparrow. And I need to have a long-overdue discussion with your husband." She crossed her arms and shifted her weight slightly atop the metal pipe.

Kara could see the old lady was getting more and more uncomfortable. Surely she'd need a bathroom soon. "My husband isn't here, Mrs. Willis—"

"That's what they keep saying. The thing is, I've come a long way to talk to him and I'm not giving up until I do."

Kara tilted her head and used her sweetest voice. "Mrs. Willis, maybe you could tell me what this is about. I'm on the PFD Pipelines Board of Directors, and I've been working with the local Creek community for months to ensure they're happy with this project and the precautions we're taking. We've established goodwill with local residents and addressed their concerns. Now, do you live around here?"

Mrs. Willis shook her head slowly and looked at the steel pipe below her for several seconds. "No, I live in Alabama with your husband's daughter, who is my granddaughter and a wonderful young woman. Her name is Skye. She's been trying to contact him for a long time."

Kara was speechless. She held up one finger to indicate the old lady should wait, then turned and walked to Deke, who'd been joined by Drew Tyler. "Pete doesn't have children, he can't have children," she hissed. "This woman is a nutcase. She's obviously here to try to extort money from him. I want her ass off that pile of steel now. Go get her down, Deke."

"Mrs. Darling, I wouldn't advise that," Drew said. "The pipe's secured, of course, but that lady could be injured if someone climbs up and tries to take her down. Believe me, if I thought it could have been done safely, we'd have tried it." He glanced at Mrs. Willis, who was sitting with her hands folded in her lap.

"Mr. Tyler, I could not possibly care less what you think about this situation. I'm busy trying to clean up your mess."

Kara shoved one long fingernail into Deke's back and pushed him toward the woman perched atop the pipes. Deke set off as slowly as he could reasonably walk. Mrs. Willis recognized what was unfolding and stood, swaying slightly, atop the stack.

The reporters sensed a dramatic ending and moved into position.

Kara turned to shoot a triumphant look at Lang, but he was gone.

Twenty-one

EUFAULA, ALABAMA

Mama and I eased ourselves down in unison onto the couch to watch what was unfolding. Neither of us said a word, glued to the television screen, where my grandmother appeared Barbie-sized atop a giant stack of steel pipes. ABC was broadcasting live from their Tulsa affiliate. It was obvious why "Kip Richmond" held a microphone and kept waving his hand to Grammy— renewed protests of the pipeline made good news, but an itty bitty old Creek woman sitting on a gazillion dollars' worth of supplies to stop it…well, that was a startling picture no network wanted to miss. "What we know at this point is that Verna Willis, a woman of Creek descent, has traveled here from her Alabama home. She's refused to leave her position on top of this towering pyramid of steel," here Kip paused to wave his hand dramatically, "until the owner of PFD Pipelines, Peter Darling, comes to meet with her. We reached out to Mr. Darling, of course, but he can't be reached for comment. Sources tell us he's in Pennsylvania today."

What they *didn't* know, so far, was why Verna Willis had made the trip all the way to Oklahoma and demanded to speak with the pipeline company owner. Very few of the millions of people watching had any idea why my heart was twisting in fear and blowing up with pride at the same time. After a couple more minutes of the standoff, *Good Morning America* reappeared and Robin Roberts assured viewers they'd keep us posted on the "developing situation" in Okmulgee, Oklahoma. She introduced Chef Michael Symon to instruct us all how to grill kielbasa. Mama and I exhaled.

"Try her cell again," Mama said.

"I will, but it just goes straight to voicemail," I shrugged and dialed for the fifteenth time.

Grammy's home phone rang and we both lurched for it. "No," Mama said. "We have no comment." She rolled her eyes at me. This was going to be a long day. We watched Michael and his kielbasa faithfully, hoping he'd wind things up and we'd find out what was going on.

Mama went to get a cup of coffee, but my stomach felt like it was in the middle of a gymnastics routine. I stared at the screen. I willed Michael Symon to burn his hand and stop cooking. I tapped my foot through five commercials. Three of them were for personal injury lawyers, a flock of modern vultures swooping through the airwaves to zero in on lawsuit lottery candidates.

Then came an endless debate about the impact of social media on mental health. It was all I could do not to scream at the TV. I got up and began to pace the room, back and forth behind Mama's patient coffee-sipping.

It wouldn't be long until GMA would end and we'd be subjected to game shows and several more emotional pleas for victims to help an assortment of Alabama attorneys. Maybe because I was telepathically demanding it so hard, Robin Roberts announced a return to its Oklahoma coverage. This time, they opened with a shot of at least a thousand people gathered along a fenced property, almost all of them waving or holding protest signs. There was a brief interview with a man named Darrell Littlefeather. He scowled into the camera and yelled over the crowd, "I'm proud of Mrs. Willis for taking a stand when so many have been silenced by the pipeline company, with its community donations and PR campaign. They can't buy their way into our consent!" He threw his fist into the air and the crowd began to chant "PFD HAS GOT TO GO! THIS IS OUR LAND, WE SAY NO!"

Then they moved on to Grammy, still sitting as though waiting for Pete Darling to be choppered in and dropped onto the pipe next to her. She stared down at something or someone out of camera range, then crossed her arms defiantly and looked away. Kip Richmond informed us a member of the PFD Board of Directors had attempted to negotiate with Mrs. Willis with no success.

Grammy sat with her hands calmly clasped in her lap. I smiled at her, knowing these people had no idea how iron-willed The Sparrow was. The camera panned down to the base of the stack where some guy was apparently going to climb up and join her. Mama and I looked at each other, not sure whether he was a fellow protester or an employee sent to physically remove Grammy.

No one was trying to stop him.

Kip Richmond said, "Mrs. Willis…" and suddenly quit talking. The picture swung back up to Grammy, who had stood and was swaying slightly. She pointed her finger down, presumably at the man we'd seen. We could hear her yell, "YOU WILL NOT…" Then we watched as my grandmother lost her balance and tumbled sideways onto her elbow. I waited an eternity, at least thirty long seconds, for her to get up to re-take her seat and continue yelling at the man below.

Instead, I heard myself scream "No!" as she tried to push herself up and faltered when her hand slipped. Grammy fell, bumping her way slowly, horribly down the sloping bank of steel pipes to the ground below. A throng of people ran to her and blocked our view.

The camera immediately returned to an open-mouthed Kip, his face glazed with fear and uncertainty. He glanced around and clutched his earpiece for guidance. Kip announced, "An ambulance is responding and we will update you on Mrs. Willis's condition as soon as possible. This is Kip Richmond in Okmulgee for KTUL, Tulsa's Channel 8."

Mama and I were screaming and crying too hard to hear the knock at the door five minutes later. Manny called Mama's cell and told her to let him in. He wrapped Mama in his arms and gathered me into them, too. He spoke quietly, telling us Grammy would be fine. She was strong and in good health. Then he tried to usher us off to our rooms to pack a few things. He'd find out where the ambulance had taken her and make flight arrangements while we got ready.

Mama stared at him like she didn't comprehend a word he'd said.

"Es-cah-yee, take your mother and help her. We'll be with your grandmother in a few hours. Go!" Manny commanded.

Wilma was in the living room when we came out, leaning on the back of Grammy's old floral couch and sobbing into a wet wad of tissue. "I should never have let her do this. I should have told y'all what Verna was planning. It's all my fault. Have you heard anything about her? Do y'all even know where they took her? Oh, lord, I'll never forgive myself…"

Mama looked at Manny, cell phone to his ear, and he shook his head to let her know he hadn't found out anything. She put her arms around Wilma. "Wilma, honey, no one can stop my mother when she's determined. We all know that. I'll call you as soon as we find out how she's doing. You stay here as long as you like and lock up when you leave." She kissed Wilma's papery cheek, and we all headed to Manny's pickup for the long ride to Atlanta airport.

Not one of us said a word. I sat in the back seat of the truck in the dense silence, my head vibrating against the little window. I kept closing my eyes and seeing Grammy tumbling down that hard metal, bouncing and hitting over and over like she was caught in an old-style pinball machine.

Twenty-two

K ara stabbed the number of Pete's cell in like she was trying to punch through the back of her iPhone. She'd tried him five times, all of which went to voicemail. She got Joseph on his cell's first ring, despising the fact she had to go through an intermediary to get her husband's attention.

He promised he'd have Mr. Darling call back as soon as his meeting took its morning break.

"Joseph," she hissed, "I don't think you understand. You go to Mr. Darling immediately and tell him I have to speak with him now. Not fifteen minutes from now. I don't care if he's in the middle of performing sexual favors for Pennsylvania's entire state congress to cement this pipeline repair contract, you will interrupt him. This is more important. Do you hear me?"

"I'll give him the message," Joseph replied, ending the call and girding himself for Mr. Darling's reaction. Shooting the messenger was one of Pete's favorite hunting activities. Joseph re-entered the conference room, avoiding his boss's eyes as he came to stand by his chair. Pete nodded at the six other men in the room and turned to Joseph with a humorless smile.

"Excuse me, Mr. Darling, there's an emergency call for you." Joseph said his piece and stepped back, trying to blend into the burled walnut wainscoting and navy linen wallpaper.

Pete didn't miss a beat. "Gentlemen, we were just about to discuss this section, I believe." He held out a sheet of paper and pointed to a paragraph with his pen.

Mrs. Darling was going to be apoplectic.

Fifteen minutes later, Pete dialed Kara's cell phone. She answered with, "You have to come here. Now. To Oklahoma. I'm on my way to a hospital in Tulsa."

Pete was panic-stricken. "Oh God, baby, what's wrong? Are you hurt? What happened?"

"I'm not hurt, Pete, I'm furious," she shot back. "Some old lady staged a protest this morning by waltzing past your guard and climbing to the top of a stack of pipe in the laydown yard. Your useless idiot Tyler let the situation develop into a press nightmare before I could get there. And then the old lady fell and I have no idea how badly she's injured. They're taking her to OSU Medical Center. It was on the *national news,* Pete. Where the hell have you been?"

Pete leaned his head against the wall and massaged his left temple. "Why are *you* going to the hospital?"

Kara gritted her teeth in exasperation. "Because PFD needs someone there acting like they care, Pete. Do you ever think about appearances? Our public image?"

"Of course I do. I appreciate your doing this, baby. I just wasn't sure why—"

"Oh, wait, Pete, there's so much more," Kara interrupted. "The lady says she's the grandmother of your daughter. Your *daughter*, Pete? How is that even possible?"

"Hold on," Pete said, "You're telling me someone says I have a daughter? Where? Who? How old is she?"

"About twenty-two, in Alabama. Now you tell me right damn now that's impossible, Pete." Kara glanced at Deke, who was driving like a maniac to the hospital at her insistence. At least they could get ahead of the story, even if the old lady died.

"Pete?" Kara couldn't miss the fact it was taking him a while to answer. "Have you ever even been to Alabama?"

"Yeah, but it was a long time ago." Pete bent his head, pinching the bridge of his nose and trying to remember the girl's name. Lisa. "I mean, I knew a girl there named Lisa—"

"You told me you never had children. You never wanted children. You had a vasectomy. This can't be happening." Kara held the phone out and stared at it, like she could change what she was hearing. She didn't care that Deke was pretending not to listen as he noted every detail of her conversation.

"I'm not saying it could be true, Kara. Probably not. Certainly not that I know of. I traveled all the time years ago. My whole life was on the road." Pete looked at the group of men down the hall, filing back into the conference room. "I'm going to have to hang up in a minute."

"Jesus, Pete, did you get laid wherever your pipeline did? Is that what you're telling me?"

Pete rolled his eyes and then closed them, shutting out everything but the information he'd prepared to close this deal. "Kara, I have to get back into this meeting. I'm sorry. We'll leave here as soon as possible and I'll find you. It'll all be okay.

I love you." Pete ended the call and turned his cell off, handing it to Joseph. "No interruptions."

Joseph nodded and followed his boss back into the room.

Three hours later, true to his word, Pete left with a signed contract in hand and flew to Oklahoma. Kara's call had given him a perfect opportunity to speed up negotiations and force a decision, as he had a "family emergency" back home. He and Joseph followed Kara's directions through the corridors of Oklahoma State University Medical Center to a private waiting room.

Kara was sitting in a burgundy wing chair, the kind important people always seemed to occupy while others in waiting rooms were relegated to uncomfortable rows. Except they were alone in this space, at Kara's insistence to the administrator they be accorded privacy. She'd managed to look like the fox being pursued by a pack of press hounds, batting her eyes at the flustered older man.

Deke stood and nodded to Joseph. They went to stand outside the door.

Pete took his wife's hand. "I'm sorry you've had to handle this alone," he began. "Is the old lady all right?"

Kara smirked. "Is that really what you think I want to talk about? The old lady is alive. She's in surgery." She shrugged and continued, "Broken and fractured bones, a bunch of contusions. One rib is broken but didn't puncture a lung. Her left arm took the worst of it, and they're operating on it. She was lucky. Now, can we discuss this thing? This child you may or may not have fathered? Why did you lie to me?"

"I didn't lie, Kara. I mean, it's possible, but I can't see how. Not in Alabama."

Kara's eyebrows shot up.

"Okay, look, there was this girl in Wisconsin. Her name was Kaitlin. And like every other girl I met back then, she thought I was just another one of the guys, making a few hundred bucks a week. That time, she got pregnant. But I personally took her to the clinic and we, umm, ended it."

Kara nodded.

"I never wanted a kid. First of all, I was always on the road. I didn't want anyone or anything to answer to. And I can't stand to be around kids, anyway. I can't even be in a room with my niece and nephew for more than a minute or two. It's the reason my brother and I don't talk anymore. I don't want to be a father or an uncle or any of it. You know that."

"Yeah, I do." Kara was tapping her fingernails on the table next to her. "And you told me you'd made sure you'd never have to."

"Well, I did. After Wisconsin I went and had the surgery."

"And when was that?"

"About 2000, I guess," Pete answered, miserable. "So I guess if Lisa Willis—"

"Oh my God." Kara sprung to her feet. "That's the old lady's last name. Willis."

"Kara," Pete stood and held her arms, looking into her eyes, "there were only a few girls, ever. I'm not exactly some NBA star. I've mostly kept to myself, my whole life. You remember when you met me? You're the first woman who loved me. And you loved me without knowing about the money. You didn't know I was the owner of this company. You thought I was some lonely guy named Otis Garfield. Remember?" He tilted her chin up with his forefinger.

Oh, she remembered. And Pete would never know how much research she'd done before she'd placed herself down the hall from his hotel room in Chicago. Never.

"So, you're saying this girl in Alabama could be yours?" Kara tilted her head to one side. "You realize all they want is your money, Pete. If the mother—what'd you call her, Lisa? If Lisa had wanted a father for her daughter, she'd have contacted you when she was a baby. So, that's all this is, a shakedown. They found out who you are and smelled money."

Pete nodded, thoughtful. "Yeah, I see your point. Although I didn't make it very easy to find me. But still, Lisa could have let me know somehow if this really was my child."

Kara pulled away from his grasp and began to pace. "Pete, there's no place in our life for some instant daughter. Every bit of happiness we've found will disappear if you get tangled up in this. It would change everything." She turned to her husband and cradled the right side of his face in her hand, stroking his jaw with her thumb. "My love, you're going to have to deny ever knowing this Lisa person. You'll have no memory of being in Alabama in the late 90s. You're going to tell them they're mistaken, and that under no circumstances will you take a DNA test or cooperate with anything they want to do to establish you as this girl's father. Any further discussion they want to have about the situation can be directed to your attorney. I have one of Gerry's cards." Kara reached into her handbag and handed it to Pete, the model of efficiency.

"What do you mean, them? I thought there was just this old lady."

"Oh no, Pete, there's an entire redneck delegation headed our way, including this purported daughter. The doctor treating Mrs. Willis says they'll arrive within an hour or two. All they want is a payoff, Pete, and you can't let them use this story they made up to get to you. Not if you want to stay married to me. We'll cover whatever the old lady's insurance won't, because your imbecile allowed her onto the property. But that's all." Kara wrapped her arms around Pete's neck and kissed her husband deeply, long enough to know she had his absolute attention, then leaned back and smiled at him.

And all Pete Darling saw was the most beautiful woman in the world.

Twenty-three

TULSA, OKLAHOMA

Pete sent Kara and Deke home before he and Joseph stopped by surgical recovery and rang the intercom buzzer to confer with someone about Mrs. Willis. They were told to wait.

Seven infuriating minutes later a petite blonde emerged, her black and pink floral scrubs the only thing that made her look like she hadn't arrived directly from her high school graduation. "Mrs. Willis has been moved from recovery to a room," she informed them.

Pete could barely contain his aggravation. "No one told us. My wife was promised we'd be notified when that happened," he snapped. "Where is Mrs. Willis's doctor?"

The young nurse eyed Pete and Joseph up and down, clearly unimpressed. She released her long blond hair from a ponytail and re-gathered it into a new one. "Dr. Mathur's in surgery with another patient," she replied, her expression flat. "Are you Mrs. Willis's family?" She made an exaggerated point of looking at Joseph's dark brown skin and then at her Apple Watch.

"No, I'm Pete Darling, and Mrs. Willis was injured on my property. Your hospital administrator, Ed Berenson, knows who I am."

"I'm sorry, I have patients who need me, Mr. Darling. You'll find Mrs. Willis in 422. I don't think her family's here yet," she said, turning her back on them. She punched a code into the door's keypad and was gone.

Pete and Joseph located 422 and swung the door open to see a small, tightly swaddled figure in a hospital bed, wires and tubes snaking from her to a variety of monitors and IV bags. A heavyset man Pete presumed to be a nurse followed them in and asked, once more, if they were family.

Joseph raised his brows at the man, cocking his head to one side. He then directed his attention to the woman in the bed. He thought he saw her blink her eyes open and shut, but decided he must have imagined it. He sure as hell wasn't about to mention it to Mr. Darling. Just please God let this day end. He needed a few hours to relax before a fresh round began tomorrow morning.

"No," Pete told the man, "we're not family. But I can assure you it's all right for us to be here, checking on Mrs. Willis."

"Sir, my patient has just gotten out of surgery and really can't have visitors right now." The nurse opened the door and gestured for Pete and Joseph to leave. "I'm sure you can come back during visiting hours tomorrow."

Pete pulled out his cell under the withering gaze of the nurse, who pointed out the sign prohibiting their use to Joseph. Joseph made a slight shake of his head and the man walked away in disgust as Pete told his PR guy to issue a statement: Mr. Darling had personally visited Mrs. Willis in the hospital and was happy to say her surgery was successful. Mr. Darling and all of PFD Pipelines wished her a fast and full recovery.

"Grammy? Grammy, can you hear me?"

Verna's whisper crackled like paper burning in a fire. "Where's the man who helped us?" she asked, her eyes still clamped shut. "Is he still here? They're getting close to finding him. Oh, no, they are going to find…" Verna's head shook back and forth, then lolled to the side as she returned to sleep, open-mouthed.

The nurse held her fingers to her patient's right wrist and smiled at Skye. "It's the drugs. She's not fully out of the anesthesia yet. Don't worry, she'll make sense when her mind clears."

Lisa glanced at Manny and said, "I wouldn't be so sure," under her breath. She squeezed his hand and laughed softly, shifting her weight in the hard little chair beside her mother's hospital bed. Then she closed her eyes and allowed a few tears to fall.

Skye stood to pace along her side of the bed, unable to think about anything but the words the surgeon had said. "A long road to recovery… she'll be in a lot of pain for a while, but we'll mitigate it as well as we can… might be ready to travel home in a few days, but I can't promise that… our goal is to make sure she recovers the use of her left arm… possible nerve damage …physical therapy… lucky…"

Skye would slap the next person in this hospital who told her Grammy had been "lucky," even if it was true. Skye couldn't look at her blackish-purple right eye socket or the line of dark crimson bruises trailing up from Grammy's tightly wrapped chest to her left ear or her fiberglass-enclosed left arm and think "lucky." She now had pins, rods and screws knitting together the reassembled bones in that arm, and Skye couldn't imagine how her grandmother could ever live a day without pain again.

"It's getting late," she told Mama. "Why don't you and Manny go to the hotel and I'll stay here with her?"

The nurse, a plump, square-jawed fifty-ish woman whose ID badge proclaimed she was "Delia" placed her hand on Skye's shoulder. "Honey, she's not going to wake up for several more hours. We're giving her a sedative in this IV. We'll keep a close eye on your grandmother, I promise. You all need to go and get some sleep so you can help her tomorrow. You can come back early in the morning and you'll be the first people she sees when she wakes up."

Skye looked at her mother. "I'm not leaving. You two go on and I'll curl up in the recliner over there." Skye nodded at the worn, beige faux-leather chair sitting middle-ish in the room, which no doubt held memories of a few thousand other bedside vigils. She walked over and turned it toward the bed, watching Delia shake her head in defeat. "I'll get you a pillow and a blanket," the nurse sighed. Manny headed to open the door, visibly relieved, and Mama bent to kiss Skye's head as she passed by. "She'll be fine, baby, I promise. You don't need to stay."

"I do," Skye answered.

Skye had somehow managed to drag the recliner between Verna's bed and the wall, positioning it so she could occasionally reach out and touch her grandmother's hand, the one that was only plagued with IV lines and not broken bones leading to it. Throughout the night various nurses had paraded in and out, most managing to do what was necessary on the other side of the bed. If not, they'd obligingly allowed Skye to keep the recliner where it was, asking her to move when they needed to reach past it. She was enormously grateful when the sun began to separate the closed blinds with the tiny, promising rays of a new day. At least she wouldn't have to try to sleep. Skye had just finished using the bathroom when Dr. Mathur stopped in to check on Verna. She returned his cheerful "good morning" with a little wave. He was a good three inches shorter than Skye with a thick head of black hair, a brilliant smile, and wire-framed glasses. She stood back and said nothing as the doctor examined his patient with a series of little satisfied grunts and nods. Then he turned and asked Skye to leave the room for a few minutes.

He saw the terror on her face and quickly added, "Oh, no, all is well, I simply want to allow some privacy for your grandmother for this part. Please give us a few moments." He nodded to his nurse, who'd been waiting by the door to show Skye out.

The hall was quiet except for a lone woman at the other end pushing a cart loaded with breakfast trays. By the time Skye could smell the sausage and eggs, her stomach pitching, Dr. Mathur stepped out and told her Verna was recovering as well as he expected and would likely wake up soon. "She'll be on liquids until tomorrow, Miss Willis, but you must be hungry for real food. Let me have a tray brought for you."

"No thank you," Skye told him. "I really couldn't eat anything."

"Miss Willis, you can and you will. No arguments. Take care of yourself so you can then take care of your grandmother, yes? She will need you." He squeezed Skye's arm and walked toward the elevator, stopping to speak to the breakfast lady.

Minutes later, as Skye was biting into a piece of toast, Verna fluttered her eyelids and tried to reach for Skye. She put the tray on a nearby table and took her grandmother's hand in hers, thrilled when Grammy's gnarled fingers wrapped around her own and held tight.

"I am so glad to see you," she stood and bent over to kiss her grandmother's forehead gently, never dropping her hand.

"Oh, Little One, I am glad to see you, too." Verna's voice was faint. "I wasn't sure I would be coming back from wherever I was." She closed her eyes and continued. "I was with one of my grandmothers, long, long ago. She was running with me. I was tied to her back, and I was just a baby. We were in tall grasses and it was so hot. She was trying to keep the men from finding us." Verna paused to swallow.

"What men, Grammy?"

"The government men. The army. They were coming to take us to Indian Territory. But my grandmother knew... that's it, she knew because she had been told by a wise woman we would never leave Alabama."

"That's quite a dream..." Skye smiled at Verna and gently squeezed her fingers.

Verna shook her head. "It wasn't a dream. I was *there*. I was that baby." She coughed and asked Skye for a sip of water. Skye held the straw to her grandmother's lips. "Anyway," Verna continued, "we came to a marshy area, where the mud sucked at my grandmother's feet. She knew the men were getting closer to us and she was terrified. And it was getting dark. She was so afraid."

"Grammy, you can tell me all this later. You need to rest your voice." Skye smoothed her grandmother's soft white hair back from her forehead. "Are you in pain?"

Verna seemed to notice her left arm and its confinement for the first time. "It's not bad. Did I break a lot of my old bones? Are my hips okay?"

"Your hips are not broken. Your arm took the worst damage, but your surgeon was able to fix it. You're going to be fine."

Verna nodded. "Did he come yet?"

"Did who come yet?"

"Pete Darling, Little One. Did he come to you yet?"

"No," Skye answered. "He hasn't been here."

"He will be. He's coming to meet you very soon." Verna's eyes began to droop. "I am so tired. I need to take a nap."

"You do that, Grammy. I'm here and Mama's here, too. She just stepped out for a little bit." Skye brushed a tear away and leaned back into the recliner, watching her grandmother sleep, saying all the words to herself she'd been saving for her Grammy. They could wait.

By the time Lisa and Manny arrived bearing donuts and coffee, Verna had settled into a deep sleep.

"I feel awful I wasn't here," Lisa said.

"I told her you'd just stepped out. She knows you came, too. It's okay, Mama." Skye took the chocolate-glazed Krispy Kreme her mother extended with three napkins and settled back to enjoy it. Manny sat where he'd been the night before, scrolling through his phone. Lisa perched on the arm of Skye's recliner.

"The restaurant is doing great," Manny announced to no one in particular. "My mother says everyone is stopping by to leave cards and flowers for Verna."

Lisa glanced at Skye. "That's wonderful," she said. "She's loved by a lot of people."

And yippee, they're buying tacos, Skye's rude brain added. She knew she should be feeling nothing but grateful to Manny Alvarez, and felt a quick stab of guilt. He'd arranged and paid for this trip for the three of them without a second thought.

"How did she seem when she woke up?" Lisa asked Skye. "Was the pain awful?"

"No, she's not feeling much pain. I think she's been on some major painkillers in this drip. They said she'll start taking them orally soon." Skye waved her arm at one of the hanging plastic bags connected to Verna. "She doesn't seem confused, either, but she started telling me about this dream she'd had. She was a little baby and her grandmother was running with her and trying to hide. Only, honestly, it sounded more like it was her mother. I think she just meant 'grandmother' in the sense of ancestor. I don't know. Grammy said it was real, she was there, it wasn't like a dream." Skye shrugged and wiped chocolate from her chin. "But she remembers what happened, that she fell. She was asking about her injuries. Oh, and Dr. Mathur came by and saw her already. He said she's doing well."

"I wonder," Lisa said, "how soon we can take her home." She said it to Skye, but was looking at Manny, who met her eyes and shook his head slightly.

"Lisa," he said. "I told you. If I need to go, I'll go. Your mother needs to take her time to recover."

"I feel bad that you're away from your business," she said.

"I'd feel worse if I was not here by your side, *mi amor*." Manny's eyes locked on my mother's in a way that excluded the rest of the world for several seconds. He blew a kiss at her.

Skye felt her donut kicking its way up at that. She wondered if she'd ever get used to public displays of affection between her mom and Manny. She sighed and concentrated on her sleeping grandmother, whose eyes were shifting under her lids.

Maybe she was back in her Alabama dream, bouncing along in a papoose.

"You promise me you'll fly home if you need to? Skye and I will be fine with Mom."

"Yes, Lisa, I promise. But my mother is a capable manager, and she has a cook to help her. Everything will be all right." Manny turned his head toward the sound of the opening door, expecting a nurse. Instead, the doorway was filled by a large black man who stood in front of a group in the hall. He scanned the faces in the room slowly, doing a superb Secret Service imitation.

Lisa called out, "I think you have the wrong room," waking her mother.

Verna moved her good hand as she blinked her eyes open, trying to point her index finger at the doorway. She said, "That's him. He escaped from the plantation near Mobile. He's a runaway sl—"

Lisa immediately reached to embrace her mother as best she could among the tubes and wires that surrounded her, yelling, "Mom! You're awake!" as loudly as possible to cover Verna's drug-addled ramblings. "How do you feel, Mom?" she asked.

"I'm definitely starting to notice this arm," Verna answered. She peeked around her daughter. "Where did he go?"

All eyes turned back to the doorway where Peter F. Darling entered with his hands in his pockets, watching them. His wife was beside him in a flash, wearing a fitted black leather jacket with a peplum waist over a charcoal pencil skirt. Skye peered around her mother's shoulder and quickly leaned back, hiding behind Lisa. Deke and Joseph stood off to one side until Pete waved them out into the hall.

"Hello, Pete," Lisa said from the edge of the recliner.

"Have we met?" Pete answered. He frowned and leaned his head to one side.

Skye put her hands to her face, unable to believe what she'd just heard. Those three words were nails hammering into her heart: *Have. we. met.* She held her breath, trying to keep quiet as the tears flowed behind her palms and down her wrists.

Manny got up and went to stand at Lisa's side, arms crossed and leaning against the recliner.

Kara chiseled the rock-solid silence by saying, "You look better, Mrs. Willis."

Verna answered, "Well, you look better, too, since you're no longer trying to trick me."

"Mrs. Willis, I was only trying to get you down safely so we could talk. I'm so sorry you fell. I sent my bodyguard to help you down, and if you'd only waited—"

"And certainly better without motor oil all over you," Verna added, and closed her eyes.

Kara's lips flattened into a tight coral line.

Lisa asked, "Why do you have to have bodyguards with you all the time?"

Pete glanced toward the hall. "Joseph came in here first out of habit. We've had some problems like the one Mrs. Willis pointed out. It's a sensible precaution," Pete answered.

Manny stared at Pete. "It's not because of the children killed by your pipeline exploding in New Mexico?" Lisa wasn't sure if he pronounced it "New Meh-HEE-coh" to claim it as his own or to supply extra aggravation for Pete.

"That was a horrible tragedy, sir, and my company had no part in it. We installed the line, but there were factors out of our control that caused the accident. New Mexico's Supreme Court reached that conclusion a long time ago. But you're right, when you're in the public eye, people can react to events like that with understandable anger, even if it's misdirected."

Pete swept his gaze up and down Manny and added, "Are you a member of the Willis Family?"

"Not yet," Manny answered, "but I love this woman, her mother, and her daughter." He put a protective arm around Lisa, who was looking anywhere but at Pete.

Verna opened her eyes a tiny bit and slid her gaze to Skye, still pressed against the back of the recliner and hidden from view. "I'm starting to hurt really bad," she said, swallowing hard.

Skye didn't hesitate. She dried her tears with her sleeve and arranged her face into a calm mask. "I'm going to get the nurse, Grammy." She somehow managed to clamber out of the recliner and get around Manny and Lisa without falling over onto the hospital bed. Skye paused to look at Pete for a second, then rushed to the door without another word, forcing him to step out of the way with her glare. She pretended Kara didn't exist, afraid she'd start yelling at her in front of Grammy and the entire room would burst into jugular attacks.

When Pete first laid eyes on Skye Willis, his immediate thought was: she looks exactly like a young version of my mother.

When Kara first laid eyes on Skye Willis, her immediate thought was: this is going to be harder than I expected.

When Joseph first laid eyes on Skye Willis, his immediate thought was: I am not going to get out of this godforsaken hospital anytime soon because that's definitely his damn daughter.

When Deke first laid eyes on Skye Willis, his immediate thought was: that is the Anti-Kara, no makeup, messy hair, cheap old jeans, and she looks beautiful without knowing it.

Skye felt the weight of people staring at her back all the way to the nurse's station. Should've pressed the call button, she cursed herself silently, but she'd wanted a faster response for Grammy, and she'd desperately needed to get out of the room. She was greeted by a nod from a young man with a stethoscope around his neck. Was he a nurse? Would she offend a doctor by asking for pain medication for her grandmother? Would she ever stop worrying so much what other people thought?

The young man rescued her from her thoughts by asking what she needed.

"My grandmother is in 422 and she's having a lot of pain. Can you please help her?"

He glanced at a screen. "I'll get someone to Mrs. Willis's room in a few minutes," he said.

Skye was suffering from a lack of sleep, an excess of worry, and the realization she didn't want to meet her biological father after all, certainly not under these circumstances. Her entire body felt like one clenched muscle. She leaned on the desk and tried not to let her voice shake as she said, "A few minutes will not do. She's my grandmother. She's in pain. Do what you would do for your *own* grandmother."

"I'm sorry, I can't leave the desk, but we'll get someone to help as soon as we can." He returned to his bank of screens and monitors, dismissing her without another glance.

Skye felt someone approaching but didn't dare look behind her. Pete appeared at her side and placed his broad hands on the counter. "Hi, I'm Pete Darling. I was told by your administrator, Dr. Berenson, as well as a member of your Board of Trustees, Senator Lee Harrow, I shouldn't hesitate to ask for help today if I need it. So, I'm asking for help, son. If the young lady needs you to get pain medication to her grandmother, I'm going to want you to do that right now."

The man didn't hesitate. He consulted his screen for Verna Willis's medical orders and nodded. "I'm on my way, Mr. Darling," he said. "She can have her next dose of pain medication now. She's actually a little past due." He followed that with a dramatic, lemon-sucking expression aimed at the back of Pete's head.

"Thank you," Skye told Pete, looking at her shoes.

"We need to talk, Skye," he said. "As soon as your grandmother's feeling a little better, come and meet me in the private waiting room on the first floor. The information desk can direct you there. Just tell them I'm expecting you and one of the guys will meet you at the door and let you in."

"Okay," Skye continued to address her Nikes. "Will it be just you?"

"Just me, I promise." Pete touched Skye's upper arm lightly and trailed his hand down to her elbow, shattering her into little pieces that fell all over the hospital floor. She fought back tears all over again.

Pete walked to Verna's room. He handed Lisa a business card, his eyes on the small figure in the hospital bed. "If you need to follow up about anything, contact this man. He's my attorney." He turned and extracted his wife, waving as they moved away.

Manny watched Lisa turn the little white card over and over wordlessly before placing it in her purse.

Pete and Kara linked arms in the hall, trailing the two burly men behind them as they headed for the elevators. Skye waited to hear the ding and closing doors of their departure before she started back to room 422.

"Kara," Pete said, "You and Deke go on and we'll meet you later today." He nodded to Joseph, who managed to look agreeable despite being sentenced to another day in the damn hospital. "There's really no sense in all of us being here."

"I'm not leaving you to talk to her alone, Pete." Kara shook her head and took her husband's hand as the elevator descended.

"I have to insist that you do, baby. This is between me and that young woman, and I promised her we'd talk in privacy. Besides, I know you have shopping to do in Tulsa. You said so this morning."

"Yes," she enunciated slowly, "but I meant after we spoke to the girl and cleared this misunderstanding up."

Pete brought Kara's hand to his lips after they stepped off the elevator, then held it to his chest. "You know you can trust me, Kara. You know what I'm going to say to her. We've been over all this more than once. You're my wife, and no one comes before you."

Thirty minutes later, Lisa hugged her daughter and whispered in her ear, "You don't have to do this. He knows damn well who I am, honey, and I don't want him hurting you any more than he already has."

"I have to, Mama. Grammy's right about that. I'll never forgive myself if I don't take the opportunity to talk to him. Look at all she went through to make it happen." Her eyes traveled to her grandmother, now snoring softly as Manny watched the two of them from the recliner.

"If you're not back in an hour, I'm coming after you," Lisa sniffed. "Okay?"

"Okay, Mama. If I'm going to be longer than an hour, I'll text you." Skye held up her phone and kissed her mother goodbye. The door closed after her with a soft whoosh.

Lisa returned to her seat on the side of the recliner and leaned against Manny. "Do you think she'll be all right?"

"Are you kidding?" Manny said. "That girl is stronger and smarter than you and me put together. Doesn't matter what he says or does, she'll see him for what he is, Lisa."

Joseph waved to Skye as she approached, swinging the door open with a nod. She found Pete sitting in one of the hard plastic chairs lining the wall. He patted the one next to him with a smile.

"I don't think we actually introduced ourselves." He extended a hand. "I'm Pete Darling, and I know you want to talk because you think I'm your father."

Skye shook his hand without a word, staring at his gray eyes.

"Anyway," Pete continued, "it's very flattering to me a pretty girl like you might believe that. And I can see how you'd notice my eye color and my height are like yours."

"Are you about to tell me it's not true? The way you lied about not knowing my mother?" Skye started to stand and Pete pulled her back down to the chair.

"I didn't lie, Skye, I don't know your mother. I don't even know how I'd have met her." Pete leaned forward and clasped his hands between his knees. "I mean, I've been to Alabama once or twice, mostly up near Huntsville, but not any time when I could have fathered a baby." He paused to look at her directly. "Truth is, Skye, it's very personal to discuss these matters, but I can't have children. Maybe someone on one of my crews used my name when they worked on a project down there. I guess that's a possibility."

"Seriously? That's what you expect me to believe, that someone used your name?" Skye threw her head back and looked at the stained ceiling tile.

"If they said they were Pete Darling, yes," he answered. "I don't use my name when I travel. I go around as Otis Garfield most of the time. Keeps people from—"

"Trying to get your money?" Skye interrupted, a stunned look on her face. *"That's* what you think this is about. Okay, let me explain something to you. I was brought up by two women who have given me more love than any one person is entitled to, and I've been taught that life is about people you cherish and pride and joy in what you do every day to make your contribution to the world. Maybe money is how you keep score with everybody else, but it's nothing I care that much about. I have never wanted a penny from you. Wouldn't take it if you offered."

"Have you been to college, Skye? You seem like a very intelligent girl."

Skye lowered her eyes from the ceiling to him. "I *am* a very intelligent girl. I don't need a degree to prove it. I read more books in a month than most people do in years. Why do you ask? Were you planning to sponsor my education like I'm a third-world child?"

Pete looked at his hands. "Most people would be thrilled to have their education paid for."

"That's true. I appreciate the thought, but I don't want money from you for school or a new dress or candy from the gift shop. If you're going to deny me, at least have the style to do it without insulting me in the process."

Pete turned to Skye and said, "I'm sorry I'm not who you thought I was."

"I can't tell you how much I agree with that statement," she answered as she walked to the door. "You're not at all who I thought you were."

Skye nodded at Joseph as she entered the hall. She waited until she was out of his line of vision to lean over and press her forehead against the wall, hugging herself. Anyone who saw her would assume she was crying over the loss of a family member in one of the many hospital beds surrounding her.

Twenty-four

TULSA, OKLAHOMA
Four Days Later

As Manny, Lisa, Skye and Verna sat in Tulsa International Airport waiting for their flight to Atlanta, a startling situation was unfolding on the phones, tablets and laptops surrounding them. By the time they landed and drove to Eufaula, #sosickofthesefuckingpeople would be the number three trending Twitter hashtag in the United States. The YouTube video it linked to would have over three hundred thousand views within hours.

Someone with the handle @TricksandTreaties had posted: "Rich white woman's disgusting RANT against Native Americans #racism #PFDPipelines #condemnhate #whiteliar #sosickofthesefuckingpeople" along with a link to the video. It showed a furious Kara Darling telling someone off camera, "I don't care if the little old lady falls on her little old Creek head. I am so sick of these fucking people. You give and you give and this is the thanks you get. Motor oil thrown on you. New demands every day. None of them cares about the environment, they only care about their goddam casino money and whatever else they can squeeze out of the rest of us, and they've squeezed more than they deserve already. I've had it with every single one of them." The video ended with block letters on a black screen:

KARA DARLING IS A
BOARD MEMBER OF PFD
PIPELINES
and is married to its president. If you find
this video repulsive, contact PFD and
DEMAND her removal. Call or write your
state representatives and
STOP THE SPREAD OF
THEIR GREED AND HATE.

National news coverage of Verna's protest and her dramatic fall had run for a couple of days but quieted after her recovery in the hospital. A few people stared in the airport in Tulsa, but Skye noticed several more gawking and whispering as they gathered their luggage in Atlanta, Verna leaning heavily on Manny's arm.

Deke was regularly private-messaging various parts of his anatomy for a couple of girls in Texas to enjoy, so he discovered the Twitterstorm first as he watched Kara and Pete eating lunch at a separate table. They held hands off and on between courses, gazing at each other and toasting with Kara's beloved Perrier Jouet champagne. The plan was to follow this celebration of love *and* the departure of the Alabama contingent with a private afternoon in their suite. They'd move into the lodge tomorrow. Life was exquisite and perfect and Deke was not about to burst those champagne bubbles.

He put his burger down and contemplated his next move carefully. Deke handed his phone to Joseph, who regarded it without expression and accepted the horrific task of showing the tweet and video to Pete, but only after they'd arrived back at the Hard Rock. Until then, he and Deke would remain stone-faced bodyguards without any indication they carried the dynamite that would blow the Darling celebration to hell and back.

Deke figured he'd be packing his bags and returning to Texas soon, and maybe that wouldn't be the worst thing that could happen. The woman he'd found irresistible had morphed into a raging, aging Gorgon in recent weeks.

Deke was tired of pretending an interest in every good-looking man who walked past for Pete Darling's benefit, too.

It would be good to be free.

Pete sat on the bed beside Kara, who was trying to talk between hysterical sobs. "I was so terrified, Pete, they were hitting the car and threatening us when we drove in. It pushed me over the edge. I was scared and yes, angry, and it boiled over into a bunch of things I shouldn't have said. You've done so much for these people, been so generous to them," here she stopped and looked into Pete's eyes, making sure he understood how deeply wounded she'd been, "and it hurt me to see how they were repaying you. I should have told you, but I knew you had so much on your mind, baby, and you were trying to close that deal in Pennsylvania—"

"Kara, do you have any idea how much your public hissy fit is going to cost us?" Pete got up and went to the bottle of scotch sitting next to the ice bucket. He poured a few fingers into a glass with his back to his wife, wondering what to say next. When he turned around, she was removing clothes from dresser drawers and folding them into her suitcase.

"I'm so sorry, Pete, you don't deserve this awful video of me out there in the world for people to gawk at and gossip over. I'm going to Texas and disappear for a while," she told him. "All that was in my heart was outrage on your behalf, and it's been twisted around to hurt you. I can't forgive myself for that." Kara swiped at the tear tracks on her cheeks and went to the bathroom to gather her toiletries as Pete closed her suitcase and threw it on the floor.

"You're not going anywhere," he said. "This will all die down as soon as the next idiot does something stupid with a gun or Kim Jong-un starts playing with missiles again or Oprah finally gets married. We just have to lay low for a day or two, and we can move into the lodge tomorrow to do it there. The place is a fortress. It'll all be fine." Pete held his arms out and Kara stepped into them, leaning her head on his chest. "And Kara," he stroked her hair, "you know you're going to have to resign from the board."

"I know," she sniffed. "All I wanted was to help you, and look what I've done." She began to sob into his shirt all over again. "I am so sorry someone is putting us through this."

Pete said, "As far as I know, there weren't that many people around you in that laydown yard. Who would video you and make it go viral? Who is this TricksandTreaties person? I know it wasn't Tyler, and it sure wasn't Deke. Who could it have been?" He ran his fingers up and down Kara's back.

"I have no idea," she answered. "They must have zoomed in from far away."

But Kara knew without question who was responsible. She also knew Pete must never, ever find out.

Kara and Pete were in the process of trying out the new leather couches, looking for the best angle for the gorgeous view outside the lodge, when the distinctive ring set for Gerald Davidson began to sound on Pete's cell phone. He nodded at Kara and went through the French doors to answer in the cool morning air. "Hey, buddy," he told Gerry. "You should be here to see this view." Pete squinted at a bird circling in the distance, wondering if it was an eagle.

"Pete, Pennsylvania's falling apart. I heard from their attorneys this morning. They're going to try to void the contract."

"You can tell them Kara is officially resigning from the board, Gerry." Pete pinched the bridge of his nose and closed his eyes. "They don't have grounds to rescind the contract. And I know the Attorney General. He's not coming after me."

"They hired outside counsel, Pete. They're claiming they can't proceed with PFD in light of the blatant racism demonstrated by one of its board members. I mean, it's *everywhere*, Pete, have you seen a TV? Been online?"

"I just told you, she's resigning." Pete looked at the bird again. It was a buzzard, and two more had joined it.

"I'll tell them, but it won't be enough." Gerald paused and added, "I really need you to fly down here and sit with me. Let's talk this through in person."

Pete held his phone out and frowned at it. "What's up, Gerry? Just say Kara sincerely regrets her remarks and is resigning from the board. They'll listen. We made a deal, and it's a good deal for them. They know that."

"Pete, I'll try. You know I will. But fly down to Dallas sometime soon, okay? I'll update you when I know more on Pennsylvania."

"Okay, buddy, I need to see about a couple things in Dallas, anyway. I'll be there in a few days and we'll get together." Pete hung up thinking it was nice his friend missed him. Pete missed Gerry, too, and would see if he'd like to come up and do some shooting in this new paradise. Kara would have the place ready for visitors within a week or two.

The buzzards swooped down onto the carcass of an armadillo and began fighting their way through its armor.

Just before Joseph was to drive Deke to the airport, Mr. Darling asked to speak with him in his study, which contained nothing more than an expansive cherry desk and chair for Pete at this point. Deke stood before him, hands clasped in front, as Pete asked, "Who's responsible for this video?"

"I think any of the TV station people could have filmed her, sir, especially if they had an extended range microphone. The only other person I can think of is Mr. Tiger, but he was gone when I looked where he'd been standing. We were all focused on the lady sitting up there and there were people milling around. I'm not sure."

"Langdon Tiger was there?" Pete leaned back in his chair and drained the last of his pre-dinner scotch, then smacked his glass onto the desk.

Deke nodded.

"That guy gives me the creeps. Doesn't he make your skin crawl?" Pete stared at Deke, who sputtered, "Oh, yeah, he does."

Deke could barely conceal his panic at the idea of discussing Langdon Tiger with Mr. Darling. He'd sooner kiss a diamondback rattler on the mouth.

"Well," Pete said, "if there were people milling around and you aren't sure who was there and your attention was on the old lady, you're fired, Deke. I won't be bringing you back from Dallas. You'd better hurry up and get to the airport." Pete picked up a random piece of paper from his desk and studied it hard until Deke was out of the room.

Pete woke the next morning and reached for his beautiful wife, her silhouette barely visible because the eastern bank of bedroom windows was cloaked in velvet blackout draperies. Kara's eyes were tightly shut against the early hour and Pete's grasp on her waist. Why couldn't the man sleep past six-thirty once in his life?

Pete kissed Kara and whispered, "Welcome to our first morning in this place, my love."

He hadn't told her about Deke yet. That could wait until some coffee lightened her morning mood. Maybe champagne at lunch.

They shared a breakfast of fruit salad and scrambled eggs on the balcony outside their room, sitting at a cute little wrought iron bistro table set the tech guy had abandoned. Kara was back to forbidding Pete the biscuits and croissants he adored, and he grudgingly accepted it was necessary. He'd grown a little heavier lately and started to worry about his health, though he'd never tell her that. Kara mentioned the need to hire a cook in Oklahoma. He figured that was going to be necessary, but wondered what local wouldn't try to poison her. They'd definitely need to search for a private chef from elsewhere, one of those California types who could make vegetables taste like food.

Kara smiled at her husband, who'd just given her permission to search for someone to cook meals worthy of the white marble table he'd yet to see. It was to be installed tomorrow along with the chandelier. The very thought of it thrilled her and she glowed as she sipped her coffee.

"Kara," he told her, "you've done a wonderful job making this place a home already. It's a showcase of your exquisite taste. You really could be an interior designer." Pete patted the table. "But can we please get rid of this uncomfortable damned thing?"

She suppressed her annoyance because the bistro set made her feel like they were in Paris and all he could notice was the seat felt hard on his huge butt. Kara reached her hand out to touch Pete's face and thank him for his compliment. Instead of the lazy grin she expected from him, Pete's eyes widened in shock as he looked past Kara at something in the distance.

A large drone hovered in place above them, about a football field away. A bright red banner cascaded from it:

KARA
DARLING
IS A
RACIST
BITCH.

Twenty-Five

EUFAULA, ALABAMA

Grammy slept most of the way home from Oklahoma and immediately took to her room in Eufaula. Mama kissed Manny goodbye, and we collapsed, exhausted, at four o'clock in the afternoon.

It was easy to slip into our usual routine the next morning, Mama off to her breakfast shift and Grammy sipping late-morning coffee at the table with me, side by side. We'd discussed Oklahoma and most of what happened there to death, so I asked her, "What was in this dream of yours, the one you mentioned in the hospital?"

She leaned back in her chair and patted my arm with her good right hand. "Little One, I don't know how to explain it, but this was not a dream. I was *in the time* of my distant grandmother. There were no cars, or even roads like we know them. The sky was filled with many birds, more than I've seen

205

at one time. We lived on a bluff overlooking a big river, but we ran away when I was very small. She was carrying me on her back, like I told you. My grandmother was terrified, running because all of us were being forced to relocate to Indian Territory." Grammy stopped and asked, "You remember the Trail of Tears?"

"Of course," I replied.

"She slipped out with me one dark night before the march was to begin," Grammy continued. "The white men chased after her. We hid day and night from them, mostly in the thick woods. My grandmother knew they would track us so she went through water when possible, trying to throw them off. It seemed we went for many miles, getting farther and farther from home. She'd brought food for us. I remember it was mostly dried meat and nuts. That lasted a few days, and we became very hungry." Grammy paused for a sip of coffee and closed her eyes. "My grandmother was carrying me because my mother was dead. A white man had killed her not long after I was born."

I stared at her, fascinated. "And you remember all this like it actually happened?"

"I remember it because it *did* happen." Grammy raised her eyebrows, which was painful to watch because her left eye was still surrounded by bruises. "It's as clear a memory as I've ever had. We ran on and on, always afraid. After several nights we came to a swampy place bordered by a forest. She thought the men chasing us had given up.

My grandmother had a net she'd been using to try to catch fish. She hadn't managed to snare a single one. That night, she trapped a squirrel with it and built a small fire in the woods to roast the meat. She was holding me in her lap, looking around the woods, listening. That's when she whispered to me she believed we were finally safe, because a wise woman had told her we would never have to go to Indian Territory. She cried as she said this and hugged me close. I'm sure she was crying for my mother more than anything."

"I'm sure she was," I said. "How horrible. Do you know why *your* mother was killed?"

Grammy said, "I think maybe there had been a battle with the village and she was caught in the crossfire. But I really don't know."

"When we were in your hospital room," I said, "you saw a black man you'd thought had helped you in your dream. Do you remember that?"

"It wasn't a dream," she frowned back. "And I'm getting to that. My grandmother told me two other things the wise woman had said. We would not have to go out west, but someday, a distant granddaughter would. She would go because of a white man. And I feel sure that's me, and Pete Darling." She set her mug down and smoothed her hair, still wild and unbraided for the day.

I wasn't sure how to respond to that, and the subject remained an open wound. "And the other thing she told you? What was that?" I asked.

Grammy looked at the heavy cast on her arm. "That my distant granddaughter would tell this story in the future, after she went to what she called 'the place near the other Eufaula'. And *her* granddaughter would tell it to many, many people."

"Me?" I pointed to myself. "Wow. I'm not sure what that means." I tried not to look skeptical. "And you had this dream…" I rephrased it when she glared at me, "this experience after you went to Oklahoma, not before?"

"That's right. I went there without any knowledge of this. It came after. So anyway, my distant grandmother and I were sitting by this fire and she was feeding me tiny bits of meat. She heard something that startled her and she jumped up with me in her arms. We hid behind a tree. She held her hand over my mouth, but I already knew to be quiet. I could feel her shaking as she held me. And we both saw a man unlike any we'd ever seen. He was very tall and his skin was the color of the night sky. He was looking back over his shoulder as he moved through the forest. My grandmother held her breath as he came closer." Grammy shook her head. "He saw the campfire and began looking around for us. He said, very quietly, 'You come out, I help you hide. Dey lookin' for me, too,' and came nearer to where we crouched. We stayed very still and hoped he'd go away. 'Listen to me, dey's troops headed dis way. Dey see me and I'm a dead man. This fire gon' lead dem right to us.' My grandmother looked at me for a minute, considering, and finally nodded her head. She stepped out of the shadows and the man looked as surprised by the way we looked as we were by him. 'I's Mose,' he said. 'I's runnin' like you. I know a safe place. Come on. We ain' got much time fo' dey be here.' My grandmother and Mose kicked dirt over our small fire and we followed the man toward the moon. There was another black man waiting in a clearing nearby. 'Dis here where we part comp'ny', he announced. 'Dey a cave over dere', he waved to his right, 'and ain' nobody find you dere. Don't come out til' you see dem troops go past. Dey gon' come dis way in a little bit. Dey lookin' fo' us, but you ain' want dem to find you neither.' My grandmother answered him with a nod in the moonlight. The man stared at us and reached into his pocket. He handed my grandmother some berries, inclining his head at me. Then he and the other man ran off. We found the narrow cave opening and hid inside. It was completely dark and we couldn't see out, but we heard the men riding by and yelling to each other after a little while. We stayed in there all night. I slept snuggled up to her warm chest. And that's all I remember."

"And the bodyguard looked like that man?" My eyes met hers, and I believed everything she'd just said, as bizarre as it all was.

"Well, I was confused at that point, and nicely drugged. It could have been any tall African-American man, and I'd have associated him with Mose." Grammy got up and walked to the little window over the sink, staring out at the gathering clouds. "All I know is that he saved us that night. Maybe I wouldn't be here and neither would you."

"Do you know what happened to that distant grand-mother? Where the two of you went, who you lived with?"

"I have no idea, other than I'm sure we stayed in Alabama. Maybe she'll invite me back again someday, and I'll find out more." Grammy shrugged. "I'm going to lie down for a while," she said, kissing the top of my head. "This arm is really hurting."

"Did you take your pain pill?" I asked. "You were due for another at 8:00."

"I did," Grammy answered. "Seems like they're working less and less." She caught my look and said, "Don't be ridiculous. I'd never take more than what the prescription says. I know how dangerous the white man's opioids are."

I was pretty sure everything bad was going to be "the white man's" from there on out, even if my beloved late grandfather had been one of the whitest men ever to sunburn in a rainstorm.

"And Little One," my grandmother added, "I'm very sorry Pete Darling isn't the man we hoped he'd be. Not the man he *should* be. I'm even sorrier I got your hopes up by trying something so crazy. It was all I could think to do."

I stood to hug her as gently as possible, but she still cringed from the pain. "Don't you ever apologize for doing something so brave and wonderful out of love for me. You're the most amazing woman I'll ever know," I said.

"That's true," she answered, nodding and kissing my cheek.

I watched Grammy make her way down the hall as I heard my phone buzz and ignored it. I knew without looking it was Sergeant Whitaker texting me from the recruiter's office, the first of many attempts for the day. I didn't know what to tell him, not anymore.

Mama and I walked into *Oro y Cena* that night completely unprepared for the changes Luz instituted during her brief reign over the restaurant. She'd left behind a large chalkboard by the kitchen; written at its top were "chores" for the servers. Our names were listed under our assignments. In the past, we'd shared these jobs informally and kind of bargained to see who did what.

Not anymore.

I wondered what else Luz had ordered in our absence, and whether Manny would override any of it. He walked out of the kitchen, wiping his hands on a towel. He kissed Mama, then nodded at the board. "Good idea, eh?" he asked.

Mama just smiled and nodded. I suppressed a groan. My name was under "FILL SALT AND PEPPER SHAKERS", which meant an extra *forever* at the end of our shift. "Lisa" was scribbled under "ROLL SILVERWARE." In addition, I was assigned "wipe seats clean" and Mama had "empty server station trash can" and "prep salads" was assigned to both of us.

"Manny, haven't we always gotten this stuff done without an assignment board?" I asked. "All of us are pretty good at splitting things up without military orders." I smirked at the chalkboard.

"I thought you were interested in military orders, Skye," he raised his brows and grinned. "Chasing after them, even."

"That's a subject for another time," I replied. "Everything's up in the air since Grammy got hurt."

I couldn't miss the look and subtle nod Mama gave him. Why not just throw confetti in the air and yell SHE'S GONNA CHANGE HER MIND? I rolled my eyes at the two of them. "Look, I haven't decided anything. In the meantime, are we really going to have demands issued in chalk every night?"

"Only until my mother stops paying attention," Manny answered. "She needs to feel she made some positive change while she was in charge, and this isn't hurting anything. A little organization isn't so bad." He turned and went back into the kitchen, Mama on his heels.

An hour later, I saw him emptying the server station trash can during a lull in business. Mama did too, and beamed at him as she said, "Manny, you did a Lisa thing!"

"Every time I take a breath, it's a Lisa thing," Manny said.

I hurried back to my one table, eager to do anything my customers wanted if it meant avoiding the thick mush between those two.

Mama went home first, tired and worried about Grammy, who wasn't answering her phone. I was filling my millionth salt shaker when Manny slid into the booth where I stood. "Sit down, Skye," he said, waving me to the opposite side. "I want to talk to you."

I just wanted to go home, damn it. I sat opposite my boss and pretended to be interested in what he was about to say, which was probably about spilling salt or the size of the lettuce leaves in my salads.

"You know I love your mother," he began.

My stomach did a barrel roll.

"And what you may not realize is that I love you, too, Skye." His eyes were dead serious, holding my gaze. "Any man would be so blessed and lucky to have you for a daughter."

Oh God, he was going to try to make me feel better about Pete...

"I never had children of my own, but I have always wanted a daughter, Skye. And I want her to be you." Manny pushed a ring box across the booth to me. So that was it: he was going to propose to Mama and wanted me to preview the ring. I opened the velvet box and revealed a small, square-cut ruby with diamonds on each side, set in white gold. It didn't look very engagement-y, and I wondered how to tell him tactfully.

"It's your birthstone, isn't it?" he asked. "July?"

"Yes, but—"

"Skye, I want to ask your blessing for me to propose to Lisa, but also for me to be your dad. The ring is for you. The one for your mother is a little different."

I took the ring out and slipped it onto my right hand. It fit perfectly. I found I couldn't look at it without crying.

"Skye, I want you to know I will always be here for you. I may not be a rich man, but I can promise you that. Whatever a father does for his daughter, whether it's helping provide for you, or offer you guidance, or tell you when you've done something particularly wonderful, or run off a boy who's bothering you—"

I couldn't look at him, either. The tears wouldn't stop.

"Manny," I choked out, "you don't have to do this just because—"

He reached over and tipped my chin up. "Skye, I have wanted to ask you this for a while now. Way before Oklahoma. That has nothing to do with it." He swiped at my cheek with his thumb.

"So, you're going to ask Mama to marry you?"

"Soon. I'm going to tell her I want to wait until your grandmother is well, and I want Verna to give Lisa away at the wedding. And I want you to be part of the ceremony, too. We'll become a family, all of us, together. Your mother has never had the big wedding she deserves. I want it to be wonderful. Whatever she wants. Wherever she wants."

"Manny, what if—"

"It's only a formality, Skye. She'll say yes. We've sort of talked about it a little." He patted my fingers near the shiny ruby. "So, will you be my daughter, Skye?"

It was hard to whisper "okay" through the tears, but I managed.

Twenty-six

DALLAS, TEXAS

Pete eased his long frame into an undersized leather barrel chair in front of Gerald Davidson's desk, legs stretched straight out and hands over his belly. Gerry was leaning forward, his face serious after their customary hand-shake/back-pat greeting.

Pete didn't have to ask why Gerry had dragged him into the office. He'd already prepared his umpteenth defense of his wife to present to his best friend. Attorney or not, Gerry wasn't going to win any argument he put forth against Kara.

Pete decided this would go a whole lot better if he began the conversation. "Look, Gerry, all the viral video stuff will blow over. I know you're worried about the company, and I promise you, we'll bounce back. This kind of social media crap dies down in a couple weeks. You saw it yourself with that hashtag MeToo bullshit."

Gerry played with a stapler on his desk, angling it back and forth with his thumb and forefinger. He didn't look up at Pete when he said, "We've lost Pennsylvania. I'm worried about challenges to the Oklahoma project. But most of all, Pete, I'm worried whether PFD is going to get any future contracts at all." He slowly raised his eyes to meet Pete's. "I don't think you understand the extent of the damage she's done."

"Pennsylvania wasn't make-or-break for us, Gerry, and I haven't heard anything outside a few rumblings with the Oklahoma project. That's not a state contract. They don't have to be all PC and shit."

Gerry shook his head. "Still not getting it, buddy. Every inch of pipeline you install in Oklahoma is going to be met with signs and chants, and likely, sabotage. Each day will present the potential for a fresh PR disaster."

"We have more security than ever in place," Pete shot back, annoyed. "It's costing thousands of dollars a day."

"Yes, Pete, and you'll finish the line, I have no doubt. But it won't be easy, and you'll be way over budget. You're going to have to eat a lot of security expenses and there'll be delays every time you turn around."

"You're not telling me anything I don't know," Pete said.

Gerry smacked the stapler down on a pile of paperwork and leaned back in his chair, lacing his fingers behind his head. "Business is going to be an uphill battle for a long time, Pete. There are companies that'll avoid dealing with PFD, more and more of them, and that's not going away. And after what Kara said… on *camera*… no state, federal or local government entity will come near you. That's twenty-four percent of your annual revenue, gone."

"So, we'll make it up elsewhere," Pete replied. "But we won't have to. I'm telling you, this whole scandal," he spat the word, "will be forgotten very soon." Pete stood and waved at his friend. "C'mon, let's get some lunch."

"Sit down, Pete," Gerry said, his eyes flashing. "You need to talk this through with me, and there's more. Don't forget, I have a substantial interest in this company, too."

Pete slouched back into the chair, as sullen as any sixteen-year-old in the principal's office. "Damn it all, Gerry, she apologized. She's off the board. She's keeping a low profile." Pete leaned forward and clenched his hands together on the desk. "And you don't realize Kara said those things… which were nothing but the unvarnished truth, by the way… because she was defending me. She was upset at the way the protesters were acting after all I'd done for them, all the checks I'd written to make their little community centers and volunteer fire departments and freaking afterschool babysitting facilities better. They'd threatened her, they'd *thrown motor oil* on her, they'd *attacked* her, Gerry. But she wasn't thinking of that. She was thinking of me, her husband, and the insults and ingratitude they'd answered my kindness with." Pete slapped his hands on the desk for emphasis, scowling at Gerry. "Me."

"Pete—" Gerry began.

He was immediately interrupted. "I don't want to hear it, Gerry. Kara's being crucified for a few words she uttered in my defense. She's suffering through this because she loves me. I never should have put her out there as the face of PFD, exposed her to the hateful shit people say and do. I blame myself." Pete rubbed his hand down his face and took a deep breath, trying to calm his hammering heartbeat. "All she wanted to do was help. I don't need you bitching at me about this, Gerry. I know how you feel about my wife. You've *never* been fair to her, not from day one."

Gerry stared at him in silence for a full minute. "I didn't want to do this, buddy. Not now and not ever."

"I'm not so sure you didn't." Pete shook his head. "You seem to love an opportunity to put my wife down."

Gerry paused to consider what Pete said, then slid open the top right drawer in his desk. He leaned toward his friend and asked, "Do you remember a kid we had here, a junior associate straight out of Baylor named Stephen Dykstra?"

Pete closed his eyes. "No. I don't know. Maybe. Does it matter?"

"He left months ago for a big firm in Atlanta. Before he did, he came in to talk to me about some, um, personal stuff."

Pete leaned his head back and stared at the ceiling. "What does any of this have to do with me, Gerry?"

"He hinted to me that Kara might have had something to do with me being framed for sexual harassment. I can't prove it. He wouldn't say much. Made it sound like he'd heard things but couldn't disclose sources."

Pete stared at Gerry. "That's ridiculous. She's not your biggest fan, but Kara would never—"

"Pete. Hold on. Like I said, he only hinted at that. But Stephen also made it clear he couldn't work here anymore because of something that happened with 'Mrs. Darling', and he wouldn't tell me anything beyond that. At the time, I thought maybe he'd hit on her and she'd threatened him. Really didn't think much about it. Kara had been in and out of the office when you were in the hospital and during your recovery, too."

Pete shook his head. "Probably got his feelings hurt. Wouldn't be the first guy to have a crush on my wife, Gerry—"

"He did tell me, though, that if I'm your best friend I should pay attention to Kara and what might be going on with her." Gerry shook his head. "I told him hell, no. That's the worst thing a best friend can do."

Pete raised his brows. "What do you mean, 'going on with her'?"

Gerry closed his eyes and exhaled a long breath through his nose. "He seemed to think Kara might…might be spending time with other men—"

"Man, I don't know what's gotten into you, Gerry, but we've been friends for too long for me to let you blow it all to hell and back with insinuations about my wife. I know you don't like her, Gerry, and you're concerned about business, but you're going *way* too far. I'm gonna walk out that door and try to forget you said any of this." Pete moved forward and put his hands on his knees, preparing to stand.

"Pete, I'm sorry. Like I said, I never wanted to have to do this." Gerry slid a manila envelope across the desk. "I'm so sorry, buddy."

Pete pushed it back at him. "I don't care what's in there. I love her, and I choose her, and I'm not looking."

Gerry opened the envelope and drew out an 8x10 glossy photo, holding it up without a word. The telephoto lens had captured the scene from a perfect angle: Kara stood talking to a man in the driveway of a contemporary wood and glass house. The man was completely naked.

The man was Langdon Tiger.

Pete snatched the photo from Gerry's hand and tore it in half. Gerry extracted another, this one of Kara in a silk robe, kissing Langdon Tiger goodnight in the doorway of her suite in the Catoosa, Oklahoma Hard Rock Hotel and Casino.

Pete took the photo from Gerry and stared at it like a 21st century Rosetta Stone, trying to piece together the meaning of the image in front of him. It couldn't be Kara. It couldn't be that preening, long-haired, manicured Tiger. None of it made sense. The photo faded in and out of blurriness as he blinked his wet eyes.

Pete sat immobile for a full minute, staring quietly and waiting for Kara to be someone else, anyone else, in the photo. He put it facedown on Gerry's desk and buried his head in his hands.

"Pete, I'm so sorry," Gerry said. "I truly am."

"You had her followed?" Pete said through his palms.

"Yeah, I did. I hired a guy to make sure what Dykstra hinted at wasn't true. I was trying to look out for you, Pete."

"Well, mission accomplished, buddy. You looked out for me, all right." Pete came to his feet slowly. "I think I'll pass on that lunch." He walked to the door and met Joseph in the hall, without one word or backward glance at his friend.

They walked in silence to the car, Pete's jaw clenched. Pete took his place in the back seat and hurriedly swiped at his eye before Joseph could see him in the rearview mirror.

"Do you want me to make any stops on the way to the house?" Joseph asked.

Pete met his eyes in the mirror. "No, something's come up, Joseph. Not going to stay in Dallas after all." Pete turned to look out the window as Joseph started the car.

"It's just… I made plans with my girlfriend tonight," Joseph said, pulling out into traffic.

"Oh, Joseph, hell, I'm sorry. Look, just take me to the airport and get your car there." Pete dug in his pocket and extracted three hundred dollars, handing it over the seat to Joseph. "I know you've waited a long time to see Lalique, and I apologize. Dinner's on me. You take a couple days here with her, too. I'll fly back alone."

Joseph took the money and said, "Thank you, that's very kind. But what about security at the lodge?"

"The place is a fortress. We won't be going anywhere." Pete was shaking his head slowly and rubbing his temples. "Kara and I will be okay."

"Mr. Darling, are you sure you have to fly back today?" Joseph asked. "Maybe you could take a little time to rest up here. Your schedule has been crazy lately."

Pete took several beats to answer. "You know what? That sounds good to me. Stop by the liquor store and I'll grab a couple bottles of scotch, then you can drop me at my house. I'll stay there until Thursday, then we'll head back together. Oh, and call Daniello's and order me an extra-large Meatsa Pizza. We'll pick it up when we get to Sunnyvale." Pete pressed the button to partition Joseph from his thoughts.

Kara ran her hand down the length of the white marble dining room table, then stepped back to admire the glittering crystals and butterflies suspended from the ceiling, lit by countless tiny bulbs. It looked like a display to be roped off in a museum of modern art.

Rarely had home furnishings inspired her to tears, but this was beyond exquisite. She moved to adjacent rooms to admire it from every possible angle.

It was breathtaking. The white metal canopy ran almost the length of the table, suspended three inches from the high ceiling. The impossibly delicate, transparent wires connected to it were bundled inside clear Lucite tubes at each end, barely noticeable. The lights, butterflies and crystals cascaded toward the table at different lengths. There were almost a thousand of them.

It was a fairy tale of lights and magic.

The team of electricians who'd installed the chandelier complimented her over and over on the beauty of it, even as they grumbled about its complexity. They, too, had never seen anything like it. Or like Kara, for that matter. She smiled at the memory.

It had all been accomplished over eight hours under the watchful eyes of a couple of Pete's local security men. Now she had the lodge to herself. She planned to have a glass or two of champagne, then video herself under the sparkling crystals and send it to Pete. Maybe she'd climb onto the table. The chairs hadn't been delivered yet, and that cool marble would make a striking, sexy place to pose for her husband.

Kara poured a large glass of Perrier Jouet Belle Epoque and went to select the perfect tasteful lingerie to remove on pristine, polished, Italian Calacatta.

By the time she pressed send on the video, her husband was snoring off the effects of an excess of Glenfiddich and pizza in his favorite recliner, curtains drawn tight against the world in his Sunnyvale study. He didn't hear the "Love Me Tender" ringtone he'd programmed for Kara's texts, though it echoed in the darkness several times.

Kara greeted Pete in jeans and a flannel shirt, albeit a tailored, four-hundred-dollar version with a mink collar and cuffs. She was barefoot and stood on tiptoes when Pete bent to kiss her.

"I thought you'd have a stronger reaction to that video of me on the table than 'pretty'," she said.

"Sorry," Pete replied. "I was a little hungover when I saw it." He turned to climb the stairs to their bedroom. "I'm going to shower and change clothes. Did you get anywhere hiring a chef?"

"No," Kara said, thinking it odd for him to ask. "I haven't even lined up an interview yet."

"That's probably for the best," Pete answered, turning his back to her. Kara watched him mount the stairs, wondering if his blood pressure was okay. Her husband definitely seemed off. She decided to begin a search for the best cardiovascular specialist in Tulsa. She'd start with a call to Ed Berenson at the hospital and make an appointment for Pete, whether he liked it or not.

It was only then she realized Pete hadn't even looked at the dining room when he came in. The meetings with Gerald Davidson must have gone worse than she'd feared.

The Glock was where Pete kept it hidden under a pile of books in the nightstand. Pete took it into the bathroom and placed it on the black granite counter, then turned the shower to a setting as hot as he could bear. He toweled off and dressed in old jeans and a sweatshirt.

He knew he'd find her in the newly furnished dining room, admiring her own latest triumph, her glory of the week, her work of art, the final resting place for nearly two hundred thousand of his dollars. It really was stunning, and Kara was, too. She was leaning on the table, talking on her cell. She dropped her call immediately when Pete walked in.

"Hey," she began, her smile as bright as the chandelier. "I missed you, Pete."

"Did you, Kara? Were you not busy with anyone else while I was gone? Langdon Tiger, maybe?" Pete eased his back down the wall to sit on the floor in the absence of the God-only-knew-how expensive chairs yet to be delivered.

Kara's eyes widened. "Are you crazy? Why would you even say that?"

Pete stared at the dangling butterflies, wondering if they could be counted. So damn many. "Don't insult me more than you already have. I've seen pictures. Who the hell stands in his driveway naked in broad daylight?" Pete laughed and turned his eyes to Kara. "Was he the only one, baby? I'll bet he wasn't the only lucky ticket holder for—"

"Shut up, Pete." Kara held her hands to her ears. "You completely misinterpreted that photo. The guy's a lunatic. He parades around naked at his house. It had nothing to do with me. I was as repulsed as you can imagine. And I can't believe you fucking had me followed."

"I didn't, actually. But let's get back to the subject at hand. What about *this* photo? Did his kissing you in the doorway of your suite at the Hard Rock have nothing to do with you?" Pete unfolded the picture he'd carried in his back pocket and held it up for her to see. He dropped it at his feet and shook his head. "I've been every kind of delusional about you I could be, Kara. Some kid named Stephen Dykstra warned Gerry about you—remember him? I'm sure you do. I've been thinking about it, and if I were a gambling man, I'd lay good money on young Stephen. You probably amused yourself with him while I was recovering from a freaking stroke. Is that right, Kara?" Pete reached into the back waistband of his jeans and extracted the gun, turning it over and over in his hands.

Kara stared in silence for a full minute. "Pete, you're talking crazy. I'd never cheat on you—"

Pete swung the Glock up and pointed it at his wife. "Answer me with the truth, Kara. You get one chance to tell the truth. And don't think I won't shoot, because my life is already over. I have nothing to lose. This house, this marriage, my company… it's all scorched earth now. So you need to tell me one damn true thing, Kara. Come on," he waved the gun slightly, "I know you can do it. You might spontaneously combust, but you can do it."

Kara blinked at Pete, terrified the man across the room was capable of things he never would have been before he went to Dallas. When this was over she would make sure Gerald Davidson was the sorriest man on the planet for what he'd done. "Yes," she whispered, "I was unfaithful to you with

Langdon Tiger. He came to my room after one of those dinners, Pete, I had no idea he was coming, he just showed up out of the blue—"

"… so you had to take him into your bed. Of course," Pete nodded. "I understand."

Kara narrowed her eyes at her husband. This was a Pete Darling she'd never seen.

"Anyway," Pete continued, "you need to get your shit and get out of here. Then you need to get yourself a flight to Dallas and get your shit out of there. Joseph will be with you to make sure you can accomplish that without trying to remove anything that's not yours. And by the way, unless it's something you wear or use to paint your face, it's most likely not yours."

"Pete," Kara took a step toward him and froze as he raised the gun, "Pete, please, I love you—"

The sound of the shot destroyed the rest of her sentence. Pete's expert aim had taken down approximately one Disney World ride's worth of butterflies and crystals, now shattered all over one end of the table and much of the dining room floor. He paused to sight the other Lucite column and brought the rest clattering down. His ears were ringing too loudly to hear Kara's shrieking.

He waved the gun at her and yelled, "Go! Get your things and take the rental car. You need to be out of Oklahoma by tonight. Gerry will be in touch with the rest. You'll talk to him from now on."

Kara was sobbing, hugging herself as she moved from the dining room. Pete knew she was lamenting the damn chandelier more than the death of their marriage, which wouldn't seem real to her for a while.

But it was.

Pete tucked the gun back into his waistband and walked to the kitchen for a beer, which he carried to the pool outside.

He'd call the security people and reassure them all was fine at the lodge, then notify Joseph to extract him to the Hard Rock later today.

Pete downed half the beer and let his gaze wander across his beloved Oklahoma landscape, one more thing on a long list Kara had taken from him.

He could start listing his properties for sale as soon as a crew finished cleaning up the wreckage he'd leave at this house.

The marble table, fittingly, would remain like a headstone.

Twenty-seven

EUFAULA, ALABAMA

The following weekend, Manny took Mama to Cheaha Mountain to propose. It was the highest point in Alabama, and he walked her out to the edge of a towering rock formation with a breathtaking, panoramic view of the emerald pines and valleys below. He left her standing there and asked an older couple from Tennessee to take a pic of the two of them with his phone—but instead of returning to stand by Mama and pose with his arm around her, he dropped to one knee on the craggy surface.

According to Mama, Manny began talking about that night the customer had been so horrible to her and she'd ended up in his arms. He said he'd known at that moment he wanted her to stay there forever.

He told her his heart was bound to hers and it always would be. That her family had become like his own. That he would be the happiest man in the world if she'd agree to be his wife.

When Manny saw the acceptance in her smiling eyes, he added he'd jump if she said no. Final persuasion was provided in the form of a glittering princess-cut diamond framed by triangular rubies on each side; he said those were to represent Grammy and me as he slid it onto her finger.

She said yes, of course, and tourists from six states rushed forward to applaud and congratulate them. They spent the rest of the weekend in a cozy chalet atop the mountain, and decided to plan their wedding there the following June.

Grammy nodded her approval at this news, telling us, "Cheaha Mountain was sacred to the Creek, you know. The word meant "high place" to them. There's also a legend associated with it…"

I glanced at Mama. Wasn't there always?

"… the local chief, Choccolocco, had a beautiful daughter named Talladega. He planned to marry her to an ugly old chief from a neighboring tribe."

Mama muttered, "Hmmm, a NASCAR Indian…she probably ran around in circles a few times a year." I stifled a giggle and Grammy ignored her.

"Talladega was deeply in love with a young brave named Coosa. The ugly old would-be fiancé knew about his rival. He took a medicine man with him to find Coosa, and they administered a potion that would make him sleep forever. Talladega discovered her sleeping lover and made secret visits to him, waiting for him to awaken, pleading with Coosa to open his eyes." Grammy paused to make sure we were following. I was waiting for the inevitable brokenhearted-Indian-princess-jumping-off-a-waterfall-to-her-death conclusion. These things always ended with waterfalls.

"Talladega was so depressed and unhappy," Grammy continued, "the ugly old chief who wanted to marry her decided he should reveal that Coosa could never be awakened from his slumber. Talladega stared at him in silence. Her father, Choccolocco, arranged for his daughter to marry the old chief after the passing of three moons. But when the wedding day arrived, Talladega wasn't there. The woods were searched along with all the hills and valleys, but no bride could be found. The searchers were about to give up when a young brave told them he'd found Talladega. She lay dead on the chest of her beloved Coosa."

"Like a certain Shakespeare tale I remember," I added.

"Yes," Grammy said, "but this is a Creek story. There's more. Although the drug had magic to keep Coosa sleeping, it also carried the power to make him grow. Over hundreds of years he has grown to become a great giant, now forming a mountain many miles long, where he can be seen from all around. The Great Spirit covered him with earth, his blanket from the cold. It planted trees to shield him from the hot summer sun, and scattered flowers all around the place where Coosa lay. And there he stays, still dreaming of his beloved Talladega, 'The Bride of the Mountain.'"

"So, Manny and I are getting married on top of a giant comatose guy?" Mama trolled.

"There is no appreciation for our ancestors in you, Talisa," Grammy patted Mama's head, "but I have enough for both of us. I think it's wonderful Manny wants me to give the bride away. I may add a little shove to show how freely I'm giving." She went off to work on the wedding dress she was insisting on designing for Mama, which was top-secret until she got a bit further long with the sketch. Her cast was due to be removed in a month and she planned to start sewing it then. I was expecting a UPS shipment of deerskin to materialize any day.

Grammy ran a hand up and down her injured arm as she walked away. Her Percocet prescription had run out a couple of days ago. Mama and I were relieved to see she was coping okay with ibuprofen and a lot of rest.

I think it helped that I'd told Sergeant Whitaker I was delaying my enlistment decision by a year.

The first time I saw Greg Varnadoe in a policeman's uniform felt like I'd failed to notice it was Halloween. He looked more than a little surreal. The fact he'd stopped me for speeding, however, was just annoying.

"Hi, Skye, license and registration, please."

"You gotta be kidding me, Greg." I rolled my eyes and reached into the glove compartment. "You're not really going to give me a ticket?"

"No," he answered, "not this time. But if you keep doing forty-six in a twenty-five, then yeah, I'll have to."

"Your uniform looks good on you," I said, watching him scribble my warning citation. "Bet all the ladies like it."

"Only the discerning and tasteful ones. Slow the hell down, Skye." Greg leaned into my driver's window enough to invade my personal space and added, "I want you to come to a party this weekend at my folks' place. My aunt and uncle are coming into town and my dad's doing a big barbeque. Friday night at about eight, okay?"

"I might have to work—"

"Actually, you don't, according to Manny. I saw him this morning."

"That is super creepy, Greg. Way too stalky for me." I started to power my window up and Greg stuck his hand on top of the glass. I wondered briefly what the penalty for crushing an officer's hand was.

"And congratulations on the engagement and your new stepdad, Skye. The guy really does care about you."

"He's not my stepdad yet, and if he's plotting my Friday nights with you, that's gonna stop."

"No, it's not like that. I just casually asked him if you were working. Please come, Skye. There'll be a bunch of people there you know."

That was why I didn't want to go. I shrugged and nodded at Greg. He released my window and watched me drive away slowly enough to leave an iridescent slug trail.

I dressed up for the Varnadoes' party, ditching my usual jeans and t-shirt for a white spaghetti-strap camisole and long, gauzy baby blue skirt. I wore heels, too, even though I would tower above Greg. Actually, *because* I would tower over Greg and any ideas he might have about romance would be dwarfed. I put my hair up in a messy bun and actually applied mascara and lip gloss. Mama's lapis earrings dangled almost to my shoulders.

I looked like a *girl*, Grammy said, an exceptionally beautiful girl.

Grandmothers are required to say such things by law.

I was glad I'd put a little effort in when I saw the crowd. There were at least sixty people milling around, all ages, and the Varnadoe family had decorated with tons of tiny white lights strung overhead and in the trees around their barn. They'd rented round tables, and each had a maroon tablecloth and matching flowers in the center, ringed by candles. I searched the crowd for a surprise bride and groom but found only Greg, who walked over immediately and thanked me for coming.

"Is somebody getting married?" I waved my hand at the decorations. Mr. Varnadoe thought I was waving to him and nodded with a smile before returning his attention to a giant smoker full of ribs and chicken.

"No, this is all my mom's thing. She hasn't seen her big sister in a long time. Mom wanted to throw an outdoor party and make sure it was up to Aunt Merilee's Savannah standards. I think she did okay." Greg grinned at me. "You look pretty, Skye."

I glanced down at my skirt. "Thanks. I'm glad I dressed up a little for Aunt Merilee. Now I'm slightly terrified."

"Oh, you should be," Greg said, sipping his beer. "Let me get you a drink. Wine or beer? There's something Mom calls Chatham Artillery Punch, too, but you'll have to sleep on the couch if you have more than one glass. I think it's burning a hole in the punchbowl." Greg nodded at a drinks table dominated by what looked like a crystal swimming pool. His mother, Ann, was carefully ladling punch into clear plastic cups from it. "That was my great-great-great-great-great-grandmother's. Supposedly submerged in a creek to escape the Yankees' pillage."

"I think that obliges me to try the punch, sir," I drawled and followed Greg to the table. Mrs. Varnadoe came around to hug me, leaving the precious punchbowl dangerously unguarded from Yankees and clumsy people. I took a cup and lifted it to Greg, trying not to choke on the first swallow. I had discovered the Southern equivalent of Long Island Iced Tea, and a few more sips made it taste like heaven in a cup. "This might be why we lost the war," I told him.

Greg took my nearly empty cup and set it down on a table with his beer. "Let's take a little break from that," he told me, "and I'll introduce you to my Aunt Merilee."

Aunt Merilee was a small woman in an expensive-looking navy knit suit and gold charm bracelet. She had a chin-length black-and-gray hairdo that looked lacquered into submission and the whitest smile I'd seen on anyone but a game show host. Her deep blue eyes sparkled at me as she placed her impossibly soft hand in mine. "Pleased to meet you, Skye. Willis, you say? Do you have relatives in Savannah? Our librarian was a Willis before she married."

I stuffed down the urge to reply that all our librarian Willises were stereotypical old maids who'd never left Alabama. "No, ma'am, I don't have any family in Georgia."

"Oh." She seemed disappointed, and I felt sorry I hadn't invented any kin for her. Within seconds, she was looking over my shoulder and calling her husband over. "Garrett, this is Gregory's friend Skye Willis. Skye, this is Dr. Leatherwood."

An extremely tall man extended his hand. I couldn't help but notice his resemblance to some actor Grammy professed to be in love with, the guy who played the dad in *Divine Secrets of the Ya-Ya Sisterhood*. "Call me Garrett," he said, his voice deep and booming. "Nice to meet you. Are you originally from Eufaula? This is a lovely little town."

"Yes, sir, I was born here." I snaked my arm behind Greg and poked him under his shoulder blade. The last thing I wanted to do was stand here and dissect my family tree for the Leatherwoods. Greg got the message, and we excused ourselves, rejoining our drinks at an otherwise empty table near the barn.

"What kind of doctor is he?" I asked.

"The kind who teaches philosophy at Georgia Southern University. Aunt Merilee just can't help herself, or maybe she's used to talking to his students." Greg shook his head. "They're really nice. Maybe a little pretentious, but nice. Listen, I need to run into the house for a few minutes. Do you mind if I leave you here? I'll be right back. Angie and them will be here soon. There are probably a few other people you know." He nodded at Jackson Latimer, who wore his usual skintight t-shirt and appeared to be helping Mr. Varnadoe grill food.

"I'm fine. Go on." Greg walked off toward the house and I headed back to the magic punchbowl for social courage, taking a cup while Mrs. Varnadoe chatted with some new arrivals. I sat back down and sipped, people-watching the same Eufaula channel I'd been viewing for twenty-two years. I heard the chair next to me being pulled out and looked over as a guy about my age unfolded himself by my side. He sat without a word, staring straight ahead.

It was impossibly awkward, sitting in silence with a stranger. At least a full minute passed before I said, "Hi, I'm Skye Willis."

"Yeah, I know. My mother saw you sitting alone and asked me to 'accompany' you while Greg's in the house." He nodded at Marilee Leatherwood, who was busy shaking hands and presumably preparing to kiss random babies. The guy stretched his arms out toward the flickering candle on the table, revealing some symbol tattooed on his inner wrist.

"What century did your family teleport from?" I laughed. "I'm fine by myself."

He clasped his hands together and announced, "I'm Len. My mom is well-schooled in Southern manners that date back to the time of that punchbowl." He inclined his head toward Greg's mother and the drinks table.

"Is Len short for Leonard?"

He smoothed black curls back from his face and frowned in the direction of his mother. "No, it's short for Cullen."

"What kind of name is Cullen?" I blurted.

"It's my paternal grandmother's maiden name. Dad comes from an old Savannah family. Didn't my mom attempt to analyze your DNA when you met her?" He laughed and settled back, crossing his arms. "She's never happy unless she can find out who your people are and connect a dot or two with our own."

"Yeah, well, I'm pretty sure our dots are on different planes."

He turned his eyes on me, and they were dark as a midnight ocean. There was a little moonlight in them when he smiled and said, "Geometry buff, huh?"

"Nothing could be further from the truth," I told him. "I hate any and all forms of math."

"Well," he took a long pull at his beer bottle, "we have that in common. I had to get a tutor to help me limp to a 'C-' in Linear Algebra this semester."

"Let me guess: Georgia Southern."

Cullen laughed. "Not for all the money in the world. I'm a junior at Auburn. History major. What about you?"

"I'm a rebellious twenty-two-year-old with no clear plan." I guzzled the rest of my punch. "What are you going to do with a history degree?"

"Teach. Probably a bunch of insolent middle schoolers at first. I had a history teacher in high school who really made it come alive for me, you know? Like, he made us all feel like we were there. He taught me to question things, too, and not just accept everything in a textbook. Mr. Tisdale changed the way I looked at everything from the American Revolution to the Vietnam War."

"Interesting," I said. "Do you like to read? I mean, for fun?"

"I love to read when I have time. Plowed through Follett's Century Trilogy last summer. Then *The Pillars of the Earth*." He turned his empty beer bottle around and around in his hands.

"I love that book. *Pillars,* I mean," I answered. "I've never met anyone outside my own family who's read it."

He locked his eyes on mine and held them, a challenge. "What's your favorite historical fiction book?"

"Either *The Pillars of the Earth* or *The Source*, by Michener," I answered instantly.

"So, do you like history, or just historical fiction?" he asked.

I smiled. "Both. I loved history in school and took every AP course I could. But I really like good historical fiction, because it always makes me want to learn more, you know? My browser history is full of stuff I've had to look up after finishing novels. I think you should use your real name, by the way. Cullen has a cool historic ring to it."

He chuckled and began peeling the label from his Coors Light. "You're the first person who's ever said that. Kids in school used to make fun of it along with my dork glasses. My parents shortened it to Len to keep me from getting regularly scheduled ass-kickings."

"I walked the Reject Path, too, if it helps. But you seem to have turned out all right. I remember Greg going through the same stuff until he started playing sports."

Cullen finished peeling the label and crushed it into a foil ball, which he rolled to me. "This is the extent of my sports activity, ma'am."

I rolled it back and it dropped into his lap, where my eyes stayed a little too long. I cleared my throat and yearned for a hit of Artillery Punch. "So, how long are you and your parents staying?"

"We're leaving Eufaula tomorrow. They want to see some other parts of the state, so I'm taking them on a tour. Little River Canyon, DeSoto Falls, Cheaha Mountain—"

"My mom's getting married there in June," I interrupted.

"Have you ever been?" he asked. "It's really pretty. Lots of good hiking trails. I've even talked Mom into camping in the state park there, and Merilee Leatherwood camps for no man."

"No, I haven't. I guess I'll see it for the first time in some horrific bridesmaid's dress."

He laughed softly. "There's a legend about Cheaha, you know. The Creek believed a jilted groom grew into the mountain after someone poisoned him to keep him from marrying a princess named Talladega." Cullen stopped talking and looked at me. "What? What did I say? Are you okay?"

"No, umm… how do you know about that? My grand-mother is Creek, and she just told us that story. It's so weird that you'd be familiar with it."

"It's not weird at all. I'm a history major with a concentration on Native American studies. I kind of live and breathe this stuff."

"So do I," I said. "I am the only person I know whose grandmother cooks sofkey and tries to foist it on the UPS man."

Cullen grinned. "Marry me," he said, then immediately tried to laugh through the weirdness. It fell all around us like a summer hailstorm.

We sat looking anywhere but at each other. Greg approached with a cup of punch for me and beers for the two of them. An answered prayer.

Greg set the drinks down and placed a hand on my shoulder. "I see you've met my cousin, Skye. What time is your girlfriend getting here, Len?" He slid into the chair on the other side of me, having nuked the hailstorm into oblivion.

"She isn't coming to the party, Greg. Thought I told you that." Cullen opened his beer and took a long swallow.

Greg pulled out his phone and handed it to me. "Isn't she pretty?" Some girl with long blonde hair and ice-blue eyes stood with her arms around Cullen's shoulders, her leg kicked behind her playfully. It was the Facebook profile pic of Amanda Abernathy, taken in front of Jordan-Hare Stadium. Everything about her screamed sorority girl. If you cut her, she'd bleed Vera Bradley.

"Yes, she is," I answered. "Have y'all been together a long time?"

Greg took his phone back and scrolled down helpfully. "In a relationship since August 2017. That's a pretty long time, isn't it?" He flashed the screen at me and replaced the phone in his pocket. "Dunno if Skye told you, but we've been close since elementary school. She's a big part of my life."

No I'm not, I wanted to scream. It didn't seem necessary to bother, though, as Cullen grabbed his beer and stood to say, "Sure was nice meeting you, Skye. Y'all have a good time. I've got some stuff to get ready for our trip tomorrow." He walked off toward the house.

I looked at Greg, who was staring at me like he'd never seen me before. "You really do look beautiful."

"It's just a damn skirt." I reached up and released my hair from its bun, rubbing the back of my sore head.

Greg set his beer down and took my face in his hands. His lips pulled at mine almost too softly to feel at first. Then he shut out everyone else under those twinkling lights with a long, deep kiss that stunned me to my toes. We came up for air to find more than a few people quickly looking away. Merilee Leatherwood was one of them.

Greg rested his forehead against mine. "You have no idea how long I've wanted to do that, Skye," he whispered. "If it took six hours of stringing lights and setting up tables, it was worth every second." He stood and walked over to two big speakers set up by the barn doors, pressing a few buttons on his phone and laying it on top of one. I recognized the opening strains of a country song from a few years back called *A Woman Like You*, and then Greg came back and held his hand out for me to dance with him.

"Haven't we made enough of a spectacle yet?" I said. "Let's just sit here for a little while." Couples were moving out under the lights, though, and I gave in and joined him in an awkward box step. I could feel the eyes and expectations of Greg's entire family on my shoulders. Everyone's eyes but his cousin's, that is. Cullen had completely disappeared.

An hour after midnight most of the older folks had cleared out and a bunch of us sat at two tables under the stars, the same stars and the same people who'd known each other forever. Angie sat in the lap of her boyfriend Keith. It occurred to me we were right back at that night by Lake Eufaula, only sober and with Greg pining for me instead of Caroline.

Mr. Varnadoe came out with a big trash bag and started cleaning up. Greg's mom was on his heels, collecting and folding tablecloths.

The antebellum swimming pool of a punchbowl had long been swaddled and carried to a safe place inside.

I jumped up and followed Mrs. Varnadoe, gathering and folding and hoping to avoid the inevitable conversation she'd start. All she said was, "He talks about you all the time, Skye. I'm glad you came tonight."

"Greg's a sweetheart, Mrs. Varnadoe." That was the best I could do, and she accepted it with a warm smile. We stacked the tablecloths, and I walked over to Greg who was helping his dad. I pecked his cheek and told him good night, knowing he was evaluating my sobriety as I did it. I guess he was satisfied because he allowed me to walk to my car alone after promising I'd text when I got home.

I collapsed in my car and leaned my head back, tired and confused. I stayed that way several seconds before reaching for the ignition.

The corner of my right eye caught Cullen Leatherwood's face in my passenger window. I stifled a terrified scream to keep a herd of Varnadoes from running to investigate. "What the hell are you doing?" I hissed as he opened the door.

He folded his long body into the seat beside me, but left the door open so I could see him in the overhead light. "Look," he began, searching down the driveway to make sure we were alone. "I didn't want to leave things the way Greg made them sound. I'm not a bad guy. I only want to talk to you a little more."

"What do you mean, 'the way Greg made them sound'? Greg submitted photographic proof you have a girlfriend. And in case you didn't notice, he managed to kiss me like we were on a Times Square billboard at midnight on New Year's Eve."

"Yeah," he said, searching my face, "I saw. And if Greg's what you want, I get it. It's just...I couldn't let you leave without saying something."

"Well, you've said it. And do not insult me by adding that your relationship with that Tri-Delt recruitment-poster girl is bad, that you were planning to break up with her already, or some horseshit like that."

He looked stunned. "No, Mandy's great. That's not what I was going to say at all. I had fun talking to you, and I thought maybe I could meet your grandmother sometime, is all. She's the one who made that protest out in Oklahoma, right? Sitting on top of those pipes? I kinda pieced it together with your last name after the things you said."

"Get out," I said, starting the car. "Get out and don't stalk me online anymore."

"Skye, I—"

I shoved Cullen's shoulder hard enough to convince him to exit. I left him standing in the driveway with outstretched arms, palms up, catching the rays of my headlights.

Twenty-eight

DALLAS, TEXAS
Three weeks later

P ete leaned back in a booth at Frankie's, Gerry's favorite sports bar, eyeing the Sunday-morning "Hail Mary" the server had just placed in front of him. The thing had a mountain of cheese, bacon, shrimp, and most of a Whole Foods produce department sitting on the glass. "I like their style," he told Gerry, popping a shrimp into his mouth. It would take a few minutes to dig down to the vodka and tomato juice, which would make it noon and socially acceptable.

Gerry inhaled deeply and pointed at a gigantic cinnamon roll being carried to the next table which looked like it supported most of a pecan pie atop it, dripping down the sides. "They call that a Bubba Bun." Pete smelled the spices and toasted pecans a few feet away and had to work to avoid drooling on himself. That had only been a problem late at night in his recliner lately, when nobody was around to see.

"Thanks for coming out, Pete," Gerry was carefully unloading the top of his drink, placing all the goodies in a neat row on his bread plate. "It's good to see you. You been doing okay?"

Pete copied Gerry's de-garnishing, suddenly in a hurry for vodka. "I guess I'm not doing too bad for a man who's lost a wife and a business he spent a lifetime building." Pete gulped his drink. "Oh, yeah, and his Oklahoma dream house."

"I still don't know why you don't keep the lodge, Pete," Gerry said. "And you haven't lost PFD. That's ridiculous."

Pete placed his hands on the table. "Actually, it's not. When we finish the projects we have going, there's nothing lined up. No one will touch us. Already laying guys off. I have to meet with the board next week, and I'm pretty sure they're going to push me to sell." Pete drained his Hail Mary and nodded at the man-bunned server across the room, who nodded back. "And I can't live anywhere near Okmulgee, Gerry. That's a poisoned well." Pete picked up a piece of bacon and nibbled at it. "And no," he raised his eyebrows, "I haven't talked to her."

"That's definitely for the best, Pete, until things are finalized."

Pete shrugged. "I think changing my phone numbers and all the locks was kinda over-the-top, Gerry. And now that you've served the divorce papers, she won't come anywhere near me. I can assure you, she's too damn mad for that."

"She's fine, Pete. The settlement we offered her will let Kara land on her feet." *And sustain her until she lands on her back or knees.* "Anyway, I have something I want you to think about."

"Yeah," Pete answered, "what's that?" He gazed up at a rerun of a Mavs game.

"Remember when Kris and I split up? The best thing I did was get away from here for a little while, and I think you should, too. And don't tell me you need to stay connected to PFD or your realtor or any of that, Pete, because we both know you can stay connected from anywhere in the world."

"Uh-huh. And where would I go?" Pete accepted another Hail Mary and began to wonder if brunch or lunch would be necessary at all. Two slices of bread and he could make a hell of a garnish sandwich.

"Isn't there anywhere you've always wanted to travel?" Gerry asked.

Pete shook his head. "Been all over Europe, and I'd see Kara everywhere we've stayed if I did that. And I'm not going on some African safari by myself. Not real interested in the Orient—"

"Yeah, we call that Asia now, Pete." Gerry began looking through the menu. "I'm suggesting that you go where I went. It's beautiful and tranquil and the people are friendly but not too friendly. No one will know who you are. It's a perfect place to be alone and reflect."

"I don't reflect, buddy." Pete was trying to decide what would go well with a Bubba Bun. "And I'm real sentimental, but I don't remember where you went or even if I missed your sorry ass."

Gerry rolled his eyes. "New Zealand, Pete. I can tell you exactly where to stay and what you can't miss. You can hike and play tourist and eat cheeseburgers the size of engine blocks. Breathe some fresh air. Watch a sunrise you'll never forget—"

"I can do all that here," Pete said. "And I am not wadding myself up into some commercial jetliner seat and flying for sixteen hours. Not gonna happen."

"...see the Southern Cross for the first time..." Gerry plowed on.

"What are you, Crosby, Stills and Nash? I'm not going."

"... see whales and penguins and learn a haka..."

"What is a *haka?*" Pete coughed the word up like a furball.

"It's a war dance with a chant. The Maori do them. You need a war dance, Pete. Some of your old fire. You're about as fiery as a damp sponge in the sink. I'd rather see you angry than hurt." Gerry took a minute to pull up YouTube and handed his phone to Pete.

He watched thirty seconds of a bunch of face-painted, grunting natives posing dramatically, then handed the phone back. "Not interested."

"You're gonna die in that damn recliner, Pete. Everybody knows what you're doing, I'm just the only one brave enough to say it."

Pete moved a celery stalk back and forth through his drink, then set it on the inedible vegetable pile where it belonged. All he looked forward to was the oblivion of an afternoon nap, which would last until five or so. Then he'd scotch-on-the-rocks his way to his evening oblivion. He glanced at Joseph, who was across the room with Lalique, watching his boss and dutifully drinking a Diet Coke. "I'll consider it," he said, just to shut Gerry up.

"I'm going to send you a bunch of New Zealand links to look over."

Pete nodded. He pointed to the Chicken Cordon Bleu Eggs Benedict on the menu and told Gerry, "I think that'll go great with a Bubba Bun."

"And a link to your cardiologist's website. Maybe a personal trainer—"

"Stop your melodramatic bullshit, Gerry. I'm fine."

Gerry studied his friend for several seconds before quietly adding, "She's not worth it, Pete. I'm sorry to say that to you, and I'm sorry I was the one to tell you in the first place." Gerry looked so sincere Pete almost felt bad for him.

"You did what you had to do," Pete answered, rubbing two days of stubble on his chin. "If I have to sell PFD, it'll be one of the hardest things in my life. But this disaster with Kara has prepared me. It really can't get any worse, buddy." Pete lifted his glass to Gerry as the server walked up to take their orders.

As man-bun left the table, Gerry leaned forward on his elbows, his hands clasped. "Pete, I know I probably shouldn't mention this, but the girl in Alabama? The one you told me I might hear from?"

Pete looked up from his drink. "Yeah?"

"Is she your daughter?"

"Probably. Look, I don't want to talk about it. I told you a long time ago, Gerry, I've never wanted kids. It's something I've known all my life."

Gerry sipped his drink and set it down. "Why, Pete? Do you mind if I ask why?"

"I do mind, Gerry, yeah." Pete frowned and shook his head. "Look, I don't need an instant, grown-up kid at this point in my nuclear-wasteland life. It's too late for that, and she made it clear she doesn't need my help."

Gerry stared into Pete's eyes, a riot of red and gray. "Maybe you need hers."

Pete woke around nine p.m. to the sound of the video doorbell. He'd given Joseph the night off, so all he could do was hope the ringing would stop. He wasn't even sure how to check the damned thing on his phone. Kara had set it all up. Pete grabbed his gun, cursing himself for leaving the gates to the driveway open. No way anyone would know he was in this dark cocoon of a house, though. He closed his eyes and waited.

The ringing didn't stop, and Pete's eyes opened wide at the thought a burglar might be testing to see if the house was empty. He trudged to the foyer, gun in hand. He didn't need a camera to see what the sidelight windows revealed from his hiding place: Kara stood at the door, obviously distraught that her key no longer worked. She rang the bell again, then pounded the door with her fist. "Pete!" she screamed, "I know you're in there. Please, I need to talk to you. Please, Pete." Kara leaned into the door, pressing her palms and forehead against it. She began to sob, choking out, "Pete, I still love you!"

He could never stand to hear her cry. Pete tucked the pistol in his waistband and started toward the door.

He stopped several feet away. Something in his reptilian brain took over, a primitive instinct for self-preservation, and instead he double-checked the security system and walked back to his study. He heard the angry squeal of Kara's Porsche tires a couple of minutes later, as he poured a drink to loosen the tightness in his chest.

He sat in his cradle of a recliner listening in the darkness, almost hoping she'd come back. After two hours, he took his drink and placed it on the nightstand next to their bed. His eyes fixed on the pillow where Kara's head should lay, her dark hair falling across her cheek, her body soft and warm, curled with her back against his side. Pete fell asleep with that image of his wife.

In the wee hours of the morning he ended up in a recurring dream: his father was chasing him up the stairs with a belt, snapping the looped leather between his hands and yelling his name. "You're gonna get your sorry ass out there and clean that mess up!" his father screamed. "I've lost count of the times I've warned you about this. Maybe you'll remember this here belt when you wanna slack off and watch some goddam TV show instead of bein' responsible." His dad caught up and pushed Pete hard against the wall, his arm across the back of Pete's neck. He yanked Pete's pants down and lashed the leather against his bottom and legs over and over. When he finally stopped to draw a breath, he bellowed, "Clean it up now or you'll be sorry!"

Pete turned around and stared at his father towering over him, refusing to cry. He was seven years old. The "mess" was an assortment of toys in the front yard's dirt walkway, where a beer-addled Mabry Darling had stumbled over them onto the low cement steps leading to the screened-in porch. His little brother Johnny sat in their mother's arms in the living room, yowling into her shoulder, but Daddy never chased him, anyway.

Just Pete.

He woke with his fingernails digging into his palms, the same as every time, remembering.

The old man died right before Pete's twenty-third birthday. Pete was working for a pipeline company in Texas. His mother begged him to come home for the funeral, but he'd told her it was impossible to get away. Pete knew Johnny would comfort her a lot better than he could.

He'd sat drinking in a little bar near Houston at the precise time they were to lower his father into the ground, listening to some twangy country song in the mid-afternoon darkness. That was the moment Pete swore he'd never have a kid. Mabry Darling would never reach out through Pete's hands and hurt a child.

Those were memories he'd never shared with anyone, not even Kara. Pete rolled over and grabbed her pillow, inhaling the tiniest trace that remained of her Russian Amber shampoo. He hugged it as he fell back into an uneasy sleep.

A week later, Pete lay in a first-class bed on an Air New Zealand flight. It wasn't the links to glorious scenery or Hobbit movie tour packages Gerry sent that put him on the plane—it was a phone call from Gerry bearing bad news—news that convinced Pete he needed to go somewhere far away, to be anywhere but where he was and anyone but who he was.

Now he accepted a fresh cup of ice smothered in scotch from a smiling older lady named Bronwyn and settled back to watch some damn Hobbit movie crap and see what all the fuss was about.

What the movie failed to supply, Pete saw from his waterfront apartment the next afternoon in Queenstown: a perfect, fully visible, vivid rainbow in the blue sky, stretching from the row of white-capped mountain peaks to his left all the way across the wide lake to the smaller brown mountains on his right. It was a vista unlike any he'd experienced, a fully present rainbow set like a jewel in a painting.

The entire front of the apartment was glass; sliding doors and windows that drew you out onto the small balcony. The living room featured a gas fireplace and cushy couches and an adjacent kitchen full of fancy appliances. A bedroom loft hung over all of this, with an additional large window on the entire scene.

The kitchen table bore a big welcome basket of chocolates, fruit, and cookies, its cellophane gathered and tied in a dark green ribbon.

Pete had to admit: Gerry had chosen well. He yawned and stretched, weary from the flight, and the man New Zealanders would know as Otis Garfield climbed the polished wood stairs to the loft for a nap.

Twenty-nine

EUFAULA, ALABAMA

"I have some for both of y'all, too," Grammy nodded and turned to inspect her hair in the mirror. Mama had added a multitude of tiny red dried-flower clips as Grammy had insisted, all up and down her lovely white braid. We'd done her makeup the way she liked, light on the mascara and heavy on the rose-pink lips. Mama and I had successfully Googled up a fringed, faux-deerskin vest so Grammy could get her arm cast through her favorite fashion statement. She wore it over the stretchiest white t-shirt we could ease onto her and a pair of her favorite bellbottom jeans. She looked adorable, ready for either Woodstock or a tribal council meeting.

Now my grandmother reached into a drawer and extracted ten more little red dried-flower clips, offering five to Mama and five to me. Her nod indicated what I'd feared: we were to wear these to the Piggly Wiggly with her. Mama swept her own long hair back on one side and clipped the barrettes in. I stuck mine to the top of my head, where they closely resembled warts.

No one was going to argue with The Sparrow about this. It was her first foray into the world since Oklahoma, a Saturday afternoon grocery trip. Grammy wanted to look her very best. I think half of her wanted to run into people she knew and the other half dreaded it. Her goal was to get through every aisle with pretty smiles and mysterious nods at our neighbors.

We would intervene and redirect if anyone started asking about Oklahoma. That was understood, particularly if Myra Burnside was there. Myra was the town librarian; ironically, silence was a vacuum to her. She stood behind her counter and stamped the card-sleeve envelopes of books all day long for half the town. Myra spread whatever "news" she heard like bubonic plague in the sixteenth century, with only slightly less catastrophic results.

I sneaked a pic of Mama kissing Grammy as she buckled her into her seat belt, noting her dried flowers looked less warty than mine. I gathered my hair into a ponytail and moved the barrettes into a clump at the top of it before we drove off.

Grammy was a little disappointed, I think, to see there weren't too many customers. We'd accidentally scheduled our trip on a Saturday during football season, which meant the entire state of Alabama would appear to have been raptured unless you were in a stadium or in front of a TV.

We made it twenty feet into the store until my grandmother remembered she'd been telling us about some Creek Indian battle earlier and needed to tell us the rest of what she'd learned. I was staring at my phone, paying more attention to Snapchat than Sparrowchat until she said, "Do you know how many innocent people died there? Women and children included? It was a huge *bloodbath,*" Grammy paused to chew a sample grape she'd plucked from the display. It met her taste test, so she carefully placed a full bag next to her purse on the shopping cart's seat.

"Mom, come on, not in the Piggly Wiggly." Mama glanced around for innocent victims of Grammy's history lesson in the produce aisle. Grammy had spent yesterday afternoon reading about the Battle of Horseshoe Bend, I remembered now. She had been broadly hinting I needed to take her to the national park there.

"Jackson's men stole the Creeks' canoes. The soldiers attacked the braves trying to swim away, about two hundred of 'em. They just shot or stabbed them with bayonets in the water. Can you imagine? That river had to be a horrible sight, running red…" Grammy let her voice trail off, shaking her head.

A lady with two small children hurried on, loudly asking the older one if he remembered where the cookies were.

Mama looked at me, her eyes pleading.

"Okay, Grammy, I understand why you want to go," I told her. "I'll take you to Horseshoe Bend next weekend, I promise. As long as I can be back by six on Sunday."

"It's less than two hours away, Little One," Grammy said. "We can leave early in the morning and see everything. It's such an important part of our history, when everything changed for the Creek. It was the beginning of the end, the battle that eventually led to the Trail of Tears. Having you there to experience it with me means so much, honey. Thank you." Grammy kissed my cheek, satisfied, and returned her attention to the fresh fruit and vegetables. Only two children were harmed in the making of our grocery trip for the week.

By the time we reached the canned foods, she was complaining of a headache. Mama and I exchanged looks, worried we'd overdone Grammy's first outing. We hurried through the rest of our shopping and Mama loosened her braid when we got into the car, thinking that might help her headache. Her long white hair cascaded down the back of the passenger seat. I grabbed an errant dried flower Mama had missed and clipped it into my own arrangement.

Grammy kept protesting she was fine and just needed to lie down. We got her settled with some ice water and ibuprofen, her broken arm resting next to her on a pillow in her darkened bedroom.

I was concerned about leaving her when Mama and I went off to work that night but she seemed fine, sitting on the couch with a bowl of soup on a TV tray table, watching Vanna White turn letters she'd guessed long before the "addle-pated" contestants.

Grammy was scheduled to get her cast removed in two weeks. Her bruises had faded to shadows. She didn't say much about her arm, but Mama and I would still catch her rubbing it absently. After the cast was taken off, she'd begin physical therapy with the goal of returning to her occasional shifts at Walmart.

If a trip to Horseshoe Bend in the meantime would make her happy, it was the least I could do.

Mama and I climbed into her car that night. I'd been riding to and from the restaurant with her in order to avoid Greg's radar, literally and figuratively. He kept texting, and I kept coming up with reasons I couldn't see him.

I told him everything but the truth, *because I'm not attracted to you* cannot be worded in a way that doesn't hit like a nail-studded baseball bat. After a week or so, he'd quit trying. A single kiss was the exact distance from years of friendship to the hurried glance Greg gave me at a gas station one day and drove away without looking back.

So, when he walked into the restaurant about eight-thirty, I hid in the kitchen. Mama rolled her eyes at me and went out to wait on him as Manny and I watched. When she started toward me with Greg at her heels, my heart sank. I knew he hadn't come to see me in that uniform on a social visit. His tears gave him away.

Wilma had come to join Grammy to watch an old, classic movie on TV, their weekly ritual over shared dessert. She placed her pecan pie on the counter and called "Verna!", but no one answered. She found Grammy slumped over on the couch and couldn't wake her. She dialed 911, begging for an ambulance to hurry.

Greg came straight to us when he heard the call. He took Mama and me to the hospital with his lights and siren on. The ER lady told us they'd taken Grammy back immediately, that's all she knew, and we needed to wait there for the doctor. She was a kind-faced older lady, but she shot around her desk and led Mama to a hard plastic chair when Mama headed toward the door to the examining rooms.

A year passed in ten minutes. Mama was glued to her chair, staring vacantly, and I paced the room. We were the only people in the medical center's postage-stamp of a waiting room. Most folks went to the bigger hospital in Dothan. Maybe they'd transfer Grammy there.

Greg came over and hugged me, telling me he had to leave but Manny was on the way. I remember thanking him and watching the glass doors whoosh to a close behind him. A second later a guy in green scrubs walked in, sitting next to Mama and taking her hand. That was the instant I knew Grammy was gone. It was written all over his tired, overworked, thirty-year-old doctor face.

There was nothing they could do, he told us. "I don't have confirmation yet, but we're almost certain your mother suffered an intercranial hemorrhage, a brain bleed," he told Mama. "It was probably caused by an undetected injury to her head when she fell and broke that arm."

"No," Mama answered, looking at me. "That can't be right. She fell weeks ago, and she was treated in a hospital. There must be some mistake…" My mother stood to walk away, her eyes focused on that oak door separating us and reality.

The doctor—the hospital identification badge hanging from his neck said, "Morris Henry, MD"—gently pulled Mama's arm until she sat back down. He turned his attention to me, his hand still on Mama's wrist.

"Did she have head pain after her fall?" he asked.

"She didn't say anything about her head hurting in the hospital," I answered. "It took us a long time to get to her. She was in Oklahoma."

I saw the recognition flash in his eyes. He blinked and lowered his gaze to the floor for a second.

"If they were unaware she'd hit her head, they might not have done a CT. Or maybe nothing showed up at that point." He turned back to Mama, whose mouth hung open.

The doctor paused, clasping his hands together between his knees. "Was your mother taking blood thinners, Miz Willis?"

"No," Mama brightened, as if this could change everything. "She's never taken blood thinners."

Dr. Henry said, "What pain medication did she have? Do you remember the name?"

"She had Percocet, but she ran out of those at least a week and a half ago," I told him. "She started taking ibuprofen because her arm still bothered her."

"I'm so sorry," he answered, shaking his head slowly and shifting his bloodshot blue eyes to me. "It's possible that may have made things...worse." He patted the sides of his chair and stood up.

"What do you mean?" Mama shrieked at him. "What do you mean by *made things worse?*"

"Drugs like ibuprofen can act as blood thinners. If your mother had an undetected brain injury, that may have led—"

I held up my hand to stop him. Mama didn't need to hear this now.

Dr. Henry seemed to understand and segued into, "This was very sudden, Miz Willis. She didn't feel the pain of it."

There was no pain for me, either. I felt like my brain and heart were wrapped in cotton.

The doctor heard Manny walk through the glass doors and watched him making his way toward Mama. He touched my mother's shoulder and nodded to the nurse at the desk as he left the room.

The older lady came over and asked if we'd like to see my grandmother. Mama shook her head at Manny, leaving him there as she and I followed the nurse through the door.

Mama and I walked to the room where Grammy's body lay bathed in soft light the ER people surely dimmed for us. She simply looked like she might be having a pleasant dream, or maybe I was having a nightmare instead.

I kissed her forehead and stroked her hair back.

Then I spotted the tiny dried flower tangled in the white cascade on her pillow. That was what made Mama and me break into a million pieces.

We spent the next few days moving through time like we were slogging through molasses. Nothing felt real. Mama and I kept waiting for her to come out of her room and dispense some Sparrowism to make us laugh. To love us. To comfort us. To encourage us. To scold us. To show us the way, the next step.

We had to find it on our own, navigate the whole bewildering maze of trying to decide what fancy box was sufficient to house our "loved one" for eternity *(what satin lining is worthy of a piece of your own heart?)* to what songs she would want played *(Tim McGraw was her only musical love and we can't play Indian Outlaw)* to what "Sunday dress" she'd want to wear *(she'd prefer her faux deerskin, we were pretty sure).*

We decided to have her cremated—she'd mentioned that preference more than once—and it was some comfort to know we could keep her remains with us, maybe scatter some in places that were most special to her.

Mama stood with me by the door of the funeral home, both of us armored in black against the kind words people kept offering. We hugged and smiled and thanked all hundred or so who showed up. We'd save our grief for later. It was too raw to share with any but our closest friends and family. Those few waited for us at the house where they'd hurried after the final words of the preacher we'd hired. Everyone was invited to stop by.

Wilma poured her grief into a baked ham, coconut cake, a chocolate cream pie, a banana pudding, and twenty-four cupcakes decorated with her vision of Native American designs in red, black, and yellow on a blue icing background. Manny and Luz had lovingly prepared some of the best chicken and dressing, mashed potatoes, green beans, turnip greens, and macaroni and cheese ever to comfort a native Southerner.

Greg and his parents came and stayed for a while, sitting in folding chairs Manny had added to the living room. A couple of my old teachers from high school, Mr. and Mrs. Bullen (chemistry married English), perched near them and made small talk. One stooped, white-haired man from Walmart introduced himself as Bernard. Grammy had always referred to him as the "greeter-geezer" with a crush on her, and Bernard was obviously hurting from her loss. Other people came, ate, hugged and left without ever telling us their names. We suspected most knew her from work.

They breathed their energy and hope into Mama and me, and we'd been as empty as two people can be. Grammy would have said something about everyone having an aura that touched other people's auras, sharing energy. All I know is that strangers comforted us without words.

Our Cousin Terry brought photos of Grammy we'd never seen: Verna at six on a black Shetland pony, as a skinny teenager sitting on a rock by a lake, knees drawn to her chest. There was one with Grammy's arm around her brother, Terry's dad. He was dressed as a cowboy and held a shiny toy pistol pointed to the sky. She was wearing a fringed suede vest and a feathered headband, pretending to strangle him. They couldn't have been more than seven and ten, we decided.

These were treasures we couldn't thank Terry for properly in a million years, though we tried. Her body stiffened when I hugged her, and I could practically hear Grammy whispering in my ear it was because she was only accustomed to the touch of cats' paws for the last twenty years. We accepted those pictures with a dollop of guilt, promising to visit Terry in Dothan.

There was a tacit understanding Terry wouldn't actually enjoy that any more than we would, and we weren't going to show up anytime soon.

Manny went to take Luz home and Mama and I sat at the table with Wilma, who hadn't really stopped crying all day.

She'd stayed busy cleaning the kitchen and forcing Cool Whip containers of food onto people as they left.

Now it was just the three people who'd loved Verna Willis the most, the ones who'd carry The Sparrow in our hearts from this day on. Mama glanced at me, exhausted and probably wondering when Wilma might make her way home. Saying goodbye to her would be really tough, the ruins comforting the ruins.

Wilma said, "I know y'all need to get some rest," dabbing her eye with a ravaged ball of Kleenex. "I'm just going to miss her so much, and when I walk out that door it's going to feel so final."

Mama reached across the table and held her hand. "You were a wonderful friend to her, and she knew how much you loved her."

Wilma turned her eyes upward. "She knows, I am sure of it. She's joined that distant Creek grandmother, exactly like she told Verna she would. Of course, when she didn't pass on in that hospital in Oklahoma, she kinda thought..." Wilma saw the look that passed between us and stopped, stricken. "She didn't tell y'all about the dream?"

"Well," I said, "she told us, but she didn't say anything about *joining* her."

Wilma's white brows knitted together in a frown. "The grandmother or whoever she was told her three things—"

"Two things," I interrupted.

Wilma considered that and nodded, closing her eyes with a sigh. "I'm so sorry. I shouldn't have never mentioned that part to y'all. Verna probably didn't want you to know."

"Know what?" Mama leaned forward and stared at Wilma.

"Oh, it's silly. You know how she was with her stories and all." Wilma dabbed at her eye again, stalling. "She didn't want to worry y'all, I guess, but the grandmother told Verna she'd be joining her, forever, after she visited the place near the other Eufaula, which y'all know is Oklahoma—"

All I could manage was, *"What?"*

"Honey," Wilma patted my hand, "She didn't pay that part no mind because she didn't die in Oklahoma, in that hospital. She thought that meant she was gonna be fine." She choked a little on the last word. "I'm so sorry I told y'all. I thought you knew. Oh, lord, I'm sorry. Lisa, Skye, I shouldn't never have said anything about it."

Mama and I sat speechless until Wilma stood to go. We hugged her goodbye as she apologized again and again.

Mama tipped Wilma's chin up with her finger. "Listen to me. It wouldn't have made any difference if she'd told us that. Mom thought she was fine, and we did, too. No one knew what was going to happen, Wilma. It wouldn't have changed anything."

Wilma nodded and climbed down the cement steps from the door. We watched her walk to her house way down the street, making sure she was home safe.

Then, without a word between us, Mama and I silently agreed we just couldn't discuss what we'd heard. I went to my room, and my mother collapsed on the couch to wait for Manny to get back.

Mama went back to work the day after the service, insisting she had to stay busy. She waited on customers morning and night as though nothing in her life had changed.

One afternoon I heard her come home after her Huddle House shift and throw her keys on the table. I was in my room, re-reading passages of a book I'd tried to get lost in.

That was when the screaming started. Mama was on the ancient phone in the kitchen. "He *killed* her!" she yelled into the receiver. "You tell him he killed *my mother!* It was *his* selfishness, his refusal to be a man that led to all of this! He didn't even have the decency to acknowledge his own daughter!"

I stood four feet away and could hear a man's voice responding, trying to get a word in. Mama yelled on. "He's responsible...he and that shitty wife of his...Pete did this, it's all on him...she never hurt anyone in her *life*..." she sputtered into sobs and leaned back against the counter, throwing the phone to the floor along with Gerald Davidson's business card.

I reached out to take her in my arms. "Mama," I whispered, "It's okay. We'll get through this together. We just need some time." I swiped at my tears and hers, too.

Mama shook her head. "Not really," she sniffed. "Wait here. There's something I want to give you." I sat down and watched her walk to Grammy's room.

Mama returned with a something wrapped in white tissue paper. "She was saving it for your birthday. She told me if anything 'happened' to her, I should give it to you." Mama placed it in front of me, her hand shaking. "You know all those months she was in her room, supposedly sewing for Luz? She was secretly working on this."

I unfolded the tissue to reveal a square picture embroidered in Grammy's perfectly stitched petit point. I could instantly recognize the old red brick church we'd visited in Africatown and the massive green oak that towered in front of it.

Mama pointed at the tree. "Do you see the little brown bird perched in the branches? She wanted me to tell you that's her. That's your Sparrow."

I ran my fingertips over the stitches and couldn't answer Mama. I couldn't breathe.

Thirty

QUEENSTOWN, NEW ZEALAND

Pete spent his first few days in the rented apartment, emerging to walk downtown and scavenge for pizza or burgers. The liquor store and supermarket were within easy reach, too, offering New Zealand's version of "American" products like Pulled Pork Potato Chips. Pete bought them to make fun of and soon became addicted to a bag a day, usually consumed with beer as he sat in front of the fireplace and tracked boats crossing Lake Wakatipu at sunset.

There was no denying the beauty of the place. On Day Four he veered off his usual food and beverage path into a waterfront park and watched black swans glide in front of the fairy-tale backdrop of the Remarkable Mountains, their peaks snowy even in the Southern Hemisphere's spring. The next morning he explored the waterfront's business district and tossed three five-dollar notes into the guitar case of an old man singing "Ring of Fire" accompanied by an enormous, shaggy, black and white dog howling along to selected verses. He went to the famous Fergburger for his third "Big Al": almost a pound of New Zealand beef on a bun with bacon, cheese, onions, aioli and other heavenly things Pete considered worthy of a twenty-minute jostle with fellow tourists to receive. The place was so crowded, most people ended up eating on an outdoor bench or standing on the sidewalk. He stifled laughter as a pimply kid with a New York accent dropped his prized burger when a vicious street pigeon mugged him for a French fry.

Then Pete ambled slowly back to the apartment and took his afternoon nap, curled up with the fake fur blanket thoughtfully provided by management.

That evening he turned sideways in front of the sliding glass door and accidentally glimpsed his belly. This kicked off a worrying spree about his health, with Pete's doctor's admonitions ringing in his ears about weight loss, nutrition, exercise, preventing another stroke, partial paralysis, possible brain damage, and the use of the word "vegetable" in two ways Pete didn't care for at all.

At that point, Pete slumped into the soft couch and closed his eyes. The truth rushed at him like a fly ball: no matter where he went, there he was: the same guy who did nothing but eat, drink, and be dreary. He could go to New Zealand or Iceland or Morocco—his marriage would still be over and his business in a nosedive. That old lady would still have died, finally pushing him onto a plane and out of the country. But what good had his traveling accomplished? Nothing changed. He might as well be in his recliner, clutching a bottle of scotch.

Pete sighed and pinched his nose, frowning. Gerry had given him printouts of local tours and attractions, which Pete hastily folded into a corner of his suitcase and forgot. Now, he walked the five polished oak steps to his bedroom loft and dug them out.

Lord of the Rings minivan tour to Glenorchy, featuring filming locations. Bungy jumping from Kawarau Bridge, the historic home of the "sport" (cute joke, Gerry). Parasailing on Lake Wakatipu (same). Day cruise on Milford Sound. Skyline gondola to Ben Lomond Mountain's peak for a view of the city. Walking trails. Day cruise on Doubtful Sound.

What the hell was a sound, anyway?

He'd promised Gerry he'd do at least a few. Pete reached for the phone and dialed the numbers for the ones that would pick him up by the apartment and allow him to stay seated throughout. Maybe there would be beer at the top of the mountain peak to accompany the view. Maybe he'd see some good stuff along with where Frodo and Bimbo posed and considered their next quests.

Pete climbed into the Glenorchy tour minivan the next afternoon still slightly buzzed from his lunch beer. The driver was a diminutive white-haired man named Ian, who told Pete and his fellow passengers he'd been born in Queenstown and promised them the best stops for local scenery as well as the Lord of the Rings filming locations. He added the tour would culminate in "tea" in the woods and they'd all be allowed to try on their choice of Hobbit capes or Gandalf's gray, hooded cloak. Pete began to scream inwardly before they pulled away from the curb.

Worse, the young boy next to him clapped loudly and yelled, "Hobbits, Mom!" to the smiling, pony-tailed woman in the row behind him. Pete pinpointed his accent to Georgia, and not the Soviet kind that would make the kid leave him alone.

"I knowwww, honey," the mom drawled. "This is so exciting!" She caught Pete's face in the rearview mirror and added, "Let's be quiet so we can hear what Mr. Ian tells us."

Pete tuned out the driver's chatter and stared out the window. The minivan wound its way upward, providing a glimpse of the same water Pete spent his afternoons by—only this view showed the length and narrowness of the glacial lake, a huge, unusually cut sapphire glowing in the afternoon sun. Ian was talking about how the lake had doubled for Loch Ness in some movie because their features were similar. The kid's eyes widened and Pete could tell he was about to ask about a monster. He couldn't get a word in, though, and his mother reached over and gently squeezed his shoulder, whispering for him to listen.

Ian announced a stop, pulling over to allow his passengers to stretch their legs. He asked the group to gather around him, waving his arm at the Remarkables' peaks in the distance. "You all may know these as the Misty Mountains," Ian grinned at the little boy. "Do you remember them from the movies?"

Pete wandered a short distance away to look at a creek and the path it wove toward Queenstown. The landscape was uneven, roughly carved, and it cradled tufts of short, puffy bushes and scattered trees in its reddish soil. The light was hitting them in such a way everything looked pastel; Pete saw pinks and pale greens and the most delicate blues far into the horizon. He heard Ian approaching him from behind, having dismissed the others for a few minutes of exploration.

"You're Mr. Garfield, right?" Ian looked at his passenger list on a clipboard.

"Yeah, call me Otis," Pete responded.

"Ah, all right." Ian looked Pete up and down, taking in his six-and-a-half feet of height. "I think you'd make a great Gandalf if you might put the cloak on for that kid and let me get some photos of the two of you in costume. If you wouldn't mind, of course."

Pete squinted at the boy who was busy picking up rocks and showing his mother. "Why don't you let his father do it? Surely that would be much better."

"He doesn't have one along," Ian said. "I think that's why they're on this trip. But I'll certainly understand if you don't want to do it." Ian smiled politely at Pete. He turned and whistled loudly. "Everyone back into the van in five more minutes, please. We have much more to see." Ian went to stand and wait for the group to board.

Pete stayed where he was, examining the water-carved ridges running at different heights around the creek. He followed the others when it was time, catching a phrase or two of French from the middle-aged couple in front of him. Ian offered his hand to help the woman up and she thanked him in heavily accented English. The woman and her two kids were back where they'd been before, allowing Pete to notice there was no man seated behind him as he'd thought. They stared openly at Pete as he ducked his head and squeezed into the minivan. He hoped it was because of his height and not a news report somewhere. It wasn't unusual for his size to both frighten and fascinate small children.

"My name is Colin," the boy told him as he fastened his seat belt. "We live in Alpharetta. I'm in second grade. My sister is Lucy. She doesn't talk much because she's only twenty-seven months old." The kid jerked his thumb behind him and Pete rolled his eyes, longing to respond that he was somewhere around six hundred months old.

Instead he said, "My name is Mr. Garfield. Nice to meet you." Then he turned his head and stared out the window, shutting Colin down as effectively as a traffic cop holding up a palm to a Buick.

The next stop was a still, cerulean lake surrounded on three sides by mountains. The sun was directly opposite the group and drew a perfectly straight, sparking white line across the water to where they stood. Pete watched the young mom squat down next to her children and try a selfie. Middle-aged Guy, whom Pete had decided to be Canadian in origin, walked over and offered to get a pic of them with the lake. The mother thanked him with a genuine smile. Pete noticed her prettiness for the first time, her blonde-and-blue-eyed Southern beauty queen pedigree trailing her like silver pixie dust as she led her kids back to the group. She stood behind her children, one hand in her tiny daughter's hair, absently curling Lucy's butter-colored ringlets around one finger. Lucy glanced toward Pete, quickly looking away when he made eye contact.

Ian began another five-minute Lord of the Rings monologue, droning on with Aragorn this and Elvish that. Pete stared off at the mountain peaks surrounding Queenstown, longing for his customary nap. Maybe he could nod off in the van.

He saw the young mom kneeling to whisper to the kids before they re-boarded. Pete was pretty sure they stared at him because they were being told to leave the big man alone.

Good.

Ian drove a mile or two and pointed out the site of a giant, super-eco-friendly development called Camp Glenorchy, created by an American tech billionaire and his wife. They'd taken a former campground and made it into permanent dwellings for some, a "holiday" (Pete's brain translated "vacation") spot for others. Pete caught words like "self-sustaining" and "solar panels" and "the efficiency of a flower, with seven petals of focus", all of which interested him as much as a Hobbit's choice of underwear. He closed his eyes and ears, managing to snooze with his head against the trembling van window.

He woke to Colin poking him in the arm. The kid was trying to alert him they were supposed to exit the van. He pointed at the open door next to him, patting Pete's sleeve. Pete took in several things at once: the mom and little sister watching him expectantly, as they couldn't move unless he did, the soft darkness that surrounded them, the enormous tree canopy shading the clearing Ian had parked in, which appeared to a small niche carved out of Hobbity forest.

"Sorry," he mumbled. "I must have dozed off." Colin didn't try to hide his exasperation as Pete moved to the exit, his joints stiff and his expression sour.

Ian laid out his late-afternoon "tea" on a giant tree stump blanketed by a brown cloth. There were Styrofoam cups (did the eco-Americans know about this?) next to a thermos of Earl Grey, sweeteners and cream in matching Styrofoam cups, slices of some dark, fruity bread on a paper plate, plastic spoons, and napkins. Ian was looking up into the pale light that filtered through, talking about the primeval forest. Pete had never experienced anything like the damp-cool, ancient feel of the place. Heavy green moss grew everywhere, bright red mushrooms sprouted on the forest floor, and there were probably enchanted squirrels waiting to serve refreshments.

Pete took his cup of tea from Ian and stirred in as much sugar as he could. He clutched his mystery-fruit bread in a napkin and moved off to the side of the tour group, whom Ian held in rapt attention as he began talking about the tangled logistics of filming backdrops in this remote location and the many months of work required to make it feasible. When he finished, he informed them they'd try on Lord of the Rings costumes after eating. "And we have someone perfectly suited to don this…" he held up a long, matted-looking white wig, "…and this." Ian pulled a floppy gray wizard's hat from a bag.

All of them turned to Pete in unison. He smiled as authentically as possible and shook his head, waving at the Canadian guy. "I'm sure Mr., uh, Mr."

"Francois", the Canadian interrupted. "And no, monsieur, you must be the one for Gandalf. The children would love to see this, no?" He nodded to Colin and Lucy, whose shining eyes were locked on Pete. Pete did his damnedest not to glare at Ian in front of his tour group, but mentally deducted ten dollars from the tip he'd planned to give him.

"Sure, sure, I'll do it," he told them. "Just let me finish my raisin bread—" Pete held his napkin at arm's length and squinted at the thing he was supposed to eat.

"It's fig bread baked with molasses," Ian supplied. "My wife made it this morning."

"Delicious," Pete said after a nibble. He did not mean it. The Kiwis had yet to learn to sweeten things enough for Southern American sweet-tea-level taste buds. He noticed the Georgia contingent wasn't too enthusiastic, either.

He wiped his hands with the tiny paper napkin, impossibly sticky after eating something so devoid of flavor. Ian asked the rest of the group to excuse them and led Pete behind an enormous tree.

"Might you, umm…" Ian inclined his own head to show Pete he needed him to bend downward. He tugged the wig on before Pete had time to ponder how many scalps had preceded his, then placed the hat atop it. He put the gray cloak around Pete's massive shoulders and stepped back to admire his handiwork. "You look perfect," he assured Pete.

"Are you ready?" Ian called to the group.

"We are!" they chimed back.

Pete stepped around the tree to find they were all wearing plain brown Hobbit cloaks, perfectly dwarfed by his size. They applauded, and he removed the hat with a flourish and bowed, holding the wig in place with his free hand. He didn't have the faintest idea what Gandalf would do or say, so he focused on smiling at the children and replacing the hat. Within seconds Colin and Lucy were by his side, grinning for photos their mother would surely Instagram as soon as they returned to civilization. The Canadians joined him for more photos, and finally, Ian took several of the pretty mom and her kids with Gandalf's long arms around them.

Pete declined several offers to have photos taken for his own keepsakes, knowing he'd live a much better life without seeing himself in a tangled white wig.

Pete's head itched, and he handed the clump of dangling hair back to Ian with no small amount of irritation. He climbed into the van and resumed staring out the window, but he could feel the children's eyes on him all the way back to the apartment. Ian stopped the van and slid the door open so Pete could climb out. He stepped down and heard the mom yell, "Wait a minute, Mr. Garfield, please!"

All two feet of Lucy stepped toward the edge of the van's open door, still attached to her mother's hand. The crumbs of whatever she'd been eating still clung to her blue-and-white striped dress, Pete noted. Lucy moved away from her mom and reached her dimpled arms out to hug Pete. He bent down and felt her lips brush his cheek.

"Thank you," Lucy whispered near his ear at a loud, toddler volume. He could smell traces of Cheerios as she pulled away, disappearing into the van. Pete watched until the taillights blended into Queenstown's heavy traffic, the reds all blurring into a watery kaleidoscope image before he blinked.

The gondola ride to Ben Lomond's peak would have been less nauseating without the Fergburger Pete wolfed down while waiting in line. He ignored the horde of Americans sampling the gigantic, tourist-trap buffet at the top. He followed a group of giggling women down a corridor and accidentally discovered large, colorful mosaics hanging on the wall. One was the famous American Gothic couple by Grant Wood. Another was some Hobbit he couldn't identify. It took Pete a minute to realize they were composed of thousands of jellybeans, apparently a partnership with a candy sponsor. The Hobbit piece had a placard proclaiming it "Lord of the Beans."

Past these was an observation deck. Pete leaned on the railing and breathed in the view of Queenstown and the mountains surrounding her. He stayed there for well over an hour, watching tiny cars navigate the streets he'd been walking daily. He pressed a button to listen to a recorded version of local history; the Maori traveled here to collect jade long before white settlers came. The area was perfectly suited to rural sheep farming, and the British prospered alongside the Maori, mostly peacefully through a series of agreements between their leaders. All that changed dramatically with the discovery of gold nearby and the subsequent rush. Queenstown's first, bustling hotel was a former wool shed renovated to accommodate the influx of miners looking to get rich.

What Pete was looking at now was worth far more than gold. The gorgeous views brought tourists from all over the world. Of course, he thought to himself, they'd also made it almost impossible for natives to afford houses here. He'd overheard a conversation between two local ladies in the supermarket. One claimed she couldn't buy a decent house in Queenstown for less than a million dollars. She was currently living in a trailer, miles from the city.

New Zealand dollars, of course, but still mighty expensive. Tourism had definitely extracted a price. He'd seen plenty of that. Same story, different place.

Just like Pete.

The entire city was bathed in crimson, pink, and orange the next morning as Pete waited for an early tour bus to Doubtful Sound. It was the one thing Gerry said he had to do, no matter what. The sunrise was so vivid Pete could practically taste it along with his coffee.

The private coach hissed to a stop at precisely 5:49 a.m. as advertised. Pete made his way to the opened doors and climbed aboard to find himself alone with a large, sixty-ish lady driver. Her auburn hair was piled into a messy bun; her dark blue uniform jacket slightly strained by her belly. He sat directly behind her to avoid seeming impolite.

"You, Mr. Garfield?" she asked, and Pete nodded and handed her his phone to show his e-ticket. She gave it back with a big grin. "I'm Gillian," she announced. "I'm guessing you're terrified you'll be the only one on this big old bus with me. Don't worry. We're picking up heaps of folks. Bus will be chocka before you know it." Gillian got up and stretched her arms behind her head, then placed her hands on her hips. She stood facing backward until another bus blared its horn behind them. She slammed her sizeable body into the driver's seat with a thud. "Keep yer bloody knickers on, Earl, I'm movin'!" she screamed into the rearview mirror. Her face immediately settled back into an easy smile as she guided the bus onto the road. "You all right this morning, Mr. Garfield?"

It took Pete a minute because this Gillian person had the strongest accent he'd heard since arriving in New Zealand, spoken at a rapid-fire pace. Hers was that strange blend of

British pronunciation and Aussie-like twang Pete heard here. "Oh, yeah, I'm fine, thanks."

"I'm a box of fluffies today, too." Gillian winked at him in the rearview mirror and Pete wondered if he'd need Google Translate to get through the day.

Their first stop was to pick up a smiling Asian woman in her twenties who wore a jacket matching Gillian's. She squeezed Gillian's shoulder as she climbed aboard, taking the seat in front opposite him. "Hi, I'm Ming," she said, offering her hand.

Pete shook her hand gently and was surprised by the grip she returned. He wondered why they needed a back-up driver. "Otis Garfield," he said. "Nice to meet you." Pete turned his head to the window reflexively, unaccustomed to conversations with anyone at this early hour that he didn't initiate and direct.

Gillian announced, "Ming will be conducting a separate tour on the boat for a group of Chinese tourists." Pete must have failed to control his grimace, because she added, "Don't worry, you'll have your own hosts and tour guide. All in the Queen's English, or as near as we Kiwis get."

Ten stops later, they had a full load of Chinese, American, and British tourists. Gillian took her microphone and gave everyone a second welcome. She said a few words about Lake Wakatipu as they passed it. "The lot of ya still look like you're asleep," she joked, "so I'm not going to talk much about what you're seeing until we get closer to our destination. We'll be stopping at a store where you can get takeaways if you're hungry, and you'll get to meet some lovely alpacas there, too. In the meantime, if you have any questions, just let us know. You're in for a beautiful day, I can promise you that. Doubtful Sound is the most special place in all of New Zealand, and you'll not ever forget it." She handed the microphone to Ming, who repeated it all in Mandarin or improvised her own presentation. Pete had no idea.

He closed his eyes for a moment, glad for the empty seat next to him. No one plops down next to a man his size unless absolutely necessary. Occasionally Gillian would point out sheep farms or native vegetation, but the perennially smiling Ming didn't translate afterward.

He noticed several herds of deer standing and staring at the passing vehicles instead of the customary leaping in front of them back home. "Gillian," he asked, "What's up with all the deer?"

She took the microphone and informed the entire group Mr. Garfield had asked about the deer they were seeing, and she was glad he brought it up. "Red deer were introduced to New Zealand in the nineteenth century and their population quickly exploded, even with all the hunting for sport. Soon they were wreaking havoc on crops everywhere. They tried all sorts of methods to cull them, but weren't very successful. The idea of domesticating the deer and farming venison took hold. We're very proud of our country's pioneering that, and all the improvements we've introduced over the years." Gillian glanced at the group in her mirror and chuckled. "In the early days, men were dropping from helicopters onto their backs to capture them for breeding. That was as effective as you might imagine, eh? Now they're raising them crossed with elk, and that's why they're so large and meaty and delicious. It's an important industry in New Zealand. Thank you for your question, Mr. Garfield." Gillian passed the microphone to Ming and maneuvered around a slow-moving car. Pete heard her muttering about a "blimmin' Sunday driver" as she shook her head and smacked the steering wheel with the heel of her hand.

The "store" Gillian had mentioned had a full-blown restaurant built in. Pete bought a large coffee and a bacon and egg hand pie, savoring every bite and wishing he could take one to McDonald's to copy. He watched his fellow tourists crowd around a group of alpacas leaning over the fence behind the parking lot, their fuzzy faces begging for handouts. He saw one of the Chinese women feed one an entire muffin, piece by piece. Not a bad gig for an alpaca, Pete thought.

Closer to their destination was one last stop, a paved pull-off Gillian chose after mysteriously announcing she wanted to show them something "unique." They filed out of the bus and stood around expectantly for a minute until three huge green birds hopped out of the woods and into the crowd, causing a couple of women to shriek.

"These are kea, wild parrots," Gillian nodded at one perched on the bus's side mirror. "We also call them the 'clowns of the mountains' because they're very smart and get into all sorts of mischief. That one on the mirror would peck all the rubber off around the windshield if I let him."

Everyone turned toward a scream from one of the American girls. She'd placed her backpack on the ground to look around and a kea was perched on it. He'd already partially opened the zipper and was tugging enthusiastically at a bag of candy. Gillian ran toward it, clapping her hands until the bird reluctantly hopped off. Pete would have sworn it glared at her.

Now there were at least ten keas gathered around, eyeing the tourists. One of the largest flew to Pete's shoe and began untying it with his beak. Pete forced himself to stand still long enough to see what the thing would do next. He laughed along with everyone else as the bird completed his mission on the first Nike and moved onto the second, the entire group watching and videoing the scene. "Will he try to take 'em off?" Pete asked Gillian.

"Most likely, Mr. Garfield, but we haven't time for him to work it out." Gillian swatted at the kea and threw a piece of toast she'd saved to distract him. "We need to get on now or we'll be late."

They pulled away with two keas on the roof of the bus, "surfing" until Gillian reached a high enough speed to make them fly off.

The man sitting behind Pete tapped his shoulder. "You sound like you're from Texas, am I right?" He leaned his face around Pete's seat.

"No," Pete responded. "I've never been to Texas." He stared pointedly out the window, hoping the man would take the hint.

"My wife and I, we're on a twentieth anniversary trip. My name's Bill and hers is Jeannie. We live in West Palm Beach."

Pete's dull, "Uh-huh" was enough to make Bill sit back and take his wife's hand, wondering what the hell was wrong with the big guy in the front row.

The bus unloaded onto a boat that crossed Lake Manapouri to yet another bus that carried the group to the small ship they'd take into the remote Doubtful Sound. The boat's main cabin was enclosed in glass, so Pete immediately settled into a seat. His fellow tourists crowded the deck, frantically selfie-ing with all the New Zealand scenery they could. Ming led her Chinese contingent to the bow to tell them all about the place. Gillian called everyone else into the cabin and introduced their guide as the ship left the dock.

Pete tuned out most of what the guide, Benjamin, told them. He caught a bit about the body of water actually being a fiord, not technically a sound, as glacial as any *fjord* in Norway. Pete was more absorbed in the dramatic rock cliffs running along both sides of the channel, towering hundreds of feet above them. Waterfalls were everywhere, many of them huge and thunderous. They passed islands of all sizes, some dotted with trees and some purely rock. Pete spotted a large number of fur seals squawking at the boat. Dolphins leapt on the starboard side and in their wake, too. He recognized a massive albatross circling nearby. It was all beautiful, and he was glad he could observe it without wind, sea spray, and people. They were outside with Benjamin the guide, running back and forth, videoing and taking pictures. Gillian was probably belowdecks, hanging out with friends she saw every day.

The ship took a leisurely route all the way into the Tasmin Sea and a man on the intercom announced this was where Captain Cook had observed the rocky entrance to the sound and pronounced its successful navigation "doubtful." Pete stood at that point and looked back where they'd been, startled by the vision: Doubtful Sound was framed by two gigantic, ominous gray rock formations like something from one of those Hobbit movies. They looked like skyscrapers. Further into the sound, Pete saw a surreal arrangement of mound shapes, each an island they'd passed, all lit in such a way their shades varied from palest silver to pewter to steel gray. The largest was dead center and midnight black, with all the others gathered around it like silent attendants. All were shrouded in mist.

Even Pete was moved to take some pictures with his phone, hurrying to the stern to jostle for position. He took his place easily, his size causing others to part automatically and make room. No one said a word to the quiet man who'd kept to himself in the cabin.

The boat turned around and maneuvered back into Doubtful Sound with Pete still among the crowd, spotting dolphins and hoping for whales. When they'd been cruising for about ten minutes, they pulled up next to an island bearing a narrow waterfall cascading at least a hundred feet.

The captain announced: "Ladies and gentlemen, I'm asking each of you to put away your cameras and phones for a few minutes and simply experience what surrounds you. Most of it is untouched by man for tens of thousands of years. Please observe some silent moments and take in what nature offers you here. It's unlike anything else in the world." Pete heard the engines shut down, immediately ushering complete silence apart from the water falling in the distance. No one moved. They barely breathed.

Pete leaned forward across the railing. Perfect, pin-drop quiet and the beauty of all that surrounded them moved everyone in different ways, but they all felt a meditative peace settling in their hearts. No one wanted to move or speak and break the spell.

The lady next to Pete clasped her hands under her chin and bowed her white head in prayer. The young man on his other side ran his fingertips up and down the railing, staring at the waterfall.

Pete closed his eyes and felt the stillness of millions of years held in the rocks around him. At some point in the utter quiet he caught himself rubbing the stubbly cheek where a tiny girl had given him a whisper of a kiss. Tears rolled down his face. He didn't even try to wipe them away. *I have a daughter. I have a beautiful, smart, kind daughter and I have to find a way to apologize to her. I have to tell her how sorry I am; I have to beg her forgiveness. That is all that matters in this world.*

Pete found Gillian at his elbow when the captain had the engines restarted, their diesel *clang* shattering the world they'd stepped into. "Are you all right, Mr. Garfield?"

He swiped at his tears, awkward and embarrassed. Pete took a deep breath and watched the island and its pristine waterfall recede into the distance. "I will be, Gillian. I will be."

Thirty-one

EUFAULA, ALABAMA

You lose someone a thousand times a day in the beginning, when you sip your coffee and turn to tell her a joke, when she doesn't remind you to take your umbrella, when she isn't there to ask if you'd like to try antelope for dinner.

All thousand are accompanied by a slight tightening of the band around your chest. With time, the band loosens and is replaced by a sharp stab.

I was still waiting for the stabbing to dull two-and-a-half weeks later. I'd resumed lunch and dinner shifts at the restaurant and used my free time to write thank-you notes. I'd given up on expressing our gratitude properly to Wilma, who continued to appear at our door with teary smiles and chicken casserole, fond memories and banana bread, hugs and beef stew.

"You should open a restaurant and call it 'The Comfort Café'," Mama told her one afternoon. "You can feel the love in every bite, Wilma, and I don't know what we'd do without you." She watched the older lady walk down the street, Wilma's shoulders hunched more than usual in her red floral housedress. Mama added the disposable foil pan she'd left behind to four others in the refrigerator. "I don't know how to tell her we have more than we can ever eat, Skye. I don't have the heart to do it."

"Just let her work through her Southern Lady Comfort Process, Mama. It makes her feel better. We can always share some of this with Manny and Luz. I'm sure they get tired of cooking."

Mama shoved casseroles together in the fridge with an aluminum crackle and screech, trying to fit the latest in. "I already *have*. If there were a homeless shelter around here, I'd donate a dish or two…"

"… except Wilma would hear about it within ten minutes and be devastated," I finished. "It's the joy of small-town living."

Mama ran her hand through her hair and collapsed into a kitchen chair. "How are you doing, Skye?"

"I'm okay. I miss her all the time, just like you. It's not getting any easier." I eyed Mama from the couch, trying to gauge her mood. I took a deep breath and exhaled my question. "But I want to ask you something. Are you and Manny still getting married in two months?"

I could tell she'd been dreading the subject by the way she looked at the ceiling, at anything but me. "Yes, we talked about it and we're not putting it off. Manny's ready to begin our life together and lord knows I need a fresh start. So do you, Skye."

I nodded, trying to keep the tears from my eyes. "So, you'll move to Manny's and I'll be here alone."

"Well…we have an idea, Skye." Mama smiled and moved to sit by me. "The insurance money Mom left is all going to you. And if you want to keep living here, you'll be able to afford it easily for a long time. But Manny and I want you to know we understand if you want to move somewhere else. Somewhere new."

I raised my eyebrows. "Okay. It's a little weird to know you've been discussing this without me."

Mama sighed. "Only because I know this house is full of Mom, Skye. She's everywhere you look. I'm not sure that'll be good for you once I move out."

"So what, exactly," I frowned, "am I supposed to do? Where do I go? What happens to Grammy's house?"

"We can sell the house and you and I would divide the money." Mama hesitated and looked at the hands clasped in her lap. "And I know a buyer."

My eyebrows shot to the ceiling. "Yeah? Who might that be?"

"Luz. She knows the house and wants to live someplace else once I marry Precious Son." Mama's eyes rounded with sarcasm. She added, "I thought maybe we could sell to her."

I clapped my hands together. "And if I want to stay here, I can pay rent to the mother-in-law you'll dump. Perfect, Mama." I stood to walk away and she pulled me back down.

"Don't be ridiculous. You'd have the money to start over wherever you want, Skye. What comes next is up to you. You can breathe and explore your options anywhere you choose. But Manny and I both think the military is the absolute wrong choice, for the record." She paused to brush a speck of lint off her black pants. "You're capable of doing anything you want, honey. And you'll have what you need for tuition… Manny thought you might want to major in Hospitality at Auburn."

I stared at her. "Please don't start that again. College is not for me. And I am surely not the only millennial you know trying to figure out what to do with her life, Mama."

She stood and walked to the window, pulling the sheer white curtain back. "You're the only one I know with the brains and attitude to accomplish whatever goal you set, plus a cushion to live on while you pursue it. Skye, waitressing in Eufaula is not the life I want for you."

"It's been good enough for Lisa Willis," I shot back.

Mama spun around and planted her hands on her hips. "I had a baby. I didn't have a lot of options at the time." She stood glaring at me for a few seconds.

"So there we are again. Why didn't you just name me 'Burden', 'Burdy' for short?"

"Enough dramatics, Hannah Skye Willis. You know damn well I've loved you every day of your life. How much reassurance do you need, Skye, to give up the tortured adolescent act? You're a grown woman!" Mama shook her head and collapsed into the chair opposite me, her face a tangle of anger and frustration.

"Sorry, I guess having a fake father followed by a disowning daddy has had a lingering effect on my self-esteem."

Mama grabbed my arm and shook it a little. "Enough. You've been using that excuse not to live your life, Skye, and it's well past its expiration date. And as much as I loved your grandmother, she coddled you and did all she could to keep you here."

"Because she actually wanted me around," I aimed the comment like a dart at her.

"That's not fair," Mama leveled her eyes with mine. "I love you more than anything on this earth, Skye, and I never want to be away from you. All I'm trying to say is, you can do better. And I want better for you, honey."

"This is all Manny. You never talked to me this way before Manny." I slammed my hand on the couch and stood, my eyes full of angry tears.

"Manny didn't even want me to have this conversation with you," she said quietly. "He said I should give you time and not mention selling the house or anything else."

I crossed to the table and grabbed my keys. "Tell him I said thank you for thinking of me. Obviously, you're not." I slammed the door in my wake and the car door, too, for added effect.

I spotted a forgotten slab of aging banana bread intended for yesterday's snack in the passenger seat. I took that little piece of Wilma's grief to the lake and fed some of it to the ducks and geese, most of whom followed me around the footpath by the water's edge afterward. They gave up and slipped back into the lake as I hiked toward the sunset and back. It was after dark when I crept into the house, tiptoeing by the light under Mama's door to avoid another conversation. I sprawled on my bed and reached for a book, the one place I could hide from the world.

Mama and I avoided each other for the next few days, nodding at one another in passing at the house and communicating with as few words as possible at work.

I had never been so miserable, so lost, in my life. It took everything I had to get out of bed each day.

On Sunday morning I rolled over and hugged a pillow to myself, willing my mind back into a dream about flying. I'd been soaring over Lake Eufaula, trying to see something sparkling in the tall grass along its shore.

Instead, I was wide awake and angrily blinking at the sunshine filtering through the blinds. I reached for my bottled water and sent a stack of books thudding to the floor. There was a printout Grammy had made about Horseshoe Bend sitting under my former book pile, "SKYE" scrawled in blue ink at the top of the first page. We'd discovered it in her bedroom among hundreds of pages she printed, most of them Creek history or sewing-related.

I got out of bed and trudged to the kitchen, carrying the papers Grammy stapled together. Mama was already off with Manny somewhere and the house was pin-drop quiet. I could do anything, go anywhere.

How boring could Horseshoe Bend be? It was, at least, a destination. I gobbled down cold pasta from Wilma's latest delivery and put the address in my phone, hoping to find something, anything, that might make me feel connected to my grandmother.

The sides of the highway became leafy-cool and green as it twisted toward Horseshoe Bend. I drove in and followed the paved car path, stopping at each informational sign to read about the battle. The park was dominated by the Tallapoosa River, the vehicle that delivered slaughter to the Creek camped there. Grammy's description was vivid in my mind. I could practically see the water running red.

Displays here seemed more dedicated to the sacrifice of the Federal troops and Allied Creek who aided them than remembrance of the Native Americans fighting to defend their freedom. Andrew Jackson ensured his future political career with this victory over the "Indians." My stomach began to clench more with every sign I read, so I began ignoring them and concentrating on the squirrels hopping around me, the babbling of the water, the remains of a massive former covered bridge in the distance. Its stone foundations still stood high above the river, silent witnesses to history, whispering things I couldn't decipher.

Instead of feeling closer to Sparrow, there was only sadness. I was the only visitor in the park aside from two old men wearing Vietnam veteran caps. They nodded and smiled politely as we passed each other.

I almost drove past the visitor center. My eyes settled on the bright blue cannon out front, and suddenly I had to ask why they'd painted it such a weird color.

There was a girl about my age behind the counter in a dark green ranger uniform. "Hi, welcome, my name is Chloe. Please let me know if you have any questions." She looked back down at whatever she was reading, her long brown hair swinging forward as she rested her chin on her fist.

"Actually, yes," I pointed at the cannon outside the glass door. "I was wondering why that cannon is painted blue."

Chloe nodded, and I realized she heard this question over and over. "It's an homage to the French, who painted their cannons light blue. You have to remember they were allied with us against the British not long before the battle took place here." She blinked at me expectantly.

"Thank you," I said, and walked over to explore a series of displays, most featuring weapons recovered from the battlefield. I looked at the souvenir section for a few minutes, settling on a refrigerator magnet to remind me I'd come here for my grandmother.

My car sat baking in an unusually hot spring sun. I turned the air conditioner on and sat waiting to cool off, not especially thrilled by the idea of driving home. The Vietnam vets pulled up beside me and headed in to the visitor center. A family with West Virginia plates parked a few spaces down, the mom handing out juice boxes and sending the dad to carry a toddler to the men's room.

I shifted my car into reverse, smiling at the mom and waving. I had to slam on my brakes to avoid a mass of medium-ish children running across the parking lot, a man in a ranger uniform chasing after them and yelling "stop!" His hand was clamped on his head to keep his hat in place. A chubby older lady followed him, clearly upset with her charges. I could see "Macedonia Baptist Church" on all their matching red t-shirts.

I nodded at the lady as she took a shortcut by my car to reach the group, wheezing for breath. She grabbed the hands of the two youngest children, yanking them into place and slowing their run to the visitor center. It was obvious they were being threatened as she glowered over them.

The ranger walked up to her after delivering his part of the group to Chloe, now standing next to the open entrance door. He glanced at my car and waved, apologizing for the wild herd of kids.

It took a moment for my brain to register the dark curls and easy grin of Cullen Leatherwood, who was already walking toward the car, abandoning the tour group to the lady chaperone and fellow ranger.

"You looking for me?" he asked as I rolled my window down.

"No, I came here without any idea you'd be here," I eyed his brass nametag. "I'm guessing you got a job?"

"Something like that." He nodded at the visitor center. "I'm volunteering here. History major, Native American Studies, twenty minutes from Auburn, remember? It's like you entered keywords in your GPS and conjured me."

"Nope. I had no idea you'd be here." I put the car in reverse and began pulling away.

Cullen threw his arms into the air. "We broke up!" he yelled. "If that's anything you care about. And I never lied to you. My cousin went out of his way to make me look bad. I'm not that guy." He shrugged, leaning his head to one side.

I stared at him.

"And you know this uniform is sexy as hell," he added. Cullen patted the baggy green pants and I couldn't help but laugh.

"Come on," he continued. "I have twenty minutes until these Baptist hellions finish their tour. There's a picnic table with our names on it by that oak tree." He waved at it for emphasis.

I closed my eyes and kept my foot on the brake pedal.

"No, seriously, I carved our names into it," he added.

"You did not."

"That is correct. I will not lose my job by defacing park property. I've thought of carving your name somewhere, though." He shook his head and looked into the distance. "Well, *that's* stupid. Okay, what I mean is… I've thought about you. I've wondered how you were doing." He stuffed his hands into the misshapen pockets of his uniform. "Hey, I'm really sorry about your grandmother. I know you loved her. And I hate that I'll never get to meet her. Greg said she was a wonderful lady." He stood there in awkward silence for a minute, then waved at the weathered wood picnic table. "Please, Skye? I'll only be a few minutes."

There was something in the way he said my name that made me park the car and sweep away leaves and acorns to sit waiting for him. The afternoon light drenched the scenery around me in golden syrup, even making the screaming children who emerged half an hour later look angelic.

Later, I would decide it was probably the first time The Sparrow had beamed down a satisfied smile on me.

Thirty-two

DALLAS, TEXAS

Pete entered his six-digit code into the deadbolt lock, turned the key, disarmed the security system, groggily stumbled to his study, and collapsed. He startled awake three hours later, automatically looking for the window displaying Queenstown's lake and mountains. It took several seconds to realize where he was. He surveyed his desk, cluttered with weeks of mail from his assistant, and groaned.

What he wouldn't give for a Fergburger and a fur blanket. Pete forced himself from his recliner and sank into his office chair, sorting through the stacks of envelopes. Some were benign, appeals for contributions or requests for interviews. The loathsome ones, carefully separated into a pile of doom, waved red flags at him about the financial state of PFD Pipelines. He shoved those aside and laced his fingers behind his head. His eye traveled to a large, pale-blue envelope bearing no return address, postmarked Chicago, Illinois about a week ago. Pete slid the letter opener through it, expecting the usual "free" gift from a charity accompanied by a lengthy explanation why his generous contribution would be a proper response to some personalized mailing labels.

His hand began shaking as he realized he was pulling a photo of Kara into view. He placed it on the desk and stared. No note, no nothing, just a polished, professional picture of his wife that could easily appear in *Vogue* magazine. She wore a deep sapphire jumpsuit, belted at the waist, and her hair looked like it was blowing in a gentle breeze. Kara was outdoors, a field of golden wheat behind her and a red barn in the distance. She was slightly leaning against an old wooden ladder (was that supposed to be a metaphor?), looking into the photographer's eyes in a way that made Pete's stomach flip.

Of course, that's what it was designed to do.

He reached back into the envelope for the third time and ran his fingers along its insides, searching for the note Kara would surely have enclosed. Empty.

Pete was horrified to find a tear running down his face, swatting and swiping it away. Something had broken loose in his heart in New Zealand. He'd felt the shift like a physical change, boiling water poured on ice. Pete wasn't sure if he'd rather find the tightness in his chest now came from some damned emotion or a problem that would show in his regularly scheduled stress test in a little less than a month. He pictured Dr. Kailash's smug, vegetarian face greeting him, waving at the treadmill.

He looked longingly at the scotch decanter sitting on a side table. Pete took his cell out and dialed Joseph, whose phone was answered by his annoyed-but-polite girlfriend, Leeka Reynolds.

She'd have Joseph call back in an hour.

Two weeks later Pete mopped the sweat from his forehead as he rolled off the bench, stepping aside for Joseph to take over the barbell. He watched his bodyguard-turned-personal-trainer slide forty additional pounds of weight on each end—a little too nonchalantly to suit Pete—and proceed to lift the bar over his chest like it was made of balsa wood.

Joseph replaced the barbell with a clank and grinned up at his boss. "You're gettin' there," he told him. "Two weeks ago you were lifting like a Girl Scout and eating cookies like one, too."

Pete patted his belly and nodded. "I'm down twelve pounds."

Joseph frowned. "Is that right? I guess we'd better head to the scale and verify." He pointed to the shiny black electronic monolith in the corner of the weight room, which dispensed fates in giant, red numerals for the world to see. Pete glanced around to be sure no one was looking. He wouldn't let anyone but Joseph witness his numbers until he broke two-forty, and that was a good twenty pounds away.

Joseph nodded and Pete stepped down, exhausted from today's workout.

"We still have the elliptical and then a cooldown on the treadmill," Joseph said.

Pete nodded grimly and followed him, watching the younger man's muscles as Joseph flexed and stretched his biceps in a gray LSU t-shirt. Pete had one week until Dr. Kailash's stress test, five weeks until he'd endure the stress test of signing his pipeline company over to a German conglomerate. Bernreuth AG had swiftly maneuvered its way into a hostile takeover of PFD with slightly more finesse than Hitler used in Poland. Pete's entire life had been meetings and workouts and pastel envelopes from Kara, always in a complementary outfit and beautifully arranged to drive spikes into his chest. She still hadn't sent him any accompanying messages, just the overt "look what you're missing" one.

Pete found himself less resistant to the Germans than he'd planned. What began as a hostile takeover had morphed into deliverance. Let some other poor bastards fight the protesters and government interference. Let them analyze and agonize over steel strength, HVL lines, and tanker transport costs. He would walk away with more money than Pete Darling and Otis Garfield combined could ever spend.

He had no idea what would come next. It was as scary and exhilarating as any project he'd ever taken on, this unknown path ahead.

After the stress test, which would surely elicit fawning praise and a clean bill of health from Dr. Kailash (or at least some appreciation for Pete's efforts), he'd continue his search for the woman missing from his life.

The phone number Gerry had recorded when Lisa called was no longer in service. Pete dispatched one of Gerry's investigators, Charlie Harris, to the Eufaula address matching it. Charlie was greeted by a plump, elderly Mexican lady, and his inquiries about Lisa and Skye met with a puzzled look and repeated head shakes punctuated by *"Lo siento, no hablo ingles."* Pete told Charlie to leave her alone after she closed the door in his face; he should locate a translator and go back the following day. Charlie found Rico eating tamales for dinner in a Mexican restaurant after a tip from a local cop. They arranged to meet at Luz's house the following afternoon.

The door opened to reveal a large Rottweiler-looking dog standing at Luz's side. She listened carefully and nodded with a cordial smile. *"Compré esta casa de un agente de bienes raíces. No tengo idea de quiénes son estas personas. Lo siento, soy nuevo en esta ciudad. No puedo ayudarte,"* she rapid-fired back at Rico. Charlie noticed her hand rested on the dog's head, and the dog never took his eyes off the two men.

Rico turned to Charlie. She says, "I bought this house from a real estate agent. I have no idea who these people are. I'm sorry, I am new to this town. I can't help you."

Luz held up a finger, gesturing for them to wait. She returned with fresh cinnamon churros wrapped in white napkins, handing some to each man with a grin. *"Para tu viaje,"* she announced. *For your journey.* She closed the door and turned the deadbolt with a loud, dismissive click.

Charlie noticed the dog push his nose through sheer pink curtains, parting them neatly to stare as they walked away. He paid Rico his hundred dollars and shook the man's hand. He threw his churros onto the passenger seat and was climbing into his car when he spotted a woman in a red housedress standing down the street, clearly watching the scene.

Might as well give her a shot.

Charlie ambled up to Wilma with his hat literally in his hands, turning the faded baseball cap over and over. "Afternoon," he began, smiling and dipping his head at her. Charlie ran a hand through his short blonde hair. "I was wondering if maybe you could help me."

"Hello," Wilma said, her head-to-toe inventory of the stranger clearly visible. "What do you need?"

"My name is Charlie Harris, and I'm trying to locate the former occupants of that house down the street." He gestured behind him. "Do you know the people who lived there?"

Wilma stared at the house. "Are you from around here, Mr. Harris? Your accent doesn't sound familiar."

"No, ma'am, I'm from Dallas. My boss hired me to find a young lady named Skye Willis. Do you know her? Or maybe you know her mother, Lisa? He's a relative of theirs and has lost touch over the years." Charlie attempted to smile with his blue eyes, hoping they might have an effect on the old lady.

Wilma blinked in the sunshine and held her hand like a visor, squinting at Charlie. "I knew Verna a little bit, but she passed away. I didn't know her daughter and granddaughter. Kinda kept to themselves. One day they were gone, and that Luz woman moved in the next afternoon. She's a Mexican lady, you know."

"Yes, ma'am, I spoke with her. Well, with a translator. Seems she doesn't speak English."

"No," Wilma tilted her head to one side, "She sure doesn't. Not a word."

"Do you have any idea where Skye or Lisa may have gone? Is there anyone you know they might have told their plans?"

"No, I can't think of anyone," Wilma said. "I wish I could help you. I'm sorry, Mr. Harris, but I need to get back on inside. It was nice to meet you."

Charlie put his baseball cap back on and tugged it into place. He held out a card to Wilma. "Thank you, ma'am. If you hear about those ladies, would you please let me know?"

"Oh, I sure will." Wilma smiled brightly and went into her house, wishing her hand hadn't shaken so much as he gave her his card. She had no intention of that damned Pete Darling finding Skye, not if she could help it.

She dialed Luz's number as the investigator drove off in his rental car. "You didn't tell them anything, did you?"

"Of course not. You think I want my son's new marriage invaded by that *cabrón?*"

"Good. I'll be down with a chocolate pie to trade you for some of them churpos in a few minutes." Wilma paused. "But you know, Luz, any investigator can find a record of Manny and Lisa's marriage. It's only a matter of time."

"Yes. I'm going to call Manny as soon as we hang up, although he already knows that man is looking for Lisa and Skye. The translator he just brought over was my nephew."

Charlie sat in his car outside Lisa and Manny's house two days later, sipping bottled water and watching a neighbor race a zero-turn mower around his lawn like he thought it was Talladega Superspeedway. The guy made eye contact and nodded every time he did a lap, obviously wondering what the stranger was up to.

He dreaded the call he was about to make to Mr. Darling. Charlie's usual investigations for Mr. Davidson were dry as the Dewey Decimal System and just as straightforward. This "favor" for Mr. Darling was a minefield of the sort of emotional crap he avoided in his personal and professional life; Lisa had cried and yelled at him before closing her front door in his face minutes ago. Charlie just wanted to go home and start chasing down transaction records and contract violations.

He tapped the button on his cell, hoping for voicemail, and was answered on the first ring.

"Did you find her?" Pete said.

"Not yet, Mr. Darling. I've just left the house of her mother, Lisa. She recently got married, and this state is not big on internet access to public records, so it took me a while to track her down." Charlie cleared his throat. "I talked to Lisa for about five minutes, and she's... well, I'd say she's very angry, sir. No need to use the words she asked me to repeat to you."

Pete sighed. "And?"

"She wouldn't tell me where Skye is, only that she doesn't live in Eufaula anymore. She said to tell you her daughter wants absolutely nothing to do with you after the way you treated her in Oklahoma. She added that if you've suddenly started to care about Skye, you can prove it by staying out of her life."

There was no response. "Mr. Darling, you still there?"

"Yeah. I'm still here. Look, Harris, you don't leave Alabama until you find Skye. No more progress reports. Call me when you accomplish that."

"Mr. Darling," Charlie began, "I'll do my best, but you have to understand this isn't a police investigation, and it isn't like you see on TV. I have no bank records, no way to track her activity, and I can't force people to answer my questions." Charlie took a deep breath. "And no one in this town intends to help me locate Skye. They've circled the wagons real tight."

"Then I suggest you get creative, Mr. Harris," Pete hung up before Charlie could say another word.

Thirty-three

HORSESHOE BEND NATIONAL
MILITARY PARK, ALABAMA

Cullen and I sat on the picnic bench that day for exactly nineteen minutes before he had to say goodbye and rejoin his tour group. He told me about his classes, his volunteer shifts as a park ranger, the little girl who threw up on his feet yesterday as he described the Creeks' pitiful lack of food (there were rumors some had eaten undigested corn kernels from animal dung in their desperation), the ninth-graders who affected nonchalance when they heard the history that took place on the very ground where they stood in ripped jeans, passing contraband vape pens or chewing tobacco when they thought they were hidden behind trees. They were his favorites, because watching them start to pay attention was such a victory.

He seemed to know I didn't want to talk much. I told him about missing Grammy and it made me cry, but Cullen was kind enough not to try to comfort me beyond a few words about how sorry he was. He never put his arms around me, he didn't even touch my hand, and I might have fallen to pieces if he had.

What he did offer me, without even realizing, was my future. I began to form a plan; I'd sell the house to Luz and move somewhere near Horseshoe Bend. I'd look into a path to becoming a park ranger. I'd start with volunteering if necessary, because I'd be able to afford it.

It seemed like a perfect way to keep my grandmother with me, to honor her, to let The Sparrow fly even if she was only a whisper of the past.

I sent him back to the visitor center with a perfunctory side-hug. He promised to text me some links to study material, a National Park Service application, and to "keep in touch." Halfway there he turned around and blew me a kiss, cocky and confident and gorgeous in the dappled light under an oak canopy.

Weeks later, I scanned the faces of thirty-two fifth-graders who were politely attentive to my account of the events leading to the Battle of Horseshoe Bend. Today's group featured two girls who endlessly braided each other's hair and a boy who kept pocketing small rocks when he thought I wasn't looking. All wore matching electric-blue t-shirts with their school's mascot, a comical tiger better suited to a cereal box.

Soon they'd climb back aboard their school bus and be dropped at the feet of Chloe Bannister, who would stand on a boulder by the river and bring the battle to life with her trademark war cries. Halfway through, Chloe would walk them a few steps to the site of the former Creek encampment. She'd bring the group to near-silence through a whispered account of the women and children who'd hidden there.

Cullen would silently paddle to the shore behind the children's backs, an invading army of one in a canoe. He'd yell something and watch their mouths drop open in shock. Their jolt to attention would be accompanied by nervous laughter and most of the boys posturing bravely for their crushes. Then Cullen would continue Chloe's narrative from the perspective of Federal troops.

I glanced at my phone to check the time. I had a few minutes before releasing the kids to the bus, so I asked for questions.

No hands shot up, so I improvised. "The battle here was the beginning of the end for the Muscogee Creek in Alabama. Have any of you heard of the Trail of Tears, which took place later?"

Most eyes turned to the history teacher, Mr. Mosley, with nods and smiles. Mr. Mosley volunteered, "We've been discussing that chapter this week."

I smiled and nodded. "Do any of you have questions about that?"

One of the girls in front elbowed the boy with wheat-colored hair standing next to her. He raised his hand and asked, "Did all of the Indians have to go out west, or did some get to stay here?"

I was accustomed to the question by now. "Most were forced to relocate because of agreements their tribal leaders reached with the U. S. government. It was rare to get around that. A few managed to escape, though. My grandmother was Creek, and she believed her ancestor ran away with her little granddaughter and never left the state." I paused. "My

Grammy was told she took the baby and ran because white men had killed her daughter, the baby's mother."

Now sixty-four eyes were wide and fixed on me, sixty-six if you counted Mr. Mosley's. "This ancestor of mine walked day and night with her tiny granddaughter, hiding in the woods. One night when the moonlight was soft, she lit a campfire to cook something for the two of them. They'd run out of food and were starving."

"What did she cook?" the rock-thief yelled out.

"I believe it was a squirrel," I told him amid a chorus of ewwws and ughs. "Anyway, her campfire gave her location away. She and her granddaughter saw a man approaching and were terrified. They hid behind a big tree. When he got closer, they saw his skin was much darker than theirs, and they had never seen an African-American. They watched him getting closer and held their breath, terrified." I saw three black boys in the middle row paying close attention to my story for the first time. "He called out to them and told them not to be afraid. He said he wanted to help them hide, because the men looking for him would be drawn by their campfire. My ancestor decided to trust him. He told her his name was Mose, and he was running away from a plantation near Mobile. They put the fire out together and Mose showed her a cave where she and the baby could hide. He had berries in his pocket, and he gave them to the tiny girl."

Now, hands shot up everywhere:

"Did Mose leave her?"

"Did Mose get caught?"

"Was Mose a slave?"

"Where was the cave?"

I pressed my palms down in the air to shush them. "The troops came by that night and my ancestor and her grand-daughter stayed safely hidden in the cave. Mose left with another man who'd escaped, and yes, I think he was a slave. I don't know if he made it to freedom, but I like to think so. He may have saved their lives, or at least saved them from having to leave the only home they'd known in Alabama."

The kids muttered among themselves. I heard "wow" more than once. A small girl standing near the teacher raised her hand. "How do you know that stuff is true?"

"I don't," I answered. "Creek history from that time is oral tradition; it wasn't written down. I only know the story as it was told to me, but I believe it's true."

Mr. Mosley held up his Apple Watch arm and pointed to the bus. "Let's thank Miss Willis for her time and for giving us a lot to discuss!" He grinned at me and began applauding; the rest joined in before being shepherded away in a buzzing, excited single file.

My stories about Grammy weren't exactly part of the official information we provided, but as long as they were presented as her memories I was allowed to tell them.

I waited until the faces staring from the back window were out of sight, then sat down on a tree stump and placed my head in my hands, finally free to cry in private. I heard Grammy's voice in my head all day long, but her physical absence was a thing that walked next to me, always there.

I knew Cullen would find me after his presentation and we'd head back to the office together. I dried my tears and reached for my backpack to fix the makeup I'd destroyed.

Whatever Disney princess scenario I'd imagined didn't happen for us. Cullen and I were good friends. He flirted with me, but he was the kind of guy who'd flirt with anyone from babies in the grocery store to old ladies in church.

That was just Cullen.

He'd welcomed me to the staff, but not like he was particularly thrilled. I kept to myself and he paid a lot more attention to the people he'd known and worked with for months. We ended shifts together with a wave. He never once asked me out, or showed any sign he planned on it.

I was so caught up in the loss of Grammy and trying to navigate my new job it didn't matter as much as I'd thought it would. I went back to Eufaula a couple of times, homesick for Mama and Manny. I'd sit in the restaurant for hours and occasionally jump in and bus a table out of habit.

One Saturday night I kissed Mama goodbye, hugged Manny, and made the drive back to Dadeville with a takeout container of enchiladas and a little tub of flan on the passenger seat. I was still spending too much time swiping tears away, and I remember it was a long, weepy ride in the rain.

I turned into the apartment complex, looking for an available spot near my door. The rain had stopped and the clouds parted to reveal a full moon. I grabbed my food and carried it upstairs, planning a midnight fiesta like Grammy or Mama and I sometimes had.

I glanced at my phone to find three missed texts from Cullen, all asking me to meet him at the park, long closed after dark. "Say yes and I'll meet you at the gate," he typed. "Please. We can sit by the river and talk. It's beautiful."

"Sorry, maybe next time," I answered. I was tired and hungry and not particularly in the mood for a national park booty call.

The following Monday evening we found ourselves closing the visitor's center alone. We watched the last guest's car turn onto the highway and Cullen used his key to lock the glass door.

Then he leaned against the bright blue cannon in front of it, crossing his arms and watching me. "Skye, I haven't been honest with you," he said. He took off his hat and ran his fingers through his hair, his eyes never leaving me.

I just stood and stared.

"I think about you all the time. That started the night I met you at Greg's, and it's never stopped. I even came to your grandmother's funeral, but I sneaked out before you could see me. And I've tried, I've tried to sneak out of everything before you really see me. Because if you see me, then it's like are we going to be a *thing* or..."

I put a finger to his lips. "You came to Grammy's funeral?"

He nodded. "I didn't think you'd want to talk then..."

"I don't want to talk now, either." I leaned forward and brushed my lips against his, the tiniest of touches, still standing inches away and looking into his eyes. I didn't move my body at all, kept my arms at my sides, and continued to explore his mouth with my own. I made myself stay still, determined he would be the one to reach for me. Cullen sighed and put his hands on either side of my head, his fingers splayed in my hair, thumbs on my jawline. He kissed me so deeply, so slowly, so thoroughly, it was by far the most intimate thing I'd ever experienced or ever would again. I don't know how long we stood there, wrapping ourselves around each other, but night fell and crickets sang and the exterior lights kicked on and we weren't aware of anything but us.

And I was his and he was mine from that moment on.

Cullen and I worked side by side, though much of it was actually his training me and several other volunteers hoping to become rangers. His voice, no matter what he was saying, seemed to reach through my skin and bones and wake every cell in my body. An accidental brush of our hands left me practically vibrating, nervous and fumbling, scared to death someone would notice what was happening between us and ruin it somehow. I was pretty sure we weren't supposed to have romances among the reverent historical markers, and getting caught might mean one of us having to leave.

I was cleaning the little theater in the visitor center when Chloe stuck her head in and said, "There's some old guy here to see you." No name, no nothing. That was all I'd get from Chloe, who I was pretty sure had a monster crush on Cullen. She giggled nonstop every time he was around and occasionally reached out to tug the dark curls under his hat, thinking it was playful and cute.

I had to act like I had no interest in this whatsoever, but I'd have cheerfully strangled her under different circumstances.

I carried the broom and mop back to their closet and wiped my hands on a paper towel, hoping I didn't reek of the pine cleaner we used by the gallon. I blinked my way into the fluorescent gift shop, trying to adjust from the relative darkness in the theater. There was only one person who looked remotely like an "old guy", and he was standing beside a postcard rack. He was a black man with closely cropped white hair. His posture had a military bearing, and he wore a dark brown leather jacket I suspected had some sort of veteran's patches on it. As I moved closer, he pulled off his sunglasses and smiled, extending his hand. "You're Skye Willis?" he asked, shaking my entire arm up and down in enthusiasm.

"Yes, sir, I am."

He swept his gaze up and down me and nodded. "I'm Bill Patterson. I was wondering if we might talk for a few minutes."

I gestured to the theater which was fairly private and available for the next half-hour or so. He followed me and took a seat to my left, grasping both armrests.

"My grandson was here on a field trip last week," he began.

My stomach flopped and sank, worried I might have caused some offense. "Oh, Mr. Patterson, I hope I didn't say anything that might have upset him…"

He patted my hand. "No, nothing like that. Lerome came home talking about you and what you said about your Creek ancestor being helped by a runaway slave. He was impressed enough to talk all through supper about it."

"Well, I'm glad it made an impression. That story is very special to me. I might not even be here otherwise, if it's true."

"That's the thing," Mr. Patterson said, "I think it is true. When I was a kid, my great-grandmother told me a very similar account, one handed down by her grandfather. He'd escaped from a plantation down in South Alabama with a friend. He told all his grandchildren about running through the night, surviving on whatever they could forage, his feet bloody and barely able to go on. Part of the story was how he encountered an Indian woman and her little girl and helped them hide from the white men pursuing them. My great-grandmother died when I was ten, but I distinctly remember her telling us, complete with dramatic pauses and her imitation of her grandfather's deep voice."

"Wow," I said, wide-eyed.

"Oh, there's more wow. His name was Mose Kennedy." Bill paused to let that sink in. "I feel sure the story is true. Never dreamed I'd meet someone who'd heard it, too."

"So, your ancestor, Mose… he made his way to freedom? He and his friend were all right?"

Bill shook his head. "His friend died somewhere along the way, but Mose was able to get to Pennsylvania. We have absolutely no idea how he did that, because this happened before there was an Underground Railroad. Bounty hunters were paid huge money for captured runaways. It's mind boggling to think he escaped them."

"Are you from Pennsylvania?" I asked.

"I'm from everywhere. I'm a military brat born on base in Germany. I retired as an Army Captain in the mid-90s, and it just so happens I was stationed at Fort McClellan, an hour and a half from here. My wife and I had grown used to the area, and our kids, too. We all ended up there. Lerome," he tilted his head at me, "is my youngest and most inquisitive grandchild. I'm so glad he came here the other day. Imagine, in the whole wild world, to have you turn up here and tell your grandmother's story." Bill shook his head in wonder, a grin across his face.

"At the risk of sounding crazy," I said, "my grandmother passed away months ago." I had to stop to take a deep breath and squeeze my eyes shut tight. "I miss her so much it hurts, every single day. We were really close. She died suddenly a few days before I was supposed to bring her to Horseshoe Bend. I found a printout about the place with my name written on it, and came here on a whim. Everything that's happened since…well, sometimes it seems like Grammy is directing things." I sighed and looked at the ceiling.

I could feel him staring at my profile. Bill stayed quiet for a minute, then said, "Do you believe in God, Skye?"

"I don't know. I think so, though he may not be the God other people worship." I felt a tear slide down my cheek.

I could see him nodding beside me. Bill leaned back and exhaled. "I stopped believing in coincidences long ago. My mama used to tell us no one crosses your path without a reason, and it's your job to find out why. Sometimes you're God's hands and heart on Earth to help someone else, sometimes they're there to help you."

I met his eyes. "And you believe you're here to help me?"

"I believe," he said, "you've been through a lot lately and needed a message from your grandmother. Maybe she wanted you to know her story is true." He shrugged. "Maybe that's my thread."

"Your thread?" I frowned.

"Another thing Mama said. We're all part of a tapestry bigger than any of us can imagine, weaving in and out and creating a glorious picture. All of us, from the beginning of time. She even sang a song about it, but I can't recall how it goes."

My mouth fell open. "Grammy told me something like that once. I'd forgotten all about it."

"I think she wants you to remember it, Skye." Bill stood and tugged his jacket into place. "Could you could give me a personal tour of Horseshoe Bend? I'm interested in military history of all kinds."

"Oh, you might want to let Cullen Leatherwood show you around. He's a far better military historian than I am. Let me go get him for you."

Bill held up a hand. "You're the only person I want on this tour. I promised Lerome I'd get you to show me around. He's expecting a full report."

By the time he left, Captain Patterson and I'd exchanged phone numbers. He wanted to contact the Calhoun County School Board and ask them to invite me to speak to a high school class or two, about much more than Horseshoe Bend. History, he said, needs to be alive and vibrant, not crumbling from a dusty text but shouted from the heart of a young person.

Thirty-four

Dadeville, Alabama

Jennifer DeWitt and her three-year-old son were in the apartment complex's small playground, killing time until Benjamin's daily raisins, baby carrots, and Cheerios at precisely two p.m.—no deviations allowed.

She shaded her eyes and squinted into the sunlight, trying to make out the license plate of a new white Ford Expedition that drove up and parked near her unit, 122. It was definitely out of place among the fifteen-year-old Nissans and Toyotas the neighborhood knew. A large man sporting a baseball cap, gray t-shirt and jeans emerged. He glanced at Jennifer and walked toward the other end of the row of apartments, stopping to knock at the door of 129.

She waited to see what would happen next. He was probably a bill collector of some kind, and Jen wasn't about to help him. He knocked again, shifting his weight from side to side impatiently. She could see he was giving up on a response.

Good.

The man climbed into his shiny vehicle and drove off. Jen made a mental note to keep an eye on Skye's place and see if he returned.

Pete drove straight to Horseshoe Bend after the apartment. He'd been told Skye didn't work there on Thursdays, but that must've been wrong.

The kid in the visitor center cheerfully informed him Skye was off today. He could come back tomorrow and catch her. The ranger-boy made a point of returning his stare to the book he'd been reading when Pete walked in, a clear dismissal.

He gave up and drove to his hotel in Auburn, unaware that Skye was a half-mile away enrolling in freshman classes. She and Cullen would celebrate that and Cullen's new job teaching American History at a local elementary school tonight at a fancy restaurant called Acre, which neither of them could really afford.

He had promised, absolutely sworn, he'd help and support her along the way. Skye was such a natural to study history, he'd insisted, it would be a crime if she didn't pursue it. Cullen wore her down like water over rock, watching Skye gradually accept the idea. He researched scholarships and found a way to get most of her tuition covered, ensuring she wouldn't have to work full time through school.

Cullen told her he'd introduce her to his former professors, many of whom had become friends. He'd tutor her in Calculus. He'd revisit the excruciating pain of inorganic chemistry. He'd do anything for the woman he was starting to think he might be sure he could possibly want to marry someday. Maybe.

After registration, they were going to tour two apartments near campus. Cullen was secretly looking for one that would allow the puppy he planned for her birthday gift next month, a tiny, fluffy shelter moppet he'd reserved and wanted to name Heruse, pronounced hey-thuSHEE, the Creek word for beautiful.

Or Rover or Spot or Dog, if that's what Skye wanted. It didn't matter, as long as she stayed as happy as she was right now. He'd watched her transform into a woman who smiled at everyone she met, who stopped, giggling, to steal a few cotton bolls from a field and put them in a bright red vase on her kitchen table, who rolled over in bed some mornings and stared at him, whispering *God, I love this man* when she thought he was still asleep.

Skye had told Captain Patterson about far more than Horseshoe Bend; she'd shared her ancestry traced to Joko, survivor of the *Clotilde* and settler of Africatown. She drew a portrait so compelling Bill Patterson had taken his family to explore the church and cemetery there. He'd also retraced the pilgrimage Skye and Sparrow made to the Wichahpi Commemorative Wall, touched the stones and felt their peace.

Captain Patterson convinced Skye she was walking, talking Alabama history, with stories no one but she could tell. He'd arranged for her to speak to three high school classes so far. She took along her petit point tapestry from Grammy, beginning by showing them the tree and church in Africatown, telling them why it was so precious to her. Each time, she came back to Cullen glowing, going on and on about the kids and how they actually seemed interested in what she had to say.

She was blossoming, opening like the petals of the pastel wildflowers in the park, turning more toward the sun each day.

Life was pretty much perfect for the two of them.

The next morning, Cullen and Skye arrived at Horseshoe Bend to find she'd been assigned to take a cart and do clean-up around the park, a job reserved for junior volunteers. Cullen and Chloe would cover the visitor center.

Skye waited until Chloe wasn't looking and gave Cullen a quick kiss. "I'll see you this afternoon," she told him. She glanced at Chloe, who was straightening postcards in a rack. "Behave yourself," she added.

"Have a good time," Cullen called after her. He meant it sarcastically, and couldn't possibly know those were the words her grandmother always used to send Skye off to work.

Skye sighed and stretched after hours in the sun. She pulled her hair into a ponytail and reached for her water bottle. The golf cart was parked to the side of the car path, and an occasional tourist would wave as they drove past.

She collapsed on the boulder Chloe normally used as a stage during presentations to groups. Her back was sore from picking up assorted pieces of paper, many of them discarded brochures from the visitor center that failed to reach a trash can. Skye wondered idly if it would be worth it to continue volunteering on weekends as she and Cullen had agreed. It might be too much, with school and whatever social life they'd have in Auburn. She was daydreaming about the apartment they were considering, a post-WWII building heavy on exterior brick and interior wood paneling. It was tiny and dark, but it fit their budget. Almost all off-campus apartments were priced like big-city penthouses, designed to be shared by four or more roommates whose parents had deep pockets.

She had no intention of sharing Cullen.

Pete walked into the visitor center and spotted a tall young man behind the counter with hair almost to his shoulders, a neo-hippie badly in need of a barber and a real job. He cleared his throat noisily before he got near the counter, announcing his arrival.

The young park ranger looked up. "Hello and welcome. Please let me know if you have any questions." He went back to stacking some boxes under the cash register.

"I'm looking for a young lady who volunteers here. Her name is Skye Willis." Pete noticed a pretty girl with apple-round cheeks and blonde hair enter the room, watching him closely.

The ranger guy—his nametag read 'Cullen'—shot a look at the girl.

"She's not working in the office today; she's out in the… umm… field," Cullen said. "May I ask what it's in regard to?"

Pete raised his brows. "It's *in regard* to family. I'm a relative visiting from Texas. Can you tell me how to find her?"

Cullen was well into his third head shake, preparing to get rid of the guy, when Chloe yelled, "Oh, yeah, Skye's working outside in the park. I'll tell you exactly where she is." Chloe pulled a brochure from a wall display and unfolded it for Pete, pointing to the area Skye should be clearing of litter.

Pete accepted the map. "Thanks." He walked to the door.

Cullen called out, "What did you say your name is, sir?"

"I didn't," Pete smiled. "It's Otis Garfield."

Cullen nodded and went back to his boxes, glaring at Chloe as soon as the man left. "Her biological father lives in Texas, and she wants nothing to do with him, Chloe. That could be him or an uncle or an ax murderer. You don't know."

"Her father's name is Otis Garfield?" Chloe's eyes rolled to the ceiling. She made a dramatic grimace and added, "How embarrassing would that be?"

Cullen slammed his palm on the counter. "I'm following him out there, just to be sure she's all right."

"Seriously? Skye's a grown-ass woman, Cullen. Leave her alone." Chloe lowered her eyes long enough to roll them again for added effect. She watched Cullen jump in his car and drive slowly out of the parking lot, about as stealthy as a rampaging elephant.

Skye wrinkled her nose at the mound of bird crap she was trying to wipe off a wood bench, a plastic bag of used paper towels at her feet. She heard the Expedition park nearby and paused, looking up to welcome the guest and offer to answer questions.

The driver's door opened. She took in his height first, and knew immediately who was climbing out into her personal world, uninvited and definitely unwanted. She gathered her cleaning supplies and got behind the wheel of the golf cart, turning the key as Pete approached.

"Leave me alone," she said. "I have nothing to say to you and I don't want to hear anything you have to say, either."

Pete positioned himself in front of the cart, holding up one hand. "I understand. I wouldn't want to talk to me, either, if I were you. But Skye, I've come a long way and I'm only asking for a few minutes of your time. Please. Let me say what I came to say and I'll leave, I promise."

Skye threw her head back, eyes closed tightly. She stepped out of the cart and waved at the bench, placing herself on the non-bird-crap end. She saw Cullen's car in the distance, silent assurance he was there to rescue her if she signaled.

"What do you want to tell me?" she sighed.

Pete settled beside her, far enough away to keep from making her uncomfortable, he thought, though sacrificing his jeans to birdshit in the process. He bit his bottom lip. "I came to say how sorry I am. I was wrong, so very wrong, to turn away from you in Oklahoma. I knew… Skye, the minute I saw you, I knew you were my daughter." Pete stared at the ground, unable to meet her eyes. "I thought my marriage would be over if I acknowledged you. Hell, I was *told* my marriage would be over, in no uncertain terms. I made a choice between you and my ex-wife, and it was the biggest mistake I've ever made. And I've made too many to count."

"Ex-wife?" Skye asked.

"Yeah, our marriage broke up for other reasons, nothing to do with you. But Skye, I swear to you, if I had it to do over I'd stand up to her. I wouldn't have lied to you. I'm not asking you to forgive me. I'll never forgive myself."

Skye kept her eyes straight ahead. "Do you know how pathetic an excuse that is, your wife wouldn't let you have a relationship with your daughter? You're a grown man, a successful man, someone used to telling everyone else what to do… but you crumpled like a weak little boy under pressure from your wife. Pitiful. And after that, you think I can respect you? Have you in my life?" Skye shook her head back and forth. "I don't want you or need you."

"I know," Pete said quietly. "I'm not here to ask that. Just to tell you, in person, how deeply sorry I am. To apologize. That's all I wanted." Pete swiped at a tear escaping his eye, embarrassed to the core. "I'm so sorry, Skye." His voice broke as he said her name. He reached to touch her shoulder, and Skye jerked away.

"You know why I can't take you seriously, Pete?" Skye spat. "The person you owe at least this much apology is my mother. And I'm willing to bet you haven't said a word to her, and you never planned to."

Pete shook his head. "All I can do is say I'm sorry. I'm sorry to you and to Lisa, and I'm sorry you lost your grandmother, Skye. It's obvious she loved you very much, and you loved her, too."

She would *not* let him see her cry. Skye focused everything she had on staying still and calm.

Pete took a deep breath, stood and handed her a piece of paper. "If you ever, ever need anything, you can reach me in an instant and have it. I know you don't want money, I know you don't want me to be a father to you, I know I've failed you in every way. But if there's something I can do for you, Skye, if there's a moment you might want to reach out to me... I'm here. I can't change what I've done, I can only tell you I regret all of it. That's what I came to say. I was wrong, and I'm sorry."

Skye folded the paper and put it in her pocket. She got up and walked to the golf cart without another word, and never saw Pete crying behind the wheel of the Expedition as she drove away.

He leaned his head onto the steering wheel and closed his eyes, asking himself what he'd expected would happen when he found her, when he unburdened himself but changed nothing at all for his daughter. It had been, as usual, all about him. Now Skye was freshly wounded in all the places she'd managed to heal, and he was even more sorry.

Pete rolled his windows down and listened to the river *shooshing* its way beside him, watched a bird perch on a tall rock. When he turned his gaze forward, he saw Cullen park his car in front of Pete's, blocking him. He hurried to dry his eyes and compose himself before the guy walked up to his door.

"Are you her father?" Cullen asked. Pete could read anger in his face, but something else, something deeper.

"Yes, I am, my name's Pete Darling. I'm sorry I lied to you."

Cullen nodded. "I can see why you would. If I'd heard your real name, I'd have known instantly. We've talked about you." He stared in the direction Skye had driven off.

"I'm sorry," Pete said automatically. "I've hurt her a lot, and I can tell she's your friend."

Cullen smiled tightly. "She's much more than a friend, Mr. Darling. The thing is, Skye has a dad. His name is Manny. He loves her like she's his own. He actually gave her a ring when he proposed to her mom. They're a family, and you don't want to ruin that."

"No one's trying to ruin anything, Cullen. I came here to apologize to her. That's done and now I'm leaving. I'll fly out tomorrow afternoon." Pete turned the ignition and raised his red eyes to Cullen's, dipping his head slightly.

Cullen tapped the roof of Pete's car and walked to his own, driving away and clearing the path for him to go.

"Why? Why would I forgive him, Cullen? He sat in that hospital, looked me in the eye, and told me I wasn't his daughter. I don't understand you, thinking he deserves to be forgiven." Skye was biting the cuticles from every finger and staring out of Cullen's car, too furious to look at him. "And the man didn't have the decency to contact me after Grammy's death. He's never said a word to my mom, and she deserves an apology, too."

"I wasn't suggesting you do it for him. I was suggesting you do it for you." Cullen swung the car into a space near Skye's apartment.

"I don't need your psychological insights, thanks." Skye slammed the door and marched toward her apartment. Cullen didn't bother to join her. "I'll see you tomorrow!" he yelled at Skye's back. If she heard him, she didn't acknowledge it. He sat staring at her front window, waiting for her to switch on a light. Apparently, she didn't intend to. He imagined Skye sitting alone in her tiny living room in complete darkness, getting angrier with him by the minute. Cullen smacked the heel of his hand on the dashboard. Damnit. He had to make sure she was all right.

Skye answered the door and waved him into the room. "I knew you were still out there. Why didn't you leave, like a sane person?"

"Can we turn a light on, like sane people?" Cullen banged his shin on an end table and winced. He felt his way to a chair just before Skye obliged by switching on a hallway light, casting a dim glow from ten feet away.

"Want a beer?" She waved her wineglass at him.

"Sure."

Skye handed him a bottle and sank into her Grammy's old couch, as comfortable as her favorite slippers. "Look, I admire your lofty principles of forgiveness, Cullen, and that you're all noble and shit, but I'm not like that."

He choked a little as he laughed. "You've got me all wrong. It's not about being noble or the bigger person or any of that. But Skye," he touched her hand, "we were so happy. Everything was coming together for you, for us. And if you don't make some kind of peace with Pete Darling, accept his apology, let him feel forgiven... well, that's going to be a pile of manure we step around all day, every day. It will be a thing, a part of our lives, randomly sucking all the joy out of little moments here and there."

"You're wrong. I'm fine. It's already forgotten." She placed her wineglass on the table. "This is how forgotten it is." Skye moved to Cullen's lap and sat facing him, offering a kiss designed to erase everything else.

He placed a hand on her chest and gently pushed her back to look at him. "Not forgotten. You won't forget what he did, ever. I want you to forgive him because it'll make *you* feel better."

"Do you know," she said softly, "how hard I searched to find him? The letters I wrote, the calls I made, never getting an answer?"

"Maybe he didn't know about them. He's probably surrounded by people who…" Cullen stopped as she shook her head.

"And even if that's true, Grammy went all the way to Oklahoma and found a way to *make* him meet with me. She did that for me, Cullen. It ended up taking her life. For *me.*" Tears streamed down Skye's face. "And he sat down and told me I couldn't possibly be his daughter. Acted like he'd never met my mom. How do you forgive that?" she whispered.

"Aww, Skye," he sighed. "Forgiveness is never about measuring the wrong against you, about weighing the injuries and calculating the moral equation. It's about freeing yourself to move on, and allowing the other person to move on, too. It's unlocking the room you're trapped in together."

She tilted her head and stared at him.

"My dad is a philosophy professor, you know. I had philosophy dripped all over me regularly as a kid. Would you like to hear about Socrates forgiving the two men who had him executed? His beliefs on how forgiveness demonstrates wisdom?"

Skye looked at her half-empty glass. "I think I'll just have another gulp or two of wine instead, thanks. But I like the unlocking the room thing. Very nice."

"Think about it," Cullen said. He reached in her pants pocket and pulled out the paper with Pete's numbers. "And if you're going to call, maybe you should call while he's still in

Auburn. You could meet him somewhere in town. Let him go home with your forgiveness."

"I'll think about it if you won't mention Socrates again. Ever." Skye drained her glass and headed to the kitchen for more.

Three hours, two glasses of wine, and four pieces of a delivered pepperoni pizza later, Skye told Cullen she'd call Pete in the morning.

"Okay," he said, "but you're going to tell him in person, not on the phone, right?"

"Does Socrates require that, too?" Skye murmured, pulling the blanket over her face as she turned onto her side. She was snoring softly when Cullen patted her foot and drove to Auburn.

Pete's room phone rang at 7:00. He almost didn't answer it, expecting his secretary or Gerry or one of the other people in his life who avoided cell phones.

"Umm, hi. This is Skye. Look, I have to work a few hours this morning but I was wondering what time your flight leaves."

"It's flexible, Skye. I can schedule it when I want." Pete held the receiver out and frowned at it in disbelief. He rubbed the bridge of his nose and swung his feet to the side of the bed. It was early on a Saturday, but he could see Auburn coming to life in the form of a few bicyclists and runners three stories down.

"Okay, well, maybe I could come to say goodbye this afternoon. Like about one? I could meet you in the restaurant at your hotel. If that's all right." Skye's hand was shaking as she unlocked her car.

"Sure," Pete smiled into the phone. "It's Italian. We can get lunch."

"No," she answered. "I'm only going to stay a minute and then go to Cullen's. I was coming into town, anyway," she lied.

"Okay. I'll meet you there. See you at one." Pete hung up the phone and reached for the antacid tablets he carried everywhere. Skye sounded as angry as she had the day before, and he wondered what she could possibly have left to say.

The restaurant was typically Italian, a dark and cozy retreat from the bright Alabama sunshine. He was grateful for that. Pete asked the hostess to make sure he and his daughter were seated in a booth where they might have a little privacy. He sat near the front door and waited, hands clasped in front of him, his head jerking up every time someone walked in.

He pulled out his cell to check the time. 1:03. 1:07. 1:11. It occurred to Pete this was her way of making a statement, offering to meet him and never showing up. His stomach roiled. The hostess, a girl who looked twelve to him, smiled sympathetically. She probably thought he was any other parent in town, visiting his college student.

If she only knew.

At 1:19, his phone dinged with a text: sry caught in traffic there soon skye.

He took a deep breath and trained his eyes on the door. When Skye came in, it was in the middle of a group of people. Pete didn't spot her at first. She'd changed out of her ranger uniform and wore a long, gauzy skirt and pale green t-shirt.

She looked beautiful.

Pete stood without a word and nodded to the hostess as Skye walked up. She led them to a secluded spot and Pete swept his hand at one side of the booth, motioning Skye to slide in opposite him. He sat awkwardly, his long legs angled out, hoping he didn't trip anyone. A boy came and took their order for water. Pete added an appetizer strictly to buy them some time.

Skye forced herself to look at Pete. "I came to tell you... I came to tell you I appreciate the effort it took you to come here and apologize to me."

Pete blinked and bit his lower lip.

She took a deep breath and exhaled slowly. "And I accept your apology. That's it, really." Skye shrugged and moved to leave the booth. She couldn't manage another word.

Pete's hand reached across the table and grabbed hers. Skye looked at the blue veins running toward his fingers, stared at the map of his blood clutching her own. She turned to Pete's face and saw a tear tracing its way down his right cheek. He was hurrying to brush it away with his other hand. Her heart hurt more in that moment than it had since Grammy died. She turned her palm up to Pete's hand, gently clasped it for a second, and let herself cry.

"You don't have to say any more," he said. "I'm just so damn proud of you, and sorry I missed seeing you grow up. And I'm more grateful than you'll ever know that you came here today. Thank you, Skye."

The server delivered water and a basket of bread. He backed away silently, embarrassed.

"Will you stay with me for a little bit?" Pete asked. "Do you have to leave right now?"

Skye hesitated. "The truth is, I don't have to be at Cullen's anytime soon. He won't even be home for another few hours."

"Then let's see if we can manage a lunch together, okay?" Pete offered her the menu she'd ignored.

"I'm really not hungry," she told him, watching his face fall. Skye looked around the restaurant, giving herself a minute to consider. "But I guess we could walk around campus a little, if you want. I don't think I told you, but I start classes here in a few weeks."

"That's wonderful, Skye." Pete put a couple of twenties on the table and stood. "Come show me around."

They ended up on the winding paths of the arboretum a half-mile away, passing in and out of the shade of enormous oaks and magnolias. Pete told Skye about New Zealand, about selling his business, about starting over. She explained all the ways her life had started over, too.

"I'm wondering," Skye said, "if you know anything about your ancestry. I discovered a lot in the process of finding you." She blinked up at Pete, his face haloed by the afternoon sun. "It's actually one of the reasons I'm going to be a History major."

"No," Pete said. "All I know is, my family's been in Oklahoma for generations. I've never done all that DNA stuff. No one's getting their hands on my private information."

Skye stopped walking and threw her head back, looking up at the network of branches above them. "There's a place I'd like to show you. It would take several hours to drive there, but maybe someday you could come back when we both have time."

"Where is it?" Pete asked.

"Near Mobile," she answered. "I'm off tomorrow, but it would be a lot to get there and back in one day. Like, leaving at a time I don't plan to be awake. And even then, it's not exactly a day trip."

"Mobile? Are you telling me I have some kind of roots there?" Pete frowned. "If that's true, I never knew about it."

"You do," Skye told him. "I think it would be good for you to learn all about it, but only when there's time to show you around. There's too much to tell."

Pete picked up an acorn, turned it over and over in his hand. "Meet me at the hotel tomorrow at ten. We'll have plenty of time."

"I don't see how," Skye said. "It's at least a five-hour drive."

"It's a much, much shorter flight, Skye. Will you come with me, show me whatever you're talking about?"

She hesitated, unsure. "Could Cullen come with us?"

"Absolutely," Pete answered.

"Is your plane big enough for all of us?"

"Yeah," he said, and threw the acorn into the air. "It is."

Cullen white-knuckled most of the flight in Pete's private jet, uncurling his fingers from the edge of the seat only after they rolled to a stop on the tarmac. He hated flying. His nerves were shot, between worrying about plunging to his death in an Alabama pine forest and about what he'd done to Skye by insisting she meet Pete yesterday. Now their lives were tangled up, and he was suddenly surrounded by this guy's money and influence. It was as uncomfortable as a barbed-wire jacket.

"I only want to show him where he comes from," she'd said. "It's important history, Cullen, and you know it. He should know and appreciate it, too."

Now he walked behind the two of them as they approached the rental car counter. He noticed there still wasn't a lot of conversation. Maybe Pete was a quiet sort of guy in his natural habitat.

Cullen suspected his social interactions had been mostly ordering others around. The man was definitely not much for small talk, as though his words were reserved for pronouncements.

Skye dropped back to wait with Cullen as Pete signed for the car. "Are you nervous?" he asked her.

"Not really," she said. "I'm going to tell him about his ancestors in Alabama, let him see where they lived and died, let him see how neglected Africatown is…"

"You're going to try to get him to donate money, aren't you? Get him to pay for the visitor center they've never built. To fund repairs and restoration…"

Skye crossed her arms. "No, Cullen. I hadn't thought that far ahead. Why is money the only thing you think of when you see him?" Skye glanced at Pete. "I'm going to show him where Joko is buried. I'm going to see if the history washes over him like it did me. I'm going to find out what kind of man he is."

Pete held up a key and pointed to the glass doors, leading to the inevitable black or white SUV.

They started toward Pete. "He really has no idea what we're here to see? You haven't told him anything?"

"Nothing," Skye answered, grabbing Cullen's hand and rushing forward.

Pete insisted on driving, because he'd been in Mobile on business and knew his way around. Skye sat beside him in front, watching his face as the realization dawned he was going to a part of town he'd never seen. He didn't say a word until they crossed the bridge and the Caribbean blues of the giant *Clotilde* mural appeared next to the road.

"You can park up there, on the right," Skye said. "It's a church, but I think their Sunday services are over. No one's around."

Pete did as he was told. He unbuckled his seat belt, taking in the sights around him. "My family lived here?"

"Your... our... distant grandmother came here on a slave ship, the last one ever to reach Alabama. She was smuggled in along with about a hundred other men, women and children from the west coast of Africa. The region is known as Benin and Togo now. It's near Nigeria."

Pete sat staring at the brick church. "I don't understand."

"Her slave name was Dolly, but her Yoruba name was *Bamijoko,*" Skye continued, "and she took it back after the war. She later shortened it to Joko. She and many of her *Clotilde* shipmates managed to find each other after they were freed. They wanted to go back to Africa, which was still fresh in their minds. They missed it constantly, cried for their families left behind. When that was found impossible, they did a different impossible thing: they created and settled Africatown to preserve the ways and language of their people. It's really the only place of its kind in the country. Can you imagine the work, the courage that took?"

"She was my grandmother?" Pete was still staring at the bricks.

"Many generations back, yes. Joko married a fellow former slave named Charles Broadhurst, although we don't think he was a *Clotilde* survivor. The town thrived for a long time, but eventually its descendants moved on, many of them to new parts of the country."

"Obviously," Pete muttered.

Skye said, "Joko remained in Africatown until her death in 1908. Her children stayed here, but her grandson Garrett fell in love with an outsider named Bettie Guffey. Bettie was both white and Creek Indian." She paused to check Pete's face, which had settled into a kind of awed wonder. He opened his door and climbed out, shaking his head. Skye followed him to the wall of the church, where he ran his fingers down the bricks.

"She was a founding member of this church. You'll find a plaque with her name out by the road," Skye told him.

"How did they… how did I end up in Oklahoma?"

"Anti-miscegenation laws would have prevented Garrett and Bettie from marrying in Alabama, so they did it in Kansas in 1922. They were on their way to join relatives in Oklahoma, probably Bettie's Creek family. Census records indicate most of Garrett and Bettie Broadhurst's descendants were still in Oklahoma at least until 1950."

"I don't know what to say," Pete told her. "I thought you were bringing me to a chimney standing next to an old plantation site or something. I'm still stunned."

Skye nodded. "I was, too, at first. And then I started thinking what an honor it was to be descended from these strong, brave people. They did what no one else could. They recreated the world they were so cruelly ripped from, the mother country they missed until they day they died."

"It's unimaginable," Pete agreed. "I'm guessing they were sold by fellow Africans to be taken to America?"

"Yes, the Kingdom of Dahomey, which is now Benin. You'll see how people feel about that when I show you the statues of a couple of Benin-Togo leaders, from a visit they made here several years ago. They're down the road, that way, next to what's going to be the visitor center." Skye pointed to her left.

Pete said. "Who's the guy depicted in the bronze bust out by the street?"

"That's Cudjoe Lewis, the last surviving founder of Africatown. He was a well-known and beloved celebrity in his time. Zora Neale Hurston wrote a book about him called *Barracoon*. I'll take you to his gravestone in a minute. People still leave candles and little gifts there."

Skye looked to the cemetery across the road, where Cullen was already walking around. She and Pete made their way across, dodging traffic. As soon as they passed through the cemetery gates, dogs began barking and howling, just as they had when Skye and Grammy visited.

Skye showed Pete Cudjoe's headstone, then told him to follow her. She walked up a slight hill, dodging fire ant mounds and avoiding stepping on graves as she went. Pete joined her under the canopy of an ancient tree, standing among slabs of concrete and marble, their markers long-erased by time.

"She's here," Skye told him. "I don't know which grave, but one of them is Joko's."

Pete bent down and traced the outer edge of a rounded headstone. "And to think I never knew." He turned to Skye, his eyes wet. "Thank you for this."

"There's a lot to learn about this place. I can recommend some books," Skye said.

"I can't wait to read them." They stood silent for a full minute, surrounded by blank memorials to countless people who'd created a vibrant community, now mostly bleak and deserted. Pete looked back at the church. "Do you think we could go in there?" he asked Skye.

"I doubt it," she said. "We can try." The two of them climbed down to join Cullen, who took Skye's hand in his and led them across the street.

They cupped their hands to their eyes, squinting to see in the windows of the locked church. All they saw were modern flower arrangements and a portrait or two no one recognized. The three of them piled into their rented Tahoe and Skye showed Pete the site of the non-existent visitor center. A worn sign announced its promise of one to come. They drove slowly past the shattered statues of African dignitaries, their heads long bashed into scattered pieces on the ground, their pedestals defaced.

Pete said, "Do you mind if we go back to the church before we leave?"

Skye held up the bag of bottled water and protein bars they'd bought in the airport. "Let's have a picnic on the steps."

Cullen swept a clean place for Skye on the end and Pete sprawled himself next to her, placing himself between the two. Pete drank a long pull on his water bottle, staring across at the cemetery.

"Like I told you, I sold my business," Pete said. "Signed the papers last week. And I have no idea what the hell to do with myself."

Skye glanced at Cullen, who sat slightly behind Pete. He shrugged.

"There was a video of Kara—my ex—saying some horrible things on the day your grandmother fell in Oklahoma. When it went viral, PFD Pipelines went into freefall. I was lucky to get out when I did. After that video, we lost almost every contract we had."

Skye shook her head "no" at Cullen. Better to pretend they'd never seen the video. It would be excruciating to talk about it now.

"Anyway, PFD has had a charitable foundation for years. I'm not going to lie to y'all, it's been about tax write-offs, not charity. But I'm thinking it's time for that to change, and we can start here."

"That would be wonderful," Skye said, her eyes misty.

"And," Pete added, "I want to rename it. Separate it from PFD. Start fresh, with a new director."

"Sounds like a good idea," Cullen said.

"I want it to be you, Skye," Pete turned to her. "I'll make it well worth your while."

Skye blinked at him. "I'm starting school, remember?"

"You could take a lesser role," Pete answered.

"No, I really couldn't," Skye told him. "I wouldn't be able to do it right. I don't know anything about foundations. What I do know is that I'm really good at engaging a group of kids. I want to stand in a classroom and bring history to life for them. I want that more than anything."

She looked at Cullen, who added, "I'm starting a job with a local elementary school, Mr. Darling. Skye wants to get her degree and do the same. And I'm hoping we will be teaching together."

Skye smiled at him and leaned behind Pete to squeeze his hand.

"I'd pay you triple what you'd earn as a teacher, Skye." Pete raised his eyebrows. "It would be a good living. You could work from Auburn, if you want. I'm trying to offer you a great opportunity."

"I know you are, Pete, and I appreciate it. But I already have one." Skye felt the warmth of the afternoon sun on her face and looked up, squinting into the brightness. "I know what I want to do."

In the towering oak that stands beside the church, a small brown bird landed and surveyed the three of them as they sat on the steps. She held tight to the branch and waited until Skye, Cullen, and Pete drove away, until they passed the painting of the Clotilde's billowing sails and began to cross the bridge spanning the Mobile River. She spread her wings and took flight, a tiny, fragile sparrow framed by a cerulean sky.

Epilogue

VIENNA, AUSTRIA

The woman made her way through a pedestrian square bordered by chic shops and boutiques. Her wool hat, the color of Vienna's most delicate golden pastries, was trimmed by a wide band of dark sable fur. Her long brown hair cascaded to just above her breasts, which were perfectly showcased in a silk knit sweater of pale cream. The matching skirt was strategically tailored to allow a view of her toned body from every angle. Her Prada boots were the precise gingersnap shade to complement the hat.

People on the cobblestones parted like the Red Sea as she approached, some allowing their glances to linger a discreet few seconds and some overtly staring, open-mouthed. A middle-aged matron smacked her husband's leg with her handbag as he stood gawping.

She had no idea a man she knew stood watching and studying her facial features, her every gesture. He followed her until she reached her hotel, enthusiastically greeted by the blushing doorman as she entered. The man waited, hidden by a statue across the street until she had time to reach the top of the marble staircase inside and press a button to summon the elevator.

He gave her a few beats to reach the penthouse, saw the lights bathe the curtains there. Then Deke took out his cell and pressed the button for Gerald Davidson's private line.

"Hello? Is that you, darling? I'm sorry, I've only just walked in," she answered the phone, her accent evoking London's poshest neighborhoods, the vowels nasal and elongated. She removed her right boot and held it, waiting for Heinz to speak.

"No, it's not Heinz, Kara. It's Gerry."

"I'm quite sure you've mistaken me for someone else." She cradled the phone on her shoulder and touched her fingertip to a panel by the bed, causing the heavy brocade draperies to open and slide on their rails to the corners of the wide room. She hobbled in one boot to the far window's edge, her face hidden by a tall floor lamp. She couldn't see anyone looking up at her. That was good.

"There are very few people in the world who can identify you as well as Deke Jones, Kara. He even has the misfortune of being able to describe your outfit like he's narrating a Paris runway. It's kinda sad in a man." Gerry was enjoying himself. "Anyway, your stay in Vienna is going to be difficult after tomorrow morning. I took that video of you, the one where you call the Creek 'these fucking people' and express your desire for a 'little old lady to fall on her little old head'? You know the one. I had it subtitled in German, and added some details at the end about the outrage in the United States, how you were forced to leave, couldn't show your face in public, that kind of stuff. Oh, and how you're staying in a Vienna hotel penthouse because you're screwing the manager, Heinz. Did you know he's married, Kara? Anyway, the video will be uploaded to YouTube and links will be posted all over Austrian social media right after. I promise you, it'll go viral in an hour or two."

"You cannot possibly—"

He laughed because she still hadn't dropped the accent. "I sure can, Kara. And I'll keep doing it wherever you go, in whatever language it takes. You deserve that spotlight you've always craved. I'm going to make sure you get it, anywhere in the world. Bye, Kara. Until next time."

—The End—

Author's Notes

S kye's ancestor Dolly/*Bamijoko*/*Joko* is fictional, though she represents the authentic *Clotilde* survivors who settled Africatown (also known as Plateau). Of course, the line of descendants ascribed to her is fictional as well. The derivation and definition of her *Yoruba* name are authentic.

Africatown is a fascinating and culturally important place, and I encourage you to explore it further. I learned about it through Sylviane Diouf's excellent book, *Dreams of Africa in Alabama: The Slave Ship Clotilda and the Story of the Last Africans Brought to America*, which I heartily recommend. (Note: *Clotilda* and *Clotilde* are acceptable spellings; I use the latter because it's on the mural in Africatown.)

In 2019, a year-long, intensive search by marine archaeologists led to the discovery of the remains of the *Clotilde* in a remote arm of the Mobile River. Efforts to preserve the history of this ship and memorialize the remarkable accomplishments of her survivors are underway. You can learn more and contribute to this vital project here:

Africatown Heritage Preservation Foundation
http://africatownhpf.s442.sureserver.com/

Horseshoe Bend National Military Park is a beautiful and moving place to visit. My representation of park rangers, their responsibilities, presentations for school groups, and the process to become a ranger are not necessarily accurate representations but my own creations to fit the narrative of Skye's story.

Providence Canyon State Park is a lovely place. The "sneaking in after dark" described in the book is COMPLETE FICTION, a product of my imagination. DO NOT attempt to sneak into the park, in daylight or otherwise.

"The place near the other Eufaula" is a phrase of my invention to refer to Oklahoma. I don't know if it's historically authentic, though it's interesting and important to contemplate how we came to have a Eufaula in both Alabama and Oklahoma.

Acknowledgments

Every author needs a trusted set of early readers. I am thankful to have the best in the world.

My mother, Patricia Poucher, is legally required to love everything I write. However, she is the most voracious reader I've ever known, thoroughly familiar with every genre of fiction, and unafraid to tell me when I've written something she finds subpar. She is my *alpha* beta reader, my beautiful, wonderful Mama.

Debbie Tuckerman, Marianne Barnebey, David Boyd, Sue McKay, Dan Brown and Savannah Duke provided me invaluable feedback through every chapter of *Tapestry*. I am forever grateful for their unique and varied points of view.

London's Rachel Lawston designs book covers the way Fabergé designed eggs. I think we can all agree *Tapestry* features one of the best examples of book cover art ever to grace a shelf. It's a huge bonus that Rachel is a lovely person who's become a friend.

Frazine Taylor is an archivist at Alabama State University, a delightful woman, a distinguished scholar with a curriculum vitae too lengthy to list here. She helped me write the chapter about Skye's Africatown ancestor. Not only did she provide terrific information, she allowed me to use her real name. I am honored Frazine is a part of this book. Here's a *partial* list of her accomplishments: She is the President of the Elmore County Association of Black Heritage, Chair of the Black Heritage Council of the Alabama Historical Commission and the President of the Alabama Historical Association. She serves on the boards of the Patrons for the Study of Civil Rights and African-American Culture at ASU, the Alabama Cemetery Preservation Alliance, the Alabama Governor's Mansion Authority and the past President of the Friends of the Alabama Archives. Ms. Taylor coordinated the African American Course for the Institute of Genealogy and Historical Research (IGHR) at Samford University, Birmingham, Alabama. In 2015 Ms. Taylor coordinated Alabama State University's inaugural biennial Genealogy Colloquium. She is the recipient of the AHA Virginia Van der Veer Hamilton Award, 2019 and in 2018 an IGHR Scholarship was named in her honor.

Frazine researched family roots and ties to Alabama for Tom Joyner, Linda Johnson Rice, Condoleezza Rice, and Epatha Merkerson for the PBS series *African American Lives 2* (2008) and *Finding Your Roots* (2012, 2019). She is the author of *Researching African American Genealogy in Alabama: A Resource Guide*, published in 2008. Currently, Ms. Taylor continues to conduct genealogy and archival workshops throughout the state.

Matthew Robinson, park ranger at Horseshoe Bend, patiently and expertly answered questions about the battle as well as other aspects of Creek history. He made our visit vibrant, as only the best historians can.

Suzanne Tapia McKay and her sister Mary Tapia Armstrong are native Mobilians who took me on a fascinating tour of Africatown (also known as Plateau). We explored the cemetery and church mentioned in this book as well as the rest of this extremely important historical site. My experience there led to a much more detailed story, and I thank Sue and Mary for taking the time to show me around.

A great joy of my life was getting to know Tom Hendrix, one of the finest storytellers ever, and the creator of the astounding Wichahpi Memorial Wall. I visited with him more than once, and his devotion to his great-great-grandmother and her remarkable journey left me in tears each time. Tom passed away in February, 2017, leaving Alabama without one of her most wonderful citizens. Skye and Sparrow visited the wall after that date, and I hope you'll indulge my rearranging time to include Tom. He was a beautiful soul. His monument to Te-lah-nay is still open to visitors near Florence, Alabama, and I encourage you to visit. It's also briefly featured in *Muscle Shoals*, one of the best documentaries in the world. Watch it! You'll get a glimpse of this lovely man, too.

Tom told me Rosanne Cash wrote part of *A Feather's Not a Bird* in the very spot I stood in his driveway one sunny afternoon. Please listen to the song. A bit of the lyrics are included in this book because it's a perfect fit *and* because she sings about Florence and the "magic wall."

A Feather's Not A Bird
Words and Music by Rosanne Cash and John Leventhal
Copyright © 2014 Chelcait Music (BMI) and Lev-A-Tunes (ASCAP)

All Rights for Chelcait Music Administered by Measurable Music LLC/Downtown Music Publishing LLC

All Rights for Lev-A-Tunes Administered by Downtown Music Publishing LLC.
All Rights Reserved. Used by Permission and
Reprinted by Permission of Hal Leonard LLC

Working on this manuscript with the talented and insightful Katie McCoach, editor extraordinaire, was a pleasure.

Thank you to designer Rachael Ritchey for making the inside of this book as gorgeous as the outside.

My husband Jay, my daughter Savannah, and my son Jason endure my endless time in the hermetically sealed writing chamber with humor and grace. They are my world, my everything.

Finally, a person experiences about forty thousand heartbeats while reading the average-length novel. Knowing you shared them with me is an enormous gift, a privilege, and I thank you so very much.

Other Books

by Beth Duke

IT ALL COMES BACK TO YOU
DELANEY'S PEOPLE: A Novel in Small Stories
DON'T SHOOT YOUR MULE

About the Author

Beth Duke is the nationally bestselling author of *It All Comes Back to You, Delaney's People, Don't Shoot Your Mule,* and *Tapestry.* She lives in the mountains of her native Alabama with her husband, Jay. Her favorite things are writing, reading, traveling with her family, and joining book clubs for discussion.

For more information, please visit

bethduke.com
facebook.com/bethidee
instagram.com/onlythebethforyou
twitter.com/bethidee

Made in the USA
Las Vegas, NV
18 August 2021

28422436R00204